THE BLACK WALL

TIDES BOOK TWO

R. A. FISHER

Published 2020 by Shadow City – A Next Chapter Imprint

Edited by Marilyn Wagner

Cover art by Cover Mint

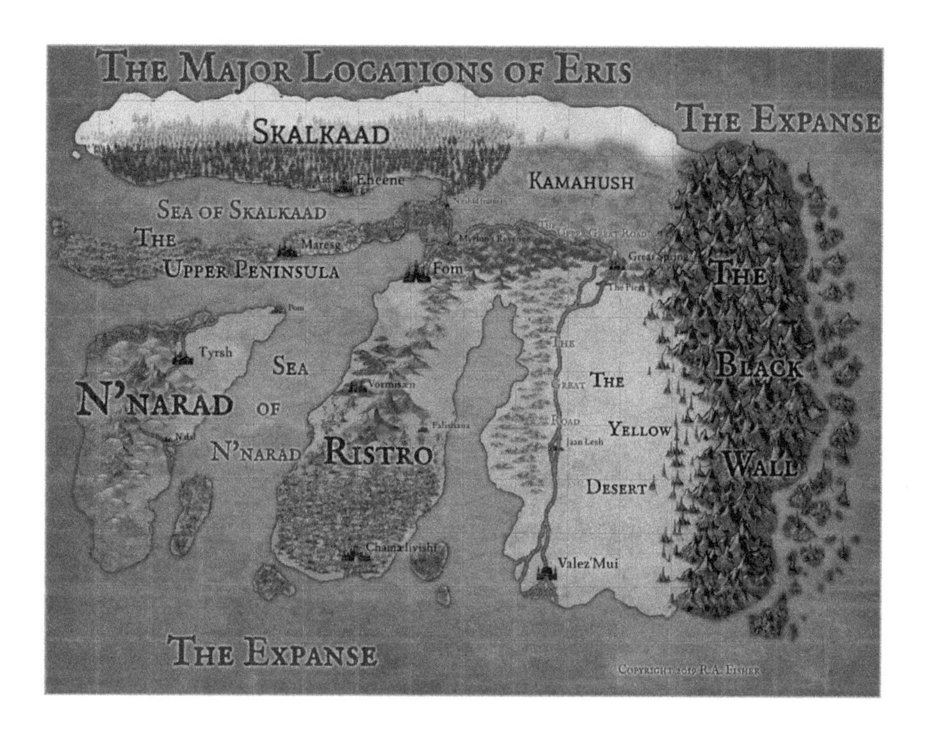

THE MAJOR LOCATIONS OF ERIS
SKALKAAD
THE EXPANSE
Eheene
KAMAHUSH
SEA OF SKALKAAD
THE UPPER PENINSULA
Maresg
Fom
Great Spring
The Pier
THE BLACK WALL
Tyrsh
SEA OF N'NARAD
N'NARAD
RISTRO
THE GREAT ROAD
Jaan Lesh
THE YELLOW DESERT
Valez'Mui
THE EXPANSE
Copyright 2019 R.A. Fisher

PROLOGUE

THE TRIAL

"Guilty." The Grace's word reverberated through the Hall.

The Grace of Fom, an angular, thin woman with hair and eyes the color of unpolished iron, waited for the echo of her verdict to die before continuing. "General Albertus Mann, you are condemned to the Pit for public viewing until dead, for sedition, treason, and the murder of Cardinal Prast Vimr. Do you have any words before you are stricken from the Books of Heaven?"

Mann, despite his condemnation, felt unexpected relief. The verdict and sentence were, of course, inevitable. Despite its ultimate success, his expedition to the Black Wall, and the valley hidden within it, had been a disaster from the moment he and his ridiculous army had embarked on the three steamships bound for Valez'Mui.

He looked around the cathedral at the center of Wise Hall, Seat of the Grace. On buttressed marble walls two-hundred hands high tapestries draped, depicting images of the Tidal Works, steamships, the thirteen harbor towers, and other glories of Fom, including several of Wise Hall, which he had always found redundant.

The Grace stood at the pulpit. Behind her rose a stained glass window from floor to ceiling—a cacophony of light and color depicting the Eighteen Levels of Heaven, from the Heaven of Stone at the bottom to the Heaven of Light at the top, represented by the sun with the crescent Eye above, embracing it in its half-circle. The seal of the Church of N'narad.

Eighteen Heavens that no longer held a place for him.

No matter, he thought. He'd stopped believing in Heaven long before he'd sunk a knife into the back of Vimr's skull.

What could he say? He was guilty of killing Cardinal Vimr. Guilty of so much more.

"Nothing, Grace," he said, voice soft and even, despite his shaking hands.

The Grace only gave a slight, sad nod. Mann let the guards lead him away.

1

THE INVASION: SIX MONTHS BEFORE THE VERDICT

Bodies lay strewn, pale against the rich brown ground. Blood muddied the soil between the trunks of massive trees, churned until its hue matched the broad, fern-like leaves grasping the sky. Long-beaked scavenger birds, red breasted with gleaming black wings, hunched in the lower branches, silent and waiting. I watched Cardinal Vimr lean down to pluck one of the long, black, wooden daggers from the hand of a corpse, the plates of his elaborate, ill-fitting leather armor sliding against each other like a film of cracked wax floating on water.

The karakh shifted beneath me. I wondered if the creature found the corpse-littered glade as terrible as I did, or if it just shared my hatred of the Cardinal. Or its attitude to our situation was as alien as its form, and its thoughts unknowable to anyone but its human companion.

Gre'pa, or as close to that as I could pronounce, was shaggy white with grey streaks, and over twenty hands tall at the shoulder. Dakar had unsheathed its tusks when we arrived in the valley. They were studded with bronze bolts, sharpened edges now dripping with gore. The shepherd sat motionless in front of me on the karakh's shoulders, and the back of his head revealed nothing about what the chieftain's husband was thinking.

I pulled my thoughts from the monstrous scavenger and forced them back to the clearing. Corpses of my soldiers. How many of them had been added this time to the ranks that would never return home from this wretched mission? How many of their lives had I spent? I tried to feel something; tried to recall my horror and shame at the first loss of life we'd suffered on this mad journey when the burning wreckage of the Salamander sank into the Sea of N'narad. But my grief since then had been replaced with a void, and now, even when recalling the Salamander, I could feel nothing.

"General Mann." The low sound of Vimr's voice made the hair on my arms stand on end, but I kept my expression even when I turned to face the Arch Bishop's adviser harnessed behind me on Gre'pa's back.

"What is it, Vimr?" I spat the words more than I'd intended.

Vimr cast a meaningful look at the bloody meadow. "I maintain that this requires a purge." Vimr's voice was smooth.

"What do you mean?" I asked, knowing the answer but needing Vimr to say it. Needed him to say it, so it would not be my responsibility. To tell myself that I was only following orders. I felt sick.

Vimr sighed, reading my thoughts on my face. "Genocide is an ugly term, and shouldn't apply to these constructs. Nevertheless, as I have said on more than one occasion, our passage the rest of the way through this valley will only be achieved with the extermination of the guardians."

I looked again at the scattering of bodies that weren't my soldiers. The karakh had mangled most into bloody strips and bone. Still, I could see enough. Shorter on average than those from outside the Black Wall, clad in soft, dark leather. Both men and women. Weapons of strange, black wood, harder than iron or ceramic. "They seem human enough to me."

Vimr shrugged. "Regardless, the histories are consistent. Whatever guardians the Ancients left in this valley were created by them. *Produced*, not born. Not, at least, in any normal sense of the term."

I felt my jaw clench, but I was facing away from Vimr, and I doubt he noticed. "I will not condone the annihilation of a people who are only defending their land. Whatever your 'histories' tell you."

Vimr sighed. "They are not *my* histories. They are, as you well know, the records of the Church—of Heaven itself. Anyway, General, I've broached the subject with the remainder of your men. They all agree that their survival and the completion of our mission surpasses any cultural needs. We—you—lead a quest passed from Heaven itself, and the locals, whether machines or men, are killing themselves in their attempt to stop you. The only difference between staying the course and bringing the fight to them is how many more of your own people you lose."

The remainder of your men. The words echoed in my head, drowning out the rest of Vimr's tirade, threatening my numbness with the only thing that would be worse: regret. Memories flooded back.

The descent into the valley strapped to the back of Gre'pa had been only a little less terrifying for me than it had been for the five hundred soldiers I'd chosen to come with, rappelling over six hundred hands to the jagged, black scree that ran to the edge of the forest. Maybe. To be fair, I've never been a fan of high places. At least the soldiers had had ropes. The eleven karakh had plunged from the grotto head first, creeping down the obsidian cliff like spiders, their massive claws gripping the cracked, black glass.

And yet the other half, who stayed in the grotto, like the thousand still waiting in the foothills of the Black Wall, had complained at being left behind. Good men. Better than me. Better than I deserved.

The first attack came while we camped at the base of the cliff that first night, whipped by wind blowing up from the south. They flooded out of the darkness like demons, slaughtering a quarter of us before vanishing among the trunks of the enormous, blood-hued trees. The canopy was so thick that even the great lens of the gibbous Eye couldn't penetrate it enough for any organized pursuit. If not for the eleven karakh, we all would have died then.

I wondered at the time—still wonder now—if those in the tunnel, so disappointed at being left behind, felt the same way as they watched our burning tents far below them and listened to the distant screams. Probably, they'd only grown more bitter as they'd looked on, helpless. In all the months since that first night, I was too much a coward to ask them.

For five days, we pushed south, circumventing the few settlements we'd found, over Vimr's protests. The villages had, at least from a distance, seemed abandoned in any case. I argued that we'd only come for the contents of a library, not to exterminate the hapless guardians who had been imprisoned in that valley since the Age of Ashes. My soldiers, for their part, followed me into the valley because they were faithful. Destined to a better Heaven should they be lucky enough to give their lives in service to the Church of N'narad.

Now more than half of them lay in a trail of corpses from the grotto to the glade where we now stood.

I studied the faces of the survivors, scattered around the edge of the clearing, standing or crouching. That meadow had become sacred. Even the karakh were reluctant to enter. Hard, tired eyes. Leather armor, some of it hanging in tatters, all now spattered with blood, their own or someone else's.

Vimr was right about one thing: These soldiers no longer served me. They no longer even served the promise of Heaven. They only wanted to survive long enough to go home.

I ground my teeth and turned, craning my neck until I could look Vimr in the eye. "I will not allow my army to commit genocide," I whispered. Then I spat. "But it is obvious that this army is no longer mine."

"Was it ever, General?"

I didn't have an answer, and Dakar, if he'd heard the exchange, didn't react.

We continued south. The terrain became rocky and uneven, but there was still no end to the massive, red trees. Twice in two days, we came across large, square patches of thin-leafed brambles covered in barbed, finger-long, thorns and tiny white flowers. The blackvine, you called it. Not even the karakh could find a path through them, and we were forced to make our way around. Both times we stumbled upon villages of small, obsidian buildings, their roofs thatched with the broad, dried leaves of the trees. Well maintained. Abandoned. Vimr ordered the buildings doused in naphtha, and their roofs burned. I watched, silent and ashamed.

The sun set early behind the western Black Wall, plunging the valley into a twilight that would last for hours. I called for a halt, anxious to finish setting up camp before the wind that had raged every night made such a task impossible. I half-expected my order to be overridden by Vimr, but the squat man only nodded like a sage from his perch behind me on the shoulders of Gre'pa.

It took two hours to set up the tents and a few hasty pickets on the uneven, root-knotted ground, but twilight still seeped, speckling the haggard remnants of my soldiers in blood-hued shadows.

I walked among my men, though in truth, it was only to get away from Vimr; there was no need for orders. From somewhere nearby but out of sight, I could hear his voice chattering and laughing with a few officers.

No, no orders were necessary. Not from me.

They set up my tent first, despite my objections, and I wandered back to sit alone at the end of my cot, listening to the sounds of my army through the canvas walls.

I wouldn't have realized I'd fallen asleep if it weren't for the scream that woke me.

An orange light flickered through the heavy cloth of my tent. Fire, I remember thinking, groggy through half-remembered dreams. The scream was sustained, inhuman, shrill. It pierced the air from every side. The tent shuddered and flapped. Wind, I realized. The screaming was the sound of the wind.

I bolted upright, and my right hip creaked in protest, reminding me I was too old for this. For all of it.

I staggered to the flap, which had become untied, now snapping in the burning gale. I forced myself to stand straight and gave my right leg one final shake, as if that would help.

Heat roiled from the south, and smoke churned between the tents on violent, stray currents. Above the scream of wind skittered other sounds—soldiers yelling in confusion, uprooted tents snapping where they fluttered, ensnared in trees, the creak and snap branches, the panicked whistles and clicks of the karakh. A black and gold Sun-and-Eye pennant of Tyrsh tumbled past, writhing like some mad spirit.

The smoke burned my eyes. A few soldiers ran this way and that between the tents, or knelt by fallen comrades. I hesitated, feeling lost, before making my way to the west side of the camp. Most of my soldiers had already moved to the perimeter to man the pickets, despite the lack of orders and the flames.

Captain Rohm was there, crouched in a shallow trench. He glanced at me and nodded a greeting as I limped down to hunker at his side, trying and failing to suppress a wince as pain growled from my hip.

"They're trying to drive off the karakh with fire." Rohm had to yell over the din. "Or just kill us."

I grimaced, remembering the Salamander. "Guess they've never seen a karakh before."

Rohm shook his head, but before he could respond, the wind surged. A wall of heat rolled over us. The livid glow to the south became a liquid avalanche of flame stampeding through a tunnel of air clear of smoke, leaping from tree to tree, devouring the whipping red leaves like locusts.

I coughed and grasped at my chest, unable to catch my breath in the boiling fumes. The air shimmered and writhed like water. Through the sheet of darkness collapsing over me, I could see Rohm on his knees, clawing at the ground.

I guess this is how it will end for us. The thought was calm. I could feel the oxygen-starved air singe my lips and tear at my lungs, smell burning hair, but it was far away. I sucked in another desperate, pointless breath.

My last breath, I thought, with a vague sense of disappointment.

A shadow passed across the wall of light. Huge eyes of gold, pupils shrunk to tiny black marbles against the glow of fire. Massive tusks bolted with bronze curved up from a flat, dog-like nose, which in turn jutted from the white face of some immense, demonic goat.

Gre'pa, smoke curling in reeking tendrils from his fur, scooped us up, each in a massive, clawed hand, and tossed us behind Dakar, who straddled the creature's neck, clinging to the brass chains pierced through its cheeks.

Without bothering to check if we'd gotten a grip on the smoldering fur, Dakar let go of the chains, leaned forward into his mount's neck, and let the creature carry us away.

I'd trained riding a karakh before the mission. Since our descent into the valley an endless week before, I'd spent every long day strapped into a harness behind Dakar, but I'd never, until that moment, imagined needing to ride as the shepherds do, without a harness, or even the benefit of the chains.

Fire and light filled my senses, and burning wind, and now over everything the acrid stench of smoking fur. My palms burned where they clung to the thick, white hair, and my legs felt like rubber. Pain screamed from my hip.

The creature leapt from tree to tree, and even through its panic it kept itself between us and the ground. I had no idea if Rohm still clung behind me, or lay dying on the forest floor somewhere behind. I could only press myself into Gre'pa, feeling the rhythm of surging muscles, while I waited to fall and be consumed by the fire that raged on every side.

Maybe, I thought, *using fire to drive off the karakh worked, after all.*

Our flight, panicked though it was, faded to monotony. I clung to the smoldering fur, choking against the rancid stench of burning hair, which was so strong that the banshee wind of the valley couldn't tear it away.

After what seemed like hours, I felt the karakh slow. The grasping fingers of branches were gone. Leaping from tree to tree was replaced with an even, crab-like amble. The wind still screamed.

I peeled my face from where I'd buried it in the burnt hair of Gre'pa an eternity ago.

Smoky, orange light oozed over the eastern peaks, which now reached almost to the zenith. Gre'pa had carried us due east to the treeless, boulder-strewn slopes at the base of the Wall. Rough chunks of obsidian ranging in size from pebbles to towns scattered to our left and right. Behind and below, grey smoke shrouded the forest of red, fern-like trees, rolling off to the north in the dissipating tendrils of wind. Beneath it, the fire throbbed orange and red and yellow.

My numb limbs failed at last, and I released Gre'pa to slide onto the lichen-encrusted rocks. There I lay, looking at the grey light of the sky with burning eyes. The karakh stepped away.

The blurry image of Rohm's face peered down at me, silhouetted against a smoggy blue sky. A light, cool breeze brushed around us.

"Rohm. I didn't know you made it." The words burned my throat.

"Right behind you, clinging to Gre'pa's ass, General. I'm as surprised as you." Rohm's voice was no better off than mine. "And I take back everything I've ever said about that glorious beast."

I tried to sit up, but the effort made my head swim, so I settled back down onto the jagged shale. My fingers felt like claws. I could still feel flames dancing along my limbs and face.

I coughed. The sound was soft and dry and sent flames into my lungs. "Who made it?"

Rohm hesitated, but I couldn't make out the captain's expression through the shadows. "Us. And Dakar and Gre'pa, obviously. Six other karakh and their shepherds. Dassik, the new Artificer, but he's burned bad. Five men in pretty good shape, and another eleven not so good. Was fifteen when we got up here a few hours ago. Now eleven, if that tells you anything. Not good at all. We'll probably be down to eight by tomorrow morning, though it looks like anyone who lives through the night will survive long enough to be killed by something else. If you want to consider that good news, go ahead. It isn't going to get any better." He ended with a shrug that might have been apologetic. "And Vimr."

I closed my eyes again. Twenty-two of my soldiers were still alive and uninjured enough to carry on. Twenty-two out of the five hundred who'd descended into the valley. Twenty-two and Vimr.

"What about the powder?" It was a question I didn't want to ask. If we'd lost the powder kegs to the fire, there wouldn't be any point in going on. I had heard no explosions, but I doubted I would have noticed them over the wind.

Rohm nodded as if he'd expected the question. "Not as bad as it could be. Eleven kegs can't be accounted for. Might still find a few where we camped, but I wouldn't count on it. Dersh and his karakh—Zha'an or something—grabbed the other half and got up here before the fire rolled through. Don't ask me how they did it."

It was the best news yet. I hoped eleven kegs would be enough to get through whatever door we'd been sent here to find. Only one way to find out.

"What do we do now, General?" I heard the question he was asking. *Can we go home now?*

I said nothing for a long time, eyes closed. Rohm probably thought I was planning some grand course of action, but my mind was blank. "Where are the others?" I asked at last, voice rasping, peeling my eyes open to look at the silhouette of my captain.

Rohm nodded past my shoulder, and I sat up enough to crane my head in that direction, wincing at pain even that slight motion shot through my head. The rocky slope we sat on fell into a crevasse fifty paces to the south.

"They fell in?" I asked, realizing how stupid the question was as I asked it.

"No, General." Rohm's forced chuckle turned into a cough. "There's water down there. Fast running stream. Fish, too, I guess, though I didn't get close enough to see any, myself. We lost everything in the fire, and we don't have enough provisions left to get back to the grotto the way it—"

"We're not going back to the grotto," I said, hating how much sense he was making. "Two, maybe three days more at the most. Faster now." *Now that there's so few of us*, but I couldn't finish the thought out loud. My voice caught in my throat, and I despised myself for it.

My army had been annihilated by its own existence. Had we just come with the karakh, we would have traveled faster. Maybe fast enough to avoid conflict. Fast enough to flee the fire. The deaths of four hundred and eighty-four men were—are—my fault. I could blame the Arch Bishop and Vimr for the others if I were the type of man to set my responsibility at someone else's feet. They had been the ones who forced me to bring that absurd army across the continent. But it had been my call to bring them into the valley.

Now they were dead. And because they were dead, the survivors could complete their mission.

I thought back to the Salamander, and the specter of death that had continued to chase me like my shadow since then. And now this. The grand finale.

Rohm's eyes flickered, but he only gave a quick nod. "Yes, General. I'll inform the others."

In the end, it wasn't that simple, because nothing is ever that simple. Of the five that included Rohm's "not so wounded," three included broken bones, and the next morning five of the burned could walk, and four others needed to be carried on litters but would survive.

For all my words to Rohm, I would not push them any further. Not for a Heaven I'd lost my faith in years before, not for the Arch Bishop of N'narad and his schemes, nor the Grace of Fom and hers.

I would go on along with the remaining officers, mounted on five of the karakh because we had a job to do. I released the rest to go back to the five hundred still waiting in the grotto, and the more than nine hundred who waited in the foothills outside the Wall. I gave the remaining provisions to those returning with the wounded, and the fish they'd caught that afternoon. I sent two of the karakh back, too, in case they ran into any more trouble. Vimr objected. I continued with my orders as if he hadn't spoken, and he fell into fuming silence.

Those that were to go back watched with blank stares as we plunged into the smoldering forest, and returned my parting salute with empty, mechanical precision. I had time to wonder if I would see any of them again, but then they were gone, behind the ethereal barrier of curling smoke and blackened pillars of the giant trees, and I was clinging to Gre'pa, thankful now to have the luxury of the harness. Vimr muttered something behind me, lost in the crack of brittle underbrush.

We traveled until the trunks looming out of the void in front of us were nothing more than shafts of shadow in the glossy haze cast by the starlight that glinted through bare branches. I intended to call a halt during the long twilight, but Vimr had beaten me too it, so I had them press on into the night, out of spite, like a seventy year old toddler.

Within an hour of setting camp, the watch reported we weren't alone. They'd heard low voices in the darkness to the south, over the pops and snaps of falling, burnt branches. The first watch had reported to Rohm, who had reported to me out of ear-shot from Vimr.

I called them over—Isam, tall, balding, and hunched, and a burly, bearded thug everyone called Keg.

"Sound like another ambush?" I asked, glancing where Vimr had waddled to relieve himself.

"Nah," Keg answered, picking at his short, ruddy beard with a thumb and index finger. "Women. Not that that means anything, I guess, but children, too. Like a town."

"A town?" I looked around at the blackened trunks. Little gusts of wind curled fingers of ash from the ground, visible in the Eyelight glaring up from somewhere beyond the eastern peaks of the Wall.

"Well, a settlement or something, anyway," Isam answered. "I heard it, too."

"They survived the fire, then?" I realized the idiocy of my question after it left my mouth.

Keg grunted.

"Who survived?" Whined Vimr's voice from where the little man lurched out of the darkness behind the two scouts.

Isam turned to face him. "A settlement or something, I guess."

"It should be purged, then." Vimr's voice was bored.

I ground my teeth. "Children and their mothers? I don't think so." I turned to the two scouts. "Keep an ear to it. Tell the next pair on watch to do the same. We'll move on before dawn. Take the long way around. With the karakh, we'll be gone before they know we're here. You hear anything—*anything*—that sounds like more than a few surviving kids and their mothers, let me know."

Nobody moved. Isam studied me a long time before he spoke. "We're with Cardinal Vimr on this one. We've had enough of these bastards, and I'm pretty sure the other men feel the same way."

"I gave you an order—"

"You can bring me up on insubordination charges if we ever get back to civilization," Isam stated. "But Cardinal trumps General, anyway, so good luck with that. I'd rather get out of here alive and let the courts decide, how about you, Keg?"

The stocky shadow of Keg dipped his head in agreement.

The silhouette of Vimr nodded as if a difficult but apt decision had been reached. Rohm watched, expressionless. I couldn't blame him. Had he argued, he'd only be tossed out with me. The men had made up their minds. The mutiny was complete.

Vimr coughed and called out into the darkness. "Dakar, is Gre'pa harnessed?"

There was some rustling from somewhere a little way to the north and a slow answer. "Er, not yet, but he can be in twenty minutes. Why? We going somewhere?" Dakar emerged from the darkness just as the tip of the gibbous Eye crested the top of the Black Wall. His grey eyes were on me, not Vimr. "General?"

I said nothing at first, trying to think of a way out. I thought about saying nothing, pretending I could wash my hands of the coming massacre with inaction.

Complacency. The evil of cowards. I could order Dakar to stand down, wait for morning and go around. And then what? If Dakar stayed loyal to me, which was likely, the five karakh would make easy work of the few soldiers and Vimr, but that... I thought of the Salamander and shut my eyes. No, I couldn't do that. Whatever happened, whomever they took orders from, they would be my soldiers. Until the end. What action was left to me? To take responsibility for the actions of an army that wasn't mine.

That was the moment I realized that was what my job had always boiled down to. Embarrassing it took so many decades to figure out something so obvious to everyone else.

"As the Cardinal said, Shepherd Dakar." My voice was quiet, sapped of will. "Harness the karakh. We move when the Eye breaks free of the Wall."

When we mounted, it was Vimr who took the place behind Dakar. The shepherd shot me a questioning look. I kept my face blank.

The village squatted on a low mesa. It was walled on two sides by fields of the black, thorny brambles, now stripped of their leaves and little white flowers, made harder than steel by the fire. South of the small collection of sunken longhouses, the ground dropped a short way before rising again into the foothills that groped the base of the Wall. To the north of the settlement, between the five remaining karakh and the base of the mesa, a circular lake burbled, edged by reeds. In the Eyelight, the south peaks glowed purple. The wind blew in sharp gusts hard enough that a chorus of cracking branches and swirling ash clogged the air and helped mask the karakh's approach. The soldiers had tied cloths around their mouths, dampened in the lake, to help filter out the ash and still-hot embers, but the karakh all coughed and sneezed, and the shepherds bore the pain along with them.

I'd harbored faint hope that any survivors would have gone into hiding, if not into their homes, then perhaps into the ash-filled forest. As we edged around the lake, my hope winked out. A line of figures appeared on the ridge above before scattering again.

"They're up there!" Vimr shouted above the din of branches and gusting wind. "Their last line of defense!"

I said nothing as we charged up the slope into the village.

A coward to the end.

The whole scene became a scatter of broken images: Pregnant women, the elderly, children, who couldn't have been older than eight or nine, trying to hack with the unwieldy, wooden halberds that the warriors had wielded with such skill. Weeping girls impaled on the tusks of Gre'pa. Old men slashed into bloody strings by a karakh's claws, faces set with resolve. Dakar looked back at me, his face pale, but I couldn't meet his gaze.

The ash-laden ground became clotted with thick, bloody mud. I felt sick in every cell of my body, and I hoped I would die before I could see the other side of the Wall and face the black tunnel the rest of my life had become. No words came to my mind, for myself or anyone else.

After sending men from building to building to ensure there were no survivors, Vimr ordered camp set at the base of the mesa along the edge of the lake.

The karakh's feet and hands were burned, and Dakar and the other shepherds coaxed them down to the shore and the cool mud beneath the reeds to coat their feet and protect them a little against the still-smoldering ground.

I leaned over to retch from where I still sat strapped to Gre'pa's rear, shaking, when I saw two figures huddled among the reeds. Small, almost child-like, I thought at the time, but clad in the clinging leather the warriors had worn. They crouched just beneath the surface of the water, faces upturned, hued violet but clear in the Eyelight, breathing through reeds.

That, I guess, was the first time you saw me, too.

I spit the last of the vomit from my mouth. The other four karakh had moved further around the lake to a flat clearing a quarter-span away. There was no one else around.

"Two there," Vimr's voice. My heart jumped and sank at the same time. "Dakar, kill them, or they may rally survivors."

"No." The sound of my own voice surprised me, stronger than it had been since Vimr had taken control of my army.

"General—" Vimr's tone was condescending, but he got no further.

Without thinking, I pulled the long, wooden dagger from Vimr's belt. The one the Cardinal had looted from the dead valley native a few days before.

I was old, but I was still fast. Fast enough, or should have been. In one quick motion, I thrust the knife up towards the back of Vimr's skull.

He twisted out of the way, and in a blur, his soft hand shot up to grab my wrist in a grip of iron.

I was flabbergasted. I did nothing but stare, useless and confused, when from behind the Cardinal, there was another flurry of motion, and Vimr lurched towards me. Dakar, almost as fast as Vimr had been, had twisted to elbow him in the back of his head.

His grip slipped on my sweaty wrist as he spun back to confront Dakar, tangled as he was in his harness, and I tore my hand from his grasping fingers.

I slid the blade into Vimr's head.

The wood cut through bone like cheese. Vimr stiffened, and he let out a short, strange, high pitched sound. Dakar released Vimr's harness with a few deft motions and watched as the Cardinal tumbled to the smoking ground.

The corpse smoldered a moment, before it ignited in a sudden flash, burning to ash in a few shocking seconds. Gre'pa jumped and waded a few dozen hands into the lake. Dakar's brow furrowed at the spot where Vimr's body had lain, now just a pile of ash a shade lighter than the ash around it, and a few fragments of blackened bone. I stared.

Dakar grunted. "Must have been a hot spot. Coals can be hotter than flame after a fire like this one." He sounded unconvinced.

I had nothing to add.

I looked toward where the soldiers were setting camp and saw Rohm standing thirty paces away. His face was pale, even in the violet and red light of the Eye, but he only gave me a quick nod and turned back toward the others.

I cleared my throat. "We were ambushed. A lone warrior came out of the reeds and threw his knife. There was no time to react, but Gre'pa finished the bastard off, didn't he?" I cleared my throat again.

Dakar glanced back, a hint of a smile on his rugged face. "That's right, General. Not a goddamned thing either of us could have done."

"Just a minute," I said. I undid my harness, slid down the back of Gre'pa, and retrieved the black dagger from the pile of ash and bone that had once been Vimr. It was made from something like wood, but undamaged by the fire or the smoking ground which, I couldn't help but notice, wasn't as hot as it should have been.

"Let's go." I looked for the huddled figures in the lake, but there was no sign of them.

2

THE DEFENDERS

PASHA TUGGED HIS SISTER UP FROM WHERE THEY'D HIDDEN under Bora lake and watched the bizarre scene play out. Her face was round, with a small mouth and wide set, slanted eyes. She was a child—not even thirty, yet—but she looked even younger. Tears mingled with fishy lake water, now black and grey with ash. Her silver eyes looked blue in the Eyelight.

Anna sucked in a breath, released a shuddering sob.

Pasha pulled her close so his body would smother the sound of her crying. His own face was gritty with soot, concealing the thick scar that ran from his right eye to the corner of his mouth. Through the blur of his own tears, he watched the shaggy, white monster scuttle toward where the other creatures had settled by the lake, far from the rest of the invaders who'd set camp just beyond their village. "I know, I know."

She turned her head away from him to watch the creature move away but said nothing.

"I think they saw us," he answered his own question lurking at the forefront of his mind. "I'm sure of it. The old man looked right at us after he threw up. The little fat man pointed and said something, and the old one killed him. Then they left."

Anna pulled away from her brother and sniffed. "What are you saying?" They were the first words she'd spoken since he'd started the fire.

"I don't know."

Anna pushed him away. Why would he save us?" Her words trailed away.

Pasha was quiet for a minute. "I don't know. And why did the man he killed burn when he hit the ground? It's not that hot."

Anna didn't answer, but stood for a minute, waist deep in the lake, looking off towards where the creatures had gone. Then she spun around and shoved her brother, hard. "And *you* killed everyone else." the sobs came, louder.

Pasha pulled her close again. She resisted, but with weak effort, and he held on until she stilled, willing his tears not to join hers. *I'm seventy-five now*, he repeated the thought, over and over again. *I'm seventy-five.* But he didn't feel seventy-five. He felt like a child who'd just lost his parents.

"You know why I set the fire," he said into her wet hair. "They came to open the Tomb. We had to stop them. We had to try." *And we were so close*, he thought. *But we failed.* The night winds had come, swept the inferno up the valley just as he'd been taught they would, but it hadn't killed all of them.

Anna struck his chest but didn't answer.

"Even father said we did the right thing." But at the thought of their father, their mother, of everyone else, the dam holding his tears cracked. They stood in the lake for a long time, holding each other and crying.

Anna pulled away first.

He wiped his face, smearing ashes into his eyes and making them burn. "They came from outside the valley."

"That's impossible. There's no one left," Anna whispered.

"We were wrong."

He thought back to what his father had said after Pasha had told him he'd set the fire. "We haven't failed. We're here, so we haven't failed. That's why he sent us to the lake while everyone else..." He trailed off, and they both fell silent again.

After a while, Anna asked, "What do we do now?"

Pasha had already thought about that. "We can't stop them from getting into the Tomb now. They would just kill us. But we can hide. Look for others. There must be someone left."

"What's the point?" She whispered. "All we've ever done is guard the Tomb. *Pretend* to guard the Tomb. If they open it, take whatever's inside, what's the point?"

Pasha swallowed. Pretend. For hundreds of generations, the people had guarded the door set into the Wall behind Suedmal from a world that wasn't supposed to exist. *Worthless guardians*, he thought. *All this time. Every one of us.* The ashes in his mouth tasted bitter.

"We can follow them, Anna. Us, and whoever we can find. We'll follow them, take back what they stole."

Their father's foundry was only a quarter span from where the invaders had set their camp, but the entrance was hidden, the chimney in the middle of the blackvine patch, which was now impenetrable with the coils of fired thorns that wouldn't grow again until spring.

The boiler pit was cold and dry. They huddled together in the blackness, waiting for dawn.

Daylight revealed itself with a single, muted shaft beaming down from the chimney hole in the middle of the round chamber. The boiler sat in the center—a single slab of obsidian carved into a bowl with the furnace beneath, where their father had boiled blackvine for three days until it turned soft as clay. Against one wall squatted the kiln, and next to it, the smooth block of volcanic glass where he had beaten the softened vines into shape before being fired. Along the walls, de-thorned rolls of blackvine cluttered, and on the lone stone table opposite the tunnel entrance lay an array of finished tiles, tools, and weapons.

Their father had claimed to be the best blackvine smith in the valley, and no one had ever disputed it that Pasha had ever heard, though he suspected all the smiths made such claims to their clans. Now, though, his forge seemed ramshackle and cold, it's spirit flitted away with the life of the man who'd spent over two centuries there working his craft.

They stayed at the forge for two days, gnawing on strips of dried bora meat and watching the shaft of light slide from west to east. Towards midday the first day, there was a low, resounding *boom* that echoed back and forth against the Wall around the valley, rolling down through the chimney hole, making the coils of blackvine stir. A few trailers of dust sprinkled from between the stone blocks of the walls. Anna and Pasha squeezed each other close. There was nothing to say. The invaders had breached the Tomb.

In the afternoon on the third day they left the safety of the forge after Pasha collected two long blackvine knives, thin and curved, from his father's worktable. Rain had washed through the night before that neither of them had noticed, dampening the ground, making it stick to their moccasins and clearing the air of ash, but it still smelled like smoke.

"We should look for survivors," Pasha said.

Anna wiped her face with the back of her hand and didn't answer.

They stood together at the narrow trail that led up the side of the mesa to Suedmal. Clouds had moved in, squeezing through the lower valleys of the western Wall like glaciers, making the sky featureless and dull. He didn't want to go back to Suedmal. He didn't want to see what had been left behind. He didn't want to voice his fear to his little sister, either, so he said, "Alright," and they continued up the path together. Towards home.

The grey smell of smoke wasn't enough to drown the stench wafting from Suedmal as they climbed the path. Anna gave a quiet little cough and pulled her vest over her nose. Pasha gave her a questioning look, but she only shook her head, and they continued on.

Animals filled the street. Rats scattered, and mourner birds took flight as the siblings crested the bluff. A family of bora rooted and gnawed at something near one of the longhouses. Revenge for a millennium of their kin being drowned in the lake below for leather and meat. Their heads swung as one towards the siblings, smooth black hides glittering in the filtered sunlight. The female's tusks jutted out and forward from the back of her lower jaw, curving upward. They were as long as Pasha's forearms. He drew his knives and struck a low defensive stance, wishing he'd taken a flat-spear from his father's forge, but she just snorted at him and led her family away to the south, unhurried. Silence returned to the village as the crunch of their hooves died in the distance.

Limbs, fragments of gnawed bone, shattered skulls with eyes pecked out by the mourners, and blackening piles of flesh were all that remained of their clan. An end to the eternal struggle to lay claim to Suedmal, the sacred village closest to the Tomb.

The invaders had tried to set the roofs of the longhouses on fire. They'd clearly been unfamiliar with blackvine and had abandoned their useless torches where they lay on the tiled roofs. Instead, they'd directed their monsters to tear the structures apart, to limited success. They'd collapsed every house, and Pasha watched with tears in his eyes as his sister tried to dig through the rubble of their home until he pulled her away. Their parents wouldn't be there, anyway. Their father would have been with one of the first failed assaults a day or more to the north beyond Bora lake. He'd gone out the same night Pasha had told him he planned to set the fire for the night winds to carry up the valley, and had never returned.

And their mother—he forced himself to finish the thought,

willing himself to anger—their mother would be out here, somewhere, in Suedmal's lone street, reduced to bones or a blackened pile of flesh. Food for hornets.

"Come on," he whispered. "Let's go. There's nothing left for us here."

She let him lead her away.

They made their way down the backside of the mesa and then up again, though a little stretch of forest untouched by the fire, though it was blanketed in ash, the green only uncovered by their footprints.

At the base of the trail that led up past the tree line, she halted and grasped Pasha's hand.

"Wait." Her voice was soft but free of the quiver that had been in it since they'd hidden in the forge.

Pasha stopped and turned to face her. "What is it?"

She said nothing at first. Pasha waited, absentmindedly running a finger back and forth across the scar on his cheek.

"Maybe we shouldn't go," She blurted.

Pasha sighed, but before he could respond, she spoke. "Why is it okay to go there now? We know they took something. Isn't that enough? Why do we have to break the second law?"

He faced her, surprised to see her dark eyes sparkling. Not with tears, but what? Curiosity. He pressed his lips together and ran a finger across his scar again, studying her face. She wanted to go. She was looking to him for a reason not to.

Find the old man, and they would find whatever he'd taken, whatever had lain at the end of the path they now stood on. But Pasha wanted to know what they'd been protecting, too. He wanted to see what was so important that the Ancestors left his people to protect it, entombed in the mountains for an eternity that had ended four days ago.

His sister must have seen something on his face that told her all she needed to know. "It's okay. Never mind. There doesn't need to be a reason." She took his hand, and together they climbed the path toward the Library.

They stood, staring at the ruin in the long twilight, each stranded by their thoughts. Pasha, about the first time he'd come here, brought by his father in the ancient ritual of adulthood less than a year ago, to show him all that the people stood for. Anna, about how her adulthood had come early, and how meaningless it was, now that it was too late.

The white door lay forty hands away from where it had been set in the Wall, its bottom resting on a black boulder, while the top of the thick disk had sunk into the mossy ground. A passage led down into darkness. A scuffling of footsteps in the dust forged a path into the shadows. Rubbish left by the invaders lay strewn to the side of the opening.

Anna broke the silence. "Let's go."

"We need light."

Anna walked over to the pile of foreign junk and poked through it. She pulled out a cage of bent brass and broken glass and held it up.

"This is one of their lights," she said. "I saw their camp."

"It's broken."

Anna examined it, standing beside her brother. "The wick is sticky. I think it'll work for a little while." She struck her flint next to the cage, and the wick inside lit with a soft, bluish glow.

She walked toward the opening in the Wall without waiting to see if Pasha was following.

He hesitated for a second, then followed his sister into the passage.

The tunnel led straight into the Wall for a hundred paces before ending in a large, round chamber, the back half collapsed sometime in the distant past. What looked like glass tables and a few rows of featureless white boxes, made of the same material as the door, were arrayed around the room. On one side, half-buried in rubble and black stone, was a machine full of triangular holes. Shards of broken crystal were scattered in front of it. If any passages had once led from this room deeper into the Wall, they'd been entombed by the c for centuries.

The siblings stood in the center of the chamber. Pasha wandered over and examined the crystal shards near the collapsed wall and wandered back again. Neither of them could think of much to say. The faint blue light from their ruined lamp was fading, and they started back towards the distant light of day.

"There's no reason we should understand it," Anna said as they reached the opening.

"No," Pasha agreed. "Those broken crystals, though. The invaders did something with them. Took them out and smashed them?"

Anna shook her head as they stopped together in the fading daylight at the mouth of the tunnel. "Why would they come here just to smash something nobody was going to find? I think those were already broken, so they left them behind."

"And you think that's what they took? The unbroken... whatever they were?"

"Maybe."

Pasha nodded. "Maybe you're right. We need to find out. Follow them and see. If they didn't find anything, we need to know that, too."

Anna studied her brother, but all she said was, "Okay."

"We'll go down a little way and camp," Pasha said. "Tomorrow we'll head north. We'll find other survivors, figure out what to do next."

"I want to leave the valley, Pasha," Anna stated, her voice quiet enough that the tunnel behind them seemed to drink the sound of it.

"I know. We'll go," he said, pulling her into a hug she didn't resist. "North, then, to find where they came in. We can look for others on the way. We'll learn the truth. We have to. How else are we going to return what they stole?"

If Anna had any thoughts on that, she didn't share them.

3

WAITING

SYRINA WAS BORED. SHE WAS USED TO WAITING IN uncomfortable places, but she'd milled around the villages in the foothills for eight weeks waiting for Mann to show up. Now she'd spent another three watching his bored army waiting for him to come back through the tunnel. She'd decided two weeks ago that watching a mob of bored people was the only thing more boring than being one of them.

Things hadn't been too bad until she'd reached the Black Wall. She'd taken the Great Road from Fom, and reasoned that if Mann and his army had somehow passed her on their way to Valez'Mui, at least she'd hear about it.

They hadn't passed her. She'd waited in Valez'Mui for three months before Mann arrived from the south. Some misplaced desire for secrecy had compelled him to travel by sea around the Ristro Peninsula, and he'd paid for it. All her intelligence said that he'd departed the Upper Peninsula with three ships, but he arrived in Valez'Mui with two, undermanned at that. The Corsairs had taken their toll.

At least back in Valez'Mui, she hadn't been bored.

She didn't have many contacts left in the Yellow Desert from when she'd done work for Ormo there years ago. Valez'Mui was a city-state of transients. Nomads, indentured servants, and the slaves who didn't survive long enough to be called residents. She was glad she didn't need too many contacts this time around, and the one she needed most was still there. On the other hand, she and he hadn't parted on good terms.

Syrina could have approached Vesmalimali as someone other than the old man who'd scammed him out of his steamship seventeen years before, but she didn't want to take the time to build a new relationship with a rogue-corsair-turned-crime lord. Not when the previous one had worked so well right up to the end. Anyway, Ves had done well for himself as the smuggler known as Whitehook. Not that he was the forgiving sort, but she hoped two decades of success had softened him enough that he wouldn't try to kill her outright. Again.

Valez'Mui was a sprawling city of intricate marble buildings and wide, palm-lined boulevards. Kiosks and bazaars filled every square, shaded by linen sheets held aloft by arches carved into flowering vines. The city of a half-million people slept through the hottest part of the day and came alive again as the sun set over the Great Road, which was so wide here she couldn't see the far shore through the haze rising from the river.

Docks lined its banks, stretching for spans past where the city ended. Behind those sprawled the warehouses of the slavers. Between the city and the desert to the east, spread the nomad camps, twice as large as the city proper, ever changing as caravans came and went with stone from the Black Wall and the marble quarries, and slaves from the villages in the foothills.

It was easy for her to track down Vesmalimali's headquarters once she'd donned the face of Smudge, the old man who'd served her in Valez'Mui so many years before. No need to worry about accuracy —seventeen years changed the face of an old man.

The black market of Valez'Mui thrived as it ever did under the eyes of the ruling Artisans, and in the past decade, the Ristroan giant with, diamonds set into his skull, had worked his way to the top of the food chain.

Getting to see him might be another matter, though, given the legion of hooligans that hung around the marble-domed mansion that served as Ves's headquarters.

But no, she thought. Someone new might have a hard time getting in to see him, but she was sure he'd want to see Smudge. She just hoped all the bodyguards meant the man had gone soft.

The hulking woman at the gate tried to send the old man away with a casual "Fuck off," but the creature was persistent, and one of the goons within the compound overheard his name.

"Did you say Smudge?" the second guard asked through the thin columns of the marble gate, carved to look like bamboo.

"That's right," the old man said, flashing a wink with one green eye.

"You idiot," The second guard addressed the gate woman. "You have a guy in front of you that says he's the one that stole the boss's steamship, and you're not going to let him in?"

She blinked. "Wait a minute. Smudge? *The* Smudge? I didn't think—"

"I didn't steal anything. He lent me that ship. I borrowed it, and now I'm bringing it back." He paused. "Well, I'm bringing him *a* ship. A boat would maybe be more accurate. Or a barge. Yeah, go with barge. In any case, Whitehook is getting it back, just like I promised. I'm just a little late. And it's a different ship."

They escorted Smudge inside to the dining room where Vesmalimali sat in a cloud of magarisi fumes. The room smelled of smoke, wine, and roasted vegetables. The pirate was fatter than he'd been seventeen years ago but otherwise looked the same. There were a few thin lines of grey in his bushy black beard, but he still kept his head shaved and set with diamonds that contrasted with his dark skin. All ten of his fingers were decorated with gaudy rings set with gemstones, and he wore a yellow and purple house robe, tied at the waist but otherwise open to show his bulging, hairless girth. Another man, the same age, swarthy, but lighter-skinned than Whitehook, thin with a trim beard and curly black ponytail, noticed the old man first and arched his eyebrows in surprise, but said nothing.

Ves nodded a bored greeting around his cup, paused, and jolted to his feet as recognition lanced through the haze of magarisi. "You? *You!*" He picked up a knife from the table, long and serrated for cutting meat, tiny in his massive hand. "You got so tired of living your miserable shit life you thought you would give me the pleasure of ending it? About goddamned time." He started unsteadily around the table.

The other man looked entertained and popped a grape into his mouth.

"Ah, good!" Smudge announced. "I thought maybe all these guards meant you'd gone soft, and I have no need for soft—I have a ship for you!" He added when Ves didn't slow.

Ves paused, suspicious. "Why come back after all these years?"

The old man barked out a laugh. "Why do you think? It's because I need someone like you. Someone who knows ships, and someone who knows the value of tin."

Smudge paused and looked at the other man, who was still watching with amused interest, sipping wine from a copper goblet. "Hello, Ash," Smudge said. "I see you're still with our honorable pirate. Twenty years and you never found anyone better?"

Ash winked at Ves. "Closer to thirty, if you can believe it. At this point, we're both just too old to bother with anyone else. And hello, Smudge. I suppose it's good to see you again."

Ves, still scowling, plunged the point of the knife into the wooden table, where it shuddered with a low twang. He flicked a hand at the two goons still flanking Smudge. They wheeled and left.

Ash stood, as unsteady as Ves, and made his way to the door. "I'll go as well. No, Ves, don't look at me like that. I'll always be your first mate, but I have no interest at the moment in listening to your business dealings, fascinating though I'm sure they'll be. You can catch me up later." He gave Ves a light kiss on the forehead and made his way out of the room with a little wave to Smudge. The pirate and the old man were alone.

"Appearances," Ves said, the word slurred under the cloud of wine and magarisi. "Turns out people here take me more seriously the more idiots I have working for me. Speaking of appearances, it looks like you've had some trouble." He nodded to Smudge's left hand, where the first knuckles of his index and middle finger ended in a knot of burn scars.

Smudge glanced at down at his hand and gave a little shrug. "Naphtha accident," he said. "Turns out I didn't need them for much, anyway."

Ves settled into the closest chair, in front of the knife protruding from the table. The wooden legs creaked.

Smudge relaxed a little. "Looks like you did alright for yourself without a ship." He cleared his throat. "Um, sorry about that, by the way. I meant to come back sooner, but, well, after your ship sank, I, uh, didn't see the point."

Ves made a low growling noise. His blue eyes looked dangerous again. "The Wave Savage sank? So, you have, what, a different ship for me now?"

"Well, more of a, uh, river barge, but yes. Well, I don't have it, but I think I know of one that's suitable and I intend to buy it for you. Um."

Ves was silent a moment. "A *river barge?*"

Smudge swallowed. "I know it's not the same, but there's a lot of tin to be made along the Great Road, as I'm sure you know. Not to mention the ten thousand Three-Sides I'll give you along with the boat. A pittance for you these days, I know, but still..."

Ves was silent for a moment. "And what do you want? You wouldn't have come back here if you didn't want something."

"At some point, I might need to leave Valez'Mui again. Maybe in a hurry. I need someone I can trust to take me to Fom. That one ride, and you'll never see me again."

Ves laughed. "You need someone you can trust, and you came to me?"

Smudge looked uncomfortable. "I'm not very good at making friends."

Ves had agreed as Syrina knew he would. As successful as he'd become selling magarisi to the locals and smuggling delezine to Fom, he was still a pirate who'd gone too long without a boat under his feet. She thought he might learn to like being a river pirate. There was a challenge in that, what with all the patrols along the Great Road. Just the sort of thing a man like Vesmalimali might enjoy.

After Mann had finally shown up in Valez'Mui, Syrina asked around and found out which route across the Yellow Desert he planned to take with his absurd army. It was an easy matter to use another old contact to ride with a caravan the same way well before him.

Too soon, it turned out, considering how long she needed to wait for him in the foothills. When he arrived, he was down to eleven karakh, and who knew how many men he'd lost. The desert people weren't very nice to outsiders at the best of times, and Mann had been involved in some sort of tribe pacification a few decades ago that had ended in disaster. Syrina wasn't clear on the details, but that was the type of thing the desert people didn't forget. The old man looked broken, and Syrina found herself feeling bad for him. She realized the army was as ridiculous idea to him as it was to everyone else, but orders were orders. That, she could relate to.

The girl caught Syrina's eye before they'd even started setting up camp. Fifteen, maybe sixteen years old. Not part of Mann's army, obviously. The guide, then. Syrina wondered if the general had resorted to forcing someone to lead him across the desert, but she didn't think that was the case. Too risky to trust someone when you've got them at knifepoint the same time you're counting on them to keep you alive. Anyway, from what she knew of Mann, he wasn't the kind to do something like that.

Well, however he'd ended up with her, Syrina could learn a thing or two. Whatever happened crossing the desert, the girl looked desperate to get away—she'd started trekking north before all of Mann's people had trickled in from the sands. Syrina waited around long enough to watch his wormy advisor protest her departure, which the general ignored. Whatever reason he'd wanted the girl to stick around, it wasn't because he liked her.

Syrina had had plenty of time to come up with a skin to deal with Mann in case it came up, and it only took an hour to put it on. A girl, about the same age as the guide, as it happened, that she'd named Chulla, from one of the countless tiny tribes that lived along the foothills of the Black Wall.

In the time it took to disguise herself, the girl had made her way to a little, nameless village a span to the north.

The people there were suspicious of Chulla as Syrina knew they would be. Strangers were almost unknown in the foothills except slavers from Valez'Mui. But they didn't like the girl, either, so she was easy to find among the dozen huts of black stone and thatch that clumped along a narrow, rapid stream flooding from the mountains. Someone had been kind enough to give her a bowl of mashed mountain grains and brook fish—a staple in this part of the foothills—and Syrina found her sitting apart from the village by the stream, eating with her hands.

"At least they fed you," Syrina said in one of the more distant dialects as she clambered over the tumbled rocks to the girl, wearing the dusky skin and tangled, pale hair of one of the settlements far to the south.

The girl looked up, suspicious. "Who are you?" Her accent was from one of the nomadic desert tribes, tinged with Valezian.

"My name was Chulla," Syrina answered, sitting down next to her. "They said I don't have a name anymore, but you can still call me that."

The girl stopped eating. "You were banished?"

Syrina nodded and held up her left hand, marred with old burn scars, and missing the index and middle finger. "There was an accident. Couldn't work. Flawed now, so not good for children, either. Not that I had much interest in those. That was a few years ago. Thought at first I'd go across the desert, see what was on the other side. More I hear about it, though, the more it seems like maybe I don't want to. Been heading north ever since."

"Why north?"

"Don't know. See what's there, I guess."

The girl nodded, satisfied, and scooped up another bite. "My name is Ginya," she said around her full mouth. "You're right to not want to go to the other side of the desert. Nothing good there. Nothing good here, either."

"So you've been there? You just came with that big crowd of foreigners, right? Who are they? Too many weapons to be a normal caravan, and too many of them to be slavers."

Ginya nodded again, swallowed, and scooped up the last bite of gruel before answering. "I came with them," she confirmed, putting her bowl down in the grass beside her. "Their guide. I wanted to get away from the city. I was a slave. Their leader—Mann, is his name—was looking for someone to take them here, so I volunteered. I traveled with the tribe a lot. Before they sold me, I mean. I know some of the tracks."

"Didn't go well?" Syrina pressed.

"It wasn't my fault, but most of them say it was. I was trying to keep them safe by avoiding the main routes, but it ended up being bad, anyway. No wonder. Everyone in Valez'Mui knew they were looking to cross the desert, and where in the foothills they wanted to end up. Nobody likes them here, least of all the nomads. They made me take one of the main routes, after. That went worse, just like I told them it would. Didn't stop them from blaming me, though."

"Why'd they come here? Seems like a lot of trouble."

Ginya nodded. "Too much trouble. Something in the mountains, I guess. I don't think any of them know what they're doing here, except maybe Mann, and he didn't seem too sure, either."

Syrina stood. "Well, thanks. For telling me I'm better off here. I need to find someone to give me some food, or catch a fish myself." She paused. "You should get out of here. That mob you came with—if they had such a bad time, they'll be needing food and supplies. They'll come here to get them."

Ginya stood with her. "Thanks. Um. Maybe we could travel together? Safer, maybe. And it's nice to have someone to talk to."

Syrina hesitated, forcing back a wave of guilt. "Sure. For a little while. Let's go."

Later that night, as Ginya slept on the moss by another glacial stream, Syrina slipped away.

You have a job to do, the voice in her head reminded her as she swallowed a lump of remorse. *As always.*

It was right. As always. And as always, Syrina didn't care. Ginya had told of her life as they walked that afternoon. Sold to an Artisan by her family who couldn't feed her, then sold again. Freed by her second master, but with nowhere to go, she'd sold herself until she found Mann, and with him, a way to escape.

And in Chulla, she'd thought she'd found a friend. One who abandoned her at the first opportunity. Syrina told herself it was for the best. The girl would be fine on her own—had learned to be hard, and would fare alright if she kept going north, where the tribes were both more sheltered from slavers and kinder to outsiders. All of those things, she repeated to herself, were true.

But it didn't matter. Syrina knew it would sting the girl when she woke up to find Chulla gone. There was a time not long ago when she wouldn't have given two thoughts to such things, but she was different now, and there was no going back, either to who she was or the girl she'd left behind.

The problem with being different now, she reflected, was that her life was the same. Only now, when she made the same choices, they added a weight to her soul she didn't know how to unburden.

When this is all done, you can retire, the voice piped as she made her way back through the sparse forest and bubbling streams to the village and Mann's camp beyond.

She couldn't tell if it was serious or not, but as far as she could tell, there was no end in sight.

Syrina waited for another week as Mann's army recovered. Sure enough, they looted the five nearby villages that lay within a day of their encampment for food and supplies. The karakh kept anyone from fighting back with more than angry words, despite the rage written in their eyes. They would have a long year or two ahead of them before they recovered from their depleted goat herds and stripped grain stores.

She'd followed at a safe distance for the next few days as the soldiers scrambled through a breach in the Wall—a narrow, steep ravine, sheer on either side, where a frigid stream tumbled down from the glaciers. The forest along the canyon floor was dense, with a few scraggly trees higher up, their roots grasping cracks in the black cliffs.

At a waterfall, flowing from a grotto at the end of the gorge, she'd now waited for almost two weeks, perched among the stunted conifers growing above the long line of bored soldiers. The peaks glistened on either side. Mann, the karakh, and half his men had disappeared into the grotto a day after they had blown out the first few layers of ice and rock with jars of powder. A few more explosions had echoed down from the tunnel over the next day. After that, for a few days, nothing. Then soldiers had poured out, repelling down to the camp below, but not Mann nor the karakh. And those that returned only settled in to wait with the others.

She started to wonder if everyone else had been killed. The only thing that had kept her out of the grotto so far—the order from Ormo to only watch wasn't enough—was because if she ran into the army coming the other way, her tattoos, which made her almost unnoticeable when combined with subtle movements of her muscles, wouldn't do anything to keep her unseen in such a tight space.

The voice in her head offered no opinion on the matter.

That damn voice. She could almost say she'd gotten used to it in the past four years, ever since it had sprung into existence the moment another Kalis, working for Ormo, had killed her owl, Triglav.

She still planned on rubbing her boss for that. Just as soon as she figured out what she and the voice inside her head were.

And she still needed to figure out *how* to kill Ormo. The first attempt had ended in colossal failure, and it was going to be harder the second time.

If anything, thinking about what she planned to do to Ormo took up time, and it was more interesting than watching hundreds of soldiers wait.

There was a burst of activity in the camp, centered at the base of the falls. A figure appeared in the shadows of the grotto, and then another beside the first. It was too dark and far away to see any details.

The figures exchanged words with a few officers below, drowned out by the white noise of the waterfall. The men in the grotto receded back into darkness before one, then two karakh appeared in their stead and scuttled down to land amid the waiting army. Soldiers scurried to get out of their way. There were people strapped to the backs of the karakh—a few with crude splints on arms or legs or both, and most looked burned.

Well, now. That *was* interesting.

A handful of others repelled down on their own. None of them were General Mann or his wormy little adviser.

Syrina half-expected the army to depart then, but these new ones only settled in while medics began treating the wounded. The karakh ambled further down the canyon whistling and clicking to each other until they'd disappeared out of sight.

She slunk down off her perch and edged closer to the encampment where she could listen, but there was a commotion around the newcomers, and she couldn't get as close as she wanted. Something about a valley, and a fire, and guardians, though there was some disagreement about whether they were human or something else. General Mann had stayed behind with the few uninjured left and the surviving karakh. The ones that had returned didn't express a whole lot of faith in their leader, but they settled in to wait for him, nevertheless.

Syrina crept back up to her perch as evening faded into a cold, cloudy night, devoid of any light except the cook fires that sprang up in the camp below, reflecting dull orange on the low clouds hiding the towering peaks around them.

Mann had disappeared into the grotto with around a thousand men. Half had returned in the first wave out of the tunnel. According to these newcomers, of the five hundred he'd kept with him, maybe, what? Twenty or thirty had survived? Whatever they'd found in there, it hadn't been kind to them. She was glad she hadn't followed.

Maybe it was a bunch of Kalis, the voice in her head quipped.

Syrina pressed her lips together, but she couldn't tell if it was serious or not, and she didn't respond.

Sometime before dawn a day later, a commotion in the camp stirred Syrina from her meditation. She opened her eyes to see white-blue naphtha light shining from the mouth of the tunnel. The whistling, clicking voices of the karakh echoed from somewhere within, and a moment later, the big white one squeezed out of the grotto with a chatter of disgust. Mann perched behind the shepherd, hanging in his harness, limp with exhaustion.

Syrina flitted down to the camp again to listen as the other karakh descended.

"... all there was, General?" Asked the man named Heine, whom Mann had left in charge of the men in the canyon. Syrina thought his tone was a bit incredulous for one talking to his superior officer. He was peering into a leather pack, which he tied up and handed back to Mann just as Syrina got into earshot. He handled it like it was heavy for its size.

Mann stood where he'd dismounted, thin and stooped. He took the pack back with a sigh and handed it to another man who'd dismounted alongside him, who sealed it into a wood and bronze shipping crate that a third soldier had brought over at a signal from Mann. *How many soldiers does it take to put a bag in a box?* she thought, but she didn't laugh, and neither did the voice.

"Yes, I am sure, Colonel." Mann's voice grated, bitter and tired. Syrina strained to hear him better. "These were the only things that could be removed at all. That weren't broken, anyway. It will have to be enough."

Heine scowled at the crate, now sealed and passed up to the shepherd, who was tying it to the karakh, using Mann's harness. "It just seems unlikely, General, that the Arch Bishop would invest so much to retrieve a handful of useless glass."

Anger flashed in Mann's eyes, but his expression didn't change from one of absolute weariness. "Then, *Colonel*," he enunciated the title, "Perhaps the Arch Bishop should have been more specific about what it was I was to retrieve from that hell pit. And if you, Colonel Heine, had such specifics, it would have been helpful of you to divulge them earlier, or even accompany us through the tunnel, rather than volunteer to supervise the men I chose to stay behind." He glanced around, now a tiny, wry smile on his face. "We could have used your expertise. Those of us who survived."

Syrina found herself smiling, too.

You might need to kill him at some point, you know, the voice reminded her.

"I'll worry about that if it comes up," she whispered under her breath. "In the meantime, I like him. Now shut up. I'm trying to listen."

But the conversation between General and Colonel had ended. Heine shambled off, looking angry. Mann leaned in close to the man he'd dismounted with—a captain, Syrina remembered him being, though none of those returned from the valley wore any insignia—and whispered something to him. The captain nodded and mounted the karakh behind the crate. The shepherd, who'd watched the whole scene from his perch on the karakh's neck, laughing silently, whistled a few soft, tuneless notes, and his mount surged forward down the canyon and out of sight.

Syrina hung around for another hour to listen but didn't pick up anything else that seemed important. Glass, she kept thinking. All of this and he came out with glass? She wanted to have a look in the crate to see this "glass" for herself but conceded that it wouldn't happen as long as it was strapped to the karakh.

A little while later, predawn light began to grope through the clouds, and Mann's exhausted army started to strike camp. Syrina retreated up to her perch, where no one would notice her.

As the soldiers began to drag themselves back down the canyon later that morning, she started to follow, but the voice said, *What's your hurry? It will take weeks for them to find a guide back across the desert. You know where they're going, anyway.*

"You know something I don't?" Syrina muttered to herself, but she stopped, looking back at the mouth of the grotto. Ropes still hung forgotten from the dark opening.

You know I don't. It just stands to reason that if someone or something gave them such a hard time in there, someone or something might not be done giving them a hard time.

Syrina had the distinct impression that that wasn't all the voice knew. "Some of the soldiers were talking about how they'd wiped them all out. Whoever they were." But she knew she'd lost the argument.

If you want to base your actions on the boasts of some soldier trying to compensate for the bad time he obviously had, it's not my problem. Only it is *my problem, so don't do it.*

Syrina grunted, but she turned around and climbed back up to her perch, one eye on the tunnel. She thought she could feel the voice gloating in its victory, but she she'd grown paranoid about things like that.

4

THE AFTERMATH

A FEW HUNDRED SURVIVORS HAD CRAWLED FROM CAVES AND blackvine forges, or from under lakes and streams as Anna and Pasha had. All of them were children or ancient and infirm. As one old man had put it, "Only children left. The old kind and the young kind."

Pasha's hopes of finding someone to go with them faded with the embers of the fire. The children couldn't help and, anyway, were the only future the valley people had, whatever new purpose they might find for themselves. The elderly either tried to convince them to stay or to leave and never come back. None thought Pasha and Anna had any hope of retrieving anything from the demon riders, and they had neither the will nor ability to come with them themselves.

Pasha and Anna saw the devastation as they traveled but still couldn't grasp it. The night wind had swept fire through the valley before, of course. Swaths of bloodfern trees lost their leaves to flame every fifty years or so when lightning struck at just the wrong spot at just the wrong time. Pasha knew some of the fires before his time had been severe, but lightning was rare enough that he'd never heard of such complete devastation. Of course, this was the first time someone had deliberately set fires at the place where the winds first swept down from the southern peaks. There were nine pockets of hidden tinder along the narrow south end of the valley, maintained by the residents of Suedmal. A last resort, Pasha's mother had taught him after he'd returned from the Tomb door with his father on his seventy-fifth birthday. If invaders came, if no others could stop them, set the fires. The last, sacred duty of the residents of Suedmal.

The winds blow almost every night, she'd told him as she showed him the pyres of dry leaves and twigs hidden throughout the forest. They're how the valley protects its treasure—if the people can't drive invaders off, the valley itself could do it.

And yet the valley, too, had failed.

Already the land was coming back to life. Anna found some of the bloodferns had tiny red buds at the tips of their blackened branches, and here and there patches of scorched, black bark were flaking away to reveal dark wood beneath, like scabs peeling away to reveal new skin.

Most of the villages hadn't been attacked, but they'd still lost most of their people to the flames and the fighting. Pasha and Anna now found lonely longhouses filled with elderly, teaching tearful children how to rebuild without their parents to guide them. They offered the siblings a place to live, but none seemed surprised when they declined. Pasha and Anna were from Suedmal, after all. Survivors from the southernmost village had a duty, however futile it might be.

On the fifth day, they came across the remains of one of the invader's camps, this one ringed by dozens of cairns. It wasn't until Anna had removed some of the stones out of curiosity that they realized that they were graves.

"They buried their dead," she said to Pasha, surprised. "I wonder if they always do that."

Pasha came over to examine the gray hand and arm clad in alien leather armor. "They didn't bury them further south," he pointed out. "We passed battle sites. Their people were just left lying with ours."

Anna considered that. "Maybe this was the last place they had time. It's respectful, I guess, in its own way. Still," she shuddered,

"Buried. How can they complete the cycle under all these rocks where only bugs and worms can eat them? How can the mourner birds gather their souls?"

"Maybe there are no mourner birds where they come from. Or maybe they don't want to return to their Ancestors." He paused. "Maybe they don't have souls. I guess we'll find out."

Anna nodded. "Yes. I want to find out."

They started to walk away. As an afterthought, Anna returned to the mound and replaced the rocks over the arm. Pasha watched in silence.

Two weeks later, they reached the long, steep scree that marked the north end of the valley. Neither Pasha nor Anna had ever traveled the full length of it before, and neither knew the names of the smattering of villages this far from Suedmal. They were all abandoned in any case. They hiked in silence, and had spoken just a dozen words between each other since they'd left the last inhabited town they'd come across a day earlier.

Pasha worried about his sister. Before the invasion, she had been the cynical joker, taking nothing seriously, delighting at pointing out the myriad of flaws she saw around her, whether those in her family or her people. The Anna he knew would have gloated through her tears that she'd been right about the absurdity of their culture; their obsession with the door embedded in the southern mountains that nobody knew how to open. But the burning rage he felt seemed to come to Anna only as a quiet, desperate need to get as far away as possible and never return.

The invader's ropes still dangled from an opening near the base of a glacier, six hundred hands or more above the sharp, black detritus fallen from the western corner of the Wall, where the cliffs veered to run south. Below, along the edge of the forest, the siblings could see the remains of the intruder's first camp, lined on both sides by more cairns. Mourner birds fluttered through the debris, and despite the attacker's attempt at burial, the stench of death hung amid the blackened trees.

"We'll rest here," Pasha said, eying the dangling ropes in the failing twilight. "Until morning."

Anna only nodded and walked back to the tree line, where she sank down to sit with her back against a soot-stained bloodfern, staring at nothing.

Pasha hesitated, wondering if she wanted to be alone, then walked over to squat beside her.

"There were so many," he said, eyes still on the ropes. "It must have taken them a long time to climb down."

She followed his gaze to the cliffs. "There are bivouacs," she observed. "Or stretchers."

Pasha peered closer. From a few of the ropes dangled small, open platforms halfway up, blending with the fissures of the Wall. "Too small to sleep on, I think. Just for resting, I guess."

"They'll make it easier when we climb tomorrow," she stated. With that, she lay down and closed her eyes.

Pasha woke with the first glint of twilight peeking over the Wall to see Anna clambering up the shale-covered slope. He felt a sudden flash of irritation and followed to squat next to her at the base of the cliff.

"Going without me?" He quipped, trying to keep his tone light, but the anger in his eyes gave him away.

Anna studied him, and he thought he saw the slightest hint of a smile nudge the corners of her mouth. "I woke up and couldn't sleep," she said. "I thought I'd come up here to wait for you." Her expression grew distant again.

Pasha's face softened. He looked up. The ropes seemed to disappear above them.

Anna followed his gaze, then shrugged. "No choice."

Pasha turned his eyes back over the valley. There were no clouds in the predawn light, and the Eye was somewhere on the other side of the world. To either side, the serrated peaks of the Black Wall sparkled in the dying starlight, and the band of glaciers began to glow a soft yellow with the sunrise that wouldn't touch the valley for hours. In the distance, the Wall closed in, then turned, so the eastern mountains blocked the southern half of the valley. The siblings' half. The forest of bloodferns was still black and leafless in the growing light, and a thin brown haze had settled in the night when the rare lack of wind had failed to blow it away.

"Let's go," he said.

Anna nodded and began scaling up the rope, using cracks in the cliff as footholds. Suppressing a sudden shake in his hands, Pasha followed.

By the time they reached the bivouacs halfway up, Pasha's shoulder's were burning. Anna rested on an adjacent platform, her own hands tucked under her armpits as she looked off over the valley, her feet dangling off the edge. Pasha climbed over to the makeshift ledge next to her, panting.

The bivouacs were made from a thick weave of bloodfern branches, snarls of ropes holding them together, made by the invaders to hoist their injured back to wherever they came from.

To either side, chips and cracks had been punched into the Wall, or existing crevasses had been widened at even intervals, like footprints of some enormous creature. He thought of the monsters the attackers had ridden. Had those things been able to scale up and down the Wall like that? He thought about asking what his sister thought of the idea but decided against it.

Up here, the air was clear. The brown haze had drifted off with the sunrise hours ago, and from this height, he could see small groves of bloodferns that still held their canopies of reddish-green leaves. Despite the sun burning above them, the air was cold.

He pointed them out to Anna. "By the time we come back, the valley might be back to normal," he said, trying to sound hopeful, but it was empty, even to himself.

"Come back." Anna repeated the words as if they had no meaning.

"Well, yes. we'll have to bring back what was taken. That's the whole point."

Anna didn't answer, or even act like she'd heard him, and he dropped the subject with a pit boiling in his stomach.

They watched the sun creep across the sky for a long time, until Anna turned to the rope, adjusting her grip and finding purchase with her feet. "Let's go," she said, and began to climb without waiting for an answer.

They reached the tunnel a short time later. The floor was slick, the ceiling jags of obsidian and chunks of blue ice. Black scorch marks streaked the walls, and rock and rotting ice lay strewn about the wide passage. The air smelled ancient.

Pasha collapsed in the mouth of the grotto and pressed his burning hands into the frozen floor. Anna slouched against the wall twenty hands further down the tunnel, but she sat up a little when she heard her brother. She wore the little smile again. "We made it," she said, and lay back down.

Pasha nodded from where he'd collapsed onto his back, looking at the uneven ceiling of the passage. "We made it," he agreed, in a whisper.

It was too cold to sleep, even with their extra layers and bora hide blankets, so they forced each other to keep moving, hands linked, groping along the uneven wall, testing each step in the blackness. Neither spoke, save when Anna mumbled a warning to Pasha about a sudden incline or chunk of stone to avoid, or when Pasha asked Anna if she was okay after one of her innumerable stumbles and falls as she led the way. Pasha lost all track of time as they staggered through the dark, their progress measured only by the short breaks they took to rest against the wall before moving on. Days, they agreed, but neither of them could say how many.

After a long time, there was the sound of rushing water, and they were forced to splash through a stream that cascaded down the center of the passage, widening until it reached both walls and they needed to slog through it. Their feet went numb with cold. A little while later, they could see shadows. The ice of the ceiling was glowing a soft, watery green.

A pale light grew ahead of them, and a few minutes after that, they were standing at the top of a waterfall forty hands high. A narrow canyon filled with stunted, gnarled pine led down and away around a bend. Ropes hung alongside the waterfall from the tunnel to the steep rock below.

They looked at each other, but neither had anything to say.

They had reached the other side of the Wall.

5

MEETING

SYRINA HUNG AROUND THE GROTTO FOR FIVE DAYS AFTER MANN, and what remained of his army, edged their way back into the foothills. She didn't have anyone to pilfer from, so she resorted to small fish, eaten raw, plucked from the pool at the base of the waterfall.

It's better than raw rat, the voice had pointed out to her.

She hadn't bothered to respond.

Syrina sat at the edge of the pool, having one such meal, when she caught movement in the mouth of the grotto out of the corner of her eye. She skirted back into the edge of the brush.

A girl's face appeared out of the shadows, and a second later, a man's. Or boy's. Syrina's eyes were as sharp as they came, but it was hard to tell from their features how old they were, and it got harder the more she studied them. The boy's scar added to the confusion. Somewhere between teenagers and middle-aged. Syrina wanted to get a better look at them. Especially the man.

He's impressive. The voice agreed. It sounded uncharacteristically enthusiastic.

Syrina suppressed a well of emotion that had risen in her belly. Looking at him gave her a sense of déjà vu, but she couldn't place why. Been away from civilization too long, she thought, although even when she'd been in the middle of Fom, she'd never found herself attracted to random strangers. But to the voice, she whispered, "Shut up. I'm listening."

The two faces—similar enough that they must be related—hovered at the entrance to the tunnel, arguing in low voices that she couldn't quite make out; just enough to know she didn't recognize their language.

That might make introductions difficult. The voice pointed out from the back of her head.

"Shut up. I've had worse," she muttered, wondering why she couldn't kill the feeling the man was giving her. She couldn't remember feeling like that since... but no, she wouldn't let herself think about that.

She was still wondering where her feelings were coming from, and trying to force them back to wherever that was, when the two figures in the grotto reached a decision. The man, then the woman, descended on the abandoned ropes and landed in the little clearing by the pool, not twenty hands from where Syrina crouched. He looked older than the girl. A little. Still, it was hard to tell. Something about them both seemed timeless, for lack of a better word.

Maybe it's thousands of years of inbreeding.

Syrina smirked at that. "Good one." She only moved her mouth, in case the siblings had good hearing, but she didn't want to give the voice the satisfaction of only thinking her response.

To her disappointment, the voice seemed satisfied, anyway.

You don't know they're siblings.

Syrina looked at the pair again, who stood in the little glade, chattering. They sounded frantic, but she supposed it could just be one of those languages that always sounded that way. Relative in height, and only a little taller than Syrina, even as short as she was. Same hair, same nose, same eyes. Of course, that *could* just be ten thousand years of inbreeding, but there was the way they interacted. Even without understanding, she would have called it familiar disdain. "Yes, I know. Trust me on this one."

The voice must have decided to trust her because it didn't respond.

They came to some resolution. Their words became more relaxed, and they started off together along the ragged trail left by Mann's army. Syrina fell in behind them, wondering when she'd get a chance to introduce herself.

She'd need to keep an eye on these two. If they were from the Wall, their ancestry could be an unbroken line all the way back to the Ancients. She thought about all she'd learned a lifetime ago at the Northern Research Initiative and Witt Pharmaceutical, and wondered if these two weren't even more important than whatever Mann had taken from them.

The pair paused at the mouth of the canyon, on the precipice that marked the start of the narrow switchback descending into the scrubby foothills and the Yellow Desert beyond. They stood on the edge, their tone a mix of awe and terror. Before them, a span below, the foothills rolled away before ending at a line of dunes. Beyond, the black stone spires of the Bones towered at irregular intervals as far as the eye could see, except to the west, where they ended in an abrupt line, beyond which the desert stretched to the horizon, all detail lost in the haze of blowing sand. The smell of stone and dust was thick.

If they'd come from within the Wall, they'd never seen the horizon before, and Syrina tried to imagine going from a place so small to a place so huge. She couldn't, and she waited while they came to grips with it.

After twenty minutes of more hushed conversation, they began down the rugged trail at a trot, bouncing over rocks and around stunted, dry trees, careless of the span-high drop they ran along. Syrina supposed that for people from inside the Black Wall, a fear of heights wouldn't do at all.

The shadows cast by the gnarled pines were growing long by the time they reached the gentler slopes. There they paused again, forcing Syrina to stay on the narrow path above them. There was a village about a half-span to the south. Not even a village, more like a few huts and sheds that belonged to a single family of goat herders. The swath of torn soil and broken vegetation left by Mann's army cut away to the northwest, and after a while, the pair headed off in that direction, as cautious and silent as Syrina.

They followed Mann's trail until dusk fell into night, and it was too dark to see. There was a vague, purple glow to the night sky, but the Eye would hide behind the peaks of the Wall for most of the night, and the starlight only thickened the shadows.

They came across a small, abandoned barn a few paces from Mann's broad trail, and squeezed through the broken door just as Syrina came around the corner to watch them. She crept to the outside wall and crouched to listen.

Syrina was good with languages. She could learn one in a couple of weeks with close observation, or at least pick it up enough to get by. But listening through a wall with no context gave her nothing. She picked up the sounds well enough, but she had no idea what any of it meant.

I think... I think I recognize this, the voice said after an hour.

"Really?" Syrina whispered to herself, incredulously.

Maybe. It seems familiar, somehow.

Syrina considered. The voice within her, at least as much as she'd determined, was a remnant from the Ancients. If the pair within the barn were from a people who had been isolated within the Black Wall since the Age of Ashes, it stood to reason that they were speaking a language related to one spoken before then. Of course, languages changed over ten thousand years, but if a group of people was isolated that entire time, without any outside influence, she wondered if it might still be recognizable to someone—or something—that spoke the language of Eris as it had been spoken eons ago.

Still, "seems familiar somehow," wasn't helpful in any practical sense, and Syrina pointed out as much.

Shut up. I might pick something up if you stop distracting me.

Syrina wasn't sure, but she thought that might have been the first time the voice had told her to shut up, rather than the other way around. She frowned but kept her thoughts to herself as the voice listened.

And to her surprise, the voice did start to pick some of it up, and as it did, she did too. A word here and there brought an image to her mind, a phrase, a feeling, and by the time the voices within the barn fell silent for the night, she thought she might at least be able to grunt out a few sounds that they would understand.

First, though, she needed a face for them to look at. She crept down the hill a little way to another scattering of huts to see what she could scrape up.

The girl of fourteen or so crept to the barn door, cautious but clumsy. The half-Eye loomed in the west, bright enough through the sparse pines that anyone looking out the paneless window could see her.

As she neared, the broken door jerked open a few hands before getting stuck, askew in its frame. A hand grasped the girl's arm and yanked her in.

The girl started to cry as she stared into the darkness of the ramshackle goat shed, green eyes wide and frightened.

The man who held her whispered a few harsh words into the darkness behind him, and a mound in the back stirred and rose, the motion sleepy and confused, revealing itself to be a girl about the same height as the intruder.

"Help. I help." The girl, still held by the man, said, studying his face like she hoped he'd understand the sounds she made. She tugged at his arm with her free hand, but the missing fingers made it too difficult to get a grip.

They must have understood. The woman said something, and the man, after a moment of reluctance, released his grip and positioned himself between her and the door.

"You (*something something*) understand (*something*)?" he asked her.

"Little." She replied, rubbing her arm where he'd held her. She had short, brown hair and delicate features. Her skin was dark, and she wore simple moccasins, leggings of goat leather, and a shirt of filthy white goat hair.

"(*Something something*) here?" He asked, staring at the girl with intense interest. The woman, who'd been sleeping in the back of the barn, moved to stand by him.

"Chulla." The girl stated, gesturing at herself. "Name Chulla."

The man nodded, gestured at himself, then the woman. "Pasha," he said. "Anna."

Chulla nodded, satisfied.

"(*Something something*) why (*something*)?" Pasha asked again.

The girl hesitated, and her eyes grew distant for a moment. She muttered to herself before refocusing on Pasha. "People from mountains. You follow. I follow."

"Why?" Anna asked.

Chulla looked to each of them, face sad. "Taken. Father, mother, taken."

Pasha and Anna glanced at each other. "They took your parents?" Pasha asked.

Chulla shook her head, frustrated, tears again welling in her eyes. "Taken. Life taken."

Understanding and sympathy dawned on his face.

Chulla wiped her eyes and nodded.

Anna looked like she was about to say something, but before she could, Pasha said, "Ours too. And they took something from us. We need to get it back. What will you do when you find them?"

The girl only shook her head and shrugged.

Anna, her expression irritated, whispered something to her brother.

He shook his head and smiled at Chulla. "You can stay with us. Understand? We won't hurt you."

Anna looked like she might object, but said nothing.

"Please, sit," Pasha said.

Chulla smiled a little, nodded, and sat next to him, while Anna sat a little apart, frowning.

The girl came from a tribe of goat herders. One of the hundreds that speckled the hills between the Black Wall and the Yellow Desert. Of the thousand dialects spoken in the desert and foothills, her tribe's was unique, as far as she knew. If anyone else had come across them, they wouldn't have been able to communicate.

The siblings had never considered that there might be more languages beyond the Wall than the one they'd heard Mann speak, but they were smart enough to know there was a lot they didn't know, and they took to the concept well enough, though Anna's open suspicion remained.

When the army—from a faraway place called N'narad—had passed through the foothills a few months before, they'd swept across villages, requisitioning whatever they needed. When Chulla's father had tried to stop them, Mann had both her parents executed.

Pasha and Anna were sympathetic. "They took something from us, too," Pasha said again before his sister shushed him.

"What they take?"

Pasha was about to answer, but Anna said, "Our parents," with a withering look at her brother. He hesitated, then nodded.

"I'm sorry," Chulla said, staring at Pasha.

He shrugged and looked away. "It's done now."

Anna watched, expression unreadable.

Pasha and Chulla talked until dawn seeped through the cracks in the walls of the dilapidated shed. After a few more harsh glances from Anna, Pasha stopped trying to tell the girl where they were from and left it as somewhere far away. Chulla didn't press. Pasha risked asking about her mangled hand, but she only said she'd lost her fingers in an accident, and he seemed happy enough to leave it at that. As they spoke, Chulla's ability with their language grew with remarkable speed, and by morning they could talk without much confusion. Anna didn't sleep, nor did she speak. She only watched her brother.

"Stay one more day," Chulla said, blinking her green eyes against the slats of daylight beaming in through the walls. It was almost noon, but the sun had only now broken above the peaks of the Black Wall.

Pasha shook his head. "They are far ahead of us. We need to follow."

Chulla shook her head and moved over to sit closer to him. He looked uncomfortable, but he didn't move away. Anna frowned from where she was pulling strips of dried meat from her pack.

"They cross the desert. It take time and only one place to go. We need find someone to cross with, too, or we die in sand. Anyway, the one in charge the army, one called Mann, go back to N'narad. We catch up."

Anna came over to sit cross-legged by Pasha, handing them each a length of the dried meat. "One place to go? You mean N'narad, where Mann is from?"

Chulla shook her head. "No, no, no. Where are you from? You don't know these things?"

Pasha seemed about to answer, but Anna talked over him. "Like Pasha said, far from here. A village. Like you." She shot her brother another glance.

Chulla looked back and forth between them. "Valez'Mui is city on other side of desert. From there, ships to Fom and Eheene and the rest."

"City?" Pasha blinked at her.

Chulla gave a little laugh. "Yes, 'city.' A village, but bigger. Much, much bigger. Millions of people, sometimes, though Valez'Mui isn't that big. So I've heard."

"Millions?" Pasha stared. "Millions of people in one place? Is that what N'narad is?"

Chulla shook her head again, exasperated. "No. N'narad is a nation. An empire." She looked at their blank faces. "Many cities, and the lands and water between."

"How many people are in the world?" Anna asked, tone disbelieving.

Chulla shrugged. "I don't know. I've been far north and all the way to ocean in the south, but I never left foothills. But I talk to many people. I hear things. Millions and millions, anyway."

"What's an ocean?" Pasha asked.

Chulla's smile grew. "Water. A salty lake that goes forever. You will see."

Pasha and Anna looked at each other. "How will we find one man out of millions?" Pasha asked his sister.

"Not as hard as you think. This Mann, many know him. Able to find, but you need to learn some language so you can talk to people. Besides me."

"Like the language Mann and his people spoke?" Pasha asked.

"Yes." Chulla nodded. "N'naradin. Many speak N'naradin. Someone in Valez'Mui can help."

"But not you?" Pasha sounded disappointed, and Anna gave a little snort.

"No. I cannot help in place I have never been. But you will find someone. I'm sure. I speak Trade, a little Valezian. Limited, but used by many who can't talk together otherwise. I teach you what I know on the way. In Valez'Mui, you find someone to help you."

Anna frowned. "How do you know? How do you know anything about what we'll find in this Valley-Me if you've never been there before?"

"Valez'Mui," Chulla corrected. "I have faith. Now," she said, changing the subject with another little smile. "I find berries for breakfast. Do you have berries where you are from? No matter. Rest. Tomorrow we find way across a desert." She glanced at Pasha, and her smile grew before she disappeared out the door.

6

THE CROSSING: SEVEN MONTHS BEFORE THE TRIAL

I let my men recover for a week in Valez'Mui once they were off the ships. The Artisans allowed them to camp along the Great Road on a wide, grassy bank to the north, as long as they agreed to make no attempt to enter the city walls. Just beyond a low, straw-hued ridge a span away to the east, the Yellow Desert began.

As you've seen, no roads cross the desert. Steam cars become clogged with sand, rendered irreparable within minutes, and downdrafts from the Black Wall hundreds of spans away drive airships into ground without warning. Sandstorms and quakes change the landscape, and from the Great Road to the Bones, none of the landmarks are permanent except the oases.

I could only pray I could trust the girl named Ginya; that she hadn't lost her instincts in the years she'd spent in Valez'Mui.

As we moved into the desert, the karakh, as always, posed the biggest problem. Their obvious joy at getting off those miserable ships turned to rage within a few days. Ginya did her best to find us shelter in the narrow, sand-choked canyons and sprawling boulder fields where we could set our tents during the day, but the heat boiling off the rocks was hot enough to cook on, and no one could sleep through the creatures' cries and clicks as they huddled from the heat in whatever inadequate pools of shadow they could wedge into. The main routes were better protected, but Ginya insisted they would be too dangerous with an army the nomads didn't want in their territory. They hadn't forgotten my previous visit to that part of the world two decades ago, nor had they forgiven it.

Dakar approached me on the third day. "General, we don't get the karakh a real source of water soon, we're not going to be able to stop them when they start killing your soldiers for blood."

I suppressed a shudder and waved Ginya over. "How far until the next oasis?" I asked her.

The girl eyed Dakar. She hadn't liked the karakh when she'd watched them come off the ships, and they hadn't grown on her.

"A real oasis? Two, maybe three days." Her eyes darted between Dakar and me. "There's a little spring though, or at least there used to be, maybe a half-day from here. It's north, though. Out of our way. You didn't bring enough water?"

"Not enough for them, I guess." I nodded toward the karakh sprawled along the base of a small cliff, panting. The other shepherds leaned against their mounts, dozing as best they could.

Ginya swallowed. "Oh."

I turned back to Dakar. "Will they wait until sunset, at least?" We camped in the shade of a crooked, orange stone spire, and the sun glowed low beyond it in the west.

Dakar nodded. "And a little after that. Until the ground cools enough to walk on again. I'll let the others know."

The spring was a line of damp rock twenty hands wide at the base of a yellowish outcropping. A pool formed along the bottom, a finger deep and about as wide. The Eye was almost full, and high in the cloudless sky by the time we reached it. Our breath clouded in the frigid, dry air.

"We should stay here tonight," Ginya said, watching the karakh scramble and fight over the sliver of water. "Let them get their fill. An hour after sunrise, it'll dry up until dark."

We didn't bring enough provisions to lose a whole night of progress, but there didn't seem to be much choice. I informed Dakar. He was obvious in his relief.

The karakh wouldn't let anyone except their shepherds close to the water. I let them have it. As long as we could reach the first real oasis in a couple of days, we'd be fine. By then, the camels would be thirsty, too.

———

In the days that followed, even, rocky ground grew harsh and jagged. Broken shards of obsidian thrust from the yellow dunes, which were blue or maroon in the Eyelight, and mounded against every windward cranny. We meandered around rockfalls and decaying, stygian cliffs that slouched amid screes of sharp black rocks.

Switchbacks around impossible terrain grew common. Three times in two nights, we needed to halt for hours while we wrangled the camels out of shallow, dead-end gulches. I'd planned for a month to cross the desert, but at the rate we were going, it would take two. At least two. We would run out of supplies long before then. To make matters worse, the Eye was waning. In a few weeks, it would be too dark to travel in terrain like that.

I began to harbor growing suspicions of our guide. Massive caravans hauling tons of raw stone crossed the desert every day. There was no way they could do that in the places we found ourselves in.

I confronted Ginya about it, but she insisted that this was the best route to avoid trouble with the nomads.

"And what will we do when it's too dark to travel by night?" I asked her, aware how much we were at the mercy of this adolescent girl.

"We should be in the dunes by then," she answered. "Easier to get lost, but we'll be able to move faster while we're doing it."

I was afraid to ask her if she was joking.

The karakh lay shuddering by the pool of slimy water, choking and coughing. It's breath came in broken gasps. Its shepherd, a man named Stadar, lay dead beside it, face purple and distorted in agony.

I stood with Dakar and Vimr, watching in the fading Eyelight. I was at a loss. Rohm was further back in the canyon with the rest of the army. The other karakh paced around the oasis, whistling and moaning.

The great body of the creature gave one last, horrible quiver and lay still.

"Another poison oasis," Vimr muttered with a meaningful look in my direction.

As much as I loathed him, I was forced to agree. We'd come upon the first a night and a half after the spring. Saved by the predawn glow in the east, which revealed the bodies of lizards and chitinous sandraks strewn about the rim of the pool, and the sticky brown leaves of the flora. Ginya couldn't explain it.

"How far to the next one?" I'd asked her then.

"Four, maybe five days," she'd answered with enough fear in her voice that I had a hard time doubting her. "But there's another two days away. Maybe less. To the north."

"So out of our way." I wasn't asking.

"Yes."

I felt trapped, helpless against this teenager who had so far led us from one disaster to another. But I had no choice, and we both knew it.

"Fine," I said. "Take us there."

And now this.

"Where is Ginya?" I asked to no one in particular, unable to pull my eyes from the dead karakh.

"Back with Rohm and the rest somewhere," Dakar answered. His eyes, too, were fixed on the grim scene in front of us.

"Someone bring her to me."

Dakar pulled his eyes away. "With pleasure." He made his way down the low hill to where the rest of the soldiers had gathered. The other karakh continued to pace around the pool.

A few minutes later, he returned, Ginya in tow, her face pale.

"Two pools of poison." My voice didn't rise above a whisper.

She swallowed. "This one too." Her eyes followed mine.

I didn't trust myself to respond, so I nodded and turned to Rohm. "How much water do we have left?"

"A day. Maybe a little more, then we drink camel blood."

I turned to face Ginya for the first time since she'd arrived. "And our next water source?"

She looked relieved to have something to think about besides the scene at the oasis as she calculated. "East. Three, maybe four days. There should be another spring north and a little west, though—"

"No." My voice was harsh. "No more rock climbing. No more dead ends. No more going the wrong way. I want out of this desert. You will take us to one of main caravan routes—the *closest* route—and you will lead us along that route until we reach the foothills."

"But the tribes—" she began.

"Fuck the tribes," I said. Rohm raised his eyebrows. "You will do the things I ask. In chains, if necessary."

"It will take three nights to get to the South Road." Her voice quivered.

"Then we will drink camel blood for two nights." I spat into the sand. "At the next oasis, you will be the first to drink, whatever corpses are lying at its banks when we get there."

Ginya stared at me, eyes wide. "You think I did this?" She asked, close to tears I didn't know if I could trust. "But I've been with you! I... How would I..." her voice broke, and she fell silent.

After one last, hard look at the girl, I turned to Rohm. "Tell everyone. We're moving on. Now."

What followed was a death march. There was no way to preserve camel blood, so we slit their throats and sucked life from their veins like vampires as the creatures thrashed and bleated. We sacrificed a hundred of the three hundred we'd brought with us. It wasn't enough for two thousand men, but any more and we'd need to abandon our tents and the provisions. Even with the loss of a hundred, we couldn't carry enough water without stopping at every spring and oasis to refill our skins. If any more were poisoned, we were doomed. But it was die later or die today. I knew it. My soldiers knew it.

Those desperate enough to drink from the animals cast dice for the chance. The losers, and the few that refused, could only hope to survive long enough to see water again.

Two hundred and thirty men died those next three nights, and we abandoned them to the scavengers. I was surprised it was so few.

Golden dunes surrounded the oasis, a lush pocket of foliage surrounded by mountains of sand. The Eye, now a fat crescent, revealed a caravan already camped there. Twenty peaked, white tents with pale blue pennants fluttering in the night breeze arranged around two sturdier wood and cloth houses— homes of the caretakers. Cook fires of burning camel dung flickered between them. It was a few hours before dawn.

When the surviving soldiers crested the dune and saw the scene, a hoarse cheer rose from the army.

The karakh whistled and grunted, and charged down the dune toward the scent of water.

A pit grew in my stomach, and the cheers behind me fell silent. The desperate sound of the shepherds whistling and calling to their mounts flitted to us from across the sand, but they were as helpless as us.

Shadows writhed through the camp as people just settling down for the morning dashed in all directions in front of the firelight. Cries of panic and terror crashed over the sound of the frantic shepherds.

The karakh tore into the camp. Tents collapsed into fires, and a conflagration bloomed, its red and orange reflection flickering in the tranquil water of the pond, a sick mockery of the sunrise two hours away.

In a few minutes, the tents and cloth houses had burned away, leaving only scattered campfires and a few smoldering tatters of cloth. I dragged myself forward, feeling, as usual, helpless. The mass of my soldiers followed behind me. Even Vimr looked grim.

"Wait!" Dakar's voice came loud and sharp from the fluttering darkness of the ruined camp.

I stopped, but fifty of my soldiers either didn't hear or didn't care over their insurmountable thirst, and charged past me towards the water.

The huge, white form of Gre'pa, red and violet under the Eye, surged from the darkness beyond the dying fires and lunged over the smoking tatters of a collapsed tent. I could make out the silhouette of Dakar standing on the creature's shoulders, pulling on the chains. His face in the flickering light of the fires was haunted.

Gre'pa tore through a dozen of the desperate soldiers like a cat killing mice, eviscerating them with a few swipes and a lunge of its tusks. The rest scattered and fled back toward the army massed behind me, their thirst forgotten. Dakar called to me, "Hold everyone back! They protect the water! There's nothing we can do."

He leaned forward and whispered something in to Gre'pa's ear before sliding down its shoulder and trotting towards us. The animal unleashed a long, warbling whistle at his back and scuttled back into the darkness around the pool.

Dakar stopped in front of me. His face was streaked with tears. "Our companions have killed our allies," he whispered.

I could think of nothing to say for a moment, choked by impotent, directionless rage. "It's not your fault, Dakar," I said at last.

I thought of the Salamander and shot a meaningful glance at Vimr. "None of it is your fault. Nevertheless, we'll all die if we don't get water."

Dakar looked past me at the army, purple in the light of the Eye. Tired faces, resigned to death. He turned and looked again at the oasis and the vague shadows of the karakh that lurked there.

"We'll fill the water," he sighed at last. "But you must camp in the dunes. They won't let anyone else near for at least a day, maybe two."

I looked back at my army, then to the Eye sinking in the west. "Seventeen of you, and almost two thousand soldiers. Filling our water will take some time."

Dakar nodded. "Yes."

"Very well," I sighed. "We'll set up here." I turned and gave the signal, but Rohm had been listening, and they'd already begun.

The men heaped their water skins as close to the oasis as they dared, and the shepherds began running bottles and skins to the pool and back again. It was less than two hours before dawn, and everyone needed to have at least one full bottle to get through the day. One wouldn't even be enough, but it was all we had time for. The camels, I hoped, would survive for another day or two, though they would get cantankerous being this close to water without getting any themselves.

When dawn broke, the air was clear, devoid of the pale haze that hung over the desert most days, and it broke over the Black Wall. Still over a week away, the foothills hidden behind the horizon, the Wall stood, looming across the Yellow Desert, any details lost to the distance, sheer, black, and gleaming. Impenetrable. Glaciers formed a band of white two thirds of the way up, blending with the puffs of cloud that drifted in front of them. The peaks, though, were sheer and black, glinting strangely clear in the light of the rising sun.

It was not my first time in that part of the world, but I doubted anyone could get used to the sight of the Black Wall.

The shepherds filled two-thirds of the canteens and skins before the sun cracked the line of peaks, and the rest before the heat grew unbearable.

My soldiers spent the day panting in the thin shade of the tents, tongues swollen, still dying. But somehow every man and woman who slept that day woke again that night. That miracle was almost enough to renew my faith in Heaven. Almost.

We spent three more nights at the oasis. After the second, the karakh had relaxed enough that they allowed the army to camp in the meager shade of the palms, but I decided we needed one more day to fill whatever we could carry with water, and give my people a little more rest.

When the assassins slid down the dunes to converge on the oasis, they made the same sound as wind-blown sand. The army around me slept, most tossing in fever. I was restless as ever, alone in my tent, and I saw nothing in the glare of daylight when I peered out the flap, suspicious of that peculiar whisper. Our attackers wore loose cloaks the same dusty yellow as the desert, invisible to my tired eyes in the brilliant light. To my shame, I returned to my cot until it was far too late.

They ignored the sleeping army and crept as one toward the karakh dozing around the pool.

I heard a puppy-like yelp from one of the karakh, and I moved back to the flap of my tent to see a knife jutting from the haunch of a scabby brown and grey creature named Lek'kt, its shepherd sleeping against its shoulder. Before I could react, five more blossomed from it in rapid succession, thrown hard enough to be invisible in the harsh light until they'd found their mark.

I shouted the same time the shepherds blinked awake, and their mounts started screaming.

Lek'kt jolted upright on his haunches, rigid in a grotesque, unnatural pose, his huge silver eyes filled with panic, dilated even in the brilliant sunlight. A moment later, one of the other karakh started coughing and wheezing, thrashing and stiff, crushing its shepherd as the man tried to scramble out of the way.

I continued to yell, though I don't remember any words that came from my mouth. My mind was uncomprehending.

The army was awake. Soldiers staggered out of their tents in confusion, squinting in the blinding sun.

"Ambush!" Dakar screamed from Gre'pa's back as his mount reared back, avoiding a thrown knife by the width of a finger. The karakh lunged as the nomad pulled another knife from her cloak, grinding her into the ground under one enormous hand as another dagger tumbled from her fingers. "Karakh!" He shouted. "Protect the karakh!"

I still stood at the mouth of my tent as a hundred of my soldiers, most only half-dressed, swarmed the attackers. The dozen nomads fought like devils, a knife in each hand slick with black grease, but they seemed resigned to their fate. None tried to flee. A few attempted more attacks on the eleven remaining karakh, but the shepherds had realized the danger and moved to the far side of the water, and the thrown knives all missed their targets.

When it was over, six karakh lay twitching or still on the ground, stiff as stone and drooling reeking grey foam. Three of their shepherds had survived the spasms of their companions but now lay sobbing against their massive bodies, helpless with grief. Thirteen nomads lay scattered around the oasis in pools of blood.

Tears again streaked Dakar's face as he dismounted Gre'pa and stumbled toward me. "Revenge," the shepherd said. His voice was hoarse. "For the caravan."

I studied the man's face, aged to look even older than mine in the past three months with the blame he carried with him, and I thought about my decision to stay one more day at the oasis.

"There is plenty of blame to go around," I said at last. "And none of it is yours. Tonight we push hard for the foothills and damn this fucking desert to hell."

I ordered pickets set from then on, but we weren't attacked again. Ginya said the tribes saw their vengeance oath fulfilled with the death of six of the karakh, but I didn't trust her.

Now that we were on one of the main routes, we moved faster than I'd dared hope the day before. Caravans heading back to Valez'Mui gave us a wide berth, and I only saw them in the distance now and again, crossing the tops of high dunes a span or two away, silhouetted in the thin light of the waning Eye. The springs and tiny settlements that survived on the constant trade from camel trains squatted abandoned in the predawn light, though I suspect within a day of our passing, the inhabitants would return. At least the water wasn't poison.

A week later, we reached the Bones—those black pillars of obsidian jutting into the sky a thousand or more hands high, scattered in a band across most of the Yellow Desert before the foothills. The Black Wall now loomed ahead, taking up a third of the sky. The dunes gave way to swirling dust devils, and long tumbles of black boulders fallen from the spires and smoothed with wind and time. On the afternoon of the second day, the sky behind us grew a hazy, brownish-yellow with a sandstorm. I realized how lucky we'd been that we'd avoided another catastrophe.

The last few weeks had been uneventful. The peaks became lost in the haze that swirled beneath them. Blasted, black rock and sand gave way to first tufts of grey scrub and sage, and then to stunted pines and dry, brown grasses. The foothills mounded in front of us, and the scattered trees grew thicker until we climbed into the thin, dusty evergreen forests at the foot of the Wall.

Scattered tendrils of smoke from cooking fires in a dozen villages rose above the trees on either side, but I ordered camp set at the edge of the forest, along the banks of a little brook tumbling down from the glaciers to die in the desert. I half-expected Vimr to countermand my order, but the Arch Bishop's adviser said nothing to me, nor anyone else, until the setup of pickets and tents was well underway.

"Where's the girl?" Vimr spat when he got near. I was walking the camp with Rohm, discussing the logistics of moving the army further into the mountains.

"What girl?" I asked. I knew full well who Vimr was talking about, but I enjoyed his reaction.

"The guide! You know that's who I mean. How many of your people did we lose because of her incompetence? Or malice."

I stopped and faced Vimr with a nodded apology to Rohm, who walked away, smirking. "As much as it pains me to agree with you, Cardinal, I think you're right. We lost far too many of *our* people—they're our people, and not just mine unless you serve some power beyond the Church? No? *Our* people it is then."

Vimr scowled. "Where is she?"

I'd half-regretted my decision when I'd first made it, but I decided it had been worth it just for the look on Vimr's face. "I let her go."

"You what? You agree that she led us to death and destruction, yet you released her without punishment? She should be burned!"

I nodded in an exaggerated gesture. "To be honest, the thought crossed my mind, but the fact is, Ginya did nothing we didn't ask of her. Nothing that can be proven. I—and you with me—told her to take a discrete route across the desert. A route that turned out to be disastrous, true, but I will not execute a teenage girl, by fire or any other means, for doing what we asked. And even you can't blame her for the oasis. In fact, she led us out of the desert before the sandstorm swallowed us. A sandstorm that she most assuredly knew how to survive, had she chosen to lead us astray.

"So, as per my agreement with her, she was free to leave." I watched Vimr's sputtering face with no small amount of satisfaction. "For her sake, I hope she heeded my advice and is now very far from here. Now, excuse me, Cardinal. I need to find Rohm. I'm sure that you agree the most important leg of our mission is upon us."

Without waiting for a reply, I headed into the heart of the camp.

7

UNREQUITED LOVE

It took three days for Chulla to find a caravan willing to take them to Valez'Mui, though neither Pasha nor Anna could figure out what the girl had offered in return. They waited a week to depart. Anna didn't trust her. Chulla seemed too interested in helping them, and Anna found her habit of muttering to herself disconcerting. Anna was sure whatever the girl mouthed under her breath was in a language different than both her native tongue, that was so close to their own, and the trade language she'd been teaching them, but Pasha told her not to worry about it. He was growing close to Chulla, despite her young age, which only fed Anna's distrust.

The caravan was massive. Nine hundred merchants and servants. Five ruling Artisans—a concept the siblings didn't comprehend—each with their own attendants and hangers-on. Thirty-six hundred camel drivers with eighteen hundred camels pulling four hundred and fifty wagons burdened with great, gleaming blocks of black stone, and a thousand mercenaries to guard it all. It was as if the whole valley had gathered in one place to cross a land far harsher than they could have imagined.

And all of them were jabbering in languages that the siblings couldn't understand.

The desert terrified them. Without the comfort of the Wall, they felt naked, but their fear eventually diluted to boredom. The caravan traveled at night and only managed eight or ten spans before setting up camp again. Pasha commented that they spent more time setting up and breaking down the camp than they did traveling, to which Chulla only laughed.

After they left the Bones, there was nothing to look at, save dunes or flat, rocky planes, and the Black Wall towering behind them, shrinking behind the horizon until even the mountains were lost in the sandy haze.

Chulla did her best to keep the siblings with the merchants' servants where they would blend in, and no one of consequence would be inclined to talk to them. She'd found some rough, goat hair shirts and leggings while waiting to depart from the foothills, insisting that their soft, black leather would draw too much attention. Anna suggested they dispose of their old clothes, but Pasha objected and bundled their belongings from the valley into their packs. Chulla had seemed too interested in the blackvine knives to Anna, but the girl suggested Pasha pack those away with their clothes if he wanted to keep them.

The Trader tongue wasn't a complete language, but Chulla said it would be enough for them to get by, as long as they weren't trying to make any friends. There were long periods where Chulla wasn't around to teach them, though, when she disappeared into the mass of the caravan and didn't come back until they were setting camp in the predawn light.

"How do you think she speaks our language when no one else does?" Anna asked Pasha during one of Chulla's absences.

Pasha shrugged. "She told us already. It's the language her village spoke."

Anna rolled her eyes. "You're too trusting. And anyway, she's too young to know so much about everything." She looked at him out of the corner of her eye and interrupted him before he could respond. "Why do you think her village speaks something so close to our language?"

He was quiet a minute. "I don't know. Why not?"

"Do you think other people from the valley left? I mean a long time ago. Long enough for their language to change, but not so long that she couldn't understand us at all?"

Pasha thought. "Maybe. We got out of the valley. Maybe there were others, hundreds of years ago."

"Or thousands."

"Or thousands," Pasha agreed.

They trudged along in silence for a while, each lost to their thoughts.

Anna sighed and looked over at Pasha.

He glanced at her. "What?"

She hesitated a moment. "I don't know why you trust her. Doesn't it seem weird to you? The way she disappears into the caravan, even though she says she's never left the Foothills before. The way she seems to know so much about the world on the other side of this—" she gestured around to the dunes and rocky screes— "even though she should be as ignorant as us. Or the way she knows this Trader language, even though she's just a child who's lived the same place her whole life."

It was Pasha's turn to sigh. "You don't know, Anna. We don't know. Maybe her parents interacted with these caravans all the time. She could pick up a lot from this many people. Or maybe everyone in her village needed to speak 'Trader' because otherwise, they wouldn't be able to talk to anyone else.

"We don't know *anything*. Why are there so many languages in the first place? Where did they come from? I thought the Ancestors only spoke one. How are there so many people in the world if life was wiped out three thousand generations ago? Is the whole world like this?" It was his turn to gesture at the desert around them. "If it is, how do so many people live on it?"

"Maybe she lied about how many people there are." But she heard how ridiculous it sounded and clamped her mouth closed.

"Then what are all these people doing?" Pasha asked, again gesturing around him.

Anna could only shake her head. "I don't want to argue with you. I'm just worried about how you trust this girl. How you seem to like her so much. Like you say, we don't know anything about the world we're in now. How can you be so sure she's on our side?"

Anna was afraid their argument would escalate and draw attention, but Pasha only sighed again. "How can you be so sure she's not, Anna? I don't know why I trust her. I look at her, and I get this feeling. like she's someone I should know. Or someone I used to know. I don't know. But this world is more dangerous than we imagined, and we'll need to trust someone. We might as well start with someone who wants to help us."

Anna pressed her lips together, thinking, *seems* like she wants to help us, but she didn't say it out loud. She knew no more than he did, so there was no point in arguing. The thing was, Chulla seemed like someone Anna used to know too. Only she was having the opposite reaction. There was something about her that she couldn't bring herself to trust. By the time they figured out whether she or her brother were right about the girl, Anna was afraid it would be too late. But there was no point in arguing about it.

They spent the final hours of the night in silence. Chulla returned as the eastern sky grew lighter and helped them set their tent. The jagged line of peaks behind them only scraped the bottom of the horizon. Another night's travel, maybe two, and the Black Wall would be beneath a horizon they hadn't known existed. Anna looked around at the dunes and cracked landscape and swallowed.

The dunes gave way to rocky flats and winding, shallow canyons. According to Chulla, they had been in the desert for a month, though both Anna and Pasha had long since lost track of time. In a few weeks, they would arrive in Valez'Mui.

The crescent Eye was lowering itself onto the line of broken hills when the house guard came pushing through the crowd of servants towards where Pasha and Anna trudged behind the others. He wore white linen embroidered in a recurring pattern of blue circles crossed with two vertical and two horizontal white lines, and a long ceramic rapier hung on a belt made of tin disks.

Chulla, who had just returned from wherever she so often went during the night marches, noticed him first and tapped Pasha on the shoulder.

"Anna," he called his sister, who hadn't noticed he and Chulla stopping. She turned. "Trouble," he pointed. Chulla looked nervous.

The man marched up and barked a few lilting words to Anna.

She blinked and looked at Chulla, confused.

The girl said a few words to the man in the same language, who gestured at Anna.

Chulla translated. "Though he knows Trader Tongue, he will not speak it. Typical. I've explained to him you don't understand Valezian, so I translate."

Anna scowled. "You speak a lot of languages."

"Anna—" Pasha protested, but Chulla interrupted him.

"No, it's okay." She turned back to Anna. "Yes. Trader and Valezian are both important. The people of Valez'Mui are sensitive, and it's better to deal with them in their own language, so I learned young, though I'm not so fluent I could teach you. Misunderstandings can be dangerous." She paused, then glanced at Pasha and added, "I'm glad you're suspicious. It is safer if you don't trust anyone."

"In any case," she continued to Anna. "You have caught the eye of Tolisho, one of the five Artisans accompanying this caravan. He asks that you meet with him. Alone."

"That's not going to happen," Pasha interjected, glowering at the guard who stood watching their conversation. The caravan dragged itself around them.

"No," Chulla said. "It's not. The Artisan, like his goon here, will only speak Trader when business forces him too. I am to go also. To translate."

"I'm coming," Pasha stated, his expression dark.

"You cannot."

At the same time, Anna said, "I can take care of myself."

Chulla looked at Anna. "You cannot." She looked between the siblings. "Neither of you can, however skilled you may be in a fight. This situation is more dangerous than you understand." She faced Pasha, "There would be nothing you could do. You won't be allowed near Tolisho. Please trust me. She'll be fine." Her green eyes sparkled at him in the Eyelight. "Keep your place among the servants. We'll return in time to set camp, if not before."

"Don't worry," Anna said, looking at Pasha, but he saw the fear hidden behind her eyes.

With that, the two girls followed the soldier through the press toward the rear of the procession.

The Artisans and their flock of retainers followed at the end of the line of camels, wagons, merchants, soldiers, and slaves. The procession was five separate caravans which, because of timing and proximity, had banded together in the foothills for security. Each Artisan rode in their own immense, six-wheeled carriage, each pulled by six camels. The wheels were huge, taller than Anna, reaching to just below the line of curtained, paneless windows, and almost five hands wide to help keep them from sinking into the sand. Anna decided that the ponderous pace of the caravan was entirely due to its leaders' conveyance.

The soldier led them to the second such carriage, which lurched to a stop as they approached. Another soldier stepped from the door between the second and last wheel and pulled the silk curtain aside. After a gentle prompting from Chulla, Anna clambered in.

The interior was dim, lit by oil braziers, the floor covered in cushions of bright green, blue, and gold silk. It was smelled of rice and cinnamon.

The Artisan Tolisho reclined in one corner. He was lanky and pot-bellied, with burnished skin and blond hair bleached almost white from the sun. There were a few lines around his mouth and eyes, but other than that, he seemed ageless in the dim light.

He gestured for the two girls to sit among the cushions opposite him. The guard standing at attention outside pulled the curtain closed and shut the door, and the carriage lurched into motion with an annoyed grunt from one of the camels.

Tolisho said something to Anna. His voice was soft and lilting, and at the end of his words, he gave her a thin smile.

Chulla translated. "He says he took note of your unique beauty some nights ago and has watched as you and those you travel with avoided contact with everyone but me." She paused. "He means he had you watched, I suppose."

Anna forced her attention to the Artisan from where it had wandered through the carriage, running her hands across the glossy silk pillows. Before stepping inside, she'd never imagined such materials existed. "Tell him, um, thanks," she said, not knowing what else to say. "Tell him I'm impressed with this—" she gestured around her. "And that we avoid others only because we have no knowledge of his beautiful language." She trailed off and gave Chulla a pleading look.

The girl gave her a reassuring smile and spoke to Tolisho in Valezian. They talked back and forth for a few minutes before Chulla again turned to Anna. She looked uncomfortable and forced a smile with a small bow to the Artisan. "He invites you to stay with him in such beautiful surroundings for as long as it pleases, and wishes to teach you Valezian himself, which you find so pleasant to hear. A translator will be found for you in the meantime, not so flawed as I." She gestured with her mangled left hand. "He offers these things to you if you are a, um. I don't know the word for it. If you've never been with a man." She paused. "He says if you've been with a woman, it is no matter."

Anna, who still sometimes had a hard time understanding Chulla's dialect, blinked for a moment, then swallowed as what he requested sank in. Chulla watched her, but the smile on her lips didn't touch the rest of her face.

"Um," Anna said at last, then fell silent again. "Um. I'm flattered, but I travel with my brother, and won't part with him. I'm very sorry to turn down his offer." She swallowed.

Chulla and Tolisho spoke again at length. Tolisho smiled.

The girl translated. "He says your brother is no concern." Her eyes grew cold. "And that his offer is not to be rejected."

Anna stared at her. "What are you saying?"

Chulla sighed but kept her tone friendly and unworried. "He will have Pasha killed and this man will make you his concubine until he grows bored. Then he'll sell you in the slave markets for a profit. It is the way of things in Valez'Mui."

Anna's heart pounded in her chest. She suddenly felt confined in the carriage that she had found so large just a moment ago. "What can we do?"

Chulla spoke, smile steady. "You'll be fine, and so will I. We'll continue speaking like this. He believes we are discussing his offer. In twenty heartbeats, run. Find Pasha, lose yourselves among the servants."

"What about you?" Anna asked. She couldn't keep the threads of fear from her voice. As much as she distrusted Chulla, she didn't want to leave her fate to this man.

Chulla's smile touched her eyes at last. "I've dealt with many dangerous men. I'll find you after the sun comes up. They won't search for you during the day because of the heat. At night it's dark, and the caravan is hectic. We'll talk more then."

Anna was shaking. "I... I'm sorry. Sorry for this. Sorry I didn't trust you. Thank you, Chulla. I'll tell Pasha what you did."

The girl shook her head. "I'll tell him myself. I told you I'll be fine. Now get out of here."

And with that, the young girl, barely out of puberty, flung herself at the Artisan, straddling him and moaning, kissing him on his mouth with open lips.

Anna stared in shock for a second but didn't wait to see what Tolisho would do. She ducked under the curtain, flung open the door, and fled into the disorganized hoard of the caravan, dodging past Tolisho's guards before they could figure out what was going on.

———

The next day, the siblings lay awake in the hot shade of the tent they shared with eight merchant's serfs. Neither Anna nor Pasha had asked Chulla how she'd arranged that when they'd started across the desert, and all she'd said was that someone owed her father a favor.

Anna had told Pasha what happened in the Artisan's carriage, and together they'd avoided the Valezian house guards for the rest of the night. Neither knew what would happen when the sun went down that evening, and Tolisho began his search in earnest.

The loose flap of the tent stirred. Chulla ducked in, stepping over and around the prone shapes of the servants.

Pasha leaped up to greet her.

Anna watched the reunion, torn between relief Chulla seemed unhurt and thinking her brother was an idiot for caring so much.

"What happened after I left?" she asked in a whisper after the girl had seated herself cross-legged next to Pasha, close enough that her knee brushed his thigh.

Anna thought Chulla blushed a little, but she said, "Not much. Less than you think. I told him he could have me instead, but he didn't care, as I knew he wouldn't. The Artisans are known for their love of perfection." She wiggled her remaining fingers. "He said there was something different about you, that my hand made me undesirable. He pushed me away and let me go, and said he would find us tonight, that after you learn Valezian, I will be like your brother —unneeded."

She gazed at Pasha. "He let me go because his plan was to have someone follow me and lead him to you, but they failed."

Anna frowned. "How can you be sure?"

Chulla smiled her infuriating smile. "I'm sure."

Pasha studied the girl, his eyes so intense it made Anna uncomfortable. "He'll be looking for us."

Chulla nodded. "Yes. And he'll have you killed. He knows you're her brother, now. He wants to make Anna his slave without interference. Then he'll have me killed, too. I've proven myself to be too much of a nuisance to bother with, translator or no."

Anna didn't like how unconcerned Chulla seemed to be with the idea of this man wanting to kill her. "I'm not going to be his slave," she said from where she lay on her stomach on the floor. "Why are we even talking about it?"

Chulla was unsympathetic. "Because that's what will happen if he finds you. Not talking about it won't change anything."

Pasha tried to give Anna a reassuring look, but it just made her more angry when he turned his attention back to the girl. "What do we do?"

Chulla leaned in, her voice low. "We move again. To the Cariz'Ali camp this time. With the cook-slaves. I got some of their uniforms—they cover the face. Plus, they're not part of Tolisho's caravan, so his men can't just walk through, looking for us. Not that they can't at all, but it will give us time while they negotiate. We can scrape by like that for the next few nights. After, we should be close enough to Valez'Mui that we'll be able to swipe some provisions from the Cariz'Ali and make it the rest of the way by ourselves. We can move a lot faster on our own."

"How do you know how far we have to go if you've never crossed this desert before?" Anna's previous suspicions came welling back.

"I've seen maps."

Anna was unconvinced. "What about all this other stuff? How do you know where Tolisho's people can and can't go? Or what Cariz'Ali kitchen slave uniforms look like?"

Chulla was unperturbed. "My village did business with many different Valez'Mui caravans before General Mann killed everyone. The Valezian are particular about how they do things. I needed to learn a lot growing up."

"So you keep saying."

"Come on, Anna," Pasha interjected. "She saved you. We can trust her."

Anna scowled, but she fell quiet again.

"It's almost noon," Chulla whispered, settling down next to Pasha. "We need sleep."

Chulla proved deft at leading them through the trundling caravan, away from the eyes of the armed men and women in blue and white. Anna worried the Artisan would start sending people to look for them without identifying livery, but Chulla reassured her that wouldn't happen. "Not here, anyway," she said. "With five Artisans in the same caravan, anyone who could be perceived as spies would cause conflict. Expensive conflict, and unwanted. You'll need to be more careful when we get to the city, though."

Again, Anna wondered how the girl could know so much, but she didn't bother asking about it.

A week went by. Their nights became an exhausting scramble from one group of servants to the next. Chulla negotiated with the head retainers of each camp, so they stayed among the last of the serfs to set their tents at dawn and were among the first to leave at dusk, when the rest of the caravan was beginning to stir in the afterglow of the numbing heat of the day. Chulla did what she could to teach them Trader. They were quick in picking it up, but the lessons became even less regular as they scrambled from group to group in silence, lest the sound of their language draw attention.

Eight nights after the incident with the Artisan, a glow rested on the western horizon, long after the sun had sunk behind the flat, rocky plain.

"That must be it," Chulla pointed. They walked with the camel drivers near the front of the caravan. "Valez'Mui."

"We'll get there tonight?" Pasha asked, staring in awe at the band of yellowish light.

She nodded. "Us? Yes, I think we can make it, if we run most of the way. You can both run, yes? The Caravan will be there by the end of tomorrow night. Maybe early the night after."

Anna was staring too. "How many people live there?"

Chulla scratched her nose, thinking, then shrugged. "I'm not sure. A few hundred thousand. More, maybe."

Anna still couldn't imagine even that many people living in one place and, according to Chulla, Valez'Mui wasn't a large city compared to others.

Chulla turned to check the Eye, a ruddy sliver looming over the eastern desert plain. "Wait here for me." She disappeared into the throng behind them.

She reappeared less than an hour later, burdened with two heavy backpacks. "Water, some food, a tent," she explained. "Just in case I'm wrong. Let's go."

Anna glanced at the camel carts that surrounded them. the drivers chatted among themselves, ignoring the trio of conspirators.

"I don't think they'll be a problem," Chulla answered Anna's unspoken thoughts. "The drivers are Nomads. They couldn't give five shits about Tolisho or the rest of the Artisans. Most of the time."

Anna's thin smile was less than reassured.

"She's gotten us this far," Pasha whispered. "Come on. Let's go." And the pair followed Chulla from the swinging lantern light of the caravan into the blackness of the desert beyond.

8

OLD FRIENDS, NEW DEALS

Syrina left the siblings after she paid a week's advance for room for them at an inn called The Chisel. She used some of the tin Chulla had "taken from her village." It wasn't opulent. It sat just a half span from the docks and two reeking textile mills, but they seemed impressed enough.

Well, impressed didn't quite cover it. Neither Pasha nor Anna could find words for the sprawling rows of tents that flooded across the plain for spans, leading to the open gates of Valez'Mui. Pasha had thought they'd been in the city and looked embarrassed through his awe when they'd finally come to the great, circular, zig-zagging marble wall, spiked by minarets rising from each point, so seen from above, it looked like thirty-five pointed star.

Syrina did her best to make Chulla impressed, too, and thought she did a passable job of it. Anna seemed to forget about the girl after they entered the city, but Syrina kept catching Pasha looking her way, smiling. It made her uncomfortable because she found herself smiling back.

She got them settled, made them promise not to leave the inn so Chulla could find them again, and fed them some lines about how the girl was going back into the camps to find some relatives. It might take a few days, so not to worry.

She felt a mix of relief and unsettling loneliness after she left them and headed towards Whitehook's estate, a few hours before dawn. She was in no hurry to see Ves, so she stopped in a little cafe for a few cups of rum to get her thoughts in order.

The attraction she felt towards Pasha was undeniable. That alone was strange enough. Kalis were human, after all, but there were layers of conditioning, through the tattoos and otherwise, that prevented attractions from popping up. What was more strange, though, was how the voice in her head was drawn to him, too. It should have been the first to mock her for it, but instead, it encouraged her, which was worse. She wondered if it had something to do with her unique status within the Kalis. She had broken most of her conditioning the past few years. Maybe the taboo against physical relationships was just the next thing to go.

I don't think it's that simple, the voice chimed in.

Syrina sighed. "No, I don't think so, either." An old man drinking alone a few tables away glanced at her, annoyed.

At least, she considered, she'd had the wherewithal to speak to the voice in Valezian. "Why him, why now?"

She almost sensed a sigh from the voice. *I don't know, but I want to be with him too. I see him, and I feel like I'm looking... I don't know. Like he's someone I know but can't remember.*

Syrina considered that. "Maybe that's it," she whispered to herself around her cup. The old man glanced her way again, scowling. She ignored him. "If you're right about them, then they've been isolated in the Wall since the Age of Ashes. If they're precursors to the Kalis, put there to protect whatever Mann took, then maybe... I don't know. It's like he's one of my kind."

Of course, he doesn't sit around in bars and talk to himself the way you do. And he's a male.

There was that. Through the sarcasm, there was truth. Neither Pasha nor Anna seemed to have a voice in their head, unless they were just better at dealing with it than she was, and men didn't become Kalis.

But there was something going on. She couldn't shake the feeling that the siblings were at least as important as whatever Mann had taken. And because of Pasha, they were becoming important to her, too.

She sighed again, paid up, and left the bar. The predawn sky blazed pink above the flowery marble arches that shaded the streets.

She took a few more detours before heading to Whitehook's. First, she went to the hawk nests near the docks, where she sent a message to both the Astrologers and Ormo about the siblings and asked what they wanted her to do about them. She wondered if she could keep the pair in Valez'Mui long enough to hear back.

With the sun just cresting the eastern rooftops to blast it's heat into the streets, she went to the ramshackle little hut where Smudge lived. There, she changed into the face and clothes of the stooped old man. After that, she dozed until dusk and walked down to the Great Road docks, where she haggled for thirty minutes with an angry, flamboyant woman over her barge, which was the only one for sale that suited Syrina's needs. Finally, she made her way to Vesmalimali's sprawling estate.

"Smudge, you rat!" Whitehook exclaimed, his smile broad, as the gate guard escorted the old man to the edge of the dining room.

The giant pirate was sitting down to breakfast. "Where the hell have you been? I've been waiting for that fucking boat you promised me for months now. I expect you have it since if you came back empty-handed, I'd have to kill you. No hard feelings and all that." He studied the old man, smiling as if he didn't care which way it would go.

"I got it, I got it," Smudge confirmed, wiping his nose on a sleeve filthy enough that it left a streak of dirt across his cheek and upper lip. "The Flowered Calf, two-thirds the way down dock nine. You won't miss it."

Whitehook stopped eating to stare at the old man. "You got me a boat called the Flowered Calf?"

Smudge swallowed. "Well, er, it's your boat now. You can paint over the name, call it whatever you want. Might want to paint over the detailing too. It's a bit, well, flowery. But it's a boat! And no one will suspect it belongs to the most feared pirate in the Expanse. Well, formerly the most feared pirate in the Expanse, since I, uh... with your last ship..." Smudge trailed off, studying the grainy wood of the table.

Ves grumbled something Smudge didn't catch and went back to eating. "Fine, fine. How far the mighty have fallen, eh? From Whitehook, terror of Ristro and N'narad alike, to Vesmalimali, captain of a river barge called the Flowered goddamned Calf.

"So then. I'm to give you a lift to Fom, am I? When do we leave? It will be good to get out of this heat-blasted town and see a real city again. Valez'Mui is good for making tin and not much else."

Smudge looked uncomfortable again. "Well, funny thing that. Maybe a little change of plans?"

Ves stopped eating again, waiting, his expression dangerous.

"No, no. I mean, nothing major. Just that it looks like there will be a couple of other passengers. A man and a woman. Or a boy and a girl. Sort of hard to tell—you'll see. They're brother and sister."

"Passengers. Great. Fine. Anything else?"

"No, I don't think so. They're chasing General Mann, the N'naradin, You've heard of him, I see. And they might—just might—be hunted by Tolisho, but he won't be back into Valez'Mui for another night, at least. But if he finds them, we'll need to leave in a hurry. And I don't think the Church knows about them, but if they find out, they'll be looking, too. But no, nothing that should be a problem." Smudge looked around the room, avoiding Ves's gaze.

Whitehook stared at the old man as if trying to decide how seriously he should take him. "I hope you're not making all this up. I was afraid my virgin voyage on the Flowered fucking Calf was going to be boring. So, when *do* we leave?"

"Soon. Not sure, but soon. I'll be back when I know. Might be short notice. Couple days? A few weeks? A month? Not too much longer." Syrina wondered how long it would take for the hawks to get to Eheene and Ristro and back. Ves seemed antsy.

"Fine, whatever. Just hurry up, will you? Been a while since I had something to look forward to."

"In the meantime," Smudge ventured, "You want to meet the passengers? They're, uh, new to the city. Kind of new to everything. I could use some help keeping an eye on them, what with an Artisan trying to track them down and all."

I'm no babysitter," Ves grumbled around a mouthful of goat haunch.

"No, no. Not like that. Just meet them before the trip is all. Maybe get someone to keep half an eye on them in case they get into trouble. If you have the goons to spare. There'll be some extra tin in it for you. Another thousand, say?"

Ves nodded and chewed. "Well, I guess I should meet them, huh?"

"I thought you might say that. I'll bring them over later tonight. Or tomorrow."

"Fine, fine," Ves said again as Smudge stood to go. "Hey, what is it you said you did, anyway? You've got a lot of tin to sling around for a dirty old man who looks like he lives in a hole."

"It's complicated."

Ves boomed laughter. "Ha! Fine. Bring them by tomorrow. And bring the tin, too."

Syrina had backed herself into a corner, and she tried to figure out how to get out of it as she walked back to the inn. She hadn't had the right equipment with her to be Smudge in the Foothills, so she'd improvised with Chulla, who wouldn't have gotten anywhere near Vesmalimali, so she'd needed to tell him about Anna and Pasha wearing the skin of Smudge. Now, Smudge needed introduce the siblings to Whitehook, but they'd never met the old man before, and she hoped they'd be smart enough not to trust him.

"Got a plan I should know about?" She asked the voice in her head.

Syrina decided the only time it stayed quiet was when it knew it would piss her off more than saying something.

And then she had an idea.

9

SMUDGE

"She's not coming back." Anna's voice was equal parts irritated and taunting.

It had been two nights since Chulla had vanished to look for her uncle in the camps. Pasha was content sitting around The Chisel and waiting for her, eating strange-but-not-awful-food they got in exchange for the triangle of light metal, stamped with a sun and crescent on one side and a man's face and a few words they couldn't read on the other. People seemed to value those triangles a lot. Chulla had advised them to keep the little sack she'd left with them hidden, and warned them that some people would kill for less. As it was, Anna was bewildered by the handful of copper balls and little metal disks she'd received in exchange for the triangle, along with two heaping bowls.

Now Chulla might not come back at all. That annoyed Anna only because it seemed like they were on their own again, but Pasha seemed broken by the idea.

"She said it might be a few days," Pasha said. His voice was petulant. They'd had the same conversation a dozen times, but Anna suspected he was losing his motivation argue about it.

"Well," she insisted, bored enough to keep goading him. "What happens if we run out of triangles?"

"Keep your voice down," Pasha hissed, looking around, but he needn't have worried. It was dusk. This early the only one close enough to hear her in the wide common room was himself.

In a more even voice, he said, "Then we'll deal with it. I don't want to leave and then have her come back to find us missing. She told us to wait. We'll wait."

Anna sighed. "Fine."

They sat for a while. No one said anything again until Anna looked at her brother, face twisted in a worried frown. "Can I ask you something?"

He turned to face her from where he'd been staring at the door.

"I don't want you to be mad, but what will we do even if we find Mann? How will we get whatever he took back when we don't even know what it is? And even if we did know, how are we supposed to get it, anyway? And then what? I don't want to go back to the valley."

She thought he'd be upset, but he only stared at the table, avoiding her eyes. "We need to go back. What else can we do?" He asked, his voice sad.

"I don't know," she replied after a moment, feeling bad for bringing it up.

"There's nothing left of our people," Pasha sighed. "Almost nothing. And even if there was, what else do we have? If I don't get back what they took, I've got nothing else. Maybe you'd be fine giving up on everything you've been taught and starting a new life. You never cared, anyway. I can't do that."

Anna knew he was trying to goad her, but she couldn't argue. "You're right, I guess. We'll try. We owe our people that much."

Pasha blinked in surprise, then took her hand and squeezed it. "If we fail and die, we'll be no worse off than we are now."

His words made her heart churn in her chest, but she only squeezed his hand back.

The bar filled as the night dragged on. Anna went back to their room to take a nap out of boredom. She left Pasha slouched at the table, eyes fixed on the door, waiting. Anna felt bad for him, even if she still found his fixation on Chulla disturbing.

She found him slumped in the same position an hour before dawn, eyes fixed on the door, nodding off. The room had cleared as locals staggered home after their post-work binging, and those staying at The Chisel crawled into their beds, already hung over from cup after cup of rum or vinegary rice wine.

"Come on, Pasha," she said. "We can wait upstairs. You'll feel better after you sleep."

Pasha grunted and shook his head, swaying. Empty cups lay scattered on the table. She frowned. Until Chulla had checked them into The Chisel, neither of them had heard of alcohol before, and she didn't like the way he'd taken to it.

"Come on, Pasha," Anna said again, putting her arm around him, determined to drag him to their room if she had to.

At that moment, the inn door swung open, and a bent old man swaggered through. Pasha, who'd been making a half-hearted attempt at standing, plonked back down onto his chair.

Anna sighed.

"Jus' minute," Pasha mumbled, nodding in the general direction of the old man, who was hobbling toward their table.

The little man's back was stooped, and his face was wrinkled and saggy with rough, tan skin. His head was hairless and covered with blotches of skin, both lighter and darker than the rest of his face. His clothes were well-cut, white linen, but filthy, and his piercing green eyes were sharp. Anna's eyes went to his left hand. Like Chulla's, the index and middle were missing in a whirl of old burn scars.

Anna remained standing behind her brother, and the little man ambled up and sat down on the free chair without waiting for an invitation.

"Anna and Pasha, I presume," he said in the same strange dialect of the valley language that Chulla had spoken.

"Uhh," Pasha confirmed.

Anna didn't respond. Her eyes wandered from his sharp green eyes to his mutilated left hand.

"My name is Calabast, but everyone calls me Smudge. Chulla's uncle. She couldn't make it back, so she sent me to check on you."

At the sound of the girl's name, Pasha stirred. "Where's she?" He slurred.

Smudge-eyed Pasha and the plethora of empty cups in front of him, the hint of a smile tugging at the wrinkled corners of his mouth. "Helping my wife with some things. Good thing she showed up, too, since I'm not as helpful as I used to be. Chulla showed up, that is. Not my wife." He grunted a noise that might have been a laugh.

Pasha nodded. "Sh's nice. Sh'looks like you." He smiled.

Smudge studied him a moment, then smiled back. Anna thought she saw something like worry pass across his face, but it was gone as soon as it came.

"Anyway," the old man continued, "I did her a favor since she did me one. Found you a way out of Valez'Mui. To Fom. It was Fom you wanted to go to, right?

"Why are you and Chulla both missing the same fingers?" Anna asked, voice sharp.

Pasha's eyes wavered to the little man's left hand. He frowned at it.

Smudge blinked, then nodded. "Fair enough, I guess. We were both caught committing the same crime," he said vaguely. "I'm disappointed Chulla got wrapped up in the same mess, and I let her know as much, but what's done is done. She was only four when I left. All fingers accounted for back then." He chortled, but there wasn't much humor in the sound.

Anna wasn't convinced. "Chulla said it was an accident."

"Oh." Smudge looked at Pasha, who had turned his eyes back to meet the old man's. "I guess she didn't want you to know she was a criminal. Hope that doesn't change your opinion about her. She seems to like you." He paused and turned to Anna. "Both of you."

Anna scowled, but she didn't answer. Pasha swayed, eyes still locked with Smudge's.

"Right," Smudge went on as if the matter was resolved. "Well, anyway, I found you a gentleman who's agreed to transport you to Fom up the Great Road. He's a long-time captain, and you can trust him. However he looks."

"How does he look?" Anna asked, suspicions renewed.

Pasha blinked, eyes bleary.

"You'll see. He wants to meet you. Bit of a big shot—again, you'll see. Just came by now to introduce myself, so when I show up here tomorrow to pick you up, you'll know I'm not some stranger out to jack you." He paused. "Or one of Tolisho's goons." He stood and gave a funny little bow. "Be here tomorrow night, midnightish." His green eyes flashed to Pasha. "I'll see you then."

And with that, he hobbled out the door.

Anna starred after him, frowning. "That was weird," she said, mostly to herself.

Pasha looked around. "Where'd Chulla go?" He belched. "She left 'fore ah'could talk t'her." He looked depressed.

Anna sighed. "It wasn't Chulla, Pasha. It was her uncle. Come on. Let's go to bed, and no wine for you tomorrow." She squatted down to shimmy under his limp arm and helped him to his feet.

Pasha was still blinking at the empty chair. "Sh's no uncle. Sh's right there." He pointed at the space between the empty chair and the front door but dropped his arm as Anna led him away.

They woke an hour before dusk. Anna was surprised to see Pasha in better shape than her. She'd lain awake until after noon thinking about their future, unable to come up with anything good about it.

When she opened her eyes, Pasha was sitting on the end of his own narrow bed, drinking water from a warped glass bottle.

He looked over at her when he heard her stir. "I feel terrible," he said. He gave her an embarrassed smile.

"You look better than you did last night. Can I have a drink of that?"

He passed the bottle to her. She drank. Even with the window shuttered and covered with heavy cloth, their room was hot.

"I've been thinking, Pasha." She said, handing the bottle back to him.

He drank again, waiting.

"You won't like this, but maybe we shouldn't go after Mann."

"We already had this conversation," Pasha said in a tone of tired condescension.

"Maybe I'm not done talking about it."

Pasha shook his head in disgust. "Fine. Talk."

Anna looked at her brother, rolled her eyes, and directed her words to the wall in front of her. "You keep saying we have no reason to live beyond going after Mann and returning what he stole to the valley."

"Anna, it was the whole purpose of our people to—"

"Fuck our people!"

Pasha stopped talking and stared at his sister with a mix of shock and disgust. She refused to meet his gaze.

Anna pressed on. The pit of flies in her stomach had opened and needed to be emptied. "Our people are failures. Our people spent thousands of years guarding something—they didn't even know what it was—We *still* don't know what—from threats that weren't even supposed to exist. Thousands of years in pointless competition to see who got to live in Suedmal—the stupid, pointless honor of living closest to the Tomb. The stupid, pointless last line of defense. The very first time—*the very first time in thousands of years*—we needed to protect it, we fail. Utterly. Our whole 'purpose' of defending that stupid door turned out to be just as pointless all those years ago as it is to us now."

"But—"

"Shut up, I'm not done. Why do you keep saying our lives have no point unless we continue that same useless mission we already failed? What about all these people?" She gestured around her.

"Who?"

"*Everyone,* Pasha. Every single person we've met on this side of the Wall. They don't have some grand reason to live, handed down by their Ancestors since the beginning of fucking time. Not one of them, including Chulla. Everyone out here has their own goals, makes their own decisions, lives their own lives, makes their own mistakes. That's what I want to do. I don't want to chase some stranger across a continent I didn't even know existed, then get killed for it because of some worthless tradition we've already failed to maintain. I want *my* life."

"Anna," Pasha swallowed, looking desperate. "If we don't go after this Mann, it makes our Ancestor's lives pointless. Everything they've done, pointless."

"Gods!" Anna wanted to tear her hair out. "You aren't listening. It *was* pointless. Our Ancestors never had a purpose to their lives beyond the one they gave themselves. Just like everyone else. I don't want to throw my life away just because the people who came before us didn't know what the fuck was going on. And I don't want you to do it, either.

"Come on, Pasha. We can help Chulla and her uncle. Or go to this other city, this Fom, and do something. Anything. But please, just admit we failed so we can move on."

"I still care where we came from." Pasha's voice came out mangled, and he had tears in his eyes. "But fine. You go. Enjoy your pointless life, with all these other pointless lives." He waved an arm at the shuttered window.

Anna was crying now, too, and stood, wiping her eyes. "I'm sorry you can be so fucking stupid."

She wheeled and stormed out of their room, slamming the door behind her.

10

UNWELCOME: EIGHT MONTHS BEFORE THE TRIAL

My hope that the worst lay behind us was absurd. I knew it when we docked in Valez'Mui, knew it long before, yet I clung to the idea like a drowning man clinging to a sinking raft. It was finally dashed by the reception we received when we tried to disembark.

It had been more years than I wished to count since I'd last set foot in the city-state. It was obvious that the relationship the Church of N'narad had maintained with Valez'Mui had disintegrated with neglect and time. The Artisan who met us greeted me with a shallow apology that only I and two others would be allowed to leave the ships, and two hundred Valezian footmen stood behind him to make sure of it.

I chose Captain Rohm to accompany me. I had grown to depend on him in the weeks following the tragedy of the Salamander. Vimr, as usual, invited himself. The rest of the men stayed behind, watching us from the decks, their faces bleak. The morning sun was already hot, the stench of sewage and vomit wafting from belowdecks overpowering even in the hot wind blowing off the desert.

I suspected if I couldn't get them off the ships soon, whoever survived the sun above and disease below would mutiny. Or, more likely, the karakh would go berserk, smash their way out of their stables, and kill everyone on the ships before laying waste to Valez'Mui.

The idea was a satisfying one.

The Artisan and his entourage—he never told us his name—escorted us to the customs house. It was a simple, square, marble building on an island in the sandy delta where the Great Road poured into the sea.

The lone room sported plain marble walls and a lone marble desk, behind which sat a thin, nondescript woman with pale eyes, draped in white linen. Two soldiers stood on either side of the room, likewise in white linen, their vests baring a purple circle with a lone, wavy vertical line through the middle—the insignia for one of the ruling Artisan families, but I couldn't remember which one.

The woman gave a curt nod of greeting. "General Albertus Mann." Her voice was bored.

I stepped forward, not bothering to conceal my scowl. There was no chair besides the one the woman sat on, so I stood. "I am sure the Artisan Council received word that our arrival was imminent."

"They did."

"So you greet all travelers with armed guards and keep them confined to their ships like prisoners? Perhaps it would have been better had we not extended the courtesy of warning you of our arrival."

The woman leaned back with an annoyed sigh. "Let me explain some things to you, General, as you seem incapable of understanding them without assistance. The Council received word of your impending arrival. Some time ago, in fact. They did not, mind you, receive a diplomatic discourse on whether we had the means or desire to house an invading army. They did not receive an attempt to negotiate a treaty on the matter. Indeed, they got the distinct impression that the Church of N'narad had no desire to come to any sort of mutually beneficial understanding at all. Instead, the council was informed, without further room for discussion, that three

N'naradin warships and some twenty-four-hundred religious zealots would require use of our scant resources for an unknown amount of time.

"Regardless of whatever your Bishop or your Grace thinks, General Mann, Valez'Mui is a free city. We feel no undue pressure to bow to the whims of religious leaders who live, without exaggeration, on the other side of the continent."

For all the times I'd wished Vimr to remain silent, I decided I could use the man's help now, but he said nothing. "We do not come as invaders, Miss...?"

"Iscez." She managed to drench her own name in contempt directed at me.

"Miss Iscez," I continued. "As I am sure the message explained to the council, we will remain in Valez'Mui—peacefully—only until we can find a guide across the desert."

"Yes. All of that was clear. What was not, and still is not clear, however, is *why* you must lead your ridiculous army across the Yellow Desert. As I'm sure you remember from your last visit here, as long ago as it may have been, although the political boundaries of Valez'Mui do not extend past the walls of our city, we have a symbiotic relationship with the nomadic tribes. A relationship without which there would be no caravans to and from the Black Wall. Without which there would be no marble and obsidian quarries. Without which you would not have your churches and palaces and statues of your Graces. Relationships without which, the city of Valez'Mui would not exist.

"So, as I'm sure even your feeble intellect can comprehend, an army invading the Yellow Desert is the same as an army invading the city that lies beyond the door behind you."

I opened my mouth to protest, though I don't remember now what I could have said, and she pressed on before I could say anything, regardless.

"And unlike your Church, we have an interest in keeping a good relationship with our neighbors, none of whom have the slightest interest in letting *your* army cross *their* desert without first knowing the reason why."

I closed my mouth. Whatever words I had planned were empty, even in my mind. As insulting as her tirade was, I agreed with most of it. I glanced back again at Vimr, hoping for some diplomacy from the man who spoke with the mouth of the Arch Bishop, but he only stood watching.

I turned back to Iscez and sighed. "So, you will not allow my men to disembark." Now, I decided, would not be a good time to bring up the karakh.

She shook her head. "It is, in truth, not even my decision. You and your companions are free to seek a guide in the city while your soldiers wait. If such a guide is found, the Council has agreed that you may sail up the Great Road, past Valez'Mui, and resume your journey from the banks of the river, where, technically, we have no authority to stop you.

"You also have their permission to continue up the Great Road without stopping, and return from whence you came."

I stared at the woman a few moments longer, willing her to say something else, before I turned and stalked from the customs house, Vimr and Rohm behind me.

Outside it was nearing midday. I could feel my skin burning in the brutal sun. The docks were all but deserted, as would the rest of the city. Valez'Mui lived in the cold of the night.

Rohm sighed. "That didn't go well."

I shook my head.

"I'll return to the ships and tell the men they must wait a little longer," Rohm volunteered. "Though I hope not too much longer. Seasickness is already being replaced by dysentery aboard The Bishop's Flame, and the holds are becoming ovens in this heat."

"Thank you for volunteering, Captain. That will not be an enviable job." I turned to Vimr. "You should return, too."

The Cardinal had the nerve to look shocked. "I will not!"

"You will. The Church is already not well received, as you may have noticed. The voice of the Arch Bishop will be nothing but another hindrance among many in finding a guide. Our men have already had their faith in Heaven shaken. By your own actions, I might add. A religious leader like yourself will be necessary for them in the days to come, and unnecessary for me. If you have an argument against this logic that has nothing to do with your discomfort, I will listen to it now."

I waited, enjoying Vimr fume and stammer before blurting to Rohm, "Come." His voice was tight. I thought I saw Rohm suppress a smile as he saluted me and turned to follow the Cardinal back to the ships.

I watched them for a moment, then turned and ventured alone into Valez'Mui's abandoned streets, seeking an inn where I could sleep off the rest of the day's heat.

I spent two weeks in Valez'Mui, wandering the markets and the nomadic camps outside the walls, returning to the ships once to give Rohm the address of my inn. It was an open-aired courtyard with high walls between the rooms and no roofs beyond awnings of woven palms for shade. During the day, the heat was almost unbearable, but I thought it would give me some sense of solidarity with my soldiers suffering in the harbor.

It would have helped morale if I'd stayed confined to the ships with the men, but the docks were across the city from the nomad camps. Far more expedient to stay near the northern walls and let Rohm come to me every morning with updates. At least, that's what I told myself.

Their condition was deteriorating. Dysentery remained confined to The Bishop's Flame, but there it had spread to one in five men, and by the fifth night, twenty had died. The healthy had the choice between staying above decks to burn to death by day and freeze to death by night or seek shelter below, where the stench was so bad it could be smelled on the other side of the docks, and the heat was almost as bad, anyway. Karakh warbled and screamed in misery.

The desert people remained unsympathetic. The few that would speak to me at all declined to guide us out of fear of reprisals from the others. Others mocked me for attempting to bring an army across the Yellow Desert in the first place.

Fury stalked me. Not toward the nomads that refused to help, but at the idiot Church bureaucracy which had decided an army was necessary for this retrieval quest, without any thought to the logistics of getting it to the Black Wall. Now two thousand men paid for its stupidity, and hundreds of others had already found their Heaven far too young.

In the end, for my weeks of searching, our guide found me.

The girl was maybe fourteen, though life had made her hands callous, and her dark face lined and rugged.

She sauntered up to the small, round table where I was choking down my breakfast of raw sandrak eggs. There was no other chair, so she leaned against the wall opposite where I sat.

I looked up as I gulped down a few mouthfuls of honeyed camel milk before the eggs made a second, even more undesirable appearance.

"You're that general, I guess."

I nodded. "I assume everyone in the city knows who I am at this point. What do you want?"

She leaned her elbows on the table, and her voice became conspiratorial. "What do *you* want? I thought you needed a guide to the Foothills. Otherwise, I guess you're not the man I was looking for."

"Are you offering?"

"Maybe."

I frowned. "You don't seem too concerned with the tribes' reaction. They won't be happy with you."

The girl shrugged and pulled over a chair from a nearby table. "Maybe because I don't have a tribe. The Kanaheed sold me when I was nine, so they can go fuck themselves. The other tribes too."

I continued to frown. "Won't your master miss you?"

She shook her head. "He died four rice harvests ago and left me my freedom with nothing else." She coughed out a humorless laugh. "Turned out I was better off a slave."

"How have you gotten by, then?"

Another bark of laughter. "Do I have to write it down for you? No free samples."

I felt my expression soften. "Four harvests? That's what, two years ago? And you were twelve years old?"

"Eleven," she said. "Things were better when I started. I could charge more."

"You still remember your way across the Desert?" I found myself wanting to help this girl regardless of her ability, but I thought of my men suffering on the ships and hardened myself.

"For a while, I was with one of the caravans going between here and the obsidian quarries. Cladutt—that was the Artisan—paid me to, you know, entertain. Spent almost a whole season like that until he grew tired of me and found someone younger. He can go fuck himself too. Anyway, I can get you to the foothills, but I'm going to stay there, so you'll need to find someone else to bring you back. If you're coming back."

I nodded. "I have men with me. A lot of men."

She shrugged. "I know. And you'll want me to entertain them, I suppose."

I shook my head, feeling my face grow red. "No, no, no. Nothing like that. Just warning you. Two-thousand men crossing the Yellow Desert might make their share of enemies. Theirs and anyone who comes with us."

She gestured at herself with both hands. "I know. Like you said, they won't be happy with me. You think I'm safe here? Every night I sit around the docks waiting to get raped for tin. I'm okay with risk."

I swallowed and nodded again. "What do you want in return?"

"Nothing. To get away from Valez'Mui, and I can't cross the desert by myself. I don't trust the tribes not to sell me again, so you're my best shot. If you leave me alone once we get to the Wall, that's payment enough for me."

I wondered if a decade ago, I would have been inclined to try to convert her to the Church in some misguided attempt to better her life. Probably. But that was then. My faith had worn thin. Even thinner since this absurd mission began. Now, I couldn't help thinking she'd be better off without Salvation Taxes and levels of Heaven.

"I'll need some time to work out provisions. Can you find me here three days from now? Same time."

"What about your army?"

"We'll meet them on the way, outside the city."

"Fine. I'll see you then. My name is Ginya. Or at least, you can call me that." She gave me an awkward salute I couldn't help but find endearing and pushed her way from the crowded common room.

11

SEARCH

SMUDGE SWAGGERED INTO THE BAR A LITTLE AFTER MIDNIGHT and saw Pasha siting by himself, eyes red. He held a cup of rice wine, but it was full. It looked as if he'd forgotten it was there. Smudge frowned.

He ambled up to the table. "Something's wrong, I guess."

Pasha looked up and caught his green eyes with his own, but looked past him, expression blank. Then he blinked. "Oh, what was it? Smudge. Sorry. Just your eyes..."

Smudge looked uncomfortable. "Where's your sister? But I suppose that's why you're sober and miserable. She pouting in the room?"

Pasha shook his head and swallowed before draining the cup and setting it down. "We had a fight." His voice was soft and ashamed. "She left. Just before sunset. She does this. She does this all the time, but she should be back by now..." His words choked off.

Smudge studied him, slanted green eyes now filled with concern. "She left the inn? Alone?"

Pasha nodded.

Smudge, without thinking, reached out and put his hand over

Pasha's, who looked up from his empty cup into the old man's eyes. He didn't move his hand.

The old man blinked at his hand, lying atop Pasha's as if surprised to see it there, and pulled it away. He sighed. "Stay here. Promise me you'll stay here."

He waited for Pasha's nod before he went on. "I'll find her. I can pull a few connections, and I can find her, but if you go out looking on your own, I'll need to find you too. So wait."

Pasha nodded again, their eyes still locked.

Without seeming to think about it, Smudge reached out and touched Pasha's face. The scene brought a few looks from around the bar, and Smudge dropped his hand.

"Chulla?" Pasha began.

Smudge stood. "Don't worry. I'll find your sister." And he hurried from The Chisel, leaving Pasha to stare after him.

Anna running off was bad enough. But in all Syrina's years as a Kalis, no one had ever recognized her before.

It didn't help that you kind of lost control, there, the voice had snarked as Syrina fled The Chisel, feeling more naked than she ever did when she was only wearing her tattoos. *But I think our feelings are mutual, at least.*

The voice's words did nothing to console her, and as usual, she had other problems to deal with before she could get to the one on her mind. Story of her life.

She hurried back to Ves's compound, forcing herself into the slow, limpy gait of Smudge, running through options in her mind.

If Anna never turned up, there would be no more doubt whispered into Pasha's ear, and he would probably do whatever Syrina told him.

But no, he wouldn't do anything without his sister. Not to mention, they were important enough she couldn't afford to lose either of them before she determined what they were. As much as she hated the idea, she might end up needing to deliver one of them to Ormo or the Astrologers, and she knew she wouldn't be able to do that to Pasha.

She needed to find Anna, and to do it in a hurry, she'd need Vesmalimali's help.

"I thought you were bringing someone for me to meet," Ves said. He sat eating next to a mostly nude, young tribesman in his dining hall. His first mate, Ash, sat across from them, sipping imported Fommish wine. He gave Smudge a nod of greeting.

Ves leaned over to his companion and said a few soft words, and the young man took one more quick bite of river fish before sauntering from the room with a haughty glance at Smudge. Ves watched his backside until the door had closed behind him.

"Should I go too?" Ash asked. His smile was innocent.

"As always," Ves answered, "You can go wherever the hell you want when you want. I quit trying to get you to do anything else years ago."

Ash smiled and looked at Smudge.

Smudge said to Ves, "Yeah, um. About that..." He shuffled in place where he stood in the doorway.

Ves stopped eating and sat back, eyebrows raised.

"It was two someones, but one of them sort of, uh, took off."

"So, I only need to take one to Fom?"

"Well, two, still. That's the thing. I was hoping you could, er, help me find the missing one. Anna. Her name is Anna."

"Ah," Ves rumbled. "You think Tolisho took her?"

The old man nodded, not meeting the pirates eyes.

"How do you know? You said she took off."

Smudge looked around the dining room at everything except the man he was talking to. Ash watched the exchange while he leaned over to slide the abandoned, half-eaten river fish over to his side to poke at with his wooden fork.

"I don't know," Smudge admitted. "But he had an interest in her, and her brother thinks she would have come back by now, and I believe her brother, so..."

Ves still looked unconvinced. "You mean this Anna's brother? I take it he's the other one I'm supposed to take. Lots of unfortunate things can happen to a lone girl in Valez'Mui who doesn't know what she's doing."

"I know. It might not be Tolisho, but either way, I need to find out what happened to her, and I can't do it alone. I don't think Pasha will leave until he knows."

"Pasha. That's her brother's name?"

"Yeah."

Ves sighed.

"All I need is for you to find out where she is if she's even alive. I know some people that can help me get her, but I can't find her without your help. I'll pay."

Ves chuckled. "Of course you'll pay. If I didn't know that we wouldn't still be talking about it."

"Thanks." Smudge bobbed his head. "After this is sorted, we can go."

Ves gave a vague wave of dismissal and went back to eating.

"See you soon," Ash said to the old man's back.

Smudge turned long enough to give an awkward wave before he closed the door behind him.

Smudge fidgeted in the foyer until a servant summoned Ves to see what they should do about him. The pirate, with a dramatic wave of his hands, declared Smudge was making him nervous and lent him a vacant room he could stay in while Ves's people looked into Anna.

Smudge fidgeted and worried, and for two days, he puttered after Ves, asking if he'd heard anything.

It got to the point that Ves was glad he got bad news just so he had something to tell him.

"They've found something." The pirate stood in the doorway of Smudge's little windowless room.

The old man had been lying on his pallet, eyes closed, but he leapt up and hobbled over to Ves, peering up at him. "You found her!" He exclaimed.

"No. No one found her, but one of my people found where she isn't. She's not with Tolisho. Not anymore."

Smudge, green eyes blinking, waited for more, then grew exasperated when he saw how much Ves was enjoying not saying anything else. "Well, where is she? What happened?"

"She *was* with Tolisho for a day or two, but she didn't cooperate. I guess she never learned how a good concubine was supposed to behave, and now Tolisho has a big bite out of his face, compliments of your friend. So he got rid of her. Either killed her or sold her, but knowing Tolisho, he sold her. No reason for him not to make a profit if the result will be the same. I've got some guys looking for her in the pens, but who knows."

"We need to find her before she's sold."

Ves cleared his throat with a sound that was more like a growl. "Don't you mean *I* have to find her? Seems like all you're doing is hanging around my house annoying me. Anyway, that's not all."

"It's not? What else?"

"Well, Tolisho is vindictive—you knew that—and paranoid. He got worried about the girl's brother coming for him, so now he's got people looking for him, too. Whatever his name is. Pasha."

Smudge's shifting green eyes froze on Whitehook. "He's looking for Pasha?"

"That's how I found out about all this. One of my people talked to someone she knows in Tolisho's organization, who told her they're checking the inns for the brother."

Smudge stared up at Ves for a moment longer, blinking. Then, he leaped up, pushed passed the big man with surprising strength, and hurried towards the front hall. "I have to get to him first," he announced without turning around.

Ves watched the old man's retreating back, perplexed. "You might want to wait until dusk. But if it gets you out of my house for a while, now is fine, too." He spoke his last words to the door Smudge had already disappeared out of, into the blazing heat of the afternoon sun.

Syrina limped down the inferno of the street, forcing herself to not charge into a full sprint. She had been analytical enough when Anna had disappeared, but the fear that gripped her when she'd heard Pasha was in danger took her by surprise. The voice in her head had nothing sarcastic to say about it, which was even more disturbing.

Smudge arrived at The Chisel an hour before dusk. The streets were still empty, and little dust devils swirled here and there in the long shadows cast by the setting sun. The common room of the inn was vacant except for the bartender, who glanced at the old man before turning back to wipe dust from the glog mugs when it became obvious he was passing through on the way to the rooms.

Smudge burst into Pasha's room without knocking. The younger man was lying on the narrow bed closest to the shuttered window but jumped up as Smudge shambled in. He clutched a long, black knife in each hand, but his stance relaxed when he saw who it was. "Oh," he said, his voice low. "What are you doing here? Did you find Anna? Where's Chulla?"

"Not quite," Smudge responded, not bothering to keep his voice down. "Getting close. You, though, you're not safe here. As far as Chulla goes, looks like you won't be seeing her again."

"What do you mean?" Pasha sat back down on the edge of his bed, tension in his voice.

"I mean, if you don't get out of this inn, you'll end up in a box at the bottom of the Great Road, so we need to leave, and there's no time for you to see Chulla again. Just me."

"I thought you said you didn't know where Anna was."

Smudge made an exasperated noise. "No. But I know she's probably still alive, which is more than you'll be if you stay in this inn another day."

Pasha refused to be evaded. "How do you know Anna is still alive if you don't know where she is? What do you mean 'probably?' What if she comes back, and I'm not here?"

"I mean 'probably,' as in probably. And she's not coming back."

"How do you know?"

Smudge took a step over to where Pasha was seated and grabbed his arm with shocking strength. "Look, you need to come—"

"I'm not a child. You need to stop treating me like one," Pasha objected. His voice was calm, but anger smoldered behind his eyes. "From what I've heard about people out here, I'm older than you."

Smudge looked like he had a few questions, but then he just shook his head. "Fine. Sorry. Look, *old man*, you need to come with me because Anna isn't coming back. She got nabbed by that Artisan who took a liking to her when you were crossing—"

"Taldishad, or whoever he was?"

"Tolisho, yeah," Smudge leaned in, voice low, still gripping his arm. "He got her, but she wouldn't play nice, so he sold her into the slave pens. Now he's got a bunch of goons checking the inns for you, and if he finds you, he'll flay off your skin and dump what's left into the Great Road. We have to go before they get here."

"Why would he want to do that?" Pasha sounded incredulous.

"Because the guy is a vindictive bastard who doesn't want you to come after him for selling your sister into slavery."

"I can take care of myself," Pasha objected, but he was gathering his things up with whatever Anna hadn't taken, and bundling it all into his pack.

"Fine," Smudge said, rolling his eyes. "As long as you don't do it here. Come on. I've arranged a safe place. We just have to get there in one piece."

"How do you know all of this, anyway?" Pasha asked Smudge's back as he followed him out the room door and down the short stairway into the common room.

"I told you," Smudge looked at Pasha over his shoulder. "I've been looking into it."

12

REQUITED LOVE

Pasha followed a few paces behind the bent form of Smudge, who hobbled down the narrow street under thin marble arches, which cast a tangle of shadows under the evening sun. Smudge was spry despite his age, and Pasha struggled to keep up.

His stomach was in knots, and he insisted with boundless stamina that he could help find Anna, but Smudge ignored him. The attraction Pasha felt tugging him toward Smudge made things even more complicated. His mind kept tracing back to Chulla and how she and her uncle had the same eyes.

Smudge led him a few blocks from The Chisel before turning down another street, into a group of nine men and women wearing the blue double-line-in-circle of Tolisho piling out of a bar, the sign to the right of the door depicting a lone, stone mug spilled under a leaning ladder. Pasha had just enough time to wonder what a place like that might be called.

The first one—a stout woman with thick arms, short blond hair and a flat face, barked something in Valezian, and Smudge stopped with a quick gesture at Pasha to hold back.

They exchanged heated words. Pasha turned away, trying to hide his face without being obvious about it.

It didn't work. One of the men standing next to the woman was staring at him. He said something to her, interrupting Smudge, and he gestured at Pasha and the two long blackvine knives he wore at his belt. They were all looking now.

The woman said something else to Smudge, her tone harsh, and shoved the old man. He fell with a cry of surprise.

She blurted a few words to Pasha. Her voice sounded like she was trying to be soothing, but he couldn't understand, and her expression was mocking. Pasha drew his weapons, but he doubted he had the skill to deal with nine of them.

"Ancestors," he whispered to himself. "I'm sorry, Anna. I tried."

The nine spread out, four on either side of the woman. They blocked the street and drew curved, bronze blades. Pasha risked a glance behind him. The street was empty until it ended at the T intersection they'd come from.

He began to back up. His knives felt small in his sweaty hands. A little closer to the intersection and he would turn and flee, and he tried not to think about what would happen to Chulla's uncle after he'd gone.

The next few seconds became a blur.

Pasha took another step backwards. He coiled to pivot and run, hoping he could out-pace them enough to force them to split up to look for him so he wouldn't need to fight them all at the same time. They continued to advance, past where Smudge still huddled in the dusty street, clutching his chest, unable to stand. Ignored. But his green eyes were sharp.

In a blur, the old man wasn't on his knees, but a streak through the mob. He flickered from one to another, faster than Pasha could follow, or they could react, and they were falling, weapons cast away, clutching throats and groins and limbs, tumbling into each other, or lying in the dust, unmoving.

In five heartbeats Smudge and Pasha were the only ones standing. Pasha felt ridiculous, clutching his knives in the middle of the street. Smudge wasn't even out of breath.

"Shut up, don't worry about it." Smudge whispered. His green eyes focused on Pasha, but he got the impression the old man wasn't talking to him.

"Don't worry about what? How did you..." Pasha trailed off.

"No. I'm going to," Smudge muttered. "Feel free to stop me." The old man muttered something else in a language Pasha didn't recognize and looked smug before he refocused on Pasha. "I'll tell you everything," he said. "But not here. We need to get off the street."

Smudge cast a meaningful look around, and Pasha noticed for the first time faces in doorways and through cracked shutters, watching.

Pasha followed the old man, who was now neither bent nor limping as he trotted through the winding streets.

People began to come out as torches were lit, the immense heat of day blown away by the evening breeze, though it still radiated from the packed ground and stone buildings.

When they fled far enough that no one took note of them any longer, Smudge led Pasha into a plain, marble cube of a building, pushing the heavy stone door closed behind them and engulfing them in darkness.

A flint sparked. A lantern flickered to life a moment later. They were in a single room, with a bundle of dusty rags in one corner that looked like it served as a bed. There were a few broken bits of furniture and a stack of clay water jugs piled against one wall. Other than that, the room was empty. There were no windows.

"Is this where you live?" Pasha asked.

Smudge had been staring at a point just left of the door, lost in thought. He blinked. "Sometimes, I guess you could say that. Not often, but sometimes." He cleared his throat, but fell silent and went over to the pile of bottles, where he unstopped one and took a long drink before handing the jug to Pasha.

Smudge watched him drink. The old man's lips moved, but no

sound came out. Pasha was disconcerted that he didn't find all the mumbling disconcerting, and he felt another emotional pull.

When he was done drinking—he hadn't realized how thirsty he'd been—he set the empty jug down, eyes never unlocking with Smudge's.

"What happened? What did you do? Who are you?"

Smudge looked to have another silent debate with himself and sighed, looking determined.

"I think you already recognized me," Smudge said with Chulla's voice.

Pasha blinked. "Chulla? I thought... the other night, I mean, I thought... but how?"

Smudge shook his head. "No, I'm not Chulla. Any more than I'm her uncle." His voice was different again. A woman's voice, but not Chulla's. Then, to herself, she muttered, "No. It's too late now, anyway. You trust him too, right?"

"What's going on?" Pasha asked. "Who are you talking to?" But as he spoke, he took a step toward the old man who sounded like a woman, who had sounded like Chulla a moment ago, in a sudden well of desire.

No, he thought. It wasn't sudden. He'd felt a pull to Chulla, though she'd been too young, and he'd felt the same toward Smudge, an old man.

Smudge put a hand up, asking Pasha to wait. Then, with a final flash of reluctance, he peeled off his face.

Pasha stared. Green eyes stared back. It wasn't as if the rest of her head was invisible as much as something he couldn't quite look at. Like grasping water, his eyes rolled off a confusing series of lines and rounded angles until only green eyes remained. All else blurred into the background until he forced himself to look for it again. Eyes, nose, ears, a small mouth. He could see her, but he couldn't *notice* her, a fact that grew more confusing the more he thought about it.

Without further hesitation, the unnoticeable-but-not-invisible-woman-who-wasn't-Chulla-or-Smudge stripped the rest of the old man's flesh and clothes off until she was just two eyes and a collection of details he couldn't grasp.

"What?" He stammered.

"Look," she said. The mirage of her body shifted, and he felt her hand take his. It was rough with callouses. "My name is Syrina. It will take way too long to explain much else, but I can tell you I've never shown myself before. Not like this. I'm assuming I can trust you because I feel like I can, and I've never felt like that before, at least about a human. I want you to trust me, so I'm being honest. Maybe for the first time in my life, I'm being honest. I was Chulla. And her uncle, which somehow you knew, I think. I've been a lot of people.

"There's some connection. Between us, I mean," she went on. "You recognized me, felt drawn to me, whatever skin I was wearing. It's mutual. Whatever I am, whatever you are." she drew closer to him, slipped her arms around his waist. He hesitated, then found her with his hands, pulled her against him.

"I knew something," he breathed, marveling at his sense of relief. "The first time Chulla came to us, there was something between us," Pasha muttered, holding her close, pressing his lips to the top of her smooth head. His heart pounded in confusion and excitement.

"I have a voice in my head," Syrina said, pulling back enough to look up at him. "It criticizes and second guesses everything I do. But even it is driving me to be with you. I'm not supposed to feel this way. About anyone. Ever. Once, there was something, but even that..." She trailed off.

Pasha pulled her close again, pressed his mouth against hers, lowered her to the pile of rags that served as a bed. She began tugging at his clothes.

He laughed.

"What?" She asked, green eyes nervous.

"I was just thinking," Pasha said. "I'm glad you're not an old man."

He couldn't make out her features, but her eyes smiled, and her face raised to his.

Later, lying in the dim blue light of the single, low-burning lantern, Syrina ran a finger along the scar that puckered Pasha's face from the corner of his eye to his chin. "Tell me about this," she whispered.

She thought he might have been asleep, but he squeezed her and opened his eyes. "We competed in the valley, to see which clan would have the honor of living in Suedmal—the town closest to the Tomb."

"The Tomb. That's the place that Mann raided, I take it."

Pasha nodded. "I guess I should have known you already knew where I was really from, and what we're doing."

Syrina smiled. "I was following Mann. It wasn't too hard to put it together. So tell me about your scar."

Pasha settled back and stared into the shadows on the ceiling. "The Felor—a different clan—had lived in Suedmal for almost six hundred years. My family, the Shent, had only managed to take it fifty or so years ago, and the Felor were still desperate to take it back. I was just a kid at the time, so I didn't take part."

Syrina blinked. "You were a kid fifty years ago? You said something to Smudge earlier about being older than him. How old are you?"

"Seventy-six. I guess people out here have short lives. How old are you?"

Syrina thought. "We don't celebrate Kalis birthdays, so I'm not sure. Around thirty five, I think, though most Kalis live to be a hundred and fifty, maybe two hundred. Who knows how long we'd live, given the chance? The work always gets us in the end. But I'm sorry, you were telling me about your scar."

Pasha studied Syrina's eyes for a minute, gave her a light kiss, and lay back again to continue.

"So all of the families competed in this, I guess you would call it a game, to weaken the villages closest to the south end of the valley so they could take over, by kidnapping members of the rival clans. Nobody was off-limits except for pregnant women. Kids were especially desirable because if they came of age while captive, they became a member of that clan.

"Those taken were treated well, under guard, away from the village that was holding them. The clans would train some of their warriors to specialize in rescuing hostages, and the others to capture rival clan members. In Suedmal, we didn't need to worry about taking over another village. We focused on defending ourselves by capturing our attackers, keeping them weak, and rescuing those few hostages another clan managed to take. If we were lucky, another village would end up taking over our strongest rivals, forcing them to move further away. And of course, any children we could hold onto long enough became ours, strengthening us and weakening them."

Syrina thought about that. "That sounds complicated. So how did anyone actually take over? Just kidnap every person in the village who could defend it and move in?"

"I guess they'd do that if they had to, but it never got that far that I know of. Eventually, a village would be so weak they would parlay with the attackers and trade villages—the losers would move to the village further north in exchange for the return of some of the hostages. Then they'd start over again.

"Except in Suedmal. If we succeeded in defending ourselves, there was nothing our attackers could offer. They needed to free the people we took from them, or else be taken by another village."

"This is what you guys did in the valley?"

Pasha nodded. "It sounds stupid now, trying to explain it out loud, but it was everything. To make sure the best were closest to the Tomb. The last line of defense. Only, nobody thought anything existed on the other side of the Wall, so it became a game that never ended. Nobody thought of it like that, but that's what it was. Anna was right—it didn't prepare us at all for the only time it mattered."

Syrina gave him a little squeeze. "So how does this explain your scar?"

"Right, so, when I was a kid in Suedmal, I was a target. There was a raid one night, and I got separated from my family. We were trained to leave the village if that ever happened. Hide in the mountains or the forest. The mountains were closer, so that's where I was, but one of the Felor tracked me."

"And he gave you the scar while you were fighting him off?"

Pasha let out a little laugh. "No, though I guess that would be more exciting. I lost her by moving higher into the mountains, where it was so rocky I wouldn't leave a trail, but on the way back, I ran into a bora sow."

"What's that?"

"I wasn't sure if you had bora out here. I guess not. They're animals. Hooved, tusked scavengers. They're what our clothes are made out of—their leather, I mean. The females are bigger than the males, and a lot meaner. She didn't give me a chance to run before she charged. I dodged, but she knocked me over. I managed to stab her in the haunch and make her flee while I was on the ground, but not before she gave me this." Pasha took Syrina's hand and gently ran her finger down his scar. "She missed my eye, or it would have been worse."

Syrina was quiet, and for a long time, there was only the mingled sounds of their breathing.

She tilted her face up and kissed him on the cheek. "It's almost dusk," she said. "Let's get you somewhere safe so I can find your sister."

13

INTERLUDE

"He succeeded," Ormo grumbled down to the Seneschal kneeling at the base of his dais, the little slip of Syrina's message still gripped in his pudgy, powdered fingers.

The Seneschal knew better than to answer.

Ormo brooded for a moment, still gripping the tiny parchment. "Has Kalis Shen returned to the Palace yet?" He asked.

The Seneschal nodded. Yes, Ma'is. She awaits your summons as we speak."

"Perfect. You are dismissed. Please send for her on your way out."

Ormo listened to the Seneschal's feet sing across his floor, the slip of paper forgotten in his hand. A few minutes later, the high doors at the far end of his Hall opened and shut, and more feet sung as the shadow of Kalis Shen approached his dais.

"Welcome back, Shen."

"Thank you, Ma'is."

He caught a glimpse of her bow out of the corner of his eye, found her brown eyes with his, and held her gaze. "I have a small task for you, now, before you rest."

"Of course. Anything."

"Send a missive to Great Spring. To the N'naradin consul, with instructions for General Mann to leave whatever treasures he found in the Black Wall with her, rather than transporting them back to Tyrsh. Use rising tensions between the Grace and the Arch Bishop as the reason, and use Arch Bishop Daliius III personal seal—make sure to use the most recent one. Let there be no mistake that this order comes from on high."

"So, no hawk then?"

Ormo nodded. "No hawks for this message. Too much risk these days. If it were to be intercepted, I fear not even a Kalis of your considerable talents could keep things from unraveling. Besides, Daliius would never send such orders by hawk. He will send a currier, and that currier shall be you. You will collect these treasures yourself and bring them to me."

"Of course, Ma'is." Shen hesitated. "May I ask you a question?"

"You know I encourage curiosity." Ormo smiled down at her.

"Won't there be problems when the Arch Bishop never receives the treasures he commissioned Mann to find? It will surely spark an investigation—"

"Nothing is sure, my dear Shen," Ormo rumbled. "I appreciate your foresight in this matter, but it is nothing you need to concern yourself with."

"Very well. I'm sorry to question you. I should have known it would be under control. Is there anything else?"

"Nonsense," Ormo's voice was kind. "Always ask questions. Never assume my knowledge is complete. That is, after all, why your kind exists. And no, nothing else."

Shen stood from where she kneeled. "I live to serve, Ma'is."

"And you do it well," Ormo said as she turned to leave.

He listened to her feet across his Hall floor, until the doors shut behind her.

Ormo sat for a time, considering. He would need to send word to Tyrsh himself, explaining the situation, but he doubted Daliius would cause problems. The Arch Bishop had, after all, organized the mission to the Black Wall on behalf of the Merchant's Syndicate.

He rose with a tired groan and shuffled to one of the concealed doors along the side of the Hall, this one behind a naphtha brazier, which led to a hidden study. There he penned instructions for Syrina in his tiny, spidery script.

He dared not tell anyone else about Syrina's news—that guardians had survived and followed Mann from the Wall. He wondered who else Syrina would tell. Kavik, likely. Wherever he was. He wished he knew who else. Wished he understood how deep her betrayal had gone.

Again, Ormo felt the unfamiliar pang of remorse when he thought of Syrina and pushed it down. It was clear she still needed him. Whoever had gotten to her didn't understand her as well as he did, and they never would. And if she could bring the Wall dwellers to him, he could test what he suspected. With a being more pure than even Kalis Syrina, well, that was one way to ease the endless loss he felt when he thought about what she'd done to him.

He'd hoped to get a complete report from Kalis Pyrdis when she'd returned with Mann, but she was long overdue. He'd spent a considerable amount of resources and time setting her up as Cardinal Vimr, not including the increased allowance of naphtha he'd promised to the Arch Bishop to ensure Vimr's placement in the expedition. Given his relationship with Daliius, that probably hadn't been necessary, but he'd wanted to make sure. It would be disappointing if it was all for naught.

Still, though, it would be worth it—worth any price—if Shen brought him Mann's treasure, and Syrina played her role in bringing him the guardians of the library.

It would be, he suspected with a mixture of pleasure and remorse, the last part she would play for him.

14

RESCUE

WELL, THAT WAS... INTERESTING.

Smudge was on his way back from escorting Pasha to Ves's place. Syrina hadn't felt like this since Triglav. Even then, well, she couldn't have done that with an owl. For the first time since Triglav's death, the emptiness inside her was gone. "You didn't object," she muttered as she ducked back into the safe house, where she'd taken Pasha the evening before, and began to peel off Smudge.

No, the voice admitted, though it sounded reluctant about it. *Look, I'm drawn to him too. It's just that the timing was a little inappropriate, don't you think?*

Syrina frowned, but she couldn't disagree. "Well," she whispered as she slipped into the torch-lit street, now naked, "It kept him from worrying about his sister for a while."

The voice lapsed into silence, but it no doubt knew as well as Syrina there were deeper repercussions. Anyway, she was thankful it had stopped bothering her about it.

It wasn't that Kalis weren't sexual. They were human, after all, even if whatever was done to them kept them from menstruating when they reached puberty. It was more that they never felt enough attraction to do anything about it, except for maybe the occasional self-amusement. Syrina had never found anyone attractive enough to have much interest in them, which had made even masturbation abstract enough that she rarely felt the need for it. Triglav had been the closest thing she'd ever felt to attraction towards anything. Pasha, though. Pasha was like Triglav in a body compatible with her own. So compatible that she was having a hard time focusing on anything else.

Aren't we getting close to the pens? The voice asked. *I don't want to kill the mood or anything, but maybe this is why Kalis are conditioned to not think about fucking.*

"Shut up," Syrina whispered, but she turned her attention to the problem at hand.

The slave pens lay outside the walls of Valez'Mui on the far side of the Great Road, out of sight from the general population. The city used forced labor in every facet of its society, but found reminders of it distasteful. Access was limited to a ferry service from the main docks or a long, marble footbridge with one foot in the Nomad camps and the other at the end of the long, run-down warehouses where they kept the slaves.

At odds with the carved vines and tiny marble flowers of the bridge was the double-row of cages that hung below it, containing corpses of escaped slaves and those that aided them, mummifying and blackened in the terrible heat. A few pitiful coughs and wheezes drifted up from a couple of poor souls locked up this past dusk, but they wouldn't survive once the sun came up.

The Pens were huge—a dozen massive warehouses each filled with two levels of cages—but Whitehook's people had found a girl who only spoke a little Trader and another language no one understood in the one called the House of Perennial Love. Syrina had never been clear on whether the Artisans were being ironic by giving their slave warehouses names like that, or just liked to dress things up for public consumption.

The House of Perennial Love was two thousand hands long and five hundred wide, built from sandstone the same pale color of the desert. It was a single high room, with double-stacked cages in five rows that ran down its length. Double barn doors stood open at either end to let in the cold night air, and bored guards lingered at either end and wandered the aisles between the pens, two-thirds full of slaves waiting for tomorrow's auction.

Slavery in Valez'Mui was a convoluted business. Often as not, people were sold by their own tribes to the Artisans, either to pay off debts or for other, more transient reasons. Others were criminals too petty to be condemned to the cages that lined the desert-side of the city walls. Some were just people like Anna—captured by an Artisan for whom no laws applied, and kept as pets before selling them for a profit. The buyers were, besides Artisans, the plantation owners that ran the rice paddies up stream on the Great Road, providing food for most of Eris, and work gang foremen running the marble and obsidian quarries that dotted the far edge of the Yellow Desert. Wherever they went, slaves taken from the city didn't live long. The quarries were just forced labor camps, and the rice paddies were dens of abuse and ripe with disease.

Syrina had an easy time slipping past the guards and dodging the patrols that roamed inside the House of Perennial Love, but as she searched the cages and found no sign of Anna, her concern grew.

With every cage checked, she slipped back outside and considered her next move. She didn't plan on going back to Pasha empty handed, but already the eastern sky was growing light. She wished she'd checked the auctions first. Anna was fit and attractive enough to fetch a good price. The slavers had probably pushed for her to be one of the first to the block the night before.

So why didn't you think of that? The voice asked.

"Shut up," she whispered, but the voice, as usual, was right.

She hadn't thought anything through because she'd been distracted by her feelings for Pasha, in such a hurry to make him happy she'd rushed out at the first hint of where his sister might be without bothering to be thorough. Without bothering to be a Kalis.

But it might not be too late, she thought as she hurried back to one of Smudge's rooms that she'd set up just inside the city walls. Technically, slavery wasn't legal outside of Valez'Mui, and it required piles of visas and paperwork that turned them from slaves to indentured servants. Such visas took time, and slave owners never departed with their merchandise right away. The quarries were far enough removed from the rest of Eris that they didn't bother with the technicalities, but Syrina doubted Anna would have been sold to them. As healthy as the girl was, she was less than a hand taller than Syrina and would be useless hauling rocks.

Anna was better suited as a house slave, either in the plantations or within the city. Tolisho had no doubt spread the word among locals that she'd be uncooperative, so that left the plantations. There, they could keep her in the house until they broke her, and if they couldn't, they'd throw her into the fields to rot.

Too bad you didn't think of all of this before.

"Yeah, too bad," Syrina muttered back, irritated, as she rummaged around the little square room, looking for materials she could use to throw together a usable face. "You said that before. Too bad you didn't think of any of this either. Too bad you seemed even more into it than me when I was fucking Pasha."

She began ironing out the beginnings of a face. The voice fell silent. She wanted to assume since it wasn't defending itself, it was pouting, but she didn't want to give it the satisfaction of thinking about it, so she turned her attention to the task at hand. She hoped the waxy base wouldn't start melting under the heat of the day.

The Visa office would have the name of the ship slated to be the next to leave up to the plantations. With luck, there would only be one.

The old woman lurched from the Visa and Export office, down the short stairway towards the slave docks. She wore a skirt of dingy, yellowed goat-hair, hiked above her knees. Her face was painted with too much makeup, thick and white, lips red and crooked, all of which failed to hide the seeping pox beneath. The flesh of her face drooped. Her hair was a tangled mass of yellow and grey, and her left hand was short two fingers, twisted like a crab claw.

Bruz'na's stomach churned when he saw her. He was loath to get close to such a foul old whore, but what the hell had she been doing in the visa office?

"Hey, lady!" He shouted from across the alley where he'd been hunkered, fanning himself, doing his best to keep an eye on both the Visa and Export office and this part of the docks without leaving the shade.

The woman either didn't hear his shout—unlikely this time of day unless she was deaf since the only sound was the buzzing of a few flies and the burble of the Great Road—or ignored him. Instead, she hurried, bow-legged, in the opposite direction, toward the docked slave barges waiting for their visas.

Bruz'na stepped into the street and felt a blast of heat on his back from the sun, which was easing its way westward in a crawl that felt like it was getting slower by the minute.

Idiot, he thought to himself. *I'm an idiot, volunteering for the day shift. "Nothing to do," I said like a piece of shit when Ghetz asked me why I'd do such a stupid thing. "Nice, quiet days." Fucking idiot.*

"Lady!" He yelled again, louder, as he came up behind her. He reached out to grab her arm but hesitated to touch the sagging flesh.

He was close enough that she couldn't pretend not to hear him anymore, and she turned around.

Bruz'na took an involuntary step back in revulsion. The old woman's face was even more grotesque up-close. It hung loose and sagging on her skull, here and there sliding at a glacial pace down toward her drooping breasts.

"What? You wan' some o' this too?" She snarled at him and grabbed her crotch.

"Ugh," he grunted and wiped the hand he'd almost touched her with on his shirt, taking another step back. "No. What the hell were you doing in the visa office?"

She released her crotch and stared at him. Her green eyes were clear beyond her hanging, diseased face, and they blinked in confusion at him. "Where?"

Bruz'na pointed at the square, single-level building.

"Oh." she peered along his finger, shielding her eyes against the sun with her wrinkled claw of a hand. "Is that what that place is?" Then she laughed. "Do I look like I care about visas? Been goin' in there for years, off an' on. When I get a job down 'ere on th' docks. Not so much these days, but sometime' this reeking ol' fleshpot's still good for a laugh." She let out another throaty cackle. "Speaking o' which, I be goin' to work, so if y'scuse me." She turned to go.

"Wait, what do you mean you've been going in there for years? It's closed. Locked, or should be." He hesitated, torn between his sense of duty and disgust.

"Yeah? Lots o' places are locked. If I can find my way in, out'a th' heat, somewheres to rest a spot an' change int'a my workin' clothes, what's it to you?"

As she rambled, Bruz'na starred at her face, fascinated and horrified. The corners of her mouth had slid almost to her chin, the left side now hanging lower than the right. Her left eye slanted downward, the tip of her pointed nose sagged to her upper lip. Her green eyes studied him.

"Ugh," he said again, no longer listening, taking a step closer. "What's wrong with your face? Is that...?" He spoke to himself as he reached out, still hesitant, to touch the wilting flesh.

"Shit," the old whore said in a different voice, and with a rapid glance around that Bruz'na had just enough time to decide was out of character, stumbled into him, knocking him off the walk into a narrow gap between the pier and a huge, docked steam barge.

"Oof." The back of Bruz'na's head struck the side of the boat with a hard thunk, and everything went black.

The old whore teetered to the edge of the dock and peered down where he'd disappeared. She nodded to herself when she saw his body, floating face-down in the gap, though her eyes looked sad. She took another look around for any witnesses.

Seeing none, she pressed upwards on her face, smoothing the sagging parts around the eye and chin. Then she again hiked her filthy, shapeless skirt above her knees and hurried off toward the barges.

The River Hulk crouched alone at the end of the furthest pier, bobbing back and forth against the fat leather fenders that protected it from the grey planks of the dock. It was wide and flat, made of green copper sheets, bulging square and low in the back where the naphtha engines rested in the Great Road, full of fuel, ready to push upstream. The poop deck was painted white to reflect the worst of the sun, and empty except for two sleepy-looking guards wearing lose, white linen, lounging half-asleep under a broad canvas umbrella.

The sagging, bow-legged prostitute had both feet on the narrow gangway before either man on deck woke up enough to notice her. Shadows stretched, but the sun was still three hands above the western buildings.

The young man on the left, head and face shaved clean, grimy and filmed with sweat, stood and glowered at the woman as she made her way up the thin plank of wood. The man on the right, with black hair and thick, wiry beard, remained seated, but he cocked a crossbow resting on his lap, and he leaned back with it, resting it against his shoulder.

"Ya' squids call up a whore?" She croaked at them, laughing, but stopped a dozen hands from the top of the plank when the bald man didn't look amused.

He eyed her up and down, face twisted in disgust. "No. No one here called you, hag. Go back to whatever sewer you dragged yourself from."

"Ha!" She barked, lurching up the plank again. "That's th' joke, innit? No one wants Saltytits. No one wants 'er poxy kisses n' dry ol' cootch anymore! Ha! But you got a friend thought it would be right hilarious fer me to come up 'ere n' offer everyone a sit n' spin 'fore yous took off up th' Road."

"Oh, gods, lady, get back!" The bald one said, drawing his long knife. He looked like he wanted to be anywhere else. The bearded one, without a word, had stood during Saltytits' speech and now aimed the bulky crossbow square into her sagging chest.

"Now," she rambled on, ignoring him. "Saltytits might be nothin' now but some joke trick, but she's honest. She been paid to come onto th' River Hulk and give th' folk here a thrill, so—"

As she blabbered on, she took the final steps onto the deck. The bald one, looking reluctant about it, did his job, lunging forward with his long knife aimed at the old woman's stomach. "I told you to get the fu—"

The old woman lost her balance and fell forward with a little cry, grabbing the hand holding the ceramic knife to keep herself from falling. Her legs twisted as she fell forward, and the motion bent the bald man's hand around to plunge his knife into his own stomach, just below the solar plexus. His curse cut off with a hiss and a little bubbling sound. He fell forward on top of the old woman, pinning her underneath.

"Tezi!" The bearded man cried out, setting his crossbow, still cocked, onto the deck before hurrying over to his fallen partner. "Tezi! Holy shit! Tezi?"

As he crouched down, the old woman moaned. "Ahh. Help ol' Saltytits up, will ya? I, eh. ugh!" Her hand lashed out from under the fallen man and seized the other by his beard.

"Ahh! Lady, Ow! I—"

"I said, 'elp Saltytits up!" She coughed and yanked down with sudden, incredible force. His head snapped forward with a sickening *pop* from his neck, and his body went limp, falling on top of Tezi's.

The old woman clambered out from under the two men. She looked around, then dragged the bearded man to the edge and dropped him into the Great Road. Then she did the same with Tezi. A broad circle of blood stained her filthy dress.

"Shit," she said to herself in a different voice, staring at the stain. She worked a minute to refold the skirt around her body, trying to conceal the blood.

No one was around to hear, and the old woman, again bent and bow-legged, swaggered to the hatch, hoping it would be dark enough below decks that not too many people would notice the blotches of red peeping out from under her oddly folded clothes.

The mid-deck was split into cabins. A large one for the dozen crew, which was the one she descended into, a kitchen and dining area the same size, and the captain's quarters, nestled in the bow. The last third of the stern was taken up by the naphtha engines hidden behind a thin wooden wall at the back of the kitchen.

It was dark. Two naphtha lamps, flames turned low, lit the first cabin, revealing dim rows of bunks where the crew slept through the day. The door to the kitchen stood open. The old woman stood at the base of the steep, short stairway of bronze grates, green eyes scanning the crew, taking count. She glided across the cabin to a peg board lined with keys and selected one before she clambered back up the ladder, graceful despite her appearance.

Above, she scuttled over to the large hatch that lay in the center of the deck, bolted closed from the outside. She pulled the pin from the latch and heaved the heavy, square door open, easing it down onto the deck with a soft thump. The stench of sweat and sewage boiled up.

Light flooded into the hold. Sounds of coughing, crying, whimpering. Faces upturned, squinting in the sun.

The old woman scowled, disgusted. The hold was packed with people. Women. Not even enough room for more than a few to sit down at a time, and it was three or four days up the Great Road to the plantations.

Her eyes flashed from face to face, looking for one she recognized. There was no sign of Anna, at least among those chained below the hatch. Grimacing, she dropped in, landing in the small open space beneath her. Dull, frightened eyes watched her.

The smell was worse. Any fresh air didn't reach through the hatch, even open.

"Help us," One of the woman said, voice quiet and hoarse. Hands grasped at the old whore, who twisted away.

"I'll get to you," the old woman whispered, her tone sympathetic. "Anna? Anna!" She began calling in a hushed shout.

"Please, help. Let us go," more cries from all around her, drowning out any response.

"Shh! Shh! Quiet! I will, but you have to—"

Go ahead, free them. It'll make you feel better and cause a hell of a distraction. Plus, no one will be sure you came in here just for one girl.

"Shit," the old woman muttered in Skaald. "Good idea."

The chains held each woman by an ankle, and old Saltytits hunched down and began unlatching each one with the key she'd taken from the cabin. A commotion began to well up as word traveled like wind through the slaves. Someone was setting them free. All the while, the old woman called out, "Anna! Anna! Where are you?" and cursing under her breath at the noise the others were making. These idiots would wake the crew.

"Here, I'm here!" Anna's voice drifted over the din from somewhere in the shadows towards the stern. The old woman unlocked the women she passed as she moved toward the voice.

There was Anna, straining against her chain, tears in her eyes.

"Who are you?" She asked as the old woman bent down to unlock the manacle.

The old woman looked up at her, and in a voice unsuited to her sagging face, said, "We've met before."

Anna blinked. "Chulla?"

Shouts of men from above and a sudden scream cut off anything else Anna was going to say. Cries of panic flooded through the hold. Women still chained screamed to be freed, while those making their way to the hatch began to mill around in fear. There was a spray of blood from above, and the body of a woman, throat slashed, fell from the hatch and landed at the foot of the ladder.

"They're getting away! Get the goddamned crew up here!" Footsteps thumped across the deck.

"I'll explain later, but we have to get out of here," the old woman said in Chulla's voice, speaking the valley language. "Follow me. Stay close."

Anna's eyes were wide, but she nodded and fell into step behind the old woman, who dodged her way through the panicked slaves towards the shaft of light beaming down from the hatch.

Another body fell and landed on top of the one lying at the base of the ladder. Then another. Blood oozed in a growing pool around the bodies. No one else was trying to climb out. The freed women crowded, frightened and uncertain, off to the side.

"Anyone who climbs out of that fucking hold is going to end up like her!" A man's voice yelled from above, and another woman with a slit throat fell onto the others. She made a bubbling sound and grasped at the air for a second before growing still.

"Stay behind me. Stay close," the old whore whispered to Anna again, mouth hovering by her ear to be heard over the screaming and weeping around them.

When they got to the bottom of the ladder, the old woman again turned to Anna. "Okay. Wait here a second." She flowed up and out of the hatch.

A man grabbed her from behind just as she emerged onto the

deck, pulling her head back, knife at her throat. She twisted around, hand over his wrist, disarming him and bringing the blade across his own throat in one motion. Blood fountained across her cheek and back, and she released the limp body into the hold, where it fell with a crunch onto the others.

At the same time, she brought her elbow into the gut of the man standing on the opposite side, doubling him over long enough that she could slash his throat open with the same knife. She dropped him down, too.

Footfalls clattered across the deck as more slavers flooded from the cabins.

The old woman paused long enough to call down into the hold, "Come on!"

She dropped the manacle key down the hatch as Anna clambered up. Then she set into the slavers rushing across the deck, ceramic knife still in her hand.

She slid among them like oil floating on water, slipping though and around them in a dance. Blood arced, men dropped groaning to the deck or toppled where they stood without a sound.

In a few moments, Anna and the old woman were alone. Bodies splayed around the deck now slippery with blood. Women began emerging into the fresh air, blinking in the sunlight.

"Can you run?" The old woman asked Anna, who was limping, favoring her left foot. The right was bloodied around the ankle where the manacle had held her.

"I'll be okay," Anna looked back at the women still coming out of the hold.

"Don't worry about them," the old woman said, pulling Anna along toward the gangway. "They'll need to manage on their own."

"Where's Pasha?" Anna asked as they ran along the docks. The sun was lowering itself onto the western spires of Valez'Mui. The city would be stirring any moment, and someone would discover the mess left behind on the River Hulk.

"He's fine. Probably." The woman answered. "I'm going to take you somewhere to hide and get you something to wear. Then I'll take you to a boat and get your brother. After that, I'll explain everything. I promise."

Sandstone buildings cluttered this part of Valez'Mui, and they stuck to the alleys until they got to Smudge's squat, only needing to duck into doorways twice to avoid police patrols. They arrived in the musty, single room just before dusk.

"Here," the old woman said in Chulla's voice and tossed some worn linen garments to Anna, who caught them and began putting them on over her tight leather valley clothes.

"You might want to ditch your old clothes. It'll be hot," she advised, but Anna just shook her head, and the old woman let it drop.

After she dressed, the old lady rummaged around in a broken trunk and pulled out a jar of thick, brownish goo. "Close your eyes," she advised. "I'm going to rub this on your face and hands. Feet and arms too. It'll make you darker—like you're from the desert." She continued speaking as she began rubbing the stuff into Anna's skin.

"It smells weird," Anna complained, but she didn't resist.

"The smell won't last, but the color will. A week, anyway. More or less. We don't have enough time to change your features, but this should throw them off enough to get you to the Flowered Calf."

"The what?"

"The Flowered Calf. It's a boat. A friend of mine will take us to Fom."

"Why do you have all this stuff?"

"Like I said," the old woman finished rubbing the substance into Anna and replaced the jar back into the dilapidated trunk. "I'll explain everything when there's time. On the boat. Let's go."

The docks were swarming with activity by the time they returned as barges rolled in and out. Further down, the slave docks had been roped off. A crowd had gathered to watch bodies being pulled from the water around the River Hulk. The two women ignored the commotion and made their way to a wide steam barge, resting low in the water. It was painted a soft lavender color over its bronze plates, with tiny green and white flowers decorating the rails with exquisite detail. Red and white roses decorated the water line.

"Who did you say this boat belonged to?" Anna asked, frowning at the flowers surrounding the hatch that the old woman had led her to.

"A friend of mine," she answered. "A pirate."

Anna's frown deepened. "What's a pirate?"

"Someone who sails around on a boat, stealing things from people on other boats." She glanced at Anna and saw her worried expression. "You can trust this one, though. I think."

Anna continued to look doubtful at the detailing of the lavender barge as they ducked into the hatch. "And this belongs to a 'pirate?'"

"Yeah, it's a long story. Come on. There'll be time to tell it later. I'll get Pasha," the old woman said after Anna settled in the tiny cabin in the stern. "Don't leave, okay? And stay away from the window."

Anna nodded, and the old woman slipped back out into the darkening night.

Syrina went back to Smudge's place long enough to strip naked again. She needed to hurry. She didn't know how long Anna would wait before taking off again, and she wasn't sure how far the investigation would spread. Anna would be safe on the Calf for a night or two, at least, but Syrina wasn't going to take any chances if she could help it.

She needed to check at the hawk nests one more time before she fled up the Great Road, but not if it would take extra time to forge a disguise and argue with the nest keepers. Better to just slip in and have a look.

The nests weren't far from either the docks or Smudge's squat. She slipped in and began going through all the little slips of paper upstairs, divided by origin, while the secretary in the lobby was busy with a long line of customers trying to send word up the Great Road about the massacre on the River Hulk.

Both the Astrologers and Ormo had responded to her in the past week. Ormo wanted her to bring one or both of the siblings to him, at her leisure.

I told you so.

The Astrologers didn't mention their thoughts on them, but they requested that she make her way to the Ristro capital Vormisæn as soon as possible to discuss things in person.

Syrina sighed. She'd been looking forward to a river cruise with Pasha, even if that wasn't what it was. In all her years as a Kalis, she'd never been able to enjoy herself as herself before, but she couldn't risk going all the way to Fom with him now and risk missing whatever it was the Astrologers wanted to talk to her about. Not if it was too sensitive to send by hawk.

She cursed their caution, knowing she might not get anything but another cryptic history lesson, but not willing to miss the chance.

Then she headed over to Ves's compound to say goodbye.

15

THE FLOWERED CALF

"Sit!"

Pasha didn't have much grasp on Valezian, but that much he understood from the way Vesmalimali was pointing at the puffy, grey leather chair in the corner of the library in the smuggler's mansion.

Pasha obeyed and tore himself from the window that overlooked the path through the garden. He slouched to the other side of the room and hurled himself into the chair, which Ves was still pointing at.

Ves dropped his hand before walking over to the window and taking Pasha's place.

Pasha sighed with an exaggerated groan. He wanted to ask the pirate what the difference was between Ves looking out the window and him doing it, but he didn't, not only because he wasn't sure how to phrase it in any language but his own, but because he was a little scared of the giant, dark-skinned man with diamonds set into his skull.

He thought for sure they'd have been back by now, and he needed to swallow the feeling that he'd not only lost his sister but also his lover. That set him thinking of Syrina, which filled him with a terror that dwarfed his fear of the pirate.

"You can stop looking so nervous," Smudge's voice said in the valley language from the open doorway.

Pasha's head shot up. Ves whipped his huge body around, curved ceramic short sword already drawn, facing the sound of the voice, which he couldn't have understood.

Pasha's eyes found Syrina's, wide and hovering near the doorway. She waved her arms around with her mouth open, doing what she could to make herself obvious.

Ves roared something and lunged at her. After a confused flurry of motion, the giant man was on the floor, legs splayed in front of him like a child in a sandbox. His sword clattered in the hallway behind the vague form of Syrina.

There was a brief, heated argument between the two in Valezian. Syrina picked up the sword and handed it back to Ves before turning to Pasha and speaking again in the valley language. "I convinced him not to try to kill me, at least for the moment, but I think there's going to be some trust issues. As for you, you need to follow Whitehook."

"Where's Anna?" Pasha asked, rising from the chair.

"On Ves's boat. You're going there now. Both of you," she added, indicating Ves with a look, as he clambered to his feet with as much dignity as he could muster.

"So. You're not coming." Pasha's tone was heartbroken.

Syrina's eyes looked sad, and she took a step toward Pasha before she glanced at Ves and seemed to think better of it. "I can't. Something came up. I'll catch up with you in Fom, though. I promise. Ves will take you that far. You can trust him. At least with getting you to Fom. I think."

"But we need your help," Pasha said, hating the whine in his voice but unable to stop it. "*I* need you. Anyway, you said you would teach us languages, so we can talk to people on our own."

This time she did step forward, and Pasha felt her blurry, rough hand take his. "I really, really wish I could come with you. You have no idea how bad. You can't understand how big this is. With you. Between us. For me. I've never—" She glanced over her shoulder at Ves, who was eying Pasha with unveiled suspicion, then leaned in and kissed Pasha hard on the mouth without finishing the sentence. She pulled him close. "I'll see you in Fom. Ves will teach you N'naradin. It's a long, boring trip along the Great Road. You'll have time to learn."

He felt her pull away. He blinked and looked around. She was gone.

Ves stared hard at Pasha as if he thought maybe Syrina was still standing with him, and he was trying to see her. Finally, he sneered and said in the Trade Tongue, "Come on, let's go. Sounds like your girlfriend left us quite a mess to get through on the docks."

"This you boat?" Pasha asked in broken Trade, looking incredulous, as he followed Ves onto the lavender deck.

"Yeah." Ves cleared his throat and frowned. The six crewmen he'd chosen from his house entourage kept their faces neutral, but Ash was shaking with silent laughter.

"Syrina said you've been sailing up and down this river—road, whatever you like to call it—for years?" Pasha frowned again at the lavender hand rail following the short stairs to the cabins, detailed with tiny white flowers. At the aft, there was a wheelhouse, the door squat enough that even Pasha needed to duck a little to get through the door, trimmed with painted roses and more tiny white flowers. Within the open hatchway, he could see steep stairs going up to the bridge and below decks. Twin stacks from the naphtha engines coughed steam on either side and behind the structure. Wide, double doors lay in the center of the deck for cargo, likewise decorated in what looked to be once an onslaught of color, now worn to a few scraps of floral decor floating on a green sea of verdigris.

"Yeah. The boat is new. New to me, anyway." Ves sounded more annoyed than he'd intended. He was trying not to stare at the gaudy paint job himself. "Haven't got around to painting it yet, and since now I get to take you and your sister to Fom, it's going to be awhile, so get used to it."

Pasha shrugged. "Not complaining. Just curious."

It had been easier than anyone had feared it would be to get to the Flowered Calf through the investigation of the slaughter at the other end of the docks. Ves's barge was far enough down the piers that there wasn't a crowd around it, and neither Pasha nor the pirate looked like escaped slaves.

Ves led him to the cabin he was to share with his sister and opened the door after a single, hard knock he didn't wait for an answer to.

"Pasha, I'm so sorry," Anna said, though she was looking at the giant pirate who had entered the room in front of her brother. "I guess this is—"

"Vesmalimali," Ves surprised them by finishing her question with a graceful bow. "Some call me Whitehook. My friends call me Ves."

Anna smiled a little smile and gave an awkward, small bow in return. "Thank you for helping us." Then she slid past the giant and embraced her brother.

"Chulla, she helped me, Pasha," Anna said, releasing her hold on him. "Only she didn't look like Chulla."

"I know," Pasha said. "She's... Well, I don't know what she is." He looked over at Ves, hunched in the doorway. "I think he does, though."

Ves blinked at him with a deepening scowl.

"Smudge..." Pasha began in Trade and stopped.

Ves needed no further prompting to know what Pasha was asking. "Kalis," he grunted. "Killers and spies for the bastards that control the naphtha. They run Skalkaad and try to rule everything else." He shook his head. "No one sees the Kalis. Most people don't even believe they're real. I had a few doubts myself up until a few hours ago."

Anna frowned. At the same moment, the Flowered Calf lurched forward with a growl from its engines. Pasha and Anna stumbled against one another, while Ves stood in the middle of the small cabin, immovable. "Then why are you still helping us?" She asked him.

Ves was quiet a moment. "Turns out, I'd worked with her for years. Before, when I first came to Valez'Mui. After all these years, a fucking Kalis turns out to be the reason I didn't end up in the goddamned slave pens or the bottom of the Sea of N'narad. I owe her, never mind my last ship she stole. Anyway, she paid me ten thousand Three-Sides to get you two to Fom, so that's what I'll do." he gave Pasha a wink. "And it seems like her boyfriend might grow on me."

He turned to go, then paused and said over his shoulder, "Not that I trust her. And you shouldn't either." His eyes rested on Pasha, who found he couldn't meet the big man's gaze. "Kalis are made out of more lies than meat." He stood in the hatchway a moment longer, staring hard at Pasha before giving Anna a smile and vanishing up the short ladder leading to the deck.

16

THE SALAMANDER: NINE MONTHS BEFORE THE TRIAL

I handed the lens back to Rohm. We stood on the port deck together. Behind us milled the hundred soldiers I'd called up from below, awaiting orders. The Corsairs were closer—two ships behind and one ahead. The dirigible that had been following us on the horizon for two days was still floating far to the west, now rendered invisible by the sun behind it, but I knew it was there. It would be closer now.

"I thought our signal flags were up to date," I said. The comment was pointless, but I felt a juvenile need to say something.

"So did I."

We'd been lucky until then. Even the karakh had been calmer than Dakar had predicted they would be, despite their confinement and the endless rocking of the ships. I'd only lost one man to them since we'd departed from the Upper Peninsula a month ago, and him because he'd been careless and went into one of the stables without a shepherd. Nobody ever could figure out why.

I was glad I'd taken Dakar's advice to modify the holds—the six weeks it took to fortify the doors and attach the chains in the Salamander and the Bishop's Flame was nothing compared to the nine months or more it would have taken to get to the Black Wall overland, a trip that would have been even more perilous in any case. Of course, there was always the Great Road. It would have been fastest, but the Arch Bishop had insisted on secrecy. I had the feeling even the Grace of Fom only had a vague inkling of what we were up to.

We weren't a secret now. Not to Ristro. The pirate in Maresg had sworn our signal flags were up to date. Maybe they had been when I'd paid four thousand Three-Sides for them, but whether he ripped us off or we'd just been too slow, it didn't matter anymore.

I snatched the lens from Rohm again. The pirates rumbled toward us, accelerating, low in the water, coughing black tarfuel smoke streaking the azure sky with thin, twisted fingers. My own ship, the White Streak, still had her deck guns, but we'd removed them from the other two to lighten them for the karakh. All three ships were large and slow—ill-equipped for a fight. They were cargo vessels, not military. The Arch Bishop's damned secrecy again.

"Suggestions?" I asked.

Rohm shuffled where he stood and took the lens again, peering through it east, then west toward where the blinding sunlight concealed the airship. "You're the general."

I didn't bother hiding my frown. "And this is my fourth time at sea in seventy years, and the first time I've faced Corsairs. So, suggestions?"

"What about the time on the Upper Great Road? Your annihilation of them is legendary."

I spat on the deck. "The stories are exaggerated. Anyway, they weren't Ristroan Corsairs. Just raiders and vagabonds from Maresg. So I'm asking you again. Suggestions?"

Rohm handed the lens back to me again and thought. The dirigible had left the orb of the sun and was now a growing black speck above it. "The corsairs expect a running fight. It's what they're used to, and it's what their ships are made for." He looked at me for the first time. "And they're used to normal cargo."

I lowered the lens and met Rohm's gaze. "Full stop!" I shouted. "And unchain the karakh!"

Crewmen called my orders back, and the engines of the White Streak rumbled and groaned as the big ship slowed. A light flashed at the top of the high signal pole in the center of the deck directing the Bishop's Flame and the Salamander to do the same.

I looked west again. The gondola dangling below the mass of the airship was distinct now. "What about that?" I asked Rohm, nodding towards the growing dot in the sky.

Rohm watched it for a minute, silent. "That," he said. "That might be a problem."

As the three N'naradin freighters slowed, the Ristro ships also eased their charge, no doubt re-planning their attack. Rohm and I moved to the bow in front of the forecastle to watch. One of the two, approaching from the west, stopped as the dirigible lowered itself over it. From a few spans away, I could see ropes drop and figures climb up to the airship like ants climbing a string. They were out of range of the White Streak's cannons, and we couldn't maneuver close enough without coming within range of the other corsairs since our only guns were the broadsides along the port and starboard. I considered running before they were ready to attack but cast the idea aside. Their ships were both faster and more maneuverable than ours, not even including the airship. I would have wagered that they were moving their people around within easy view of us because they hoped that's what we'd do.

We could be run down or watch, helpless, and they knew it.

The sudden growl of an engine to the port of the White Streak yanked me from my thoughts. To my horror, I saw the Salamander turning to flee, ponderous and low in the water with the weight of the karakh.

"Did I order a fucking retreat?" I blared, helplessly, at nobody in particular. "Signal the goddamned Salamander! Tell them to hold their position!"

It was no use. I never figured out what was going through Captain N'staid's mind when he commanded his ship to flee from a goddamned airship. I've since just accepted it was inexperience. Rohm was the only officer who'd faced the corsairs in anything more than a skirmish before, and that just as a sailor. I suppose, like everything else, it didn't matter now. N'staid finished his laborious turn and began pushing away, out of formation.

The airship began circling to intercept the Salamander, leaving me the choice of either turning to defend my rogue commander or staying in position to protect ourselves and the Bishop's Flame. I chose the latter.

The Corsair vessel that had disgorged its personnel onto the dirigible remained a few spans away, while the others began to close. They were almost identical. So low in the water they looked like they might sink, hulls and decks of copper plate painted an iridescent cobalt. Tarfuel engines concealed within sloped humps in their sterns growled, and black smoke boiled from twin stacks.

As they got closer, I could see the grappling cannons arranged at the bow, the pirates lined behind them ready to board. Their crafts were half as high as our big cargo freighters, but that was what they were used to.

The White Streak kept shifting beneath me as Admiral Nyr tried to maneuver the guns into position, but the smaller ships kept outside the arc of fire until they reached our hulls, and the handful of shots the cannoneers tried all missed their mark.

I cursed the karakh. Without them, our ships would had the advantage in firepower, if not experience. We would have at least met on equal ground. I wondered how useful the creatures would be in a fight at sea, compared to the guns we needed now.

They rammed our ships at an angle, the impacts simultaneous, or at least near enough that the sound came as one long, sickening, metallic groan rolling across the water. Behind us, the dirigible closed on the Salamander, which was now veering back much too slowly to matter. I had never been fond of captain N'staid or his inflated ego, but the desperation he must have felt then was palatable.

The stutter of the steam-powered grappling cannons being fired in succession brought my mind back to my own problems. The Ristroan grapples could better be described as anchors, huge and weighted with stone, launched high over our rail before crashing through the polished wooden planks of the deck. There was a faint whirr of the hydraulic spools, and the bronze chains grew taut.

At the same time, the White Streak rumbled and began to turn again. I imagined Nyr spinning the wheel in desperation, trying to pull our vessel away from theirs. Dull metallic thunks reverberated up from where our ships connected as the pirates attached clamps to our hull.

The hundred soldiers that had been milling on the deck, nerves frayed from the endless waiting, charged to confront the invaders scaling up the chain.

"Back!" Rohm shouted, his voice high and frantic. "Everyone back!"

The soldiers at the rear of the charge hesitated as the rest careened forward. Four figures appeared at the chains over the rails, their faces concealed by long-nosed, insect-like masks with round, tinted lenses over the eyes. I caught a glimpse of brass rods wielded in the hands not gripping the chains, then the view was shrouded by four long gouts of blue-white flame.

The fire incinerated the front line to pillars of ash where they stood, while those behind them staggered away screaming, coated in burning naphtha. Our deck ignited in rolling balls of yellow and white. The gouts from the fire throwers died almost as one, and the masked figures repelled out of sight back over the deck. A moment later, the rest of the corsairs poured over the rail in a choreographed assault, oblivious to the flames, and waded into my panicked N'naradin like armed dancers into a mob of frightened children.

A series of reports rolled across the sea from the stern. I spun to see the aft of the Salamander burning. Distant figures rappelled down from the airship spouting streaks of blue fire.

All of it happened in less than thirty seconds from the first moment their ships contacted ours. Thirty seconds to be overrun by a force an eighth the size.

Not quite.

There were five karakh on the White Streak. The Bishop's Flame held thirteen of the monsters in her hold, the Salamander twelve.

The cargo doors set into our deck exploded open with such force they sent both N'naradin and pirates sailing over the rail into the churning black water. Gre'pa, leading the other four karakh on the White Streak in a volcano of rage, erupted from the hold.

The karakh's pupils first contracted in the firelight, then dilated in rage as they cast their goat-dog heads around searching for the source of the flames. One shepherd whistled, and his mount leaped, from a standstill, forty hands over the fight around the open hold to the rim of the deck where the chains led to the corsair ship. With another short hop and a series of clicks, it dropped over the edge. Screams welled from below, not quite drowned out by the sounds of fighting.

Gre'pa and the other four karakh remained above and set into the corsairs, tearing through them, flinging them from the deck in a frenzy I couldn't follow.

There was a tremendous explosion. The shockwave was strong enough to topple combatants and almost tossed me into the sea from where I was running along the rail opposite the chains. A blue-white fireball rolled up from the corsair ship. The chains went slack. I saw the outline of karakh and rider rise from the blast and dissolve in boiling light.

The White Streak lurched, now free of the smaller ship holding it, and began to turn to the port.

The fire blocked my view of the Bishop's Flame, but I could see the Salamander as we came parallel, about a half-span away, its deck an inferno. Shadows of soldiers and karakh moved among the flames, and the dirigible still hung low over it. It was impossible to tell which way the tide was turning in the fight from this distance, and fire and smoke shrouded the view from the lens I still clutched, too much to make any sense of.

I spun at the unexpected roar of cannons from our port broadsides. A second later, the airship hovering over the Salamander exploded and crumpled like paper, crashing into the center of the Salamander's burning deck. A blinding white flash flickered across the water, and a moment after, the guns on the White Streak fired a second time.

"Cease fire!" I screamed, voice shrill, over the clamor of fighting that spilled across the deck and the dying echo of the guns. I began running toward the cannon batteries, my bad hip lancing pain. "Cease fire! Who gave the order to fire on our own ship?"

Rohm staggered up to me out of the flickering light of the fires still burning across our own deck. His face was streaked with ash and blood, but none of it seemed to be his. "Vimr," he said, a shadow across his face despite the light all around us.

The cannons fired again. Across the water, there was another explosion, and the Salamander sagged into the sea.

"I said, cease fire!" I felt spittle fly from my lips in my impotent rage.

"Cardinal Vimr gave the order, sir," Rohm repeated. "Acting on behalf of the Arch Bishop." He wiped his face. "I couldn't countermand the order. He said the Salamander was lost."

I stared at Rohm a moment, mind blank, then stalked passed him to where N'eeral, the Master Gunner, was supervising the destruction of the Salamander. I didn't know the man—It took me a moment to remember his name—but it came to me as I approached, and I growled it at him without bothering with his title, which I recalled hearing he was rather proud of.

He turned to face me, his eyes resigned and sad. "General," he began. "Cardinal Vimr has declared the Salamander a total loss and ordered—"

"Decide now whether you are my man or the Cardinal's." My voice was calmer, though I still needed to shout over the din. "But continue to fire at your surviving comrades on the Salamander, and I will kill you where you stand, my place in the Heaven of Flowers be damned."

N'eeral heisted for the briefest moment and ordered the cease fire. The roar of the cannons died. My stomach twisted when I saw the remnants of the Salamander. It tilted in the water, wretched and burning, the collapsed airship entwined across it like brass vines with leaves of fire.

"Where is Vimr?" The fight was dying down on the White Streak, and my voice was low, but it still carried over the grind of the engines and the clicks and whistles of the karakh.

"In his cabin, sir," Rohm answered as he came up beside me. He wiped at his face again. The air smelled of metal and smoke and salt water.

Without another word, I turned toward the steep stairs in the aft castle that led to the officer's quarters below the bridge.

I ran into Vimr at the base of the stairs. "Why have the cannons—?" He began before he looked up from the steps and saw me. "Oh, General. Shouldn't you be on the deck directing the fight? How goes—?"

I backhanded his pudgy face so hard he staggered backward off the bottom step, almost falling into the corridor. He had the nerve to look shocked. I almost hit him again, then thought better of it.

"I was doing just that, Cardinal, and would still be doing just that had I not been so desperate to circumvent your orders to fire on our own men." I thought of the burning wreckage of the Salamander reflecting on the water, and decided hitting him again was warranted. I gave him a second backhand across the other side of his face.

He stumbled back with a whining sound but still didn't fall. I raised my hand a third time, satisfied myself with his cowering flinch, and lowered it again.

Vimr's voice was calm. "The Salamander was lost, General. I saw it with my own eyes. Swarming with Corsairs, tethered to the airship above. The airship, which was still a danger to the White Streak and the Bishop's Flame, unless you think they would have satisfied themselves with crippling, capturing, or destroying only one vessel?" He paused for what seemed like he thought was dramatic effect, but when I said nothing, he continued.

"After the airship was destroyed, there was still the matter of the Salamander itself. How many Ristroans would it have taken to seize control of the wheelhouse and turn our ship into a weapon to be used against us? Or, more likely, just steal it. You realize that's how they get their naphtha? They don't care about N'naradin merchandise—they raid our ships for the fuel."

"There were a dozen karakh on the Salamander, and over five hundred men," I countered, my voice soft.

"The karakh, I'm sure you will agree, would do a poor job of defending the interior of the ship once the corsairs made it that far, which they no doubt already had. You think your men, fighting in tight corridors, would fare well against the fire throwers? Would you risk not only those men but those on this ship? Those on the Bishop's Flame? You may think me soft, General Mann, but I have seen the Corsairs before. I have seen what they are willing to do. First hand. They could not be allowed to take the Salamander. Hate me for it, but know what I did, I did for the good of the majority and the good of the mission at hand." He stood, staring at me, as if daring me to strike him again.

I felt my jaw clenching and unclenching of its own accord. My mind flailed for some flaw in his logic, but for all my touted experience as N'narad's great General, I had no experience against the Ristroan pirates, and we both knew it.

"If your orders ever result in the death of even one more of my people," I said, my voice a whispered growl, "I will kill you myself."

I stalked back up the stairs before he could respond.

The Salamander was gone. By the time I emerged from the aft castle, only a few smoldering deck boards drifting a span away marked where it had once been. All four life boats had made it away safely, saving an even two hundred soldiers from the deep, but more than three hundred were lost, including the ship's crew, and all of the karakh. It astounded me—still astounds me—that the Church continues the practice of forgoing rescue boats on its fleet in favor of more firepower and the crew to man it.

Gre'pa had suffered burns over its arms and lost a chunk of its right hand, but Dakar reassured me that the creature would regenerate its missing fingers by the time we reached Valez'Mui.

I cursed myself, cursed Vimr more. Vimr, at least, had lost favor with most of the men, though that proved not to last. Not long enough.

I hated myself for the uncertainty that consumed me on whether Vimr had done the wrong thing, and prayed to a Heaven I no longer believed in that we would have better fortune once we reached the haven of Valez'Mui.

17

GREAT SPRING

The Yellow Desert passed by, ever on the right, alternating between flat and dunned. On the left, the scrub-covered landscape Ves called the Salt Hills rolled by in great white mounds, streaked Yellow with sand blown across the Great Road, specked with yucca and sage.

The river forked the morning of the fifth day, the left narrow and swift, the right wide and slow and shallow. Both sides were lined with rice paddies, sprawling estates sometimes visible in the distance beyond them. A town sat at the fork, but the Flowered Calf didn't slow. Ves took the right, careful to stay in the center of the sluggish current.

After another ten days, the weather turned cool as the river bent east to run parallel to the brown, desolate mountains to the north, edging closer, day by day.

A cold wind blew from the east, dragging the scent of winter behind it. Ves gave the siblings a pair of hooded coats of rough grey wool, but neither put them on, relieved at the turn of weather after months in the intense heat.

As they traveled, Ves, good to his word, begin to teach Anna and

Pasha N'naradin. He was kind to Pasha and cordial enough to Anna, who started standing with him on the deck, watching while he gave orders to his crew. They shared their meals of salted rice boiled in river water and wrapped in seaweed in Ves's quarters, but they avoided the subject of Syrina.

After that, it took a little over three weeks for the Flowered Calf to reach the long queue of other riverboats anchored along the south side of the Great Road, and Ves commanded his crew to pull along the shore. Their pace had become slower against the ever increasing current, with the Naphtha engines grinding at full power. Ves said they would need to buy more naphtha in Great Spring, but after that, it would be faster since they would be going down stream. "Good thing, too," he'd said, but he didn't elaborate.

Kiosks and wandering vendors lined the ramshackle pier along the bank, hawking everything from clothes to skewers of meat and misshapen bottles of a fierce-smelling, amber liquid, one of which Ves purchased and took a long pull from.

"What's going on?" Asked Anna, emerging from their cabin, Pasha trailing behind her. "Are we in Fom?"

Ves laughed and handed her the bottle. She took a drink, coughed, then took another one. She handed it back to Ves, but he nodded to Pasha, who took his turn with it.

"Not even half way yet," Ves answered, watching the siblings drink. "That's enough. Meant for you to have a taste, not drink the whole goddamned thing." He winked at Pasha as he took the bottle back.

"This here is a queue for the locks that'll take us up to Great Spring. Not too long, today, from what I hear. Another day, maybe two, and we should be headed up the mountain."

"From what you hear?" Pasha asked. "Don't you do this all the time?"

Ves stared at him a moment and took another long pull from the bottle. "Work to do," he said, turning to disembark onto the pier. "Why don't you look around a bit. We'll be here a while, and Ash'll take care of everything on the Calf. I won't leave without you." He disappeared into the milling crowd of stevedores and river folk.

Anna and Pasha glanced at each other. "Shall we go look?" Anna asked.

Pasha frowned. "I don't think so."

"Why not?" Anna asked, turning from where she was heading for the gangplank.

"What happened last time you went out?" Pasha asked. "It's not safe."

"That was a long way away, Pasha. It'll be fine."

"You don't know that. We don't know that. The Artisans are powerful. Tolisho or the slavers could have someone here looking for us. Come on. Let's go back to our room." Pasha scanned the crowd passing on the shore. No one was paying attention to them.

Anna scowled, but she followed him below without arguing.

The Merchant's Locks that took ships up and down the Dry Mountains to Great Spring were an engineering marvel that rivaled the Tidal Works of Fom. Maybe even surpassed them, Ves said, since the Tidal Works had been around longer than anyone could remember, and the Locks had been built less than four hundred years ago. Before then, barges needed to dock in the string of now long-abandoned towns along the Great Road and caravan up an arduous switch back to the city above, sometimes taking over a week if they carried stone from the quarries. Now, despite the need to wait in the queue for more than a day, the locks could take larger loads up the mountain in eight hours.

Each lock was over five hundred hands high, their doors and gears made from salvaged non-metal from the ruins that dotted the surrounding plains. They were operated by massive, naphtha-driven steam machines donated by the Merchant's Syndicate.

Each lock was four thousand hands long, split down the middle with buoys to separate the outgoing and ingoing vessels. Thirty such locks wound their way up the mountain, filled by the torrent of water flowing out of the Great Spring.

Anna, Pasha, and even Ves marveled speechless at the spectacle as the Flowered Calf rose in the lock and passed through each open door, sometimes waving to the crews that hailed them from the barges heading down toward Valez'Mui.

A few hours before dusk, they arrived in the Free City of Great Spring.

A vast lake of warm water in a place where it never rained flowed at the crest of the Dry Mountains, so deep that Ves claimed no one had ever found the bottom. The center of it boiled outward with such force that sailing across it was impossible, even for the biggest steam barges, giving both the lake and the city on its shores their name.

The massive, ever-erupting geyser fed two rivers—the Great Road, up which they had come, and the Upper Great Road, which led west and north to Fom and the Sea of Skalkaad, creating a border between the Wastes of Kamahush and the Dry Mountains. It was the only maintained land route between east and west and gave the City-State of Valez'Mui a reason to exist.

The city of Great Spring sat on the western edge of the lake, sometimes called Little Fom because of the perpetual fog rolling off the warm water and clashing with the cold mountain air. The smell that wafted from it was a mélange of fish and mud, accented with the faint scent of incense. They could smell it long before it came into view as the Flowered Calf skirted the edge of the immense, lemon-shaped crater.

They could hear waves ten hands high crashing into the rocky shore, invisible through the fog but close at hand. As they approached the docks, Anna could make out the lilting language of Valez, the sing-song of N'naradin, and abrupt chatter she took to be Skald.

She asked Ves which clan Great Spring belonged to, a linguistic error he chuckled at.

"Great Spring is neutral," he answered. "Skalkaad and N'narad both pay mountains of tin to run cargo up and down The Great Road, and the Artisans in Valez'Mui pay them even more."

He caught the worried look on Pasha's face and rumbled a chuckle. "Don't worry about them. They don't come here. Not often, anyway. That's the great thing about being rich, right? You don't need to go anywhere when you can pay someone to go for you."

Pasha smiled back, but the worry didn't leave his face.

"I want to see the city," Anna said an hour after they'd docked at the customs harbor. "We have a few hours, at least. Ves said it might even take until tomorrow sometime to do all the paperwork and refuel."

Pasha frowned. Ves and Ash were in the customs office, paying fees and arguing with officials. The crew was nowhere to be seen. Pasha assumed they were all in town, drinking. "We don't know who's after us."

"No one knows about us, Pasha. Not here. Ves said not to worry about it." Anna glared at her brother and rubbed the short hair on the back of her head.

"I'm not a child," she pressed when Pasha didn't answer. "Not by anyone's standards outside the valley. I don't need you to decide what I can do, and I'm tired of being on this boat, so I'm going. Are you? We'll be careful."

Anna rose, her eyes twinkling, and ducked out the cabin door.

"Wait," He said. "I'm coming with you."

She spun, took a step toward him, and gave him a hug. "Good." She led the way onto the dock.

The quays and a few blocks beyond were humid and warm from the spring, but beyond, ice coated everything, and the wide, stone streets were filled with freezing fog. The thin air was the only reminder that they were high in the mountains. It was an hour after the sun had set over the peaks, and naphtha lamps flickered on either side of the street. Their pale-blue light succeeded only in filling the town with a grey, featureless glow.

The town clawed up the sloping crater until the mountain became too steep, and the city ended at a line of scree, short grasses, and old snow. Great Spring was long and narrow, sandwiched between the peaks and the lake. The whole basin was above the tree line, but the streets were decorated in sculpted, gnarled shrubs and short pines.

Buildings were one and two stories high, made from the same grey-brown rock as the basin, so it looked like the city was carved from the mountain itself. Streets teemed with a mix of traders and the surly men and women they employed to drive their barges up and down the Great Road.

"I bet you could use a drink," Anna smiled at Pasha as they passed one of the crowded pubs halfway up the hill, near the edge of the narrow city. This one depicted a fishtail poking out of a stylized pot. "Me too."

Without waiting for a reply, she ducked into the bar.

Prelate Sy N'dal stewed over her drink, a knot of worry in her chest. A messenger had arrived not ten minutes before she'd left the Consulate, stating that the Grace was sending a force up the Great Road from Fom to take control of administration in Great Spring.

She thought she'd been done with this mess when the first damned messenger had collected those glass rods that Mann had left with her. Mann had lost half his army getting them, and not even he knew what they were. But he'd seemed eager to hand them over when Sy N'dal had given him the Arch Bishop's missive.

Something bad was going on between the Grace of Fom and the Arch Bishop of Tyrsh. Bad enough that the Arch Bishop didn't trust anything important going through Fom, or even along the Great Road. And it was about to get worse.

As she brooded, she happened to look toward the door of the Boiled Fish just as the young siblings wandered in. Foreigners weren't uncommon in Great Spring—hell, locals were rarer than foreigners—but these two caught her eye. Not that young, she corrected herself. But there was something ageless about them that made them stand apart from the press.

It was while she was contemplating this that she noticed the man's weapons—two long, curved daggers stuck into his belt, made of polished, black wood.

The report General Mann had given her at the Consulate had been one-third confusing and two thirds unbelievable, but there was one thing he'd been clear on. The people who'd resisted him at the Black Wall had used wooden weapons. Black wood, he claimed, strong enough to cut through metal. She looked again at the knives, and the ageless faces of the pair standing at the bar, poking through their coins, and a chill went up Sy N'dal's spine.

She'd been careless, staring at them, a fact she realized too late when the man looked her way, eyes widening before leaning over to the woman and whispering something, nodding in her direction.

The woman glanced toward her with more subtlety than her brother. They tossed back their drinks and made their way to the door.

Cursing her black and gold prelate robes that made her too obvious, Sy N'dal trailed after them, leaving her drink unfinished on the table.

She hurried out the door, trying not to make a scene. The two siblings were already disappearing in the mist down the hill toward the docks. She looked around for a city guard, or better yet, one of the

N'naradin patrols that kept an eye on the area around the consulate a block further up the hill, but all she saw were the usual stevedores and naphtha pumpers that wandered Great Spring this time of night.

The pair disappeared into an alley, almost out of sight in the fog. Sy N'dal swore, drew the sword she hadn't used in twelve years, and followed them.

———

"You're sure?" Anna asked as they hurried towards the docks. "Maybc it's just a coincidence."

"I don't think so. Those colors were all over Mann's camp in the valley, and that symbol too—that crescent Eye over the sun. And on the coins. The triangular ones."

Anna still hesitated, forcing Pasha to slow his pace. They ducked onto a narrow side street. The few passersby ignored them. "If you're right, maybe she can tell us where Mann went."

"We know where Mann went," Pasha's half-whisper was exasperated. "Syrina said he went to the city called Fom."

"If we can trust Syrina."

"We can. I can. Come on, let's go."

Anna stood her ground, a stubborn look setting on her face. "Pasha, stop being—"

"It's her." Pasha's voice was flat.

Anna turned to see the woman in black and gold approach from the main boulevard. She had a long, curved ceramic sword in her hand.

The woman barked a few abrupt words at them in N'naradin, too fast for them to understand. Then, seeing the blank looks on their faces, switched to broken, accented Trader.

"You. Stop. Questions. Need come with." She edged toward them, sword raised.

She paused in front of Pasha, a blade's length away, her sword leveled at his chest. "Come," she said again.

Anna groaned.

Pasha, with a speed that surprised even his sister who'd watched him train countless hours with the blackvine daggers, dodged around the woman's blade and slit her open from sternum to hip. The arc of blood made a thick, wet sound as it sprayed the ground, and Anna felt something warm and sticky cover her arms and face as the woman's bowels tumbled through her robes. The woman collapsed, a look of surprise on her face, and curled around the coil of intestines splayed on the ground, moaning once and falling silent.

"What did you do?" Anna muttered, staring in shock before turning to Pasha to take the knife from his shaking hand. A black pool spread from under the corpse, melting the frost. *So much blood,* she thought, her hands numb. *So much blood.*

"She knew who we were." Pasha's voice was weak and as shaky as his hands.

Anna had turned again to stare at the body, but she nodded. "No. You're right. I know you're right. She would have taken you. Us."

Pasha swallowed. The dark pool had stopped growing.

A boy, perhaps ten years old, dressed in rich-looking furs against the cold, stood in the mouth of the narrow side street, staring at the scene with wide, terrified eyes.

"Pasha," Anna whispered, looking at the child.

That small sound seemed to break a spell cast over the boy, and he turned and fled up the hill.

"What did you want me to do? I couldn't... I mean..." Pasha hadn't realized how bad he was shaking until Anna tried to hand his knife back to him, and he dropped it.

She picked it up and put it in her belt, under the coat Ves had given her, after wiping it on the woman's robes. The numbness had spread from her hands into her body and mind. "No, Pasha. I know. I didn't mean..." She trailed off, not certain what she'd meant. "We need to get out of here."

"Yeah," Pasha agreed, hugging himself with shaking arms. "Let's go."

18

THE ASTROLOGER

VALEZ'MUI WAS THE ONLY STATE THAT TRADED WITH RISTRO without copious tariffs or convoluted laws, so it was easy for Syrina to find a freighter carrying marble and obsidian to take her to the capital of Chamælivishi, near the southern tip of the Ristro Peninsula. She didn't see any reason for a disguise, instead just settling in to meditate in the hold behind the huge slabs of rough, uncut black and white stone for the two week journey.

She'd never been to Chamælivishi. Although it had been the city she'd been sent to when she'd gone to the pirate nation several years ago, she never made it that far. She could only hope that in the years she'd been away, word had gotten around that a Kalis was working for them now, and she'd receive a better reception than last time. Anyway, this time she was invited.

Chamælivishi, like the other cities of Ristro, was not on the coast but a few spans inland behind a protective ridge of dense, jungled hills. The port for the Ristro capital was the largest in the country, but still small compared to the ones in Fom and Eheene—a series of floating platforms rigged to the cliffs with a web of ropes and pullies. A large encircling seawall protected it from the worst of the tides.

The capital was a sprawling maze of elevated walkways, canals, and bridges spread over a vast marsh. The largest buildings had been erected from marble on the irregular hills, although none were taller than three stories. The smaller residences, shops, and trades were sandstone and wood, resting on stilts jutting from the murky water. Mangrove trees, huge in their own right but tiny compared to those on the Upper Peninsula, grew throughout, and vines with a rainbow of flowers hung everywhere. A cacophony of songbirds competed with the sounds of the city.

It took Syrina the better part of a day to make her way from the creaking docks over the hills and through the maze of bridges and cobbled roads to the sprawling Administration Center, a series of six marble buildings on six islands, connected by covered bridges spanning over the swamp. She wasn't sure of protocol this time around, now that she was working for the Astrologers in a semi-official capacity, so, after a moment's hesitation, she just walked in.

Like within the government buildings in Vormisæn, there were gaslights every fifty paces, hooded with a deep purple shade that made the tattoos on Syrina's body glow an iridescent blue. She wasn't surprised when, less than five steps into the main hall, a voice boomed in accented Skald, "We are sure you can imagine what will happen if you take one step further."

Syrina stopped.

"Now, state your name and the reason for your intrusion." A figure emerged from a doorway halfway down the long hall. He wore a plain white robe, and his head was shaved, but she couldn't tell more than that in the dim, purple light. The sounds of people trying to be quiet came from shadowed alcoves lining the ceiling.

"Kalis Syrina, if you want to be formal, but you don't need to be. Syrina is fine. I guess you're expecting me, or you wouldn't be asking my name.

The figure down the hall gestured for her to follow. "Come."

Syrina noted that the soft mutter of people hiding above didn't go away.

The man led her to the end of the hall and out through a heavy wooden door carved with flowers, where a courtyard waited.

It must be nice to live in a country where the weather is so nice they can do all their business in gazebos, the voice commented.

Syrina ignored it.

The courtyard was a perfect circle, with winding footpaths snaking through flowerbeds shouting a cacophony of colors. A round reflecting pool lay in the middle, and in the center of that was the marble gazebo, its dozen pillars carved like entwined blossoms holding up a dome of woven stone vines.

The man gestured for her to stop at the end of the causeway, just as she'd done the last time an Astrologer wanted to talk to her, though this time she stood at the center of a mosaic of a ten-pointed star set into the flagstones. The sun was going down, and the sky was pink with twilight. This Astrologer was younger than the one in Vormisæn had been.

Maybe he's an intern.

"You're the Astrologer here?" Syrina asked.

"One of them. Now, we are sure you wonder why you must come all the way here, yes?"

"The question crossed my mind," she said, thinking of all her missed time with Pasha. She wondered how he was doing, then felt the voice in the back of her head goad her thoughts back to the present.

"Of course." The Astrologer took his seat in the center of the gazebo. "We will first tell you news of the world, which, I hope, will answer your question. Then we will tell you what we do know about the objects which this General Mann removed from the Black Wall, over the objections of their caretakers."

"Okay," Syrina said, wondering why Astrologers felt the need to tell her everything they were about tell her, instead of just getting to the point.

"The Grace of Fom has sent a missive to the Arch Bishop of Tyrsh declaring Fom's independence from the N'naradin theocracy," the Astrologer began. "In response, the Arch Bishop has ordered a full third of the Second Armada to blockade the Port of Fom. The Grace, in retaliation, has sent a sizable portion of her own forces up the Great Road, intent as she is on seizing N'naradin assets and gaining control of Great Spring, thereby rendering the Arch Bishop's blockade, for all intents and purposes, ineffective.

"Although war has not been declared in official capacity on either side, we have no reason to doubt that this is the beginning of a long and bloody conflict."

"Oh," Syrina managed, her mind again jumping to Pasha, traveling the Great Road with a pirate, utterly naive.

"As we suspected would happen," the Astrologer continued, "All messenger hawks along the Great Road north of Jaan'Lesh, including those flying from Valez'Mui, are being intercepted and killed by both sides as they attempt to disrupt each other's communications. Hence, the necessity of calling you here in person.

"As for why we asked you here," he went on. "We conducted extensive research after we received your message as to the nature of General Mann's mission. This 'glass' he has retrieved from the valley in the Black Wall is, we do believe, a sort information archive detailing... Well, we cannot know what information it holds, but it would, without argument, be of great interest to all of us— the Church of N'narad and the Merchant's Syndicate included—to find out. The means of accessing such information as is contained therein, however, is not clear." He blinked at Syrina, waiting.

She hesitated.

He already knows about Ormo's play room, the voice said.

Syrina could see it was right. She'd mentioned it last time she was in Ristro, after all. "I might have an idea about that."

The Astrologer nodded. "We have no information as to either these artifact's whereabouts or General Mann's, whom we lost track of after he arrived in Fom, though we have heard rumors he has been arrested and is awaiting trial. This arrest, if true, may or may not be linked to the Grace's rebellion and the good general's service to the

Arch Bishop of Tyrsh in obtaining these treasures, but further information from Fom is no longer forthcoming.

"As for the Artifacts he once possessed, we can only assume they have either been delivered to the Arch Bishop of Tyrsh or intercepted by the Grace and taken to Fom, who may or may not know their significance. Either way, until we learn more, it is best if you focus your attention elsewhere."

"Such as?" Syrina asked, her thoughts again jumping to Pasha.

"These individuals who followed General Mann out of the Black Wall. We believe them to be significant, and doubtless, the Merchant's Syndicate thinks so as well. However, the High Merchants out-class us in their knowledge of such things, to say the least. Things like the Kalis and the sleeping minds that dwell within you. We would hope you would deliver one or both of these people to your former master Ormo, observe his actions to the best of your formidable ability, and share what you learn with us."

Syrina frowned. "Isn't that risky? I mean, you're asking me to hand a significant advantage to Ormo. What if he learns something from these two that surpasses what he learned from me?"

"Would that not please you, to gain further self-knowledge, such as that no doubt would be?"

"Well, I guess that depends on what it also gave Ormo."

And what Ormo might need to do to Pasha to get it.

Syrina didn't risk an answer to that. She hadn't allowed herself to think about it, but the voice had forced it to the fore. She didn't want to mention her feelings for Pasha to the Astrologers either because she couldn't even explain them to herself, and she didn't want them to think he would be a liability.

"We have concluded after much discussion and debate since receiving your message that the knowledge gleaned will be worth the risk when combined with your, shall we say, supervision over the matter."

"Okay," she said, after thinking a moment. "They were on their way to Fom. I'll find them and see what Ormo wants done, then get back to you."

As long as they didn't get caught up in this civil war.

"This is agreeable to us," the Astrologer said, surprising Syrina by standing and offering a little bow. "Until we meet again, may the tides carry you."

"Uh, you too," Syrina said, already thinking about the fastest way to Fom and Pasha.

19

MYRION'S REVENGE

They huddled in their cabin, waiting for someone to find them. Pasha shook and rubbed his hands together. They were both sure some city watch or police patrol would come to haul them away, or for Ves to return and throw them off his boat for endangering him and his crew. But Ves and the sailors remained in the city, leaving the siblings alone with their fear.

"I killed her," Pasha whispered after hours of silence. He'd been unresponsive until then. Anna had resigned herself to just sit next to him on his bed, hand on his shoulder. She felt awkward, trying to comfort him.

"She knew who we were," Anna repeated his words to him. Sound without meaning.

Pasha shook his head and let out a shuddering sigh. "I've never killed anyone before."

"I know."

"I didn't know it would be like that."

"I know."

Pasha shuddered again. "We're in trouble." His voice dropped to a whisper. "I panicked."

"I don't know if we needed to kill her or not," Anna whispered. "No idea. And I need to stop thinking about it and so do you. It's done. All we can do is deal with it."

Pasha sat motionless a long time, then nodded and looked up at her, squeezing his hands together. He took a deep breath. "What do we do?"

Relief welled up when she studied his face. There was a glint of his old self in his grey eyes. "I don't know," she said. "I guess we wait here for Ves to come back and hope he doesn't turn us in, and then we get out of here. He's all we've got."

"He's not all we've got, Anna. We've got each other. And Syrina is..." He trailed off when he saw her frown. "Anyway, Ves isn't all we have, and I think we can trust him. Whatever you think of Syrina, I think Ves is too scared of her to leave us here."

Anna nodded, but the frown didn't leave her face. "Maybe you're right. We'll see."

Ves didn't leave them. His crew began to trickle in before first light, and the pirate himself staggered on board just as the sun lit enough of the fog to show it was up. He knocked, poked his head into their cabin, and blinked at them with red, tired eyes. Then he ducked out again, and the Flowered Calf disembarked ten minutes later. Anna and Pasha thought he'd been too drunk to know about the murder until he called them into his small galley with another knock, his face grim. His eyes were still red.

After they had sat in silence for another meal of rice and some kind of reeking pickled fish the crew had picked up in Great Spring, Ves studied each of their faces, then gave a quick nod.

"I guess it was you, then," he said around a mouthful of soured eel.

"Us?" Anna asked. It was a pathetic attempt at innocence, and she knew it.

"Look," Ves continued, reaching across the table to grab another rice ball, "I'm not saying she didn't deserve it. Hell, from my experience, those Church officials deserve to get shanked more often than not." He paused to take a long swig of sour beer. "I'm not judging you. But this makes things more complicated." He paused. "You know that, right?"

Neither Pasha nor Anna could think of anything to say, so Ves continued. "Someone watched you do it. You see why that's a problem? If you want to go around gutting N'naradin high-ups in alleys, you're not going to get any complaints from me, but you need to be smart about it. Smarter than you were last night. Right?"

They nodded. Neither could bring themselves to look at Ves, and neither had touched their food.

"All we can hope for is that they won't be looking too hard for you guys when we stop in Myrion's Revenge. If they do, well, like I said. Complicated. Are you going to eat that?"

Without waiting for a response, he reached across the table to grab both Anna and Pasha's untouched bowls of eel. They watched in silence.

The smell seeped into everything they owned, even before they dared going above decks. It was the smell of old oil and ammonia and rotting mud.

The locks going down the north side of the Dry Mountains weren't half as impressive as the ones they had ascended from the Yellow Desert. These ran parallel to the mountains and eased them down over the course of a day, into scrubby, miserable-looking lowlands.

The following morning, just before dawn, a stench woke them from their restless sleep. The smell seeped into everything they owned. It was the smell of old oil and ammonia and rotting mud.

Anna woke first, coughing. "What *is* that?"

Pasha sat up, rubbing his eyes. They burned, and rubbing them made it worse. He joined his sister in a hacking cough. "I don't know. Maybe Ves did something?" He stood and threw on some of the clothes Ves had gotten for them in Great Spring before following Anna out the door.

The sky was a greyish, green-yellow that felt like it was only a dozen hands overhead, even though the barren, brown mountains to the south were visible five spans away. The river bank was steep and ten hands high, rocky and rust-colored, with a few twisted, sickly brambles and weird, stunted bushes sprouting along the edge. The river itself had taken on an iridescent sheen. To the north, the landscape was a flat expanse of cracked, rust-colored mud with the occasional bulbous, twisted bush, and scattered groves of grey, long dead trees. Beyond the horizon, the putrid hue of the sky seemed to billow up like smoke.

Ves stood on the starboard side of the deck, watching the bleak scene. He turned as the siblings approached. He was wearing a complicated mask that covered the lower part of his face, with a long, wide tube that hung from his mouth. His eyes were red and watery.

He gestured for them to follow, and they went below to Ves's cabin. He removed the mask and rummaged through a trunk in the back of the room a moment before producing two more.

"These help. A little," he said as he fumbled with the straps and helped first Pasha, then Anna, adjust them over their mouths. "Good thing the boat came with these, or we'd all choke to death before Myrion's Revenge."

"What do you mean, 'came with these?'" Asked Anna, voice filled with suspicion. "Isn't this yours?"

Ves paused from adjusting Pasha's straps, frowning. "Sure, it's my ship. Now it is, anyway. If it wasn't legit, they wouldn't have let me through Great Spring, right? Just new. I've been off the water a while, that's all."

"How long is a while?"

"Anna—" Pasha started to interject.

"It's fine," Ves sighed. "Might as well be straight with you, since we're in this shit together. Quite a while, yeah? Ten years, maybe longer."

"It's been ten years since you've been up the Great Road?" Anna sounded incredulous.

"No, I said it's I've been off the water ten years. I was an ocean captain. This is my first time up the Great Road."

"Never? You've never done this before?" Anna's voice hovered on the edge of anger.

"Nope."

Pasha eyed the pirate. "So why are you doing this now? Where did this boat come from, then?"

Ves turned to Pasha. "It came from your girlfriend," he said with a wink. "And I'm doing it now because she bought me the Flowered Calf and paid me a big fucking sack of tin to take you to Fom, so that's what I'm doing. I can't say you haven't grown on me, anyway.

He paused and added, "If I were you, I'd be more worried about why a Kalis is so interested in me than about where this ridiculous goddamned boat came from.

"There," he said as he finished adjusting Anna's mask. "Not perfect, but it should help you breathe good enough when you're on deck. We'll get new filters when we stop in Myrion's Revenge."

Anna signed. "What is this place, anyway?"

"This, my adorable companions, is the glorious nation of Kamahush. Never been here before, and I can't say I have any desire to come back after seeing it once, but I learned a little about it back in Ristro, when I was supposed to learn history and all that.

"Come on," he gestured for them to sit around the small table and pulled a fat bottle of brown liquid from a shelf above his bed. "It's the sort of story that's better with a drink." He paused. "As if there's any other kind."

Ves only placed the bottle in front of himself after taking a long drink, face twisting as he swallowed. It was Anna who reached across the table to grab it. She guzzled and, coughing, handed the bottle to Pasha.

Ves watched in silence until Pasha passed the bottle back to him. He took another drink and raised it in a wobbly toast. "Makes the time go by slower, but at least you don't remember any of it." He set the bottle down.

"Kamahush was once where they grew most of the food for Eris. Green rolling hills. Rice, fruit, goats—they raised it all and fed the world. At least, if we can believe the Astrologers. Now, they're a bunch of cunts, but they're goddamn obsessed with history, so you might as well believe them on this one. Jewel of the fucking world, Kamahush was, getting rich of off Skalkaad and Ristro alike.

"Until the day it all went to shit. I don't know what happened. If the Astrologers can't say, I doubt anyone else can, either. Something ripped the whole country to hell and sent the rest of Eris into a mini-Age of Ashes five, six hundred years ago. Around then. Whatever happened, the crater it happened in is still smoking this toxic shit, though they say it's not so bad as it used to be."

Anna and Pasha waited for more, but Ves only sat there, motionless save for the occasional pull from the bottle, staring at nothing.

Pasha broke the silence. "That's it? That's the whole story?"

Ves blinked at him. "What else is there?"

Pasha made an exasperated grunt. "How should I know? It's your story. Just, the way you built it up I thought you'd know more than 'it was a nice place until it wasn't.'"

Ves shrugged and took another long pull from the bottle, then belched. "Don't know what to tell you," he slurred. "You know as much as I do now. One last fart from the Age of Ashes eight thousand years after the big shit."

At that, Ves closed his eyes and settled back against the wall, hand still resting on the now-half-empty bottle, a little frown on his wide, dark face.

Pasha emitted another frustrated groan. Anna just shook her head as together they went back to their cabin.

The siblings didn't leave their quarters again except for silent meals with Ves until the Flowered Calf lurched to a stop, twelve days later. The sun was at its zenith, throwing pale, greasy light through the little brass-framed portal of their cabin. Ves still found time to give them N'naradin lessons a few times a day, but he was occupied with navigating The Flowered Calf through the unfamiliar waters of the Upper Great Road. Except for checking in on Pasha once in a while and the brief lessons, he left the pair alone. They were nowhere near fluent, but Ves said they knew enough to get around.

There was another lurch. They picked up the voice of Ves wafting down from above, followed by another voice, male. Both were speaking N'naradin.

"Can you understand them?" Pasha asked. "You're better than I am."

"I don't know," Anna said, pressing her ear against the door. "Don't—wait. Something about Great Spring."

They glanced at each other. "She failed to... something," Anna translated. "I don't know. It's muffled."

There was the scrape of the sealed door opening and footfalls on the ladder to the cabins.

Anna gave him a desperate look and backed away from the door.

It opened to reveal a large man in black robes trimmed with gold. Behind him lurked two even larger men in leather jerkins, embossed with the sun-and-moon symbol of N'narad. They hefted long brass hammers with spikes protruding from the hilts. Pasha saw Ves behind them, looking nervous.

"Come with me," the man in robes said in clean Trader. Anna nodded and winced at the hesitation on Pasha's face, but he only eyed the guards and complied. The robed man disarmed him and led them up the gangway.

Myrion's Revenge was a N'narad supply depot on the southern edge of the Wastes. Forty or so rotting stone and mud shanties huddled like undead children between the decaying orange arms of the mountains. In the center of the town, a bigger, cube-shaped building of rust-colored stone lurked above the huts, windowless and dismal.

Their escort herded them onto decaying rowboats, and from there onto shore. The stench of rotten eggs was overwhelming, even with the masks. There was no dock, and anchored barges bobbed along both sides of the river. From the banks, paths of moldy boards led up to the structures above. Lining the shore, dozens of tall gibbets with corpses hung by their feet dangled in various states of decomposition. No, Anna saw. Not all were corpses. A few lived, moaning and swaying where they hung, upside-down, over the putrid water.

A handful of scabby-faced children sat against moist, muddy walls, staring at them with too-large, yellow eyes. Through a cracked door, Anna caught a glimpse of two naked men—one piecing the other's back with long needles coated in black liquid. As they neared the big stone building, she saw an old man load the bloated corpse of a woman onto a handcart from the filth piled between corroded brick walls.

Once inside, their escort led them through a room piled high with crates that smelled of cured meats and barrels covered in condensation, through a maze of hallways, and to a small office.

Their escort instructed them to wait in the hallway with a gesture. There was no place to sit, so they leaned against the wall. Neither spoke.

The soldiers pushed Ves into the office first, closing the door behind him. The huge man tried to give the siblings a reassuring look, but neither of them found it convincing. Muffled voices came from the other side of the door.

After a long time, a different guard came out and directed Anna and Pasha to enter and sit down on two of the plain chairs of unpolished, grey wood that lined the back wall. Ves sat on another and greeted them with a brief nod. The hammer-bearing guards moved to stand to either side of the door, while the man that had escorted them went to stand behind a dour-faced woman sitting behind a stone desk. He set Pasha's blackvine daggers in front of her with a gesture of finality. The room was dim, lit only by a few rows of candles lining shelves along the walls.

The woman's skin was creased and had a yellow tinge to it. Her hair was grey and dull, but there was a tired youth to her eyes that made Anna suspect she was much younger than she looked. Like their escort, she wore robes of black and gold, though hers were more faded.

"Tell me, where are you from?" she asked in Trader. Her voice was raspy and harsh.

Both Pasha and Anna looked at her blinking, pretending to not understand.

She turned to Ves. "You, then, pirate. These two here are your only cargo. What brings you down the Great Road with nothing but a pair of desert rabble?"

"I told you. Passengers," he said, a forced lightness to his tone that didn't touch his face. "Well-paying passengers. So what did you do to end up in the biggest shithole of a town in all of Eris? Something bad, I bet."

"Indeed." Her tone remained flat.

She turned back to the siblings, this time lifting one of Pasha's knives and making a show of examining it before placing it next to its twin and casting her hard gaze at them. This time she spoke in N'naradin. "I will leave the choice with you. You may answer my questions, for I suspect you understand them well enough, or you can stay in this 'shithole town'—for that is something your pirate is most assuredly right about—long enough for you to watch your Corsair friend join the ornaments that line our shore. A process that can take days. After which you can join him. One at a time, while the other watches. Siblings, I presume? You bear a certain resemblance. Well, regardless, you at least hold some affection for each other to come all this way from the Black Wall. As I understand it."

Anna did her best to maintain a blank, uncomprehending look, though she understood enough to have a knot of fear in her stomach. She could feel Pasha's eyes on her, but she wouldn't meet his gaze.

They were doomed. This woman, whoever she was, knew everything. She was only trying to confirm it to appease whatever convoluted laws required her to. And if they didn't confirm it for her, she would kill Ves. Not just kill him, but hang him to die, suffering and scorned, by his feet above a poison river. Anna wasn't ignorant enough to call Ves innocent, but he'd helped them. Remained silent about their crimes when he could have spoken up, even now, when it would save his life.

She thought about what she'd told Pasha before she'd run away, about finding their own purpose. Now, neither of them would get the chance. Only, maybe this *was* their purpose. To let this strange, surly man live on, rather than let him die in agony before they met the same fate.

With a wave of relief that surprised her, Anna began talking.

Pasha tried to interrupt his sister twice when he realized she was telling the woman everything in a competent mix of Trader and N'naradin—he hadn't realized how much of the latter she'd picked up. Anna just raised her voice to talk over him the first time. The second, one of the hammer guards, took a step toward him, and Anna only stopped long enough to hiss in their native language, "She already knows," before returning to her story.

The nameless woman nodded through it all, expressionless, save an occasional raised eyebrow. When Anna finished, the man standing at the woman's side whispered a few words into her ear. She nodded and gestured to the flanking guards, who took a step toward the captives. Pasha understood enough to know Anna had left out Great Spring, but he doubted it would matter. They had his knives, and probably the report from the boy who had witnessed the murder. At the woman's prompting, Anna had even explained blackvine to the woman—what it was, and how they sculpted it.

"I thank you for your honesty in this matter," the woman said, still without emotion. "Due to lack of evidence against him, the Ristroan Vesmalimali's sentence it suspended unless further proof that he had knowledge of any crimes is obtained."

She looked at Ves for the first time since the questioning began. "Tread careful, pirate."

She then gestured to Anna and Pasha. "These two I sentence to death by drowning for the murder of Prelate Sy N'dal of Great Spring, to be carried out at dusk in two days' time." Her voice still held no emotion.

Ves leaped to his feet, rage on his face. Both guards stepped toward him, but he ignored them. "What?" He bellowed. "Death? Don't they get to defend themselves?"

The woman blinked, surprised. "They are not citizens, nor even aspiring to become faithful to the Heavens. In this light, anything they could say in their defense cannot be trusted. As for leniency based on their—or rather the girl's—cooperation, they will be drowned, not suspended in the river swings. Given the boy's lack of cooperation and the girl's conspicuous omission of details about the murder of a prelate, I judge my sentence to have just the right amount of leniency."

She paused. "You have a startling amount of interest in the well-being of two foreigners you claim just booked passage with you. You already have their payment for your service, yes? Is there anything else you wish to divulge?"

Ves scowled but shook his head and said nothing as the mace bearers escorted them out of the office.

"You may return to your barge, pirate, but you do not have permission to leave Myrion's Revenge until their sentence is carried out," the woman called to their backs before a guard pulled the door closed.

"I'll get you out," Ves whispered to Pasha. Then the guards

pushed them apart, and escorted the siblings through a narrow outdoor passage and a metal gate, into a small, stone building. They shoved Pasha into a cell on the left, Anna into the last on the same side. Pasha could make out a motionless figure in the cage across from him but couldn't make out details, and whoever it was didn't move when they came in. There were no lamps or torches. The only light filtered from the slats in the gate they'd come through.

The guard who'd escorted Anna to the end of the block passed Pasha's cell without acknowledging him. There was a clang, a metallic click, and another clang, followed by black silence.

Pasha's mind whirled, but it always came back to first Anna, then Syrina. It was his fault. He'd regretted killing the woman in Great Spring before her body had hit the ground. He couldn't unsee the look of surprise on her face as her bowels spilled onto her feet.

Everything had seemed so clear as she'd approached with her sword drawn, as if in slow motion. But real clarity hadn't come until after, when the woman's soul had fled her body and a quiet sickness had overtaken Pasha with the sudden, unavoidable knowledge that he had ended her life.

He had tried to justify it to himself, and to Anna, who'd justified it back to him with his own hollow words. He knew she didn't believe them any more than he did. The woman had known about them—she'd been hunting them, as deserving of death as General Mann.

But now, alone in the dark with his thoughts, he knew he'd made a mistake he'd pay for with his life. Worse, Anna would pay for it, too.

Pasha decided that he'd tell them the truth—it had been him and him alone. He would beg them for his sister's life, even if that meant a painful, slow death in a river swing.

His mind made up with the peace of finality, Pasha closed his eyes, and waited.

20

THOSE WHO CARE

Ves allowed himself to be escorted back to the Flowered Calf. His mind was racing. There was a time he could have taken the two hammer-wielding guards flanking him. Or at least, there was a time he would have thought he could. But his years in Valez'Mui had made him soft, a fact that he wanted to blame Syrina for, but he knew better. He could have kept the hands-on approach to his business the way he had with his pirating, but he'd grown used to others doing things for him. At first, because it was expected of him, and it helped his reputation. Eventually, though, he'd grown to enjoy staying behind his walls while everyone else took all the risks. He'd always been good at hiring competent people. It had never been a problem to let them do all the heavy lifting.

But it was a problem now, and he wasn't going to get himself killed trying to deny it, no matter how much he wanted to save Pasha and Anna from the death awaiting them.

Once aboard his barge, he gave his escort the most sarcastic goodbye he could muster and retreated to the cleaner air below.

"Casting off soon, boss?" Alishepishai's voice was uncertain.

Ves grunted. He'd told his crew to leave the siblings alone while they were on board, but he regretted it now. His people would be surly when he told them he wouldn't leave their passengers behind in the most wretched town on Eris. All of them but Ash, who would give him that infuriating, beautiful smile and not say a goddamned word.

He'd been better off when Pasha and Anna were only passengers, but in the time he'd spent with them, they'd become more. They were friends. He should have made them part of the crew. Then his people would be raging to get them back as much as he was.

Second regret of the day, he thought. "No, sorry, Ali," he said, noting her little frown and giving her a look that said he was done talking about it.

She took the hint, nodded, and left. "I'll tell the others," she said, without turning around.

"Yeah, you do that," Ves said to her back, his mind already piecing together a plan as he retreated to his cabin.

He'd no sooner closed the door than there was a knock. "What?" He shouted, as he uncorked a fresh flask of rum.

The door swung open, and Ashmarirai, his first mate, best friend, and lover of twenty years sauntered in and seated himself in the lone chair at the cluttered desk, pushed against the wall under the grimy portal. He didn't turn the chair, but straddled it, leaning one elbow on the back and giving Ves a coy look while gesturing with his other hand for the bottle.

"I didn't say you could come in," Ves said, as he took a swig and handed it to Ash, uncorked.

He took a long drink and passed it back to him. "Ali says we're sticking around. No doubt to do something stupid, like rescuing your passengers."

"Our passengers," Ves corrected. "Yeah, that's right." He took another drink and passed the flask.

"They worth it?"

Ves paused. "I guess they must be."

Ashmarirai didn't hide his smirk. "You sure you're not just scared of 'Smudge?' Everyone knows who that old man really is, and rumor has it, her and that kid we're hauling are a thing. And no, before you ask, I didn't start it. Though I might not have helped keep a lid on it."

Ves grunted and passed the bottle back. "Three fucks, Ash. And here I was, thinking you strolled in here to be your usual quiet-ass self. How long have we known each other?"

"Too long." Ash took a drink.

Ves nodded. "Too fucking long."

"And you'd have it no other way."

"Nope," Ves grunted. "Well, it's not 'Smudge' I'm worried about, or whatever she's calling herself these days. It's those two." He made a gesture towards the portal above Ash's head and the wretched town beyond. "Spend enough time with someone, they grow on you. You know that. Why the hell else have we been together so long?"

Ash raised his eyebrows but didn't comment.

"Anyway," Ves went on. "They're not kids. Hell, I think they might be older than me, even if they don't look it or act like it. They're important. Important to the Church of N'narad, important to the Merchant's Syndicate. Important to the fucking Astrologers, too, I'd wager. Important enough that I'd rather none of those assholes got their hands on them. Because after spending all this time with them, they're important to me, too, and I don't want to see them drown in the stinking Upper Great Road."

Ash paused, took a drink, and handed the bottle back. "Okay," he said.

Ves nodded again and took another drink. "Stop looking at me like that. It's my own goddamned fault. I kept treating them like passengers after Great Spring, even after I decided they were more than that. Should have been drinking with you and the rest of the crew instead of sequestered away in here, like scared fops. They're friends, Ash. And you know how I treat my friends."

Ash nodded again, his face serious. "What do we do?"

Ves leaned back. "How many granados do we have?"

Ash coughed a laugh. "What, you want a frontal assault on the only solid building in Myrion's Revenge?"

"Not a full assault. Visibility is shit in this town. Shouldn't be too hard to get behind administration and blow a hole in the wall of that dilapidated prison."

"We've got a full case, plus Malisai has three more if she's willing to part with them, so that makes fifteen."

"Mali can keep hers. Shouldn't take but two or three, the way this shit town is falling apart. Hell, if we had time, we could just wait until the rain rotted the wall away for us. It's not like—"

A concussion rattled the glass in the little round portal. The Flowered Calf pitched first one way, then the other, casting most of the knickknacks, scrolls, and books scattered on the desk onto the floor.

Ash and Ves looked at each other and bolted down the gangway and up the stairs.

Behind them, midstream in the Great Road, a N'naradin warship anchored, its dog-headed guns turned on Myrion's Revenge. There was another series of cracks from the cannons, and a second later, five explosions ripped through the town, turning up the ground in giant mushrooms of rust-tinted mud. One shot hit the dour cube of the administration building, and a quarter of the front wall collapsed into a rolling cloud of brown dust.

Ves and Ash stared, speechless. "The Flower of Heaven," Ves mumbled to himself, noting the warship's name. "One of Fom's." Louder, he said, "The Grace is taking the Great Road."

Another barrage fell onto Myrion's Revenge, pounding into administration and the mud shanties around it. The ground was burning in places, their view shrouded in smoke. What was left of the main building was only visible now and then with errant swirls of the breeze. Cries and shouts welled up, and the stench of the churned, burning mud was overpowering.

The Flower of Heaven began lowering landing craft into the Great Road, full of soldiers, while a pittance of the Bishop's men staggered from the smoke, weapons drawn, to meet them on the banks. Both sides ignored the Flowered Calf and the other merchant barges, all now swarming with panicked crew trying to flee.

"We're not making it through this shit to the prison," Ash said. He looked up at Ves, ready for him to object.

Ves stared into the smoke and fire, now masking whatever was going on beyond the riverbank. More cannon shots ripped overhead, and a second later, there was another series of explosions somewhere in the town. "No. We've got to get out of here."

21

THE GRACE'S WAR

Smoke. Fire. Screams and darkness. Pasha was in the Valley again, his body heavy and cold amid flames.

He opened his eyes and closed them. Reality rushed back, and the darkness pressed him into the slimy cell floor.

He opened his eyes again, felt something sticky and warm run into them, and squinted against the smoke. The distant screams and faint yellow flicker of flame didn't fade. A fierce pain throbbed through his head.

"Pasha! Pasha! Pasha!" Anna's hoarse voice, screaming his name. The battered cell door clattered and swung outward, but it wasn't Anna who stood there. A man, tall, shirtless and emaciated, yellow hair and vast, wild beard that hid his face except for sallow, blue eyes.

He chattered something in neither N'narad nor Trade and made a quick gesture Pasha didn't understand.

All at once, Anna was there, helping him up, saying, "Pasha, you're hurt. He's hurt. Help me! Please help me!"

The last was in the valley language, but the man helped nevertheless, hefting Pasha to his shoulder while Anna took the other side.

"What's—" Pasha managed before the ground shuddered, and the air filled with dust and a subsonic rumble. He stumbled, and something dripped in his eyes again.

"I'm hurt," He mumbled, realizing someone had already said that. Anna. Anna had said that. Anna was here. He gave her a little squeeze under his shoulder and felt a wave of nausea.

"Shh!" Anna hissed, even that sound full of concern. "We're going to the Flowered Calf. We're getting out of here."

"No!" Pasha said with more conviction he thought possible before he was aware of why he said it. "My kn—" He coughed and started again. "My knives." He found his strength through the brown haze that clouded his mind. "Our father made them."

"No. Please, you're hurt."

"And the notes. She wrote down everything you told her."

"Pasha, we don't know what's happening! We have to—"

"I'll meet you."

"Pasha!"

But he was already pulling away from her and the man, running, blinded by the smoke, his only thoughts on his father's knives and the notes the robed woman had written. His sister's pleas faded and then cut off with another ground-shaking roar.

Pasha made his way back to the central building. He wasn't aware how far they'd gone. He'd been fading in and out of consciousness while Anna and the stranger carried him. Even now, reality swam. He swallowed the rank air in coughing gulps, staggering back and forth, leaning on mud brick walls for support like a drunk. Three times he fell retching, his mind blank with the pain in his head and lungs, and the mud made his hands itch and burn. The air was filled with the stench of sulfur, the streets deserted except for a few broken corpses lying half-hidden in their camouflage of orange slime. It was harder to breathe than he remembered it being.

The front door was unlocked and unguarded, and Pasha collapsed in the entrance after slamming the door behind him, not caring who found him there, sucking in the cleaner air in ragged gasps.

His head throbbed, but it was clear now.

He eased himself to his feet, fighting to pierce the roar in his ears enough to listen for any signs of life, hearing none. An occasional explosion still shook the foundations and brought down a dusting of mortar from between the orange-tinted bricks, but otherwise, all was silent. To his right, the hall lay in ruins, but ahead and on the left, the walls were cracked but intact.

He tried to think back, remember if they'd come across any fighting on their way through town, but he only remembered explosions and corpses. Where was everybody? Who was attacking? Well, he would find out when he made it back to the Flowered Calf.

He sneaked down the hall, pausing once to stumble against the wall and force the building fog from his head. As time and place began to seep back, he heard the hum of voices.

They were coming from the same little office he and Anna had been led to. Or was that further down? Eyes squeezed closed, he wiped the blood trickling down his forehead with the back of his hand.

He put his hand on the latch and waited. When the next explosion—more distant this time—shook another rain of mortar loose, he jiggled it. Not locked. He listened to the intensity of the voices, decided they weren't going anywhere after a nerve-wracking moment of silence, and took a deep breath. Again, he waited, struggling to keep his mind focused.

One minute. Two minutes. He swallowed, ignoring the burn in his throat. The voices paused, and he heard shuffling. Pasha stepped back, fighting down panic, deciding whether to flee or fight, knowing he needed to decide now.

The hall collapsed before he was aware of the tremendous roar in his ears. The shock of the explosion forty hands behind him tipped him into the wall, and before the dust had settled, the door slammed open, and two dazed men in black and gold robes halted in their tracks and stared.

Pasha was faster. Adrenaline had rushed in. He flew into the first one —the one standing during their interrogation—as the priest got his sword out from under his bulky robes. In two quick moves, Pasha twisted the hilt out of his hand and thrust it into the chest of the other man, still standing in the doorway, who coughed, burbled, and slid down the wall to the floor.

With his left hand, Pasha grasped the wrist of the first, twisted him around, and pressed the bloody edge of the sword against his throat. He found it heavy and clumsy. His vision swam, and he realized it might not matter what weapon he carried if he came across anyone else.

"You know me?" Pasha asked in Trader.

The man nodded and swallowed against the blade. "Foreign prisoner."

"Where is our equipment? My weapons?"

"Ghh." The priest squirmed once and settled when the sword drew blood. "Consul Craymith's office."

"Where you questioned us?"

"Yes."

"Where in the office?"

"I don't know. I don't know if they're still there. She wanted to look at them."

"Is she there now?"

"No."

"What's going on here? Who's attacking?"

"Fom."

Pasha debated getting the priest to explain, but he didn't have time, so he brought the hilt of the sword hard across the back of the man's head. He tried not to think about the man's odds. Better than Pasha's had been, locked in a cell, he told himself.

Killing grows easier the more you do it. He thought of Syrina but pulled his mind away.

He made a quick check of the room the two men had emerged from, found a rack for five gas masks, and took the last two. The series of clasps and straps looked even more complex than Ves's had, but he could cover his face with it on his trip to the Flowered Calf, and Anna could use the other one.

The door to the office was ajar, the room empty. His knives lay abandoned on the desk. A few pages of the notes the woman had taken during their interrogation were scattered next to them. Anna's bag sat on the floor next to the desk, its contents of clothes dumped out into a pile.

Pasha grabbed the daggers and stuffed the papers into Anna's pack. He glanced around for the rest of the notes, but he didn't see them, and he didn't have time to look.

He came across the living twice on his way back through Myrion's Revenge, fighters rushing to the ruins of the central building. Both times they ignored Pasha, either mistaking him for one of their own under the mask or not caring in their panic. He pushed past them, carried by his fading adrenaline, the haze pushed aside.

A war teemed at the docks. It was the first sign of real fighting he'd seen, but he still couldn't tell what was going on. Half the boats tied in the river had been scuttled, making an obstacle course of tarnished brass stacks and dented copper hulls. Bodies and bloody chunks littered the steep bank and tumbled along the dilapidated wooden walkway.

There was no sign of the Flowered Calf, and Pasha didn't see the flowery hull among those scuttled in the river. The rotting wooden path the guards had rowed them to ended in a ragged splinter of old wood and rough stone nails. The Great Road made faint, sluggish lapping sounds. A huge ship anchored midstream, beyond the broken hulls of scuttled ships, and cannons shaped like dog's heads smoked, though they'd fallen silent. Figures in the haze still fought—Pasha heard the clatter of ceramic and metal blades. More soldiers, these in red and white, rowed from the warship, landing along the banks and rushing into the mist-shrouded town. In the chaos, no one noticed Pasha.

"Anna!" Pasha called out, voice muffled by the ill-fitting mask, no longer caring if anyone heard him. He wandered in a little circle at the end of the shattered path along the bank. "Anna!"

After a minute, he heard her voice. "Pasha! I'm here," she called back as she stepped out from behind the beached ruins of a river barge that had been torn in half, the twisted, jagged holes in its hull smoking in the thick air.

He ran to her, threw his arms around her, relieved to feel her grip him back. "I'm sorry, Anna," he mumbled through the mask.

She coughed and pulled away from him. Her breath was shallow and pained. "Here," he said, handing her the second mask. "Put this on. The fighting must have stirred up something into the air."

Anna only nodded as she fumbled with the straps and let Pasha help her fit it over her face.

"Thank you," she said, her voice reverberating through the hose in the mask, its lenses making her eyes two disks of silver. "Ves is gone. The boat, gone."

"I knew he would leave us here," Pasha said, without conviction.

Anna looked around at the ruined ships and broken corpses half buried in red and yellow mud. "I don't think he had a choice."

He followed her gaze but only gave a slight nod. "We need to get out of here, too," he said. "Where's that man? The one who helped us out of the prison?"

"He took a little boat, rowed toward one of the ships trying to sail away. He wanted me to come with him, but I wouldn't leave without you." She hesitated, flopped her arms, helpless, and turned towards the ruins of one of the sunken barges.

Pasha followed her eyes, confused until understanding seeped into his sluggish mind. "We need to get out of here," he stated again.

It was her turn to nod. "I was looking at Ves's maps," she said. "There's a road. Or a path. West through the mountains to Fom. It looks shorter than the river, but I don't think many people use it."

Pasha looked at the hazy line of mountains that began a span to the southwest, rust-red, streaked with yellow, bereft of even scrub or cactus. "No," he said, "Probably not. Let's go. It's better than staying here." He glanced at the ruin around them. "Anything is better than staying here."

22

ORDERS: FIFTEEN MONTHS BEFORE THE TRIAL

My first meeting with the Arch Bishop of Tyrsh, infallible ruler of N'narad and Voice of the Heaven of Light, did not take place in the Grand Cathedral, or even in the nearly-as-lavish-and-closer-to-home Wise Hall in Fom. Instead, he came to me in a small, simple church on a cliff overlooking the Sea of N'narad in Pom, on the Isle of N'narad. At the time, I was disappointed I wouldn't see Tyrsh for myself. Believe it or not, even after almost seventy years of service to Heaven, I'd never had an occasion to go there. I reminded myself the honor of meeting Arch Bishop Daliius III should be enough.

The Voice of the Highest Heaven was smaller than I'd imagined him. Smaller, and younger than the image stamped on the N'naradin Three-Side implied. The soft roundness of his face was set off only a little by the stern, dark haircut, tinged white at the temples. He sat on the floor at the foot of the alter bearing the iron-bound Book of Pom, speaking in a quiet voice to one of his aides sitting next to him, but he rose as I entered. The motion was strangely graceful under the heavy red robes of his station.

"General Mann," he said, giving a slight bow of greeting. "It has taken us too long to meet." His voice was soft.

I kneeled, head bowed, as was expected. "You honor me, Your Worship. I am dismayed that you were so inconvenienced to meet me here, rather than in your home in Tyrsh."

Daliius had a wry expression as he gestured me to stand. "I should apologize that I do not greet you with the pomp our greatest general deserves, which would have been mine to give had we met in Tyrsh. Alas, time is of the essence. Besides, there are many ears in my Cathedral, and I mistrust that all of them have the best interests of our great empire in their hearts."

I caught myself giving wary looks towards the twenty guards, advisers, and retainers gathered in the small temple, but the Arch Bishop only smiled. "All those present here can be trusted. Implicitly."

I felt my face grow hot. "Of course, Your Worship."

"Now," The Arch Bishop went on, gesturing for me to step forward, "We are pressed for time. I am sorry to cast further niceties aside and discuss why I called you here.

"Have you ever been to the Yellow Desert, General Mann?"

"Yes. when I was young. The Grace sent me to—"

"Yes, yes," the Arch Bishop waved his hand. "I do not care why you were there. I am asking you to go back. All the way to the Black Wall itself."

"Of course, Your Worship. Caravans cross weekly, at least, unless something drastic has changed. Once in Valez'Mui, it should be a simple matter for me to—"

The Arch Bishop made the same casual gesture. "You will need an army with you."

"An army? I don't—"

"And karakh. I've arranged for thirty to rendezvous with you on the Upper Peninsula as soon as your ships and men arrive and are ready to depart. Three ships. Freighters, for you'll need the space. I've arranged for a shipyard to remove the cannons on two of them to accommodate the karakh. Unfortunate, but my naval advisors insist weapons won't be necessary if you take the proper precautions. The ships should arrive in Pom within the next three or four days. I trust you will be ready to leave. You may find you will need to make further modifications once your soldiers and beasts have been gathered. Trust that any costs will be covered."

My mind whirled. I was still trying to grasp the logistical horror of crossing the Yellow Desert with an army and thirty karakh, never mind the diplomatic ramifications. "Thirty karakh? Forgive me, Your Worship, but that is insane. I'm sorry I don't understand. Is this an invasion? There is nothing in the foothills of the Black wall but quarries and goat herders."

"General Mann, did I say anything about the foothills?"

"No, Your Worship. I mean, I just thought—"

"No, I did not, because you will not be stopping in the foothills. You will pass beyond them, into the Black Wall. You will need the karakh for this, and you may need them and an army to deal with whatever you find there."

"Through the Wall? Your Worship that is impossible."

"Nothing is impossible if Heaven wills it. And General, Heaven wills this.

"Cardinal Vimr will accompany you." The Arch Bishop turned and gestured to the portly, nondescript man he'd been speaking to when I'd arrived. He stood and bowed first to the Arch Bishop, then to me.

The Arch Bishop turned back to me. "You will have erstwhile command of this endeavor, but the Cardinal speaks with my Voice. Is that clear?"

"Yes, Your Worship." My voice sounded small in my ears, even in the perfect acoustics of the little temple. Nothing had been clear, but I didn't know what else to say.

"Good. Vimr will provide you with details. Now," the Arch Bishop continued as he strode from the church, his retainers, advisers, and hangers-on shuffling after him. "Best get some rest. You look forward to a long journey, though with the Highest Heaven's mighty blessings it should not be a difficult one. The Book of Flowers awaits your name upon your return, General Albertus Mann."

I watched the procession slack-jawed as it filed from the little church. The door swung shut behind them. Outside, the muffled static of surf against cliffs rose through closed windows behind the alter.

I tried telling myself the will of the Arch Bishop was the infallible will of Heaven, but the idea seemed hollow when weighed against the hell I imagined when I thought about taking an army to the Black Wall. Not just to the Wall, but *through* it. I couldn't silence the voice creeping up from my subconscious, which kept whispering that the Arch Bishop was, in fact, an idiot.

It had been a long time since I'd been to the Upper Peninsula, and I'd forgotten how hot it was. My white and red linen shirt hung like soggy drapes, and my eyes stung with sweat. The sky was leaden.

Sett'ks, or something close to it, was favored of the two karakh, and the first to break into the clearing, blowing a high, weird whistle as it tossed its head, shaking spittle from its tusks and jowls. The chains in its cheeks rattled. It was in its prime, while its rider, M'Ket, whom the chieftains had introduced to me the day before, was a friendly, sociable fellow I found myself rooting for. Sett'ks' hair was red-brown spotted with black, and it had brows that arched over the huge, yellow owl-orbs of its eyes that looked almost comical, if not for the tusks that jutted from its protruding lower jaw, reinforced with brass bolts. Even covered in their leather sheathes, they looked deadly.

When the Church had informed the tribes that a chieftain's husband and twenty-nine other shepherds and their mounts would accompany me, they had set up a series of competitions to determine who would be selected to lead them. This was the last of the games.

I stood with sixty or so women—chiefs of the lesser tribes that didn't have enough karakh to compete—along with their husbands. Only boys could bond with karakh because, they say, the mating instinct is too strong in the females, and males can only bond with other males. The women stand at the head of the tribes of the Upper Peninsula, while their husbands lead their fellow shepherds who together form a sort of cult. They explained all this to me my first day there, despite my assurances that I had dealt with the tribes before. They chose to treat me like a child because of the child-like errand I was asking them to go on.

But I digress.

We watched from a high platform at the edge of a glade of dry, grassy ground amid the enormous mangroves, some a thousand hands high, which covered most of the Upper Peninsula and the lands to the east. A variety of sliced fruits and exotic meats lay spread on wooden platters, though I had declined such a feast on the previous days. This last day I felt obligated to take a few nibbles of some sort of raw, salty meat, even as my stomach churned. I decided I would stick to the fruit and the endless supply of rum.

The rival shepherd emerged from the opposite side of the clearing. They told me he was once one of the strongest, but overthrown years ago. Dakar was his name. One chief who stood with me told me that his karakh, Gre'pa, used to be as grey as the slate sky, but was now almost pure white, and one of the largest of its kind. Karakh grew throughout their long lives, and Gre'pa was ancient.

"He's old," I said to Vimr, who stood at my side. Even then, there was something about the round, plain, little man I couldn't bring myself to trust.

He nodded and eyed Dakar from under his own dark tangle of eyebrows, but didn't respond.

The two shepherds nodded to each other, the karakh clicked and whistled. The creatures' talons were wrapped in a thick, velvety material. It was not to be a fight to the death—a fact I found comforting.

I dreaded the quest before me no less than when I had first received my orders from the Arch Bishop, but despite my misgivings, I thought then I might at least learn to live with Cardinal Vimr. I at least imagined that he was on my side. An army through the Yellow Desert, though, that idea haunted me, as did this strange, absurd need for secrecy that kept us from taking the Great Road to Valez'Mui.

And now this. Using a conquered people who trained and rode the most dangerous animals in the world as mercenaries had never sat well with me, and I still wasn't convinced such monsters were as necessary as the Arch Bishop had made them out to be. All I saw before me was the dangerous burden I had been saddled with.

But I did find the fact that they fought for the honor of accompanying me on this insane mission somewhat comforting. Over the centuries, about half the karakh tribes had taken up the Faith and joined the ranks of names written in the Books of Heaven. I wondered if those that came had been promised a higher level like I had, and supposed it was probable. As shaken as my faith had become over my long years in service to the Church, the promise of the Heaven of Flowers upon my successful return had been comforting. The tribes people must feel the same way about the Heaven of Feasts or Water, or whatever token they had been offered.

There was no prelude, no speeches. At some invisible signal, the two beasts lunged. The crowd waiting around me on the platform let out an undulating cry. I took a long drink of rum from my wooden cup and gave a nod of thanks to the young man who refilled it.

M'Ket went low, Dakar high. Gre'pa reached out with all four limbs to catch itself in the wide branches of one of the towering mangroves some two hundred hands from where we stood.

It was a mistake. Gre'pa miscalculated the catch with its felt-wrapped claws and found no purchase. It swung over the branch like a gymnast and hit the ground forty hands below with a grunt, reaching up with its left hand just before it landed to catch Dakar and easing him back onto its neck. It disappeared into the trees, M'Ket and Sett'ks bounding close behind.

I swallowed a bubble of disappointment. The rules said that the fight could range anywhere on the Upper Peninsula as long as victor dismounted his opponent in the clearing below the platform. I realized now it could take days, while the spectators had nothing to do but drink and eat under the trees and lead-grey sky.

So I drank and waited, and thought about these shepherd clans of the Upper Peninsula, the most volatile of subjects within the N'naradin Theocracy.

There were dozens of small clans revolving around the karakh. There had been hundreds once, but N'narad had subdued them by burning the forests. That had been well over six-hundred years ago, before the fall of Kamahush. The forests had grown back, but the Church had shattered the clans, and they had never recovered. Two hundred years ago, the Arch Bishop granted them autonomy after a brief, bloody rebellion. The Church had allowed them to keep their customs because both the Grace and the Arch Bishop both saw use in a people like the karakh shepherds, but they were still required to bow to the wills of both Fom and Tyrsh.

The bond between karakh and herder occurred between about one in twenty of the clansmen. A boy was chosen at birth, and a newborn karakh would be taken from its mother, the two raised together as siblings. If a karakh was more than a few weeks old, the bond wouldn't form. Life expectancy was about the same for humans and karakh, and the bond was for life.

The karakh are never tamed, so it is said, but between themselves feel a fierce sense of camaraderie. When conditioned young, that loyalty is transferred to the human child. If that bond is broken by either distance or death, it can never be reformed, and the karakh becomes wild and needs to be put down. Any herder who loses his karakh goes mad with grief, and he is expected to end his own life.

The idea was unsettling, and it added to my mounting concern about bringing such monsters across the continent with an army I didn't want to lead.

A crash from our right dragged me back to the present as the red monster Sett'ks exploded into the clearing in a trail of foliage. Almost simultaneously, Gre'pa erupted from the forest behind us and hurled itself ten hands over our heads, showering us with heavy branches and the leaves and fronds that drifted down after them. The mob let out another cheer. Vimr ducked, arms covering his head as the creature flew over us, a gesture which brought snickering from around us. The servant who had been standing at my side, waiting to refill my cup, turned to offer Vimr a drink, though the Cardinal had refused one when we'd arrived. The boy had mocking look on his face, and the gesture brought more raucous laughter.

Vimr fumed and turned his attention toward the fight.

In the center of the clearing, M'Ket led his mount in a somersault, and in the same move sprang to the side and made a swipe at Dakar just as the old man landed.

Too quick for Gre'pa to react. Two mammoth claws sheathed in cloth caught Dakar in the ribs. He went flying sixty hands before he rolled on his shoulder, head tucked down, to a stop at the edge of the glade.

I climbed down the steep, uneven spiral stairs to the clearing and strode out to where M'Ket and his karakh hovered, panting in the churned mud and tall grass.

Before I came within twenty paces to congratulate him, M'Ket turned his beast and ambled into the woods and out of sight. I stopped and looked around, confused, feeling foolish.

Dakar limped toward me—I was surprised he was even alive, but, except for the limp and a few scratches, he seemed uninjured. Gre'pa eyed me and emitted a long, high whistle from deep in its throat I associated with a growl. I tried and failed to mask my nervousness at the creature looming over me, and looked at Dakar, who grinned.

"I'll meet you at your ships in three days," he said. He made a few clicking noises in the direction of Gre'pa, who stopped whistling.

"Um," I said, feeling even more lost, and looked to where M'Ket had disappeared.

Dakar laughed. "What? You thought traveling half-way 'round

the world on some idiot mission from the Church was a prize?" He laughed again.

"Three days, Mann, or whatever you're called. I'll be there, and I'll tell you a thing or two about karakh and boats you're not going to like."

Dakar whistled, and Gre'pa lurched over and scooped him up to set him on its back. While we had talked the creature had removed the wrappings around its claws and sheaths over its tusks, and I realized they were smart enough to know when such protection was no longer needed. Then they, too, disappeared into the forest.

"Coming, General?" Vimr's voice called from behind me. It began to rain.

23

THE FIGHT

NOBODY NOTICED THE SIBLINGS WALK OUT OF MYRION'S Revenge. Once, just a few steps out of view of the docks, A soldier had stumbled from an alley, shouted something, and began running toward them through poisonous, ankle-deep mud. He got within a few dozen strides from Anna and Pasha when a crossbow bolt passed through his neck and out the other side. His body fell and slid through the reddish muck a half-dozen hands before coming to a rest face down. They never saw who had shot him, nor another soul before they found the rutted, narrow path leading up a steep canyon on the far side of town.

They climbed into the barren crags of the Dry Mountains. Pasha and Anna had been so relieved to have found each other, to be free again against hopeless odds, that they were getting along better than they had since they were children, swimming in the lake and squirting each other with water blown through hollow reeds. That afternoon and into the cold, windy night, they filled their time with comfortable silences, smiles, and playful banter.

But by the next morning, cold, hunger, and thirst had dulled their elation, and they awoke from a restless night, exhausted and scared.

The old irritations had returned before they set out to follow the western track through endless shards of rust-tinted stone.

That afternoon, when Anna again asked Pasha how he planned to find Mann, she wondered later if she hadn't been looking for a fight. Maybe, she thought, she'd been hunting for a way to take her frustrations out on him when he gave the answer she knew he would give.

"I'll find Syrina," he'd said. "She'll help us."

And she'd responded just as predictably: he was an idiot for thinking he could find her, much less trust someone who's entire life had been based on lying, killing, and manipulation.

They spent that night in angry, sullen silence, and what few words they shared were laced with spite.

Hunger and lack of sleep combined with desperate thirst over the next four days. Anna found herself picking old wounds, her rage toward her brother growing, she thought later, only because it didn't have anywhere else to go.

So when they reached a T-intersection neither remembered from the maps, how it ended shouldn't have surprised either of them.

"Fom is this way," Anna stated, matter-of-fact, pointing down steep switch-back to their left, blocked here and there by screes of small rock slides.

"No," said Pasha, his voice tired. "Look. This way is more used. Everyone who uses this road will be coming and going to Fom. Obviously." He gestured to the path to the right, wide and rutted, following the line of the mountain they had been hiking, until it disappeared behind the terrain less than a span distant. "Unless you think both Ves and Syrina lied about how big Fom is, that's the main road."

"How the fuck do you know?" Anna shouted, cursing at him in N'naradin because she knew it would annoy him. "Why are you acting like you know where we are? You didn't look at the maps for more than five seconds because you blindly trust that witch Syrina to save you. How do you know where 'most people go?' Did she tell you which way to turn on this path in the middle of nowhere before she left you, never to be seen again? I looked at Ves's maps. I fucking studied them. It's this way."

She saw his face turn red as he looked up to the sky, which had been a featureless grey-yellow since they'd left Myrion's Revenge. Telling direction from the sun was impossible. He shook his head and pointed again down the wider path. "That 'witch' saved your life. Convenient to forget that whenever you want to be right."

Anna sighed. Done with it all. "We should split up, then."

"What?" The word was a shout, a sudden look of desperation settling on Pasha's face. "Over this? Over this stupid argument? Why now, Anna? No. Not when we're stuck in the middle of nowhere." There was an echo of a whine in his voice that stabbed Anna with guilt and annoyed her at the same time.

She sighed again. "It's not just this, and you know it. I've been thinking about it for a while. Since Great Spring. Even before, when I left the first time, but more since—" She trailed off, reluctant to wound her brother with the woman he'd killed.

But she picked a different route and pressed on. "Think about it. They're looking for a brother and sister coming from Valez'Mui. Even if that's the only description they have, it's enough as long as we're together. However we dress, we can't hide our faces, our accents. They'll find us. We're not from N'narad. Not from Great Spring. Not from Myrion's Revenge. Not even from Valez'Mui. According to Syrina, where else is there? It doesn't take a genius to put the rest together."

"Not here, Anna." His voice was choked. "We have a long way to go, and we don't know how to get there. Neither of us can do this alone. Anyway, if Fom is as big as Sy— As big as they say, there should be plenty of people to blend in with. We just need to get there."

"That's another thing I've been thinking about. *Still* thinking about," Anna's voice was soft now. She felt a blind need to finish what she started. "Why are we doing this? This General Mann, he seems important, right? How are we going to get close to him, even if everyone wasn't looking for us? Even if we find Syrina, and even if she helps us? What's the point? Let's say you get to Mann. Let's say you kill him and somehow get whatever he took back. Then what? You're going to take it back to the valley and spend the rest of your life guarding it? The door to the Tomb is broken. Nothing will change the fact that we're here." Anna gestured around her. "Out here, away from everything we know. Why can't we just get on with our lives?

"And not only that," Anna talked over whatever Pasha was about to say. "They know about the valley. They know about our home. They know how to get there. They know about the fucking blackvine. You think you can just go home and guard whatever it was they went to so much effort to steal? Everyone in the valley is dead, Pasha, or near enough. It took them a week to get through us the first time. *A week*. Our people threw their lives at them, and it didn't even slow them down. Next time they'll just walk in and kill whoever's left. Including you.

"There's nothing left there for anyone out here unless you put it back. You want them to kill the last people left? Because that's what you'd do—give the fiends out here a reason to go back to our home. What used to be our home." She took a deep breath, looked like she was about to say something else, and stopped.

Tears welled in Pasha's eyes, and Anna felt a wave of regret.

"Why all this now?" He asked. The words came out in a groan. he looked away from her, took a breath, and wiped his face with his hands, but when he turned back, his face was set, and his eyes were dry.

"Look around you, Anna. Even if we weren't following Mann, even if you don't care, we still need to get away from here. If you want to get on with your life—whatever that means—are you going to start here?"

Anna looked a long time down the winding, scree-cluttered path before turning back to Pasha, tears in her eyes. "It has to be here. I can't do this anymore."

She turned and started down the mountain, slipping once or twice on the loose rocks. She refused to look back but listened for the crunch of his footfalls as he followed her like he always did.

They never came.

Two nights later, dying of thirst, in the clarity that came in the final moments of life, she decided that of all the reasons she'd ever had for leaving her brother, she'd never see him again because of the stupidest one.

24

THE PIT

PASHA HAD FLITTING MEMORIES OF THE DAYS BETWEEN ANNA walking away and waking up in a hole, lying on stones smeared in shit.

He'd stumbled on for most of that first day, away from where Anna had half-fallen down the steep, switch-back path. At first, he didn't want to give her the satisfaction of following like he always ended up doing. The way he always let her win. Spoiled, he'd thought. Since she was born, she'd been spoiled. He stopped as the yellow clouds grew black with night, wondering if he should turn back, but it was too late, and he knew it. He had no food nor water. If he doubled back, he wouldn't survive past the intersection she'd left him at.

He found a hidden spot behind a boulder—a shallow hole big enough for him to curl up in. Out of view of the road, he'd thought, but he woke in the orange predawn light with four men standing over him, speaking N'naradin in harsh voices. Pasha's tired mind grappled with the language and failed. They wore uniforms and red sashes with the Sun and Moon motif across their chests.

He pretended he was asleep until the first man reached toward him. Pasha lashed out with his knife, burying it in the man's belly and kicking another in the groin before the other two grabbed him and tied his hands. Pasha watched, numb, as the man he'd stabbed writhed and cursed, one hand holding the wound in his gut with bloody fingers while the other hand groped at the hard-packed, rocky dirt like some separate, mindless animal.

The one who tied him spat with rage. "You'll rot in the Pit, now."

Pasha, his fatigue and confusion pushed away by fear, understood that.

That one led, while the other two lagged with their injured comrade. Pasha stumbled between them, numb, hands tied behind his back, feet tied with a cord so he could only shuffle over the rough ground. He wondered if the man he'd stabbed would live.

They came to a low, bunker-like outpost, and the men shoved him inside and led him to a cell so small he could neither stand up nor lie down. His escort and a trio of other soldiers spoke for a while. Pasha couldn't hear everything but overheard enough. They had no idea who he was. They'd come across a man sleeping in the mountains and stopped to ask him questions about the battle at Myrion's Revenge, thinking he was a refugee, but he'd attacked them.

One came in and injected him with something from a thick syringe with a narrow bone needle, and everything went black. Pasha's last thought was wondering if Anna was dead yet.

When he awoke, he was still bound, bouncing alone in the back of some sort of wagon. It was hot and smelled like urine and feces. The only windows were high slits on three walls, blocked with wooden slats, so small Pasha wouldn't have been able to fit his head out of them, even if he could stand.

He had nothing else to do, so he lay down and slept, his head pounding with thirst.

Pasha had gravel in his throat, and more slid around behind his eyes when he regained consciousness. He was disappointed to find opening them didn't make the feeling go away.

He lay on greasy stones that reeked of sewage and old garbage. A susurration of voices echoed around him, and louder jeers and shouts came from above. He sat up and looked around. He was in an enormous, domed room, illuminated by five circular holes a hundred hands above. Dying, grey daylight scratched through narrow grates. Vague shapes of people peered down, silhouetted against the light, shouting, laughing, and pissing.

Seven hallways lead from the chamber, dark and barred with thick, tarnished bronze gates.

About twenty others sat or stood around the huge chamber, in small groups or by themselves. No one spoke above a whisper if they spoke at all, and they filled the room with the hiss of conspiracy.

There was no sign of Anna. Only men.

No. In the gloom, he saw the bodies of two women, naked, face down on the opposite side of the room, but both were too old to be his sister. He slumped down with his back to the wall, stomach churning.

A drain in the center of the concave floor served as a latrine, surrounded by moldy rinds and animal bones. A finger's-width of sewage coated the floors along the walls and gelled in patches around the room, the muck getting thicker as it oozed toward the drain. Pasha couldn't remember a good smell since he'd left the Black Wall. Except Syrina. But he forced his thoughts away from her.

He studied the others. The men he shared the dome with were gathered in three loose groups, and three, besides himself, that hunkered alone.

Seven people, scrawny and broken, sat together along the curved wall to his left. They made the least amount of noise, and Pasha got the impression they'd been there for long time. At least longer than the others.

Another group of four men clustered near the wall to his right. They were well-dressed, and by the way they spoke together, Pasha suspected they knew each other from before. They eyed the others in the chamber with open suspicion, and when they noticed Pasha watching, they dropped their voices lower.

Three other men hunkered across the room opposite Pasha, chatting as they looked around, laughing and jostling as if passing a bottle. Ristroan. Dark-skinned, and one had green gems set into his head, though they weren't as large and plentiful as Ves's diamonds. The second had a large mop of black, curly hair and an enormous beard. That one saw Pasha watching and gave him a sarcasm-laced salute. The last was blocked by the others, leaning with his back to the wall. Pasha could tell he sported an enormous gut, but not much more, and at the bearded man's attention, he looked away.

A few others sat or stood like Pasha, alone and frightened, or resigned. Most wouldn't meet his gaze.

And then he saw General Mann.

Pasha stared, sure at first it was some trick of the light or a hallucination—a side effect of whatever they had injected him with. But the image didn't waver, and the old, wiry man with the loose jowls didn't look like someone else the more Pasha looked at him. It was that face from the valley, lit by fire. The face he'd never forget.

"Yeah, that's him. I don't know whether you could say it's lucky you found him here, though, in the only literal shithole worse than Myrion's Revenge."

Pasha jumped up and twisted around to face the source of the familiar, amused voice, mind trying to bend to the improbability of it.

Ves nodded to him, grinning a smile that didn't touch the rest of his face. The bearded man who'd saluted him earlier and the other Ristroan stood watching on the other side of the room. his smile was sardonic behind the beard. He saluted again.

Pasha's mouth opened and closed, but no sounds came out.

"Yeah," Ves agreed, somehow managing to make his whisper echo in the cavernous chamber, "I'm surprised to see you, too. Full of mixed feelings about it, since I was looking my ass off for you. But, like you finding your general, I wouldn't call it good luck, given the circumstances."

"You left us," Pasha stammered at last.

"Indeed," Ves nodded, smile gone. "They escorted me all the way to the Flowered Calf. I intended to go back, even had a plan to get you out. Not a good one, as Ash will no doubt attest if we ever see him again. But a plan. Then the attack happened, and we needed to run or risk losing the barge and everyone on it, including me. We made it back the next day, but the administration building was in ruins. A few survivors said some prisoners had escaped into the mountains towards Fom, a few others on some of the fleeing barges, those that hadn't been sunk. I decided you and Anna would either be resourceful enough to make it all the way here or die somewhere else, so I came to Fom to figure out which it was."

"We're in Fom?"

Ves chuckled. "Yeah, you made it, so congratulations. Through the middle of Fom and into the Pit. Here to entertain the peasants above by fighting over scraps of rotting food. How did you manage to get all the way here and be just as oblivious as you were last time I saw you?"

Pasha scowled, but he told him.

Ves frowned. "I'm sorry to hear about Anna. I hope she's still out there, and somewhere we can find her. My tale is altogether less interesting. Got to Fom. Then I got drunk, got recognized, and netted."

"Recognized?"

Ves smiled. "I was a pirate for years before settling down in Valez'Mui, you remember. Mostly I preyed on Ristroans, but I didn't shy away from an easy N'naradin steamer when opportunity presented itself, which was often enough. I ended up with quite the reputation, compounded by my more recent business."

"What did you do in Valez'Mui, anyway?"

Ves glanced around. "Lots of things. One of them was making

delezine and shipping it up the Great Road to Fom and the Foreigner's District in Eheene."

"What's delezine?"

"Little rocks. Looks like salt. You smoke it, then spend the next two or three days awake and crazy, and most of that time looking for more delezine. Nasty shit. Illegal most places for a reason, but there's boatloads of tin to be made, and if I hadn't done it, someone else would have."

Pasha could only blink, dumbstruck. "Who are they?" he gestured toward the other two Ristroans watching them from the other side of the Pit.

"The two poor bastards I happened to be drinking with when I got caught. Never met them before then. The one with rocks in his head is named Fanalasasai, and the beard with a man attached to it is Telesandasari. Brothers or best friends or something. You could get away with calling them Fan and Tel if you ever get around to talking to them. They've been in Fom for a while. They know how foreigners feel about Ristroan names."

The two noted Pasha's attention, and Telesandasari gave another sardonic waive in his direction, but neither made any move to join him and Ves.

"As for your bastard of a general there," Ves went on, "He got here two days ago. Maybe one. Who can keep track? Someone tried to shank him with a splintered camel bone that first day, but the old man knows how to fight. They've left him alone since. Don't know his story. Must have been some fall from grace." He laughed, though the humor in the rumble sounded forced. "So to speak."

"They should have tried when he was sleeping," Pasha whispered, hatred boiling on his face.

"They did."

Pasha didn't respond, but he kept his eyes leveled at Mann, who was still leaning against the wall, eyes closed, with a small smirk etching a crooked line across his scruffy, grey face.

"Anyway," Ves said, "You might want to talk to him before you try to stab him. He won't have what he took from you here with him, but he might know what it was and where it is."

Mann seemed to sense their attention and turned toward them. After a moment's contemplation, his eyes widened in surprise, but he made no move to stand.

Pasha glanced at Ves. "How long have I been here?"

"Not long enough for me to notice until now. Last batch got dumped in here less than an hour ago." He nodded towards the fops huddled together, watching. "Must have been with them. Guess you were sleeping off whatever they shot you up with."

Pasha, grinding his teeth, hesitated, then stood to saunter over to where Mann sat. His leg had gone numb where he had hunkered on it talking to Ves, and the resulting limp robbed him of whatever dramatic effect he'd been hoping for. After hovering a minute while Mann stared up at him with a look of resignation in his eyes, Pasha squatted next to the old man, reluctant to meet his gaze.

"Didn't expect to see you here," Mann said. "Suspect you want to kill me. I'll make it easy for you if that makes a difference."

Pasha squeezed his eyes closed, trying to hide his surprise at Mann's demeanor, and said, "So you know who I am?"

"No. But I recognize you. I remember seeing you that night. In the lake with a girl."

"My sister." Pasha fought down a sudden well of sadness and didn't let himself say anything else.

Mann nodded. "I thought so. I hope she's well."

Pasha swallowed. "I don't know."

"Sorry to hear that."

Pasha hated the sincerity in the general's voice and tried not to let it sway him.

"So I guess you followed me," Mann went on before Pasha could think of anything to say.

Pasha nodded.

"I knew. I hoped, anyway, on the way back, that it wouldn't be the end of your people. You know, I'm old, and most of my life is one long series of regrets, but what happened in the Black Wall is the one that haunts me. I suspect it will until my last breath, which I suppose is near enough. Except for killing that sniveling fuck Vimr," he added. "That might have been the most useful thing I've ever done, even if it landed me in here."

Pasha thought back to that fire-lit night in the valley when he and Anna had watched the general stab the little round man in the back with a blackvine knife before riding away. "He saw us, and you killed him."

Mann shook his head. "I didn't save you if that's what you're thinking. I mean, maybe I did, you and your sister, but the rest of what happened in that valley... no, I didn't save anyone."

"What happened?" Pasha asked. "You took something from the Tomb. Why? It's why you were there, right? You got what you went for."

Mann laughed, but his expression was bleak. "Like I said, a life of regret. You, what? Want to know about it before you kill me?"

Pasha met Mann's gaze. "What happened to... whatever you took? I need to get it back. I need to know why you came all the way across the world to take it. And then, yes, I'll get it back. And kill you."

Mann nodded. "Fair enough," he said. "You want to know everything? Maybe I should start at the end and work backwards, so if you decide to finish me off before I'm done talking, you'll still know what I know about those goddamned glass rods a thousand men died to get."

Pasha nodded, hating how easy Mann was trying to make it for him.

"What about him?" Mann asked, gesturing with his head behind Pasha.

Pasha turned around to see Ves hovering over his shoulder, listening. "He's with me."

Mann shrugged and told his tale.

Mann had drawled on into the evening, his voice barely above a whisper to keep it from carrying to anyone else. Both Ves and Pasha had been too enraptured to find a reason to interrupt.

"After all I'd been through on the way there, my trip home seemed like the easiest thing I'd ever done." Mann's voice grew hoarse as he went on, and his audience of two needed to move closer to hear the conclusion.

"I paid everything left in the expedition coffers to make sure the caravan we'd attached ourselves to wouldn't screw us over. I still didn't trust the pasty, beady-eyed Artisan who'd said she was in charge, but she was true to her word."

"Once in the city, I told my men they were dismissed if they wanted to be. As far as I was concerned, they'd earned their place in whatever level of Heaven they wanted, whatever they did with the rest of their lives, but only a handful walked away. The rest piled onto the barges I requisitioned for the trip up the Great Road. The Arch Bishop hadn't been specific about the return trip, and I didn't care anymore how many people learned of our expedition who didn't know of it already.

"I reported to the consulate in Great Spring, but I couldn't guess the extent of the fissure between Fom and Tyrsh. There's always been tension there, old as the Church itself. But war? I didn't think it possible.

"I should have been suspicious when I received the sealed missive to leave everything I found in the valley with the Prelate in Great Spring." Mann shifted where he leaned against the cold, weeping stones of the Pit. "After all the Arch Bishop had done to secure those goddamned prisms, or whatever they were, I should have known he wouldn't just order me to leave them at the embassy in a neutral state unless there was something very wrong. To be honest, I was so happy to get rid of them. I didn't let myself ask any questions."

"Wait," Pasha said. "You left them in Great Spring? With whom?"

Mann shrugged. "The Prelate. Sy N'dal. They're not there anymore, though." He shrugged again. "I don't know where they went, after. I assume Tyrsh, though with everything going on, and now finding you here, I can't be sure about anything. I'm sorry I didn't ask."

"This 'Prelate,'" Pasha pushed, his voice tense, "What did she look like?"

"Mm. I don't know. Middle-aged. Blond hair, brown eyes."

"Black and gold robes?" Pasha asked. "White sword?"

Mann nodded. "That sounds right. The sword comes with being a Prelate. Everyone over lay priest and under Arch Bishop wears robes like that, if they're part of the Church of Tyrsh and not under the Grace. Why? You meet her?"

Pasha was squeezing his hands together, not looking at Mann or anyone else. "You didn't hear?" His voice was soft. "I killed her. I didn't know. She wanted to arrest us. I was so close." He trailed off.

Mann studied Pasha a long time. "Maybe. I doubt she had them in her pocket, though. They would have been gone by then. The Arch Bishop didn't wait around to send someone for them, I'm sure, what with all the trouble. After I heard about the war, I assumed that was why he wanted me to leave them there. Otherwise, the Grace would have them now."

Pasha looked at Mann again. "Why are you here? The Pit, I mean? For killing that other man—Vimr, you called him? Or for working for the Arch Bishop?"

Mann laughed. "The first one. Throwing me in here for working for the Arch Bishop would make too much sense. No, I got tossed in the Pit to die because Captain Rohm, the only goddamned officer I trusted, ratted me out for killing the Cardinal."

Ves, blinked. "But he was the Bishop's man, right? Why should you get punished for killing someone she'd want dead, anyway?"

"It was the betrayal, she said. A crime under Heaven. Vimr, for all his failings, was still written in the Highest Book. I sent him to the Heaven of Light without anyone asking me to. Like I said, throwing me in here for working for the Arch Bishop made too much sense."

Pasha was silent for a while, though he never took his eyes off Mann. "Why you?" He asked at last. "I mean, why does everyone seem to know who you are? When everyone talked about how you were this famous leader, I didn't expect, I don't know. You."

Mann smiled. "You didn't expect a tired old man?" He shook his head. "Public relations, I guess."

Ves interjected. "You brokered peace with the upstart karakh tribes. And wiped out the river pirates raiding every other barge along the Upper Great Road, what was it, twenty years ago?"

Mann nodded. "And wiped out the town of N'zahid when I did it. That didn't win me a lot of friends with the big merchant families."

Ves grunted. "That was one of those merchant collectives on the Upper Delta, wasn't it? Never made it that far north back in my sea faring days, but no, I don't suspect you made many friends. Good way of getting rid of pirates though—burn down everything of value so they don't have anything to steal."

"That wasn't what happened." Mann retorted, his voice soft, and left it at that.

Ves grunted again.

Mann turned back to Pasha. "A few things, I suppose. A disastrous negotiation with some upstart desert tribes. Nothing I could have done, looking back, but they still sent me there with five hundred men, four hundred of whom found Heaven before they made it back across the Yellow Desert. I suspect they sent me knowing it would go wrong. Needed to make a show of trying to restore the flock. I was there so they could have someone to blame when it didn't work. The Church is infallible, you know, but I'm not. That's why they kept me around. Someone to blame. Not that that kept me from blaming myself, too. Not for a long time."

Pasha found he had nothing to say through the conflagration of mixed emotions that raged inside him.

Ves sighed and stood. "I hate this fucking country," he announced. "No matter who's in charge. Going to see about getting us out of here." He wandered off toward the group of Ristroans, who'd were still gathered on the far side of the cistern, watching.

At that moment, the din from the people above grew more fevered, and Pasha looked up to see the crowd of silhouetted figures growing. Insults echoed down with a rain of debris.

Ves, with the other Ristroans following behind him, walked back over to where Pasha stood at the wall, staring up at the spectacle. Mann watched with a sad look on his face.

The smattering of refuse turned into a rain. Rotten meat, chicken bones, and slimy bread crusts came pouring down in a torrent of urine and feces to splatter around the drain. Laughter and hoots, echoes distorted by the curved walls, haunted the room, loud enough that the prisoners needed to shout to be heard over them.

The pit came alive as everyone except the fops and Pasha's group rushed to the center and began scavenging and fighting over bits of garbage.

"Oh, God," Pasha said.

His words were to himself, but Ves nodded. "Fom. City of games. Karakh arenas, dog races, public executions. Those things take a lot of tin. Throwing shit at the prisoners in the Pit and watching them eat it, that's free."

Pasha stared at the frenzy in the center of the room. "How can people live on that?"

Ves looked at him out of the corner of his eye. "They don't. But they try anyway. I hear you're older than you look. You've never been hungry before? *Really* hungry?"

Pasha didn't look away from the scene playing out around the drain. "No. I guess not."

Ves nodded toward the group of fops, who were watching with disgust. "Neither have they. After they've been here a few days, a week, they'll be in there, too. And us. And that'll be the end of it."

Pasha tore his gaze away to give Ves a questioning look.

"It is not only shit and piss they throw down, like that wouldn't kill us eventually. Some of it is poisoned. Some do-gooders, or maybe it's the worst of them, even throw down real food. It's hard to tell the difference between a poisoned apple and a good one."

Ves's rictus smile was anything but reassuring. "Don't worry. We'll be out of here before then. Probably."

A couple of the men crouching near the now-dwindling stream of garbage moaned and fell over, one vomiting a long stream of black bile before continuing to heave his empty stomach and groan in pain. A vulgar cheer rolled from above.

"Some die every time," Mann said. "When I got tossed in here, I don't know, two days ago, maybe? There were twenty-five, thirty down here." He let out a dry, humorless bark. "They'll need to toss some more people in soon, or the crowd won't have much of a show." He shrugged. The din from above began to fade, or Pasha didn't think he would have heard him. "They always do."

Pasha and Ves both looked at Mann, but it didn't look like anything else was forthcoming. Pasha turned back to Ves and said, "How do you think we'll get out of here?"

Ves looked around the room a moment, then asked, "You see my crew anywhere down here? It's because they're not. They're up there." He pointed up to the distant grates. "And they always think of something."

25

THE WRONG SIBLING

Syrina searched for Pasha with growing desperation. She'd been delayed for weeks in Ristro. Smugglers had canceled their runs because of the N'naradin civil war. Most of the fighting so far had been limited to the Sea of N'narad, blocking Ristro's shipping routes, so she needed to take a schooner around the west coast of the Isle of N'narad to Maresg, and then a camel train to the N'naradin border. From there, she caught one of the frequent dirigibles along the coast to Fom.

The ship was faster, but the route was four times as long. Combined with the slow pace of the camels, she arrived in Fom over six weeks later than she'd planned. She headed straight from the airship tower across the city through the far-reaching suburbs northeast of the Lip, to where the docks lined the southern branch of the Upper Great Road.

There, she found the Flowered Calf tarnished but intact from its trip across the continent. Abandoned.

It was easy for Syrina to access the harbor records. The barge had docked two months earlier with captain and crew, and no registered passengers. Her concern grew. No one had returned since the day it had docked, at least as far as the Great Road Port Authority was concerned. The port fees had been paid to the end of that month, after which it was slated for scrap.

She could trust Ves to do whatever the hell he pleased, but Pasha and Anna were supposed to wait, and the voice in her head hadn't been forthcoming with encouragement about why they hadn't arrived at all.

There was a chance they hadn't been registered out of caution, grew tired of waiting, and sneaked into the city. Despite the heightened security due to the war, she had no doubt they were capable of it. But in a city as big as Fom, she had nothing to go on except the flowery ship, so she hung around the bars that ringed the docks. She thought at least Ves would turn up for his boat before the Port Authority junked it, so she could ask him what had gone wrong.

It was with a mix of relief and terror that Syrina saw Anna appear one afternoon in the doorway of the Pilfered Cat, a bar built out of warped driftwood, held together by the collective despair of its occupants.

Syrina was half-drunk and wearing the face of a nameless, forgettable female stevedore, a fact the voice needed to remind her of when she bolted up and began staggering in a loose run towards Anna.

She slowed her gait to a fast amble to where Anna hesitated in the doorway, silhouetted by the gloomy Fom daylight.

"Looking for someone?" Syrina said in N'naradin with a gravelly voice.

Anna eyed her before turning away to scan the half-empty room. "Not you."

Syrina smiled. Ves had at least done a passable job teaching them N'naradin.

"You sure?" Syrina asked, this time in Anna's native tongue.

Anna blinked, head whipping around to take in the nondescript woman's slanted green eyes, her own widening.

"You." She managed.

Syrina nodded.

"Did you find Pasha?" Anna's voice was a whisper.

Syrina's heart sank, and she wondered about the hesitation in Anna's voice.

Something's happened, the voice pointed out.

Syrina wanted to punch it for stating the obvious, but before she could respond with something snarky it added, *She feels guilty.*

Syrina fought down her own swarming emotions to study Anna's face like she should have from the start, and saw the voice was right. Her eyes were red and rimmed with black circles, and the light behind them was haunted.

"Come on," Syrina said. "Let's go somewhere we can talk."

They ended up back on the Flowered Calf where, Syrina reasoned, they would only be interrupted by someone they were looking for.

"We fought," was all Anna said after they'd settled in their old cabin.

Syrina sighed. She still wore the grungy stevedore face, but her voice was her own. "Where did you leave him?"

Anna swallowed. "I was sure he'd follow me. We've always fought. I always leave. He used to always follow. Since we were kids. When I saw he didn't, I was stubborn. It made me mad, I guess, that he hadn't followed me in Valez'Mui, either. Then some refugees from Myrion's Revenge found me, and I couldn't go back even though I wanted to. I would've died if they hadn't found me. I couldn't go back. No food. No water. So I went with them." Her words came out in a stream, tears on her face. "I would have died," she whispered again.

Syrina's throat caught, but she asked again, "Where, Anna?"

"In the mountains. Somewhere between here and Myrion's Revenge. There was an intersection. The only one on the whole goddamned road. He wanted to go the wrong way. I was sure it was the wrong way." Anna wiped at her face with her hands.

Syrina forced her voice to be calm. "I know the place. I think so, from all the maps Ormo forced me to study. The other road goes to Fom, too. It goes back to the Great Road and then follows it the long way around. You came through the vineyards, right? On the south side of the city. Where they grow grapes?"

Anna hesitated, then nodded.

"Pasha's road was longer, but safer. It gets to Fom on the north side, not far from here."

"I know," said Anna. "I figured that out. I just came back from there. I stole supplies and walked up the road for almost a week, looking for him. His body. I went to where I left, but I didn't find him.

Syrina pressed her lips together. "If you didn't find a body, he didn't die. Not up there. No animals in those mountains to drag a corpse away, and travelers would have taken his stuff and left him."

"But he never made it to the boat," Anna protested. "It was the first place I checked. I sneaked in at night. Nobody had been here in a while."

"No," Syrina agreed.

"So we can look for him? You'll help me, right?" Sudden hope bloomed in Anna's eyes.

This one needs to go to Ormo, the voice interjected, surprising Syrina to momentary silence.

Think about it, it went on. *If you find Pasha, he's never going to let you deliver his sister to anyone, but you have to deliver at least one of them, right? To keep up appearances and to see what he can learn. About us. There's a connection between you and them, and if it's obvious to me, it's obvious to you. Besides, the Astrologer asked you to.*

You won't give him Pasha. Neither of us want that. So unless you want to give up and settle down on a farm somewhere with him and his little sister who doesn't even like you, now might be your only chance to keep doing what you've been trying to do since the first time you went to Ristro.

"Syrina?" Doubt and suspicion danced on Anna's face.

She only nodded and muttered in Skald, eyes unfocused, "So, lie?"

You're a Kalis. Your life is a lie.

Syrina closed her eyes against the cloud of guilt that rose in the pit of her stomach. "Yeah, Anna, sorry. Just thinking out loud. Can I ask you something?"

Anna gave a reluctant nod.

"If Pasha made it to Fom—and I think he did—would you trust him to survive here on his own for a while?"

"Yes." There was doubt and confusion still written on Anna's face, but no hesitation in her answer. "He's stubborn, but he's cautious. Most of the time." She gave Syrina a meaningful look that the Kalis pretended not to notice. "But why? Are you saying we can't look for him?"

"I want to find him too. You can't know how bad. But I don't know how. There's six million people in this city, Anna. If he doesn't come to the Flowered Calf, I don't know how I can find him. And if he hasn't come here by now, I don't think he will. He can't, or he won't. I can't sit here and wait to see if he'll show up. Not after what you told me. And if he does, we can leave a message for him to wait."

"Where are we going?" The buds of suspicion that had settled behind Anna's eyes bloomed.

"There's someone who can help us, but he's far from here. In Eheene. Where I'm from."

"If he's so far, how can he help us?"

"Because he has resources, contacts. Like you wouldn't believe. Look, Anna. I know you don't trust me. If I were you, I wouldn't trust me either. But whatever it is I feel for Pasha, it might be new, but it *is* real. I need you to at least trust me that far. For Pasha's sake. I would never hurt him. Not ever. And I need your help."

"Why would someone like you need my help?"

"Because the guy that can help us, he's my boss. Ormo. I've mentioned him. But, well, we're not on the best of terms anymore. So maybe if you come, and you tell him about the valley—I mean everything, your culture, the blackvine, all of it—maybe he'll trust me again enough to use some of his resources to help us find Pasha. And Anna, his resources are *unfathomable.* If anyone on Eris can help us find your brother, it's him."

Anna was quiet a long time. "I'll just need to talk to him?"

"Tell him everything, Anna. Everything you know about where you're from and your people."

"Okay. I trust you. At least as far as Pasha goes. I'll come." She paused. "What about Ves?"

"Ves?" Syrina said, putting a smile on even as the black hole of guilt in her chest threatened to suck her inside-out. "That guy will outlive all of us. I hope he and Pasha are already together, and that's why we can't find them.

"Come on," Syrina pressed on before she could second guess herself, filling her voice with confidence she didn't feel. "We have a long way to go, and I want to see Pasha again at least as bad as you. Let's get out of here."

26

THE PIRATE'S PLAN

THE NEXT AFTERNOON ONE OF THE GATES BANGED OPEN. FOUR soldiers with heavy crossbows stomped through and took position on either side, eying the prisoners while seven blindfolded men stumbled in. Six other guards collected the corpses, contorted around the drain in the center of the room, and the bodies of the two women, pushed against the far wall. The door clanged shut.

A few hours later, the same thing happened from a different door, and nine more men were pushed in.

"Is it usually men?" Pasha asked.

Mann answered from where he crouched, coughing against the ooze-covered wall. They squatted together, mostly not talking. The other Ristroans hovered nearby.

"Almost always. Women don't fare well here. They need to do something pretty bad."

"What about them?" Pasha nodded at the door where the guards had filed out with the bodies. "What did they do?"

Mann shrugged. "They were dead when I got here. Murdered their children, maybe. Or kidnapped someone else's and cut off their legs to send them out begging. It happens. Like I said, it needs to be bad to end up here."

"Do they always come from different doors?" Ves asked, as Mann slid down again to curl against the wall, eyes closed, as if answering Pasha's questions had drained the last of his energy. Earlier, he'd lain like that for hours, and they thought he'd died until they saw his chest move with shallow breaths when they moved closer. Pasha had surprised himself with his reaction upon thinking the general dead. It was a mix of relief and sorrow, but the relief stemmed from the thought that he wouldn't need to kill him if he was already dead and a resolution to the tempest of conflicting emotions.

Mann struggled to sit up again, a wracking cough tearing through his body before he could answer. "I've only been here a day longer than you. More or less."

He paused and slumped again, but then sighed and began to talk, eyes closed. "They use different doors, in case anyone tries to escape, so no one knows which goes where. Some go out, some go to tunnels the high tide floods every ten hours. Some get choked with steam every fifteen minutes, scalding anyone in them down to their bones. The rest lead to a maze of corridors and doorways so vast you'd never find your way out. Of course, I don't know if any of that is true, but it's what people say."

He opened his eyes and blinked up at Pasha. "If you're still planning on killing me, best do it in my sleep. Just in case I have any last-minute second thoughts and try to stop you. And you'd better hurry, or the Pit is going to do it for you."

Pasha blinked down at the old man for a moment, torn, but Mann had closed his eyes again, and his breath became shallow and even. He turned back to Ves, who was smiling.

"How come you're so happy all the time?" Pasha asked, annoyed. "You know how we're getting out of here?"

Ves laughed a laugh Pasha was sure only existed to irritate him more, and said, "I told you, I have faith in my crew. The last two feedings, I've heard one call down. They haven't forgotten. But they'd better hurry. I'm getting hungry."

But another day went by, and Ves grew surly and disinterested in conversation, and Mann grew weaker, always sleeping or coughing. Pasha began to watch the rain of garbage, urine, and feces with a different kind of interest as his stomach knotted, and the only thing he had to fill it was bitter water licked from the walls.

The next morning, just as the spectacle of the feeding had begun, Ves started to laugh. He shouted something up in Ristroan, his booming voice echoing like drums around the cistern, paused, and laughed again, this time so hard he doubled over, hands on his knees. Pasha had listened for a response from above, but couldn't discern anything through the cacophony of jeers from above and the fighting below.

Ves regained his composure and sauntered to where Pasha stood, waving the other Ristroans over. He gave Pasha a cataclysmic slap on the back, still chuckling. "We leave tonight."

"But wait, how?" Pasha asked, rolling his shoulders against the burning ache that radiated from where Ves had hit him.

But Ves was already talking to the others in rapid Ristroan, voice quiet, swallowing back laughter.

At last, Ves spoke to Pasha again. "The guards search everyone who throws anything into the Pit. They dig through even the most disgusting chamber pots to make sure nothing comes down that could be used as a weapon against the guards.

"None of my people were aware of that, so the most obvious plan was thrown out before they could try. Hence the delay." He chuckled again, then cleared his throat, and forced a serious look on his face, betrayed by the creases around his mouth.

"But they noticed people were allowed to shit into the Pit

without inspection. It was another day while they gambled to see who had the honor of delivering unto me our means of escape."

"So." Pasha wasn't sure what to ask.

Ves nodded.

"What are they... sending down? I mean, it can't be very big, right?"

Ves grinned. "You'd be surprised. But there was quite the debate over who the bearer of this gift would be. As for what it is," he lowered his voice, though because he didn't want anyone to hear or for dramatic effect, Pasha didn't know. "A Ristroan grenado. One of the ones I'd planned to use to rescue you from Myrion's Revenge, as it turns out." He paused. "Seems you've been ending up in jail a lot since leaving Valez'Mui."

"A what?" Pasha had a decent grasp on N'naradin, but he didn't know the word.

"A bomb. A little one for throwing."

"Is that even possible?"

Ves answered with a shrug, his smile growing broader. "They say they've worked out a system. Something to help things along, as it were. I didn't ask for details."

"Well, okay, but isn't it dangerous? I mean..." Pasha trailed off, at a loss for words.

"I would think so, but, again, they think they have a system. Though they're not confident enough about it to attend tonight's feeding. Except the purveyor."

"How did they tell you all that? I couldn't hear anything."

Ves winked. "The Corsairs spend a lot of time on other people's ships. We can't trust that nobody will know Ristroan, unlikely though it may be. So there's a code, I guess you could call it. Whistles, clicks. Like a karakh. Combined with a few words in different languages here and there, it can convey quite a lot."

"All of that?" Pasha was incredulous.

"Well, some of it. The rest we'll call conjecture. It's got to be close to reality if I know my crew."

Pasha shook his head but decided to change the subject. "Then what? According to Mann, we can't know what door to go through, even if you can blast it open."

Ves sighed and looked over to where Mann slumped, unconscious. "I suppose that's why we'll bring him along. He might know a way if he lives long enough."

"Might?" Pasha's voice was high with exasperation, with a good mix of terror thrown in. "That's it? It's never going to work."

"Could be. You can stay here, fighting over rotten, shit-encrusted food for the entertainment of strangers until you die gagging on the floor, and someone drags you out and throws you into the sea. Because that, my friend, is your other option. Anyway, you have until tonight to decide." He sat down, back against the wall, eyes closed, smiling.

Pasha joined Ves near the center of the Pit that evening, curiosity overriding his worry about all the things that were, he was sure, about to go wrong. Ves had been right. Better to die here, blown to chunks by a bomb dropped out of a pirate's ass, than be reduced to an animal before dying anyway.

The shouts and jeers began, and the most desperate of the scavengers moved in, although none seemed desperate enough to face Ves, and he and Pasha had one edge of the waiting circle of prisoners to themselves.

"How will know what's for you?" Pasha asked.

Ves didn't look down from where he was peering up at the portal as if trying to pierce the gloom with force of will. "I think we'll know."

A moment later, they heard the first, echoing, screaming grunt tumble down from above. A woman's voice. Ves smiled. "Ah, poor Alishepishai. She always was bad at gambling. Too many tells."

One last bellowing, curse-filled grunt, and a second later something heavier than the normal stream of rotten trash streaked down and struck a one of the fops on the temple, knocking him face first into a heap of shit and rotten pork. A few moved toward the object but backed off with a growl from Ves, who pushed the unconscious man onto his back as he bent over to pick it up.

He sauntered back to Pasha and held it out for him to look at. The size of a clenched fist, egg-shaped and lumpy, made of white ceramic. Pasha found himself relieved it was smaller than he'd imagined. He wondered how Alishepishai had made her way through the crowd from wherever she'd first hidden it, but decided it was something he wouldn't be asking about.

"That?" He asked. "Is it big enough to blast through one of the doors?"

Ves shrugged, his demeanor blasé. "Who knows? Shall we ask your friend?" Ves nodded to where Mann lay in a fetal position against the wall, back to the room. He'd been mumbling to himself in and out of sleep, unresponsive. Pasha suspected he had a fever.

But as he approached, Mann stirred. "I think you're almost out of time. Better make up your mind," he rasped without turning from the wall. "About killing me, I mean." He coughed.

"We're getting out." Pasha paused. "You're coming with us. Or at least telling us which door will get us out of here."

Mann choked on his feeble laugh. "Didn't you believe me when I told you I didn't know where any of these doors go? Because I don't."

"There's nothing you can do to help us?" Pasha said, anger directed at his own hope more than the old man. "You saved us back in the valley. For what? So I can die with you here?"

That got Mann's attention, and he sat up with a slow groan and squinted up at Pasha. Filth from the Pit floor coated one side of his face. "What happened in your valley, it was wrong. My biggest regret, like I said." He hacked and spit something large and bloody off to the side where it hit the bars of a gate and stayed there. "A long lifetime. Almost over now, thank the Heavens."

"And now?"

Mann sighed. "I'm from the Lip, originally. Don't know if I ever told you that before. You probably don't even know what that means." He paused and nodded toward Ves, who had again moved up behind to listen. "But he does.

"The Lip is almost all tunnels, up and down and every which way. Not just under the north side of the city like most people think, but into the sewers in the older parts of town. Sometimes into forgotten parts of the Tidal Works. A kid in the Lip with a lot of time on his hands gets to know those tunnels."

He stopped long enough to clear his throat, force out a cough and another bloody glob, not as big as the last one, and continued. His voice bubbled. "Some of those tunnels went into cisterns like this one. Not nearly as big, not so many damn doors, but otherwise the same. Some of those were proper cisterns—held fresh water in the old city, but most were abandoned, replaced with the Tidal Works as the city grew and the Works with it. Those—no way out, except a maintenance door and a well at the top.

"Some of the others were built with the Tidal Works. To manage tides, storm surges, broken boilers, that sort of thing. They'd get the water out of the streets and the tunnels of the Works, then drain when things got back to normal. Most of those ended up abandoned, too. As time went on, the Tidal Works got more efficient, and they came up with better ways to control floodwater. They drained through the bottom, though, those runoff wells. Through a skinny grate that led to the sewers, or sometimes down to the deepest levels of the Works. Sometimes straight down all the way the sea water at low tide." Mann closed his eyes and hacked.

"A grate at the bottom of the room, huh?" Ves said, looking toward the pile of rotten refuse that surrounded the small drain.

Mann nodded. "I'd wager they locked that hole good when they turned this place into a prison. Not sure how you'd crack through it." He eyed Ves's girth. "Not sure you'd fit."

Ves smiled. "There's a solution to that."

"What?" Pasha asked.

"I'll go first. If I get stuck, no one else can leave without me." He winked at Pasha, gave his arm a friendly squeeze, and sauntered back over to the watching Ristroans.

Pasha looked down at Mann. "Are you coming with us? I mean, if this works? I won't kill you."

Mann looked up at Pasha a moment, then began struggling to get to his feet. After one final debate with himself, Pasha reached out a hand and helped him.

Mann nodded his thanks, his surprise plain in his rheumy eyes. "I guess if I'm dying anyway, I'd rather not die in this hole, given any choice about it."

"I wouldn't get too excited," Pasha said. "This is going to be a disaster."

27

GOING HOME

Syrina tried not to let Anna's wonder at Eheene get to her; tried not to think about what came next. Winter fire slashed the twilight in hues of green the evening they steamed into the docks at the Foreigners' District, mixing with the blue-white aura of naphtha light shining over the wall that separated the District from the city-proper.

The journey had been uneventful. Surprising, considering the turmoil that had enveloped the world south of Skalkaad. Syrina had dressed as a Skaald low merchant's daughter for the trip, run away to Fom, now going home because of the war. She told Anna it would explain both their destination and their wealth. To the few who'd asked, she said that her hand was the result of her ignorance—scalded to the bone by a steam vent less than a week after she'd arrived in the Crescent City.

They'd bought passage on a barge to the northern delta of the Great Road. From there, Syrina paid a fisherman six hundred Three-Sides to carry them across the Sea of Skalkaad, into the muddy dregs of the Foreigners' District. There, they'd heard the Grace had gained control of the whole of the Great Road, and in response, Tyrsh had blockaded the northern delta along with the Bowl of Fom. Any smugglers caught trying to dock at the Lip were sunk, and now even Ristroan pirates avoided the region. There was a rumor that a few of the Tyrsh flagships had broken off from the main force long enough to demolish the crude breakwater protecting the Lip from the worst of the tides, but Syrina had no idea if it was true or not. There was one even more unbelievable story of a lone steamer running the main blockade across the Port of Fom, sinking several Tyrsh navy ships before blowing itself up in the Sea of N'narad.

The voice had been silent, but she could feel its presence in the back of her mind like someone watching, hovering wherever she wasn't looking. Since it had said its piece about handing Anna over to Ormo, it hadn't had much to say, but Syrina knew it was much less torn about it than she was.

Anna didn't think much of the drab, filthy Foreigners' District, which to her seemed not much different than the worst sections of Fom. But her eyes had widened as they'd passed through to Eheene after Syrina flashed the gate guards some papers that kept them from asking questions.

The neat, even lanes of the marble city sprawled, glittering in the green winter fire and the violet light bulging on the south-eastern horizon from the Eye that hadn't yet risen. The ubiquitous upturned hands holding their flames, ranging from abstract and angular to lifelike, flickered blue or white over doors of marble and brass, or heavy wood, or, in a few cases, even iron.

Anna stared, absorbing it all, as speechless as the voice in Syrina's head.

As they approached the gates of the Syndicate Palace, though, with its black and white edifice looming a block ahead, unlit by flame, the voice spoke.

Stop regretting what we knew would need to happen the moment you saw these two come out of the Wall. You want answers? I want answers. This is how we get answers.

Syrina sighed and muttered under her breath in Skald with a

glance over at Anna, who seemed too engrossed in her own thoughts to notice. "You already said that. I'm not disagreeing with you, am I? It doesn't mean I need to like it."

I just thought, this being as close as we've come to getting what we want since that night in the alley in Fom, you'd be a little more enthusiastic.

Syrina bit her tongue and said nothing. That night in the alley in Fom. When Triglav had been killed by a crossbow bolt she could have stopped, and a voice in her head had replaced the one thing she'd ever loved.

No. That wasn't true. The owl hadn't been the one thing. Before him had been Ormo. And now there was Pasha.

Her mind turned back to Anna as they approached the looming black iron gate of the Syndicate Palace, set with its white spiral, flickering turquoise with the dueling lights of the sky.

It opened on hidden hinges as they neared, and swung closed behind them as they stepped into the courtyard. Guards walked the parapets and flanked either side of the gate, watching.

"I guess Ormo is expecting us," Syrina said, as unfamiliar discomfort washed over her.

"How?" Anna whispered, her eyes on the sprawling crescent-shaped palace before them, the fifteen spires of the High Merchants silhouetted by the writhing light of the winter fire, now laced with blue and purple along with the green, mirroring the rising Eye. The flagstones of the courtyard were, like the rest of Eheene, black and white marble, laid out in another stylized eight-armed spiral. The center was a fountain of stone so white it glowed, With fifteen right hands at the top of fifteen long arms. Their palms were upturned, and from them spilled thin streams of water that tinkled into the shallow pool below.

"The gate. At the Foreigner's District," Syrina answered, wondering if she was right. "The documents I showed them included a message to notify Ormo. Not that anything told them it was me. Just that it was someone he would want to talk to."

"Does this happen every time you come back?" Anna asked as Syrina led her toward Ormo's Tower and his Hall beneath it.

Syrina shook her head. "This is the first time I've used the gate. I always just come in, well, as myself. Without company. The guards never knew I was there."

Anna frowned, but she nodded, her eyes still on the scene around her as they walked unchallenged into the palace.

Syrina felt a visceral loathing as she stepped onto the chirping obsidian floor and saw Ormo perched atop his dais at the end of the vast room. She hadn't seen him since the day he'd told her about Mann and the N'naradin plan to scale the Black Wall. Over a year ago. An eternity. Then, she realized now, she'd still harbored some vague misgivings, but time had erased any doubt about how she felt. Time and Pasha.

He doesn't know how much we hate him, the voice reminded her. *At least we'd better hope he doesn't. Try not to give it away.*

Syrina didn't risk an answer but swallowed and said, "Ma'is Ormo. I'm glad you knew I was coming. It's been a long time."

She held her breath at the lack of his usual cordial welcome, but as she neared where he sat, he stood and said, "Indeed. I didn't recognize you dressed so. When last we spoke, I thought you at the peak of your abilities. Your skills have improved beyond what I thought possible. I have missed you. And you have brought a friend, I see."

Syrina breathed a silent sigh of relief at his tone, even as she reminded herself it didn't mean anything. She looked over her shoulder at Anna, who hovered half way to the dais, brimming with uncertainty.

"Yes," Syrina said, gesturing at Anna to come closer. "This is Anna. She comes from a valley, hidden within the Black Wall since the Age of Ashes." She turned back to Ormo to give him a meaningful look, much easier to do wearing a face on top of her own, and she saw his eyebrows arch, enough to be noticeable in the deep shadows under the hood and the geometric black and white pattern on his face.

"I see," he said. "A special friend, indeed."

He turned to Anna and said in N'naradin, "You are from a very unique place, Anna from the Wall. Can you tell me about yourself?"

Anna glanced at Syrina, who gave her an encouraging nod, swallowing another surge of regret. "Yes. I'll tell you everything you want to know."

"I'm sure you will," Ormo said, a smile in his voice. "Come, Syrina. I'd like you to join us, too. I am sure things will come to light that will interest you. And I may need your assistance."

"Where are we going?" Syrina asked before she could stop herself. She felt the voice wince at the insubordination.

Ormo seemed indifferent. "My laboratory. Yes, that's the one," he added when he noticed Syrina's glance at his dais and the chamber she knew hid beneath it. "The place where Kalis are made."

Syrina didn't bother hiding her surprise and he let out a chuckle she was sure wasn't real. "Yes. I failed to mention that the last time you were there, but that was under much less fortunate circumstances, as I am sure you remember."

He turned and shuffled to the back of his dais, his feet twittering across the obsidian floor like a flock of tiny birds.

"Syrina?" Anna asked in the valley tongue. "Where are we going? You said he wanted to ask me about the valley. Why can't we do it here?"

Syrina swallowed. "It's fine, Anna. He's eccentric. We need to go with him, so he'll trust us enough to help find Pasha. Come on. He's not the kind of guy who'll wait." She put her hand on Anna's back and led her to where Ormo stood, holding the door, a sudden, almost overwhelming fear rising in her chest.

The voice said nothing.

28

BROKEN BONES

The blast left Pasha's ears ringing, and all else muffled to silence, even crouched with his face against the wall and hands pressed to his ears. Shouts welled from the hole above from a vast distance. Through watering eyes, he saw most of the other prisoners, unprepared for the explosion, lying about the cistern, writhing in shock or unmoving.

Ves, the other Ristroans, and Mann all recovered faster than Pasha, and Ves grabbed him by the arm and shoved him towards the smoking hole in the center of the room. Anything the pirate or anyone else might have said was lost to the pounding that echoed through Pasha's head.

True to his word, Ves heaved himself down first, his mouth implying that he was screaming curses.

Pasha looked down the hole, wiping at the tears streaming from his eyes. The walls of the shaft were thick with wet, moldering sewage, which at least made an efficient lubricant. Ves's huge body scraped against all four walls of the shaft. It looked like notches that once served as a ladder had been carved in the ancient stone, but they had been filled by the drip of waste. The pirate didn't use them in any case, other than as leverage he could use to push his way downward an arm's length at a time, spluttering and cursing.

Forty hands down, Ves stopped and wiggled as if stuck. He called up something to Pasha, lost to the tinnitus, and then dropped, disappearing in darkness.

Pasha felt a rough hand shove him into the hole. "You're next," Tel shouted over the endless tone roiling through Pasha's head.

Better than dying here. Pasha repeated the mantra to himself as he eased into the hole, fingers slipping, then finding purchase on the foul stone ladder. He was glad Ves's mass had scraped the walls clean and scooped the largest chunks out of the groves he could use to navigate down.

It was too narrow to see anything but glimpses of the black void beneath him, so when he edged his foot down to the next notch and found nothing but air, his fingers lost their hold. He plummeted into darkness.

He fell twenty hands into greasy, cold water, chest deep and rushing. The floor underneath was slick with slime, and he lost his footing and fell face-first into the black water. He groped and slipped, trying to find purchase in growing panic, when he felt a huge hand grasp him and drag him upright. He leaned against Ves, spluttering, when a splash behind him announced Mann's arrival.

Pasha felt the old man's weak fingers grabbing at him, and he reached down to pull him up.

There was another enormous splash that threatened to knock Pasha and Mann over where they stood, braced against the current, and a baritone cry of pain. A second later, Ves hauled Tel from the flood with one hand. The man's face was contorted in agony. He coughed through a frenzy of curses.

"They fucking got him," he shouted at no one in particular. "The fuckers got Fanalasasai! Just as I was going in. They tried to grab me, but I jumped. Fuck!"

Pasha was surprised to see what looked like genuine sympathy in

Ves's eyes, but all the big pirate said was, "Come on. We have to get going, or they'll grab us, too."

The torrent was too strong to fight, so without discussion, they started down the tunnel with the current, holding onto each other to keep from slipping on the treacherous floor, running their other hands along the slimy walls to navigate in the pitch black. Tel couldn't put any weight on his ankle, so he hopped, clinging to Ves.

"At least the water is pushing us towards the docks," Ves said, shouting over the rushing water and the ringing in their ears.

"Unless the tide is coming in," Mann observed.

Ves grunted, and they trudged in silence after that.

Before long, they realized that Mann was right—the water was rising. They felt regular side passages on either side as they half-staggered, half-swam along, but the water flooding out of them made exploration impossible. It took all of their dwindling energy to stay upright in the drink, now almost to their shoulders. No one tried to talk. The only sounds were the rush of the water and the occasional spitting and spluttering when someone slipped and coughed up what they'd inhaled, salty and rancid.

As the tide reached his chin, Pasha wondered if it really would be better to die here in the blackness, rather than in the Pit above.

There was a sudden grunt in front of him just as his feet left the slick floor. He began to tread water, his hair scraping the slimy ceiling. A second later, the current pushed him into Ves and Tel. Mann, coughing, drifted into him.

Again, Pasha felt Ves's big hand grab his arm. "Up, you miserable sons-of-bitches," Ves yelled. "We've been going across when we should have been looking up! Now grab on! I can't hold both you and Tel forever."

"Quit your bitching," came Tel's voice from somewhere above Ves. "Don't need my ankle for this. Stop pushing me and grab the others."

Ves guided Pasha's arm into the hole in the ceiling where he dangled, and a carved notch that felt the same as those they'd used to climb down from the Pit.

Pasha, too weak to climb with just his arms, grabbed the groove with his other hand and dangle there, the swirling flood pulling at his waist and legs.

He heard Ves grunt and felt him straining in the tight space, and he sensed Mann being guided to an identical rung carved into the stone opposite him.

"Can you climb, old man?" Ves shouted to Mann, who could only answer with a stream of hacking coughs.

Ves swore, and Pasha felt Ves shift as he dragged Mann upward.

Pasha realized he wasn't going to get any help, so, shoulders burning, he began to drag himself up the black, vertical shaft. After a few rungs, the walls became less slick, and after a few more, they became rough and dry. Once his feet found purchase, he stopped, leaning against the opposite wall with his feet braced on the ladder, trying to rest his burning arms. He was shaking with hunger. Above, he could sense Mann and Ves, but after a minute, he heard them climbing, and Ves called down, "Come on. There's a door. Let's get the fuck out of this reeking shit hole."

The door was locked but it was made of moldering wood, and Ves squeezed past Tel, braced his back and arms against three sides of the shaft, and kicked it hard with both feet. The door crumbled. An even, yellow light poured from the opening, making them all blink and squint after the blackness of the drainage tunnel and the dimness of the Pit before.

They dragged themselves in one at a time. Ves went first, before reaching down and helping the others. They found themselves in a stone tunnel filled with machinery, pipes, levers, and gauges, lit with a series of yellow orbs strung along the low ceiling. The floor was rough rock, covered by uneven wooden planks, better maintained than the door had been. It was hot, and Pasha could feel dense humidity roll over him, even before he'd pulled himself into the passage.

They were coated in thick, black algae.

"This stuff is—" Tel began, scraping at his arms in disgust, seated with his back against a row of pipes, when shouting erupted from their left, followed by the sound of running footsteps clattering on the wooden floor.

"Hey," a woman's voice called, as a trio of people rounded an intersection a hundred hands down from where Pasha, Mann, and Ves stood flanking the broken door. The word was in N'naradin, but it carried an unfamiliar accent. "You can't be down here. Where the hell did you come from?"

The question turned into a rhetorical one as the group approached, and she saw the shattered exit to the sewer. Two men stood a little behind her, one much older than the other. All three were coated in grease. They wore matching shirts, red under the filth and oil, that bore the Sun-and-Moon motif of Fom in yellow on the breasts. The woman had dark skin, and her hair was cut short, black under the dirt.

Mann coughed and stepped forward, pushing past Pasha. "Tidal Works maintenance, aye?" He asked and spit a bloody ball of something into the gaping doorway and down the shaft.

"That's right," the woman said, filled with self-importance. "And you can't be here." She eyed Ves, brow furrowed. "What you doing climbing out of the tunnels?"

Pasha looked at his companions. Mann, covered in black filth, looked bony, pale and withered, while Ves was the opposite in every visible way—hulking, dark under the slime, though the filth concealed the gems embedded in his skull. On the floor behind them, Tel sat, still scraping the algae from his arms and face. His right leg stretched in front of him, wet pant leg pulled up. The ankle was swollen to half the size of his foot, the dark skin mottled purple and black.

What, Pasha wondered, could their excuse be?

"Garlon," the woman said after ten seconds of silence, her

nervous eyes never leaving Ves. "Go report this and bring help. These guys are skulkers from the Lip or worse."

Ves turned back to Mann as if to say something, then wheeled just as the younger man named Garlon turned back the way they'd come, and slammed his full mass into the woman. She careened into the older man. Without stopping, Ves charged into Garlon, who had half turned in surprise before Ves hit him. The young man's turn made him fall crooked, and Pasha heard a pop as his knee twisted at an impossible angle. He cried out as Ves fell on top of him. The pirate clambered to his feet.

"Come on, you dumb cunts!" Ves bellowed, as he dragged Tel up. Without checking to see if anyone was following, he ran down the passage, carrying the other Ristroan over his shoulder. The woman and the other man were still trying to untangle themselves where they'd fallen.

Pasha and Mann hurried behind Ves into the hissing, clanging, steam-filled maze of the Tidal Works.

They fled through the tunnels, turning this way and that, with no plan other than to lose their pursuers and avoid any more. Twice, they stumbled into groups of workers without warning, but both times Ves bowled them over before they could ask questions. He led the others up and down corridors and stairways, and then down a rusty iron ladder to a corridor where the glow globes were sparse, and only a few were lit at all. The area seemed, at least for the time-being, unoccupied.

They found an alcove lined on two sides with an array of ceramic vertical pipes that hissed and ticked with heat, and slumped to rest, gasping and shaking against the crumbling, red-brick wall at the back. Broken pipes and valves lay strewn in one corner.

"Where are we?" Pasha gasped, after a hundred heartbeats, still trying to catch his breath and calm his shaking hands.

"Fuck if I know," Ves said, as he bent over Tel's leg to examine his ankle. "But I don't think anyone else knows, either. They'll be looking, though. We need to find an exit."

They both looked at Mann, who hunkered against the wall, coughing, head down, forearms on his knees.

He sensed their attention and looked up.

"I wish you would stop looking at me like that," he said, voice hoarse. "There's ten thousand spans of tunnels under Fom. What makes you think I'd know where we are?"

Pasha sighed and closed his eyes, leaning back, but Ves continued to glare.

Mann mirrored Pasha's sigh and stifled another cough in the crook of his elbow. When he finished, he said, "You know how I always got out when I ran around the tunnels as a kid? Keep going up."

Ves stared at the old man. "Fair enough, I guess."

He turned back to Tel's leg. "Bad break. Wish to shit Ashmarirai was here. He's the stitcher, not me. I'll set it as best I can and drag your ass out of here, but you're not going to walk right. Ever again, I'd wager."

Tel winced at that but nodded. "Do what you have to."

Ves sauntered over to the pile of broken ceramic pipes, selected a few, then went back to Tel and tore off the tattered, muddy pant leg at the knee. He tied it all into a passable splint. "It'll have to do," he said.

Tel nodded.

Ves got to his feet with a groan. After a second, Mann followed suit.

"Who put you in charge?" Mann asked Ves, as the Corsair hefted Tel under his arm. The bearded Ristroan was pale, his eyes focused on nothing.

Pasha answered, rising to his feet, still shaking. "I don't want to be in charge, and until a few days ago, you were everyone's worst enemy.

Tel's barely conscious. That doesn't leave anyone else, does it?" He followed Ves out of the chamber.

Mann smiled a little and followed, coughing into his sleeve.

It was as easy as Mann said it would be. Once in the disused section of the maze of machinery, it was a simple matter to avoid workers. Voices, shouts, laughter, and even too-regular banging and clanking sent them in the opposite direction. Mann pointed that there were many unmanned things in the tunnels that might make such noises, but it was better to be on the safe side. Exits to the city above peppered the Tidal Works, and they found their way up through an old, waist-high square door, so warped in its frame it was impossible to open until Ves, in a fit of desperation, smashed the thing off its hinges.

They emerged in a cold, fog-drenched alley adjacent to a packed street, less than a span from the port. It was nighttime, though judging by the amount of people moving about the main street, it wasn't late. The low clouds reflected the yellow light of the city and cast everything in a gold twilight. Ves eased Tel onto the damp flagstones. "What now?"

"Should we go back to the river?" Pasha asked, when Mann told them where they were.

Mann shook his head. "I don't think so. They're expecting us to take the river. Unless something changed while we were in the Pit, the port is under blockade—the Great Road is the only way out of the city. That and the roads, but those will be patrolled, too, if whoever took my place knows what they're doing. The Arch Bishop knows the only way to break Fom is to cut it off from everything else. The port is the big one, and he's got it. Now he'll be working on the only two roads worth a damn and the river. The fighting at the mouth of the Upper Great Road will be fierce by now, if it's come to that, and there's no reason to think it hasn't."

As Mann talked, they ventured into the bustling street and made their way west. Pasha realized he didn't need to worry about the three of them blending in. The blockade had trapped everyone in Fom, and people from all over Eris flooded its streets. No one paid the four of them any mind, even coated in crusts of black filth as they were.

"So then, what are we going to do?" Pasha asked Mann, who coughed and looked at Ves, eyebrows raised.

"We need money," Ves said. "And food. And somewhere to rest a bit. Preferably in that order." He nodded to Tel, who lolled against his shoulder. "After that, My crew has a ship at the port, so that's where we'll go." Ves smiled.

"You have a plan for the blockade?" Mann asked.

Ves shrugged. "I wouldn't call it a plan. You might call it... well, you might not call it a plan, anyway. But we'll come up with something that will make people remember us!" And with that declaration, he hefted Tel and trudged towards the wide band of inns and bars that surrounded the port. Pasha and Mann followed.

"I don't want anyone to remember me," Pasha said to Ves's back, but it didn't elicit a response.

"No," Mann agreed. "People remember me just fine, and look where that got me. I don't like this not-a-plan already."

Ves must have heard their conversation—they were only a pace behind him, but he ignored them. The teeming crowd thinned to almost nothing as they neared the shuttered port towers,

As the towers loomed into view through the drizzle three blocks away, Ves slowed. It was getting late, but the city behind them buzzed. Here, where in normal times the inns were full, and the crowds ebbed and flowed with the tides whatever time of day it was, things were quiet. A handful of wealthy-looking merchants wandered between bars, and most of the inns were half-full with people who had enough tin to keep paying for their rooms, but most of the deck hands and sailors that normally frequented the area had moved off to the Lip while they waited for a way out of Fom. City guards patrolled in groups of five and stood on every corner. None had taken notice of the escapees yet, but Pasha imagined it would only be a matter of time.

Ves and Tel limped ahead. Ves stuck to the shadows and alleys until they had a clear view of the port towers. The huge doors at their base were closed and barred, and a dozen guards with crossbows and bronze blades stood at each one.

"Are they looking for us?" Pasha asked.

"Could be," Ves said. "Wasn't expecting all this, anyway."

But Mann was shaking his head. "I doubt they're here for us. There's plenty of Tyrsh loyalists in the city. I'm surprised they haven't already done more damage. Or, maybe they have. Not something the Grace would advertise, I guess." He coughed into his sleeve.

"Probably," he continued after a minute, "they're worried about some of them going down to the water and causing mischief. Or maybe the Grace has a plan to break the blockade, and whoever is leading the charge doesn't want to be interrupted."

Ves frowned. "It doesn't matter why they're here."

"No," Mann agreed. "It doesn't."

"Is there another way down?"

"It will all be guarded at least as well," Mann frowned. "They're worried about someone sneaking in from the blockade, too."

Ves was quiet a moment. "I'm goddamn hungry, and I need a drink," he declared, and without waiting for agreement, he strutted from the alley and into the nearest bar, dragging Tel along with him.

"How do you plan on paying?" Pasha asked, hurrying to keep up and thinking about food. Mann followed a dozen steps behind, coughing.

Ves slowed his pace, then stopped. "Shit. You're right. I forgot about that. All those years being rich in Valez'Mui made my head soft." He looked around, then started walking back towards the city center, paused, and eased Tel down onto a damp stone bench in front of a shuttered import license advocate's office. "Better if you wait here," he told him.

Tel only nodded and leaned back against the wall.

"Where are we going?" Mann asked, as he stumbled up to the others, between coughs that sounded like he had bloody gravel in his lungs.

Ves looked at Mann, then Pasha. "Don't shit where you eat," he stated, then marched again towards the city, not looking back to see if anyone was following him.

They followed Ves for ten minutes, wending through streets and alleys until the Port Towers were lost from view, and the crowds had again thickened. He stopped and turned to Pasha and Mann.

"If you don't want a part in what comes next, you'd better go back and wait with Tel."

Pasha glanced at Mann, but the old man was coughing into the crook of his arm so hard Pasha wasn't sure he'd even heard. "What comes next?"

Mann stopped coughing but only scowled.

"We need money, right?" Ves asked, his deep voice a harsh whisper. "These people have money."

"You're going to rob someone?" Pasha asked, incredulous. "We're not criminals."

Ves boomed a sudden laugh, drawing a few stares from the pedestrians around them. "Speak for yourself. Oh, right, never mind. You can't because you're a criminal too."

Pasha's face tugged downward to match Mann's, who stood watching the exchange in silence. "You know what I mean. I don't want to rob anyone."

Ves laughed again. "What else did you have in mind? Getting a fucking job? We need money. Now. Even if we leave tonight, Tel is in no shape to come with us. He needs a doctor, and even an illegal stitcher on the Lip is going to cost tin."

Mann looked at Ves a long moment, suppressed a cough, and turned to Pasha. "I'm going back," he stated. Then he turned and walked toward the port, shoulders shaking with his ceaseless, silent cough.

Pasha watched him go, hesitating, before turning back to Ves. "You need my help?"

"No. But I could use it."

Pasha hesitated again, then nodded. "Tell me what to do."

Chorl Averas' heart leaped into his throat when he saw the small, swarthy man marching toward him, shouting in some harsh, alien language, eyes full of murder. He scanned the thinning evening crowds for city guards or Church watch, but there were none around. Never were when you needed them. Just when you didn't, when they came marching into your shop to demand where this or that had come from because it had been "reported stolen." Never when some filthy foreigner was about to murder you in the street. Everyone else just crossed to the other side, heads down, unwilling to get involved. Who could blame them?

"I don't understand you," Chorl mumbled as the man stopped in front of him, still shouting. He knew it wouldn't do any good. The man pointed at the bulge under Chorl's shirt, where he kept the sack full of his profits for the day, and shouted again. He reeked of old sea water and sewage, coated with some sort of black-green slime he'd only made a half-hearted effort to scrape off.

"I don't understand. Please." Chorl stammered, deciding to play dumb, hoping a guard would happen by.

Just as he was about to give up with one last, desperate look around the street, an enormous shadow loomed out of an alley and marched toward them. A giant, dark man, almost as filthy as the foreigner. A Ristroan, Chorl realized. *I'm going to die here,* he thought. *Right now. I just want to go home.*

But the Ristroan didn't confront Chorl. Instead, he grabbed the foreigner by the neck and hurled him into a pile of rubbish heaped at the mouth of the same alley the big man had emerged from. Then he turned to Chorl and said in passable N'naradin, "Son of bitches like that give foreigners a bad name. Did he hurt you?"

Chorl shook his head. "Thank you. No, I'm fine. I think he would have killed me if you hadn't got here."

The Ristroan nodded. "Could be. Things have gone to shit since the blockade." He paused. "Some people might think help like that would be worth a little tin." He smiled.

Chorl hesitated, then nodded again. "Yes. Yes, of course." He reached into his shirt and grabbed four Three-Sides. A lot more than he'd meant to, but he felt awkward putting them back, so he handed the lot of them to the Ristroan, who took them with a nod of thanks.

The big man looked towards the alley, where the foreigner now stood and stared at them, hatred in his eyes. "Sad to say he might cause you more trouble. How's this? You double what you gave me, and I'll walk you home myself."

Chorl looked at the man in the alley, then back at the pirate.

"I'd bet if I'm with you, he'll leave for easier pastures. No telling what he might do, though, if I were to walk away. Especially since he watched you pull out the tin. You should be more careful."

Chorl looked at the foreigner again, then nodded a third time with a sigh. "You're right. Of course. Thank you. Thank you for everything. It's not far."

He led the pirate down the street with one last fearful look at the raging stranger standing in the alley. He didn't notice the pirate's wink in the same direction.

They got some stares as they walked into the Grace's Inn, although it was probably because of their filth, which the drizzle had failed to completely wash off. Tel was doing a little better, but he was still pale and shaking.

They settled into an empty table near the door. The attention wavered, then dropped. The innkeeper—a young man, who looked like he'd spent the first half of his life on the deck of a ship, brought a bottle of local wine and four cups.

"Better make it two bottles," Ves said. "And whatever you've got to eat. A lot of it." The host complied.

"Why didn't you just rob that guy?" Pasha whispered. He wouldn't meet Mann's gaze.

Ves smiled. "Never use force to take anything somebody will give you." He winked at Mann, who frowned and coughed into his sleeve.

The pirate eyed the room, pouring for himself and drinking. "No one's running to tell the guards about us yet, anyway." He set into the platter of roasted pork, rice, and grapes the innkeeper had set down on the table along with the second bottle of wine.

"What are we going to do?" Pasha asked. He took a drink but didn't taste it, and began stuffing his face with meat and grapes the moment it touched the table.

In response, Ves turned to Mann. "It's been a while, so refresh my memory. The piers down there—" he nodded his head in the direction of the port. "They're not connected along the cliffs, are they?"

"No, no connections between the towers. Just the piers running straight to the underground entrances with water between. That way, no one wanders over to the wrong customs tower, and they can keep track of who came from what ship."

Ves nodded. "And the cliffs—how high are they?"

Mann was already shaking his head. "No, no. Not what you're thinking. Two, maybe three hundred hands, depending on where and the tide. Too high. If your crew is down there, why don't we just go the way they went?"

It was Ves's turn to shake his head. "First of all, because I'm not sure how they got down there. We talked about getting a guide before I got nabbed. Someone to take us through the tunnels. Ash even talked about going through one of the drains beneath the low tide line. They're all part fish. They could do it if it's not too far."

Mann shrugged. "Maybe. Don't know anything about that. Those drainage tunnels might be big enough to squeeze through if they can hold their breath long enough. Gated under the piers, though."

"We thought of that, too," Ves said. "Talked about bribing someone with a key. Don't know what they got around to doing, though. Goddamned blockade went up the day after Ash got a ship. Haven't even seen it myself yet. Right after he paid for it, I got tossed in the Pit. We have to find our own way down."

Pasha began shaking his head with Mann. "That's crazy. We can't jump. And anyway, once we're down there, then what? We can't get out, right? Why would we kill ourselves just so we can get stuck?"

Ves smiled at Pasha and winked. "Still better than dying in the Pit, Yeah? And I told you. We're not going to be trapped. I have a plan."

"You said it wasn't a plan."

Ves didn't answer.

Mann continued to protest. "The water is only twenty, maybe thirty hands deep if it's at low tide. Even if the fall doesn't kill us when we hit the water, which it will, it's not deep enough."

Ves shrugged. "We wait for high tide, or close to it. More water, less fall. Easy, yeah? You just need to know how to go in. Feet first, cross your legs." He laughed. "And don't inhale when you hit the water. I'd show you," a shrug, "but no time."

Just as Ves began working on the cork of the second bottle, there was a shout at the door. "Them! There they are! That Ristroan and that desert vagrant he's drinking with. I saw them go off together!"

Ves jumped up, knocking the table with his hip and almost toppling the half-opened bottle, before he snatched it and whirled. Pasha and Mann rose at the same time.

Pasha didn't recognize the speaker, but Ves muttered "Shit," under his breath. "I guess someone saw our performance after all."

Their accuser was an iron-haired woman wearing a red linen dress under a finely-cut leather rain cloak. Four watch stood behind her, brandishing crossbows and ceramic long knives.

The guards nodded and pushed past the woman to surround the accused. The Grace's Inn, already only half full, began to clear out. Any patrons who didn't leave stood back to watch.

Ves didn't hesitate. He swung the bottle at the closest guard, clocking the man on the temple. He crumpled, bleeding from his nose. The cork, which Ves had almost worked out, came free, spraying him with deep red wine in the face and across his chest. "Damn it, not the good stuff!" He bellowed as he gave another guard a hard shove with both hands—one still clutching the bottle—into the third. One fired his crossbow as he fell, plugging the bolt into the wall behind Mann. The watchmen fell together over an empty table, which collapsed in a crack of splintering wood. "Goddamn it!"

He swung the bottle at the last guard, who had drawn his knife halfway out of the scabbard. She tipped herself back, avoiding a blow to her head, but not fast enough. The bottle caught her jaw with a crunch and, now empty, shattered. She fell to the floor, clutching her face, blood pouring from between her fingers.

Ves charged at the old woman, who's indignant expression had transformed to equal parts terror and regret, and she fled into the night, crying for help.

Ves turned to his companions, who stared in as much shock as everyone else. He laughed.

He's insane, Pasha thought.

"Remember, you bastards, keep your legs crossed, feet first! We'd better hope it's high tide now because we're not waiting around! Sorry we couldn't do more for you, Tel, good luck!" He tossed the pouch of tin coins to the other Ristroan, who caught it with one hand.

"You son of a bitch," Tel shouted at the retreating figure of Ves, but the bearded man was laughing, too. "Guess I'll go hobble off to an alley to hide. Involving me in your crazy bullshit." He picked up a broken table leg and used it as a cane to limp out the door.

Pasha watched him leave over his shoulder, feeling bad for him but not knowing what else he could do.

"Hurry the fuck up!" Ves turned to shout back at him. He

charged into the night towards the customs towers, shouts and cries echoing off the buildings and the low clouds.

Despite his size, Ves was faster than both Mann and Pasha, and they lagged together as they followed the huge pirate across the open park that ringed the towers. Ahead they saw Ves yell, stumble, then begin running again. A moment later, something whistled by Pasha's head. He saw the group of city watch who'd been guarding the closest tower lower their crossbows to reload as row of soldiers behind them lined up to take aim.

Pasha felt Mann's wiry arms embrace his waist in a tackle, and they went down just as more bolts buzzed and clattered on the paving stones or thunked into the muddy grass. Mann cried out, and Pasha saw a bolt buried in his wrist to the fletching, the barbed, tapered head jutting from the other side.

"Forget it!" Mann shouted, scrabbling to his feet and pulling Pasha up with him. "Up, goddamn it! We need to be over the edge before they shoot again!"

Pasha got to his feet, half dragged by Mann, and looked ahead. Ves had already disappeared over the cliff. The teams of guards on both sides were reloading or aiming their crossbows, and he saw, with a glance over his shoulder, at least three teams closing in from the city.

Mann, who was now five paces ahead of him, disappeared over the edge. Bolts hissed behind Pasha as he leapt from the cliff and plummeted down. On either side, he could make out rows of ships crowded against the piers, some lit with crews stranded on board, but most dark. Beneath and ahead of him, the darkness of the water swept away. In the few seconds of his descent, he tried to make out Mann or Ves but saw only blackness.

At the last moment, he heard Ves's voice in his mind, "Cross your legs, you idiot!" He tried to do so, but too late, and he hit the water at an angle, right leg first. White fire exploded up from his knee to his shoulder, followed by numbness.

"Oh well." The thought was far away. He was aware he was underwater, but couldn't bring himself to care.

Strong hands gripped him, pulled him up. He struggled but couldn't move his right leg, so gave up and let himself be tugged into the pale, yellow light.

He was dragged through the water, which he thought might be cold, but it, too, seemed a faraway thing. Distant shouts surrounded him, until he was yanked underwater again, and everything went dark.

Ves, a dozen hands away, saw Mann hit the water and bob up a moment later, struggling with his hand, which had something jutting out of it. Pasha came down a few seconds later, flailing, and hit with one foot extended. Ves saw his leg collapse. Mann was treading water nearby, a pained look on his face. The old man gave a vague wave, and Ves saw the crossbow head glint in the unnatural light of Fom reflected from the clouds.

Ves swam over to where Pasha had disappeared and groped around where the splash still rippled outward, until he felt him floundering ten hands below the surface. He grabbed him and dragged him upwards.

Pasha murmured something. The young man's leg floated out to the side at a sickening angle. The glint of bone jutted from his knee, and the water around it bloomed red.

Ves grimaced and wondered if the boy would even make it to the ship so Ash could do something about it.

No, not a boy, he reminded himself, if what that Kalis girlfriend of his had said was true.

With the thought of Syrina, Ves's stomach churned. He had no desire to explain to her how Pasha had died in his arms.

Ves began swimming as hard as he could towards the end of pier

13, where his new ship was moored, wondering what her name was, and then he wondered if it would even be afloat long enough for it to matter. He needed to get out of the habit of going through ships so fast.

Mann was following, but dropping behind, and Ves stopped swimming for a few seconds to let the old man get within earshot. He'd bet with himself the disgraced general would be the first to die in their mad escape. He'd have put money on him not even making it out of the Tidal Works if he'd found anyone who would've taken the bet, but it seemed nothing could kill Albertus Mann, least of all the Grace.

Ves shouted, "End of thirteen! And you'd better goddamn hurry because we can't wait for you even if I wanted to, which I don't!"

Mann responded with a flailing series of gestures that Ves didn't understand, but there were footfalls on the piers around them, coming closer at a run, so he couldn't worry about it. Would be a shame, he thought, if Mann made it all this way only to drown in the Bowl of Fom like a rat flushed by the tide.

Shouts from above. Ves put his hand over the nose of the semi-conscious Pasha and dived down, under the prow of a small fishing boat, and emerged on the other side.

The towers loomed on the cliffs, their numbers painted in faded numerals twenty hands high. Twelve. One more to go. He changed his angle to head out, then across, just as a few bolts clanged against the hull of a schooner on his left. The water swallowed a few more with tiny, soft splashes in front and behind him. Cursing, he dived again, wondering how Mann would get to the right place in time.

He dragged Pasha above water into the tight space between the hulls and the pier and paused long enough to make sure the injured man was still breathing. Then he pulled himself along the rotting wood with his free hand to the end of pier twelve, praying to a heaven he both hated and didn't believe in that none of the ships would bump into the dock with he and Pasha still between. Running foot-steps surrounded him, but in the enclosed space between pier, hulls, and water, the sound rolled until it was impossible to tell which way it was coming from.

And then he was out. The Bowl of Fom flooded before him, the high sea wall a span away, the gap between the two lighthouses more or less open, though from his angle he could glimpse a handful of N'naradin naval vessels off to one side.

The blockade. Enough fire power to sink whoever came through the gap, which they'd no doubt mined.

Good, Ves thought as he waved back at the figures on the ship hailing him from the end of thirteen. It was what he'd imagined they'd set up, and he'd come up with just the plan for it.

Ves swam over to the side of the ship. The Sea Boon, he noted. A fucking sail boat. Ash had bought the first he'd found, and no chance to find anything better, but a fucking single-masted sail boat? Embarrassing, he thought. Once they got out of this mess, he'd need to work on getting a proper steamship under his feet again.

He called up, "Ash! Ash better be up there!"

A moment later, his lover peered over the side. "Ash!" He yelled again. "Hoist this one up, and careful. His leg's in a bad way. You're going to need to clean and set it, and you're going to need to do it on your own because we need to get the hell out of here an hour ago!"

"What about the other one?" Ash yelled down while signaling some of the others to lower a makeshift stretcher of planks lashed together with rope. Ves began dragging Pasha's unconscious form onto it.

Ves looked around while he secured Pasha's limp body. "No sign, and we can't wait. Too bad, too. I was beginning to like him."

"Someone's coming down the pier!" Another voice called down—a woman's voice Ves didn't recognize. Must be one of the new crew they'd picked up while he was stuck in the Pit.

"Hold your goddamned fire!" Ashmarirai yelled at someone out of view on the deck. "Pretty sure that's the other one!" Then he called down to Ves, "Old man, bolt through his arm—that's the other one, yeah?"

Ves grimaced. "Goddamn it, yeah. Leading the whole fucking garrison right to us. Well, nothing to do about it—as soon as he's on, set out toward the gap."

"What about you?" Ash called while he pulled the stretcher bearing Pasha over the rail and out of sight.

"You'd goddamn better pick me up," Ves shouted as he swam toward the end of pier twelve. "Let me get ahead of you, and sweep me up when you pass my fat ass. I'm taking care of this fucking blockade!

"I hope." He added under his breath as he reached the last boat at pier twelve—a single-masted wooden yacht that needed three people to sail.

Fuck it. No need to sail it. Just get it through the gap in front of the Sea Boon.

To his surprise, a shout greeted him as he pulled himself onto the deck. "You fucking pirate, get the hell off my boat!"

A half-dressed man, middle aged, balding and bearded, was charging at Ves with a bronze fire ax clutched in both hands. His bare chest was dark and leathery as if it had been at sea without a shirt on it for twenty years.

Ves dodged, a little slow, and the blade peeled the skin away from his left shoulder. He swore and twisted around, using the sailor's momentum to shove him off the deck and into the bay.

"Sorry, friend," Ves shouted without looking down, untying the ropes that tied the boat to the pier. "You're not going to want to be on this thing in a minute."

The boat started to pull away, but Ves heard a scrabbling at the hull in the same place he'd pulled himself on board. He jogged over and kicked the man in the face just as he popped into view. "Sorry again," he called, taking the wheel.

He looked back, happy to see the Sea Boon pulling away from the dock just behind him. A gaggle of city watch had indeed followed Mann and were now pelting them with crossbows, but his crew stayed low, and it didn't look like anyone had been hit.

Ves turned his attention back to the sea wall and the blockade beyond it. Now he could see rows of barrels floating low in the water just beyond the gap, strung together with ropes and thick logs to keep them afloat.

Powder kegs, he thought. Wasn't this going to be glorious?

He started to laugh.

Mann watched the man named Ashmarirai pull Pasha's leg until the shin bone jutting from it slid back in with a reluctant sucking sound. Pasha groaned and burbled a little, but even that extreme pain wasn't enough to bring him to consciousness.

Mann felt sick in the pit of his stomach. It wasn't the injury—he'd seen worse, much worse, after all. But he realized looking at Pasha that his whole identity, his whole idea of what redemption meant to him, was wrapped up in this man from the valley. He and his sister, who might be the only survivors of the genocide that Mann didn't condone or direct, but did nothing to stop.

Ashmarirai grabbed a flask from a man standing next to him, who was just about to take a drink from it. The man didn't object. Ash took a long drink himself, then poured a generous amount of clear liquid onto Pasha's still-seeping leg. Mann could smell the alcohol from where he stood, a dozen hands away. Whatever it was, it was strong. Pasha writhed and mumbled in what Mann took to be his native tongue. He thought he caught the name "Anna," but it could have been his preoccupied mind toying with him. Heaven knew it had been doing enough of that since he'd climbed down the cliffs into the valley in the Black Wall, two lifetimes ago.

Ashmarirai was older than Mann had first thought. His hair was black streaked with lines of silver and pulled back into a tight ponytail that looked like not one hair had escaped. His eyes were and brown and hard, set into a face darker than Pasha's but lighter than Ves's.

He glanced up at Mann as he worked. "Should've rappelled down the vineyard cliffs and swum like the rest of us."

Mann couldn't read his expression to know if the pirate was serious or not, so he just gave a little shrug. "Wasn't an option," he said.

Ash grunted and went back to work.

After cleaning the wound, he took another drink and put the flask down beside him long enough to sprinkle black powder from a pouch onto Pasha's leg. The man he'd taken the flask from was watching as intently as Mann, and made no move to pick it up.

Ash sparked a flint above it, and Mann winced as the powder ignited in a bright flash and sizzle of roasting flesh. Pasha screamed and started thrashing, his eyes open, uncomprehending and wild.

In a flash, the man watching was down on his knees, holding Pasha by the shoulders, and Mann was with him, pinning Pasha by the hips and uninjured leg. The Ristroans glanced at him, and Ashmarirai gave him an almost imperceptible nod before going back to work. He pinned Pasha's broken leg by the thigh with one hand, while with the other he took yet another drink, and doused the cauterized wound. Without exchanging words, the man holding Pasha's shoulders moved down to take Ash's place, still holding Pasha's right arm by the wrist. He looked at Mann and nodded toward the flailing left arm, and Mann moved up to hold it, kneeling on Pasha's hip while doing his best to hold both Pasha's left arm and uninjured leg, which kicked at Ashmarirai as he set two wooden planks against the front and back of Pasha's broken knee, then wrapped the entire thing in a long strip of white cloth.

When Ash was done, he took one last drink, then poured the rest of the flask into Pasha's mouth. Pasha coughed and gagged, then lay still.

The three of them stood, and Ash looked at Mann. "The Bowl of Fom is dirty," he said in accented N'naradin. "He might live. He might not." He nodded toward the prow. "We all might live. We might not."

Mann looked. He saw Ves on the smaller boat nearing the gap in the sea wall, carried by the outgoing tide. Beyond, a web of objects floated low in the water, flanked by hulking Tyrsh gunships, gleaming in the Eyelight, three to a side.

Ashmarirai shouted something in Ristroan, and there was a flurry of activity among the crew as they all donned black cloaks and began readying a pair of lifeboats at the stern, likewise painted black. One of the crew handed Mann a cloak and tossed another over Pasha's still form.

"Help," Ashmarirai said. "Into the little boat. In case things go wrong." He shrugged, blasé. "I love Vesmalimali, but often things go wrong."

Mann helped heave the makeshift stretcher carrying Pasha over to one of the black lifeboats, his attention transfixed on the smaller ship in front of them. A small, non sequitur voice in his mind pointed out he hadn't coughed since he hit the water, although his breath still bubbled in his chest.

As Ves closed the final hands to the gap, he turned from the wheel, sprinted to the stern, and leaped into the water. He shouted something lost to the sea, laughing.

They were moving fast. Ashmarirai shouted something at the woman at the wheel, who's lined face was almost as grey as the thick dreadlocks that flopped behind her in the wind Mann hadn't even noticed.

The woman banked the wheel hard to the starboard, and Ashmarirai and a trio of men tossed the ends of knotted ropes into the sea from the port.

Two of the ropes grew taut, and the four of them began to pull. Moments later, Ves, spluttering and giggling, climbed aboard.

"Watch!" he shouted to no one in particular and spun to face the oncoming gap of the sea wall.

There was a *crunch* from the smaller boat and an enormous flash of light that didn't die away. A deep, endless *foooom* rolled across the water and hit the Sea Boon in a wave of heat that singed the hair on

Mann's arms. A wall of blue and white fire, almost as high as the wall on either side of it, rose to meet them.

"Fucking naphtha?" Ves bellowed, again at nobody in particular. "Why the fuck would the bloody, goddamned Syndicate give fucking Tyrsh fucking naphtha mines?!"

The last seemed directed at Mann, but without waiting for an answer the old general didn't have, Ves charged over to the wheel as the grey-haired woman dove out of his way.

He had a point, Mann thought. The Syndicate sold enough naphtha to N'narad to power their ships, but there'd always been hard caps on how much to keep N'naradin power in check, and they'd never sold weapons. Naphtha didn't burn without flame, so making mines that triggered on impact was tricky. As far as he knew, only the Syndicate was capable of building such devices, which meant either the Arch Bishop had figured out his own way of weaponizing fuel and gambled, risking shortages in the process, or the Merchant's Syndicate was backing the Arch Bishop while paying lip service to the Grace.

Well, Mann thought. If he somehow lived through the next few minutes, he might end up living long enough to figure out which one it was.

"Fuck it!" Ves shouted, spinning the wheel until they were headed toward the wall of fire. "Douse yourselves, you cunts, and don't get into the water until we're out the other side!"

Mann found himself with the frantic Ristroans, hauling up buckets, drenching themselves in the few moments they had.

And then they hit the fire.

Heat slammed into Mann like a physical wall, pounding him down to the deck and blasting the pathetic layer of water he'd covered himself with into steam. The air sucked out of his lungs, leaving nothing to replace it with but an inferno. Others around him collapsed to the deck, curling into balls, but they were abstract, far away figures. He was only aware of his hands turning red, smoking before his burning eyes.

And then they were through. The air rushing into his gasping lungs was ripe with the stench of burning hair, making him gag and cough. His throat was raw and his eyes burned. Tears streamed down his face, stinging his cheeks. The hair on the backs of his now-red hands had curled into tiny singed balls, his fingernails he'd let grow too long now ended at his fingertips in melted, blackened blobs.

Fire surrounded them. Someone was yelling something, and he realized he was still curled on the deck.

"—Burning! Get on the fucking raft—" The shout was cut off with a massive explosion that send Mann sliding backwards across the deck to slam feet first into a lifeboat. He got half way to his feet before another explosion shattered the front of the Sea Boon to splinters, causing it to buck forward. The lifeboat began sliding towards the buckled bow, and Mann rolled out of the way just in time. He had the wherewithal to grab the back of it and let it drag him off what was left of Ves's ship, still embroiled in flames, the hull coated in burning naphtha.

He hit the water hard enough that it knocked the wind out of him, but he held onto the back of the lifeboat with his good hand. The entire world seemed to be a solid wall of light and flame.

A hand grasped his and yanked him aboard. Pasha's lifeboat, he saw. And Ves. And the man that had helped Ashmarirai set Pasha's leg. They were all hunkered low around Pasha, black cloaks over their backs and heads. As soon as Mann was on board, Ves went back to manning the oar opposite the other man, who was rowing as fast as he could while staying down.

"Get that goddamned cloak over your head," Ves growled in a harsh whisper. "Or we're as dead as everyone else." Tears streaked Ves's face too, and Mann realized they weren't from his burning eyes.

Mann collapsed where he was, throwing his cloak over himself, then rising to peer over the stern at the scene behind him. Fragments of the Sea Boon and the smaller ship still burned on the water just outside the wall of naphtha fire, which was as intense as it had been when it erupted. A few more cannons on the Tyrsh ships fired into the debris, then fell silent. There was no sign of the other two lifeboats.

"Dead?" He managed. His throat was raw, and his voice cracked like hot stones.

Ves glowered at the question and wiped his face before turning from Mann back to the fire between them and Fom.

They rowed through the night, first west, then north, edging their way back toward the coast. Mann watched the naval ships until they were nothing but distant outlines framed by the fire, which still didn't dwindle. He waited for one to turn to follow or fire on them, but the dull black paint on the lifeboat did its job. The night had grown overcast and still, as black as the tunnels under Fom had been, except for the burning water and the glow of the city far to the southeast, glittering on the horizon, lighting the clouds above it in gold.

No one said anything for a long time until Ves spoke, his voice soft and hoarse, "Most of them had been with me since Valez'Mui. Ashmarirai, since... He'd been..." Ves's voice choked off, and he sucked in a ragged breath. "Goddamn it Ash," he whispered to himself. "Goddamn it."

They rowed on in silence toward the coast north of Fom.

29

INTO THE VOID

Ormo led them down the narrow stairs beneath his dais to the white door, which opened into a room lined with levers, switches, and gauges connected to a maze of brass pipes running along two walls. Two padded, leather reclining chairs, fixed with straps at the ankles, wrists, and neck, sat together on the right. Above one chair was a lone, round screen surrounded by brass, flickering with the image of a passing landscape from far above.

"You got some furniture," Syrina quipped. "And more brass pipes. They tie the room together."

Ormo rustled. "After I learned there were people who came to us from within the Wall, I hoped I would have guests. I tried to accommodate such a possibility. As for the pipes, it turns out old machines require a great deal of power, and I saw to it they would get all they need. Please forgive the clutter."

Anna froze just in the door, wide, frightened eyes glued on the chairs. She whispered, "What is this place?"

"I don't know," Syrina answered honestly.

"Oh, but you do," Ormo said, as he shuffled to one bank of

controls and began fiddling with dials and levers. There was a hiss, and the pipes began to tick and rumble. "I told you."

"This is the room where the tattooing happens?" Syrina felt the voice's intense interest.

"One of them. Only ten of the Fifteen can create a Kalis. The other five, despite any pretenses of equivalence, depend on those ten for their servants."

Syrina couldn't suppress her suspicious frown. "Why are you telling me this now?"

And why is he telling you in front of her?

Syrina glanced at the Anna, who stood frozen in place, eyes even wider than before, looking ready to run. The same thing had occurred to her.

Before Syrina could answer the voice, silent or otherwise, Ormo answered. "Why did I grant you that gift those long years ago, which changed both you and our relationship? Remember what I told you then? The risk was worth the reward, and so it is again.

"I will need your help for what comes next. Or rather, the help of the mind who lives within you." He pulled a pair of long prisms from a cabinet. They sparkled in the steady, white light. At their cores were thin, iridescent blue lines of dust, like threads of moss, glowing or reflecting the ambient light.

She heard Anna's breath catch. "General Mann's treasure. From the Black Wall."

Ormo nodded, his expression invisible under his hood.

"But how?" Syrina couldn't help herself from asking. She trailed off, irritated at the pleasure Ormo took from stumping her, his most prized investigator.

"Intercepted," he stated and seemed to enjoy adding nothing else.

Syrina knew there was more to it. Ormo was flaunting it—showing her how much influence he had, draped it in mystery to keep her in her place. She fumed and longed for the time she could do something about it.

"Anna, my dear," Ormo said. "Of course you recognize these.

Generation upon generation, guarding such a treasure, even never having looked upon it, but you recognize them, deep within your being. And what a treasure it is. After all you must have gone through, you must be curious. Come. Sit." He gestured to the chair. "I will show you. Kalis Syrina, you too. Take the other chair. We three will embark on something that has not been done since before the Age of Ashes."

Anna let Syrina guide her, expression blank, her motions robotic. "We're not just going to talk, are we?"

Syrina found she couldn't answer, and only shook her head. But the woman from the valley wasn't looking at her—just staring ahead at the chair as if it were a gibbet. Syrina swallowed, realizing that to Anna, that might be what it was.

She felt the voice calm her, steel her nerves. *If not Anna, it's Pasha going to that chair. Remember that. Always remember that.*

"I'm sorry, Anna," Syrina managed, but the words were empty.

The girl froze, and Syrina thought at first she might try to flee, but Anna just turned to look at her, eyes fierce. "I left Pasha," she stated, her voice a harsh whisper that caught in her throat. "I deserve this. More than he does." She brushed passed Syrina and sat, waiting.

Syrina still hesitated. She could feel Ormo's smile. Insincerity buried behind a mask of benevolence. "My Kalis," he said. "You will be pleased to know I was right. *You* were right. The being which lives within you, or at least those like it, which the Ancestors created, existed to assist them with machines such as this one. These intelligences are how they interacted with their technology. And now, at long last, these mysteries—" he gestured at the screens around the room, "And those even greater artifacts left forgotten in the world and above it, can again be ours. With Anna's help, and with yours."

"But you already have me," Syrina said, not yet taking a step toward the empty chair. "Why do you need Anna?"

"Because," Ormo answered, turning from Syrina and taking three paces to another bank of levers, pipes, and gauges, "Your Preas Prohm is unique. Diluted over hundreds of generations and then... remixed, shall we say? Such an act has caused it to, for the lack of a better term, *evolve.* And, since you brought me Anna—someone who's blood can be traced all the way to our origins, undiluted, there's no need any more to take unnecessary risks with you.

"But, Anna's Preas Prohm is dormant. Unhoned and dull after generations of disuse. We must awaken Anna in a way that avoids all the unpleasantness that was required for your journey. And for that, my dear Kalis, I need your help. Now come. Enough talk. Sit. Let us begin."

He doesn't trust you, the voice pointed out as if it wasn't obvious. Syrina climbed into the chair next to Anna. *Probably something to do with that time you tried to kill him. He might be right about my alterations, though. Maybe if I hadn't been more or less dead for eight or nine thousand years, I'd understand what the hell is going on.*

Syrina didn't bother answering. There wasn't anything to say.

That's another reason you can be glad we brought Anna here, the voice carried on as Syrina settled into the chair and Ormo began tightening the straps on Anna's wrists and ankles. The girl's eyes were closed. Syrina saw her wince a little at Ormo's touch, but it was impossible to tell what she was thinking. Nothing pleasant, anyway.

"What's that?" Syrina responded to the voice in her mind, forcing herself not to even mumble. She didn't want to give Ormo the satisfaction of knowing she was talking to it.

If we hadn't brought Anna here, it would have been us sitting in that chair. And I'm willing to wager whatever is about to happen, it will be a lot worse for her.

Then Ormo settled something on Syrina's head and slid a wire into the nape of her neck, and the world spun away.

She stood in an infinite room of glass. The ceiling seemed low, yet she couldn't reach it. If there were any walls, they were lost to the horizon. The floor reflected the ceiling and vice-versa like smooth, grey mirrors, lit from nowhere and everywhere.

Next to her stood a figure, female and hairless. Like the ceiling and floor, it was a metallic, grey reflection, lacking details. Lacking tattoos. And with that realization came another as she saw herself in the liquid mirror of the floor, its surface rippling outward from her bare feet like water that wasn't wet: She too lacked tattoos and false faces. Syrina found herself lost in her own reflection, in a face—her real face—she'd never seen.

"Hello," the form standing next to her said, breaking her from her reverie.

"You're the voice, aren't you?"

"I guess we're long past calling me anything else, huh? This is how I've shaped myself through your thoughts. Is it a wonder I look like you?"

It wasn't, and Syrina said so.

"We're not alone." The voice gestured.

Two other figures stood. Anna—a younger version of herself, looking around in fear and wonder, and another behind her, standing close. Grey and metallic like the voice, but vague and indistinct. A feminine mass lacking arms or legs or a well-defined head.

"How is this possible?" Syrina whispered as Anna spotted her and began a few hesitant steps toward them. The mass slid behind her, silent and unnoticed.

"I'm not sure, but this is familiar. Ormo somehow used the technology that made your tattoos link us together—me and you with Anna and her own voice, such as it is."

"My tattoos." Syrina found herself again fixated on herself as she studied her hands, small and calloused, worn beyond their age. All ten fingers intact.

"I know you." Anna's voice brought Syrina back to where they were, and she turned to look at the girl. Maybe only sixteen in this place, and with a face as confused an innocent as a child's.

"Yes," Syrina answered.

Anna nodded and turned around to look at the silver form hovering behind her. "And this—I know this too, I think."

"You might," Syrina replied.

"It's a part of you," the voice said. "Like I am to her." It nodded toward Syria. "That's why we're here—so you can know each other the way we do. It can help you."

Anna nodded again. "Good. I think I'd like that. I'm sorry I didn't trust you, Syrina."

Syrina's stomach churned, but she said nothing and kept her face neutral.

"Well, then," the voice said, its tone matter-of-fact, and reached out to touch the form behind Anna.

Everything after happened so fast Syrina had a hard time sorting out the order they came in.

The Anna-shape collapsed down into a thin, vertical, silver line, then exploded outward into a sphere, then back in again, into a silver mirror of Anna the same way the voice was to Syrina.

"Corrupted," it said in a metallic, emotionless tone. It waved a hand at Syrina's voice, its face twisted in loathing. Then: "Connection. Transferring to Variable Geosynchronous GL-Kappa-Nine. "

The endless mirrors of the floor and ceiling fell away. The ceiling rose until it was a sphere, immeasurable in its vastness. At the same time, color bled into its perfect, gleaming surface until it was the Eye, looming above, the hurricane of its pupil glaring down at them, while a billion stars twinkled into existence around it, flooding outward.

At the same time, the floor collapsed to become another sphere, color swirling into form—a broken mass of browns and blacks and greens, surrounded by a deep blue, all covered by swirls of white.

Syrina stared down. It was all at once, very, very cold.

"Eris," the shape of her voice said next to her.

Syrina tried to answer, but she couldn't breathe. There was a building pressure growing inside her. It forced her lungs to exhale and then kept pushing. Pushing everything out into the impossible cold darkness.

"It's in your mind," the voice said. "Calm yourself. It's all in your mind."

Syrina fell. She wanted to scream, but her lungs were an empty, crushing weight inside her chest.

And then she was in the chair. A strap on her arm had broken, and she struggled against the other while flailing with her free hand. Something tugged at her neck where Ormo had inserted the wire. Hot, red, fluid sprayed out of the severed connection as she pulled it away before her tattoos closed over the wound. Not a wire. A tube.

Her eyes followed the broken strand to where it led into Anna's neck after splitting, the thicker branch leading into the non-metal white device covered in pipes and levers beneath the circular screen above them, now showing the same view of Eris that Syrina had just experienced. The room was hot and full of steam.

Anna was screaming.

"It worked!" Ormo was laughing. It was the first time she'd heard the sound—a high-pitched coughing that made her think of some horrid, dying bird. "Out!" He shouted at Syrina. There was a screech of machinery, and the view screen zoomed in, plummeting to a fuzzy white mass on the left side of the jagged shape that was the continent of Eris. Anna's screams rose in pitch. Her eyes were eyes open and rolled back.

I'll kill him, she thought. Right now.

But as she stood, the room spun, and she knew she would have fallen if the voice hadn't cleared the vertigo so she could stagger like a drunk to the door.

No, not right now.

Behind her, the grey image coalesced into a crescent shape of crisscrossed lines and brown and black squares, faint, indistinct specks moving within it like the shadows of ants.

Fom, the voice said. *He's using Anna to watch Fom.*

"How?" Syrina asked, her voice hoarse, as she stumbled up the long stairway into Ormo's empty audience hall. The braziers in the corners had been turned all the way down, and the mass of his dais and throne was nothing but an indefinable dark shape among the deeper shadows. "How is that possible? Fom is always covered in clouds."

I don't know, the voice admitted. *But I know other things now. A lot of other things. Let's get out of here and away from that asshole because I think they're the kinds of things you'll want to know.*

Syrina ran from the hall into the Palace courtyard, peeling off the false skin of the merchant's daughter she still wore, leaving it scattered behind her. Anna's screams echoed in her mind long after she couldn't hear them anymore.

The daystar we were in, it's not just something Ormo can look through.

They were the first words the voice had spoken since Syrina had left the Syndicate Palace. Not just left—fled. She was okay with that. She could still feel the immeasurable cold and the awful, internal pressure in the dark above Eris. Knowing she hadn't really been there didn't help. Somehow that it had all been in her mind made it worse.

She hunkered in the drainage chamber under the docks in the Foreigner's District that she'd used a hundred times. The last time she'd been here had been with Triglav, after her blundered robbery of Xereks Lees. The memory, even these years later, brought a familiar knot to her stomach, but she shook it away. Not now. Like usual, she had other things to worry about.

"What do you mean?"

Anna can move it around over the continent, maybe further. Anywhere. Find anything. Listen by watching the vibrations in the air. See heat through walls and ceilings. I don't know what else it does, or how it does them. I was connected to it the same way Anna was—Anna and that thing inside of her. Well, according to it, I'm the thing, but that's not the point. You would have been attached through me, too, if you hadn't freaked out. Maybe that was for the best—I'm not sure I could have pulled us out on my own. Anyway, Ormo can use Anna to learn anything, watch anyone, now.

She remembered Anna's screams. They still echoed around her, in this cramped drainage chamber five spans away.

"I need to get her out of there," she stated. "Whatever she's doing for Ormo needs to stop. Never mind the fact that it's all my fault."

No arguments here, the voice said, to Syrina's surprise. *Maybe Ormo was right about whatever I am—maybe I "evolved." But I'm glad I'm not that thing that's in Anna. That was a machine. I don't know if Anna can control it or not, but I bet Ormo can. If not now, he'll figure it out. Maybe that's what the Ancients made us to be—slaves. It makes more sense than whatever I am. But screw that. I enjoy independent thought.*

"For once, I agree with you," Syrina mumbled.

Still, you—we—can't just bail her out. Ormo will be ready for that, and now he has Anna. She may or may not help him against you, but I'm not willing to find out.

"Pasha," Syrina stated.

We're on the same page, for once. Ormo won't expect him, and if Anna can free herself from his control at all, it'll be easier if her brother helps.

"How about that," Syrina said, rising from where she hunkered. "We're finally starting to get along."

30

MARESG

PASHA SIPPED HIS BLOVEY WINE, A BROWN, EFFERVESCENT concoction fermented from the enormous mushrooms that grew at the bases of the mangrove trees in miniature forests. It was high in alcohol and mildly hallucinogenic, and tasted like mud and urine. Not that anyone drank it for the taste. Eyes closed, he listened to the sounds of Maresg—the incessant creaking of branch and rope, the lapping of waves at the base of the trees, and the sounds of humanity, which matched the sounds of every city, everywhere.

Ves sat down in the chair next to him with a dramatic groan and a thunk of his own misshapen glass on the flimsy wood table. Pasha opened his eyes. The pirate was looking away from him, off into the shadows of the mangroves, and after a moment, Pasha followed his gaze. It was just after noon, but this low in Maresg, shadows drenched everything on all but a few days out of the year, when the sun angled just right to peep through the maze of bridges, buildings, and branches above. Less than fifty hands below, the waters of the Expanse flowed around the humped fingers of the great roots, where the warped, round lumps of the blovey mushrooms clung to them like boils.

Sudden shouts rose from the other side of Sheets, the bar where they'd been spending their days, as the crew of chainmen began lifting the great, weighted wooden chain across the canal, blocking the shortcut through the Upper Peninsula until captains paid their toll.

"A dozen ships, yesterday, and that'll be six today, already," Ves stated without looking away from the shadows of the forest. "I wonder if the war is bleeding up north."

Pasha shrugged. "Good for business, I guess."

Their journey to Maresg had been easy after getting through the blockade. Ves had navigated up the coast until they met a fishing boat just setting out in the thin, grey light of dawn the morning after their escape. Ves "persuaded" the three-man crew to trade them their fishing boat for the black raft. At least, that was how Mann had described it. Pasha had been in and out of consciousness and had no memory of either their escape from the Bowl of Fom or the days that had come after.

It had taken a week to reach Maresg, and they'd been there ever since. The three had stuck together without discussion, long after they could have gone their separate ways. Long after the few other crew who'd escaped the naphtha fire had.

Not that Pasha could have gone anywhere, at least not for the first few months. A fever almost took him their first days in the tree city, but he'd fought it off. His leg had healed well enough, although he still limped, and now always would. The pain just below his knee was a throbbing, ever-present thing, but blovey wine did wonders for that, even if it made his memories of Anna somehow both painful in their clarity and their distance.

As for Syrina, he still maintained she'd somehow come for him, although he'd learned to keep his hope private since neither Ves nor Mann had anything pleasant to say about it.

And so over three months after washing up in Maresg they were drunk by noon and unconscious by midnight, waiting for nothing any of them would say out loud. Pasha had grown sure they'd be doing the same thing in four more months. And in six.

"Now that is interesting," Mann said, just coming through the balcony door of Sheets and pulling up a chair from an empty table to plant it between Ves's and Pasha's.

They both turned to him. The cough that they'd all thought would kill him had faded by the time they'd requisitioned the fishing boat and vanished within a few weeks of their arrival in Maresg, and he seemed to have gotten healthier every day since. Ves had joked that maybe it was the Church that had been killing him, but Mann had just agreed and let the subject drop.

"It's a Skaald ship today," the general said, eyes on Pasha. "And it didn't pass through after paying the toll. It docked."

"That doesn't mean anything," Pasha said, but he was already heading out the door.

Syrina reflected that the port of Maresg was like the illegal docks along the Lip in as much as any captain who docked there needed to be three-quarters insane. Maresg was nothing more than a web of bridges, ropes, and shacks tying the Upper Peninsula to the mainland. The only solid ground within fifty spans were a few hills to the west, blanketed in dense jungle, so the port wasn't a port at all. Just a place among the arching roots where boats could anchor beneath the tangle of wooden chains, pulleys, and ladders so cargo and passengers could be raised and lowered in and out of the city.

Syrina hadn't planned on catching a ship to Maresg—just one that would pay the toll to pass through, but she overheard a captain brag to a waitress in the Cranky Maiden that he'd moored in Maresg over a hundred times, and was due back in two weeks, despite the turning weather. Not that the weather was turning for a few more months. If he'd impressed the woman with his lie, she hid it behind her veneer of aloof, polite boredom.

Syrina, however, had been thrilled and hadn't even bothered with a disguise. She'd just trailed the man all the way back to his ship—a black, wide, cluttered naphtha engine freighter called The Broken Storm.

They'd departed the next day, and she'd had little difficulty keeping out of the way and nicking the occasional snack from the mess on the trip to Maresg.

She needed to keep reminding herself that she didn't know if Pasha was in the tree city. The story of General Mann breaking out of the Pit along with two Ristroans and a man from the Yellow Desert had reached the Foreigner's District while she was looking for a ship. She would have bet the rest of her fingers on her left hand that the fat man with diamonds in his head was Ves, though what the pirate was doing with Mann was an interesting puzzle. The stranger could have been anyone, she kept telling herself, but she knew in her bones it was Pasha.

The other story that had persisted, the one about the run through the blockade, could have been anyone, too, but it had Ves's name all over it. Things like that were why she'd hired him in the first place.

Of course, that ship had been destroyed by the Tyrsh navy right after running the blockade, and rumor had it there'd been no survivors. Still, if anyone was going to survive something like that, it would be Ves and anyone with him. And she knew Pasha was still alive. She could feel it. Maresg was the only place they could go.

Syrina spotted Pasha in the crowd waiting on the uneven platforms above before The Broken Storm dropped anchor, as if instinct had forced her eyes onto his distant face. He peered down amid the swarm of dock hands and freight managers readying the pulleys and cranes that would lift the cargo from the deck.

She scaled up the knotty, smooth bark of the closest mangrove tree, across an overhanging branch, and down a wooden chain to land six paces behind him, just outside the press of people watching the ship below.

"Pasha," she called out, her voice almost inaudible above the din of activity around them, but he turned, and his eyes found hers. Despite waiting for this moment for months, anticipating it, letting it play out in her mind over and over again above the gentle mockery of the voice, she found her heart in her throat.

His arms were around her so fast she was almost unaware of his moving toward her, and she gripped him back, conscious of the frightened looks around them and not caring, but after a few seconds, she nudged him away.

"You found me," he said in the valley tongue, his eyes locked onto hers.

"I told you I would."

"How?"

"Rumors and a lot of lucky guesses."

"Anna." He stopped, as if not sure what else to say.

"We need to go somewhere to talk."

He studied her eyes, face suddenly pale, but nodded and led her by the hand away from the docks, toward a crooked stairway leading down into the maze of platforms that made up lower Maresg.

"You're limping," she observed.

Pasha shrugged, still holding her hand. "I was in Fom. Leaving was difficult. It's a long story. I'll tell you about it." He paused. "After you tell me about Anna."

Syrina nodded, her heart again in her throat, this time for a different reason.

Ves and Mann glanced at Pasha as he walked back into Sheets, then did a double-take as he held the door open, and a small, hard-to-place figure followed him in.

"Well goddamn," Mann said at the same time Ves muttered, "Shit."

Pasha smiled. "I told you she'd find us."

Syrina stood next to Pasha, her tilted green eyes watching the two men as they tried to track her. They widened in surprise when they landed on Mann. "You, I was not expecting to see. There were rumors, but..." She faced Pasha. "A lot *did* happen in Fom."

Pasha nodded. "Yeah. A lot."

She snuggled under Pasha's arm and blinked at Ves. "Hi, old friend. Is Ash sleeping one off somewhere?"

The Corsair's face fell, and he looked away. "I guess you could say that," he said, voice quiet.

"Oh, gods, Ves. I am really sorry to hear that."

Ves didn't meet her eyes. "Yeah. Me too."

Syrina looked around the empty room, but they were the only ones in the bar. Even the bartender had stepped into the back room. "I need your help," she said.

"Is this about Anna." Pasha's tone wasn't a question.

Syrina bit her lip and didn't look at him. "I made a mistake. I thought it would be worth it if I learned what was going on with, well, me. It turns out, I did learn. A lot. More than I expected. But it still wasn't worth it." She trailed off, her last words a whisper.

"What did you do?" Pasha's voice was tense. Ves and Mann said nothing, but both studied Pasha with concern etched around their eyes. Pasha wondered if they were anxious over Anna, or because they were afraid of what Syrina might do.

"She's with Ormo," Syrina said. "And I need your help getting her back." She looked at Mann and Ves. "All of you, if you're willing."

"I'll come," Pasha said, without hesitation. "But I don't know how much help I'll be. I can't even run. Much less fight, if it comes to that."

Syrina squeezed him. It felt strange, such casual affection from someone so hard to see. "I know," she said. "I still need you. Anna will need you, too."

Pasha nodded and looked at the other two.

"I need your help again, Vesmalimali," Syrina said again.

"I'm sure you do," Ves said, wiping his face and clearing his throat. “And I’m sure you’ll pay me for it. Still not coming for you, though.” He nodded to Pasha. “But I’ll come for him.”

Mann just nodded, his intentions clear.

“We should go,” Syrina said. “Soon. When can you finish whatever business you have here?”

Ves barked a laugh. “You’re looking at whatever business we’ve had in Maresg since we got here. I think I can speak for all of us when I say we’re ready to go whenever you are. You got a ship already?”

Syrina shook her head. “Not yet. I just got here. But it shouldn’t take long.”

31

ALLIES

It took Syrina two days to get a ship. Longer than she'd have liked. It was a small, fast sloop with the inscrutable name Tar's Gamble, easy enough to crew with the four of them as long as one of them was Ves and they didn't hit any storms. Ves had complained about "another fucking sailboat," but it didn't stop him from taking over as erstwhile captain as soon as they were all aboard.

On the trip to Eheene, Syrina told Pasha everything she'd learned. Part of her wondered if she was trying to justify delivering Anna to Ormo, but if he judged her, he hid it well. He just seemed tired. And sad, whether because of Syrina's actions, his leg, or some less obvious reason she couldn't tell, and he didn't say. She wanted to ask him, but she was too afraid of the answer. She tried not to let that get to her, but it did.

Give it time, the voice encouraged her. *Once you get Anna away from Ormo, you'll have all the time you need.*

The voice was usually right, but this time Syrina wasn't so sure. She'd ruptured something between her and Pasha, and she didn't know if it could heal. She wanted to blame the voice—it had been the one who had argued for her to bring Anna to Ormo. Deep down, though, she knew she'd had a choice. She'd allowed it to convince her. The rub was, she would have regretted not delivering Anna to Ormo, too. Now she'd be planning how to get the girl away from Pasha, instead.

Sometimes there's no good choice. Deal with what is, not what might have been.

"Shut up," Syrina mumbled without conviction.

"How did your parents find each other?" Syrina asked Pasha one night. There was a lot of things the voice had told her in the days following the chair, but among them, this was at the forefront of her thoughts. "I mean, how did anyone, you know, get together in the valley? Marriage, or whatever it was you had."

"I don't know," Pasha said after thinking about it for a minute. "People just met and knew right away they were meant to be together. Like you and I. I thought it was that way for everyone, but I guess not."

"What if two people meant to be together were on opposite sides of the valley? What if they never met?"

She felt Pasha shift where she nestled against him. "I think there's more than one person for one person, if that makes sense. It just worked that some people were attracted to others, and it was mutual, and that was that. Sometimes two people would be together their whole lives. My parents were like that. Often there were others, though. Nobody saw anything wrong with having children with different people."

Syrina pressed further. "What about men who like men. Like Ves. Or women who like women?"

Pasha shifted his weight so he could look at Syrina, who was looking up at him with green eyes in their nest of swirling, indistinct lines. "Even then, there'd usually be someone else—someone of the opposite sex that they'd meet and have children with. They might still like men more, or women more, or whatever, but that didn't stop them from being with the people they were drawn to. What is this about, Syrina?"

"Something the voice told me. About what it learned of my—our —past. The voice, it's a machine, sort of, made up of millions of tiny machines. To reproduce, it needs to find someone with compatible machines inside them, and they would, well, for lack of a better word, force their carriers to be attracted to each other. That's what happened with Triglav, I guess. Some accidental by-product of the Syndicate's experiments on Kalis.

"So it stood to reason that your people, who were left in the valley by our Ancestors, are all carriers of the same machines, undiluted."

"But nobody had a voice in their head that they talked to," Pasha protested. "Not that I know of."

"No, but you're skilled beyond what almost anyone is out here, and you live a long, long time. Way longer than a normal human, unless they're a Kalis. And you live twice as long as most of us. If it takes a lot to recognize the machine inside of you, to wake it up, then maybe nobody knew about them. They still might have driven your unconscious to be with certain people so they could reproduce themselves."

"But you said only women can become Kalis," Pasha said, sitting up, his face tortured.

She wondered what was upsetting him, but she persisted. "That's another thing the High Merchants got wrong," she said. "Lots of people—both the ruling Ancestors and their military and civil servants—had these intelligences in them. They all became the ruling class by default. These internal machines, the Preas Prom, were how they interacted with their technology. Normal people lived shorter lives and depended on those with nanites—that's what they called them—for almost everything. They became a separate, lower caste, able to see the wonders around but only able to interact with the most simple of them.

"The Kalis—or whatever the Ancestors called them back then—the women like me with the tattoos—were a very, very small part of that society. Some secret military force. After the Age of Ashes, it just happened to be some of the only technology the Syndicate could save, so they misinterpreted the whole thing. I mean, they spent a thousand generations trying to make a Kalis like me, but they neglected the male half of their breeding programs. It's a wonder that they ever managed to produce some version of what used to be. Parents being deep in love from the moment they met was the only criterion they understood. It took thousands of years, millions of attempts, before they got it right by freak chance."

"So did this voice of yours tell you why we got left in the valley in the first place? Was it really to guard the Tomb, or library, or whatever you want to call it."

Syrina shook her head. "No, it didn't say either way, but it makes sense, based on what the Astrologers in Ristro told me once. Before the Age of Ashes, a faction of the ruling class wanted to help the people prepare for the oncoming disaster. They didn't tell me as much, but I think they wanted to spread what they knew, maybe even the nanites themselves, to help people survive. The other larger faction, what became the Merchant's Syndicate, wanted to hoard their knowledge; hide it away and prepare, so they would have complete control over whatever was left. I think the library and your guardianship over it was part of their plan. What better way to keep their knowledge out of the hands of those who wanted to deliver it to the masses? Only, it worked too well, and after the Syndicate recovered from the Age, they'd forgotten about it."

Pasha was silent for a long time. Syrina sat up to and put her arms around him, but he pulled away.

"You're saying whatever is between us is just 'forced' by artificial minds living inside us? That it's not real? That what was between my parents—or anyone in the valley—that none of it was real?"

Syrina sighed, at last understanding. She again moved to hold Pasha. His body was tense, but he didn't pull away a second time. "Pasha, I've been thinking about this a long time. Since Triglav. Isn't it real? I mean, think of your feelings. Think of your parents' feelings. They're there, right? They exist. Does it matter where they come from? People who don't have these nanites in them, they fall in love too, right? Where do those feelings come from? Do you think it matters to them? Why should it matter to us?"

Pasha studied Syrina's eyes for a long time. "You're right," he said, his voice soft. "It doesn't matter." And he moved in to kiss her.

Syrina knew her plan to rescue Anna would be unpopular, so she plotted out retorts to any objections. What she wasn't prepared for was her own emotional baggage.

"No. No way," Pasha said, tone flat. "I'm going with you. That's why you found me, right? To help."

She signed, annoyed at the pang of guilt. "I promise you I would have found you, regardless, Pasha. You know that. But we need to be fast. *Fast.* In and out with Anna before anyone catches on, which I don't think will be possible, in which case we'll be running from I don't know how many Seneschal and Heavens only know how many Kalis."

"You can't handle that by yourself. Not while protecting Anna. I can help."

"Pasha," Syrina tried to be gentle and failed. "You can't run. If I have to, I can carry Anna through the Papsukkal Door. I think she can handle it if everything I learned—everything I told you—is accurate. But I can't carry both of you."

"Then I can help Ves—"

"No." Syrina made her voice firm, even as the dismal look on Pasha's face squeezed her heart down into her gut and held it there. "It will be dangerous. If something happens, we won't have time to look for you, and If I lose you—" She stopped and swallowed. "I can't lose you."

Pasha said nothing, looking somewhere past her into the wall of the galley where they sat around the captain's table.

Ves cleared his throat, making such a show of being uncomfortable that Syrina was sure he was enjoying it. "To be clear," he rumbled. "You want me to cause problems."

Syrina nodded, relieved that she had a reason to look somewhere besides Pasha's tortured face. "Like I said, there will be I don't know what all after us by the time I get Anna to the Foreigner's District. The bigger the trouble you can stir to cover us, the better. Riots. Fires. You won't have a lot of time, so whatever you can cook up."

Ves grumbled a laugh. "Don't underestimate me, Kalis."

Syrina smirked behind her tattoos. "Never."

She turned to Mann. "Can you—" She sighed. "Can you make sure Pasha stays on the boat?"

Mann nodded, face neutral, as Pasha stood and stormed out of the room, trying and failing to cover his limp as he did so.

Syrina tried to comfort Pasha in the three days before they reached Eheene, a skill she'd be the first to say she was terrible at. Ironic, she thought, that if she'd been playing some role wearing a stranger's face, she'd have all the right words at just the right time, in just the right pitch to ease his mind. As herself, though, talking to someone she loved, she was lost. She wondered if that was how normal people blundered through life, or if they got better at it with practice. Probably the latter, she decided. Otherwise, everyone would be miserable.

They still spent their nights together, and most of their days too, drawn to each other like chunks of magnetic stone connected by a force greater than either of them. But there was a chasm now that no physical closeness could bridge, and it twisted inside Syrina and made her feel more helpless than she'd ever been.

Get Anna, the voice advised the last night as she stood alone on the deck, watching the spume off the waves and thinking, of all things, about Triglav. *Reunite him with his sister, and he'll forget about all this.*

"I don't know about that."

The voice shrugged in her mind. *Better than watching him get cut down before you even get to Anna, and you know that's what would happen.*

Syrina couldn't find an answer to that truth, so she didn't respond, and watched the waves glint in the light of the rising Eye. She forced her mind blank.

And for the first time in her life, failed.

32

THE RESCUE

"I NEED YOUR HELP," VES RUMBLED, TEN MINUTES AFTER Syrina had disembarked alone into the Foreigner's District.

Mann glanced at the closed cabin door where Pasha was moping.

Ves rolled his eyes. "You're more useful to me than you are here, babysitting a grown man who could leave if he wanted, whether you try to stop him or not." He followed the old man's gaze toward the door and raised his voice. "He knows he's useful here because his sister needs him to not get himself killed. After whatever shit she's been through, he'd better remember that."

Mann sighed. "What do you have planned?"

"That's more like it. She needs a distraction, right? A goddamned riot, she said. Well, I was thinking. Remember how the Bishop's barricade outside Fom was using naphtha mines? And we wondered how the hell they got them, right? Either the Arch Bishop's people somehow came up with how to trigger them while they're floating in the goddamned ocean, or else the fucking Merchant's Syndicate isn't as neutral as they're pretending to be."

Mann nodded.

"Well," Ves continued. "Let's say the Grace found out it was the

Syndicate, and she didn't like her enemy having secret allies, so she decided to do something about it. What do you think she'd do?"

Mann thought. "I don't know if she'd send a fleet up here if that's what you're thinking. Spreading her forces thin like that. Risks that big aren't her style, even if she could get them through the Upper Great Road Delta."

To his surprise, Ves grinned. "See, you know that. You're goddamned General Albertus Mann. I didn't know that. And nobody knows what the hell is going on at the Delta—it's all old news by the time it gets up here. And you can bet your balls nobody lurking around the Foreigner's District in Eheene knows anything about any of that, either. Not anyone with as much clout as the famous traitor General Mann."

Mann nodded. "So you want me to convince everyone that the Grace is coming here to blow the hell out of the harbor. I don't know. Even from me, that's a stretch in the time we've got."

Ves's grin grew wide. "Not just coming here. *Here*. Right now. I'd need to argue the point and explain how I'd know such a thing to every bastard I talked to, then go off and do something about it and hope everyone back on shore decides to believe me after I'm gone. People will recognize you. Enough of them. And the ones that do won't even bother asking how you know. You turned against the Grace and escaped from the fucking Pit, or so they say."

Mann frowned again and looked back at Pasha's closed door. "Even if I could convince anyone, then what? I do what Syrina told you to do while you stay here and drink?"

"No, old man. Like I said, I'll make your story believable. I'll be in the harbor. The Grace's fleet is already here." He gave Mann a wink.

"Why wasn't I informed about this sooner?" Ormo stormed down the marble stairs of the mezzanine surrounding his foyer, unpainted face shrouded by his hood. His steam car grumbled in the courtyard, door open, the shadow of Kalis Shen waiting beside it.

He was glad Shen was back. If any of his Kalis were a match for Syrina, it would be her.

Kalis Lydia, dressed in the skin of a common servant, winced at the question. "It was the rain, Ma'is. The signal triggered as it should, but the rain and low clouds masked it from our vantage. Kalis Charisi was on watch in the Financial Square, and even she almost didn't notice it. She came as fast as she could."

"Where is she now?"

"She used the Papsukkal Door, Ma'is. She's resting."

Ormo lapsed into silence as he climbed into the back of his long, black and white steam car, gesturing for Lydia to drive and Shen to ride beside him. He would have liked Charisi to be there, too, for what was about to come, but it couldn't be helped.

Since Anna had come to him, he couldn't lock the door beneath his Hall. His Kalis needed access, and anything that would keep Syrina out would have kept them out, too. Instead, he'd installed a warning system. He'd used the guise of street maintenance to rig a trigger between the door beneath his dais to the chimney of a small mansion he owned, a quarter span from the Syndicate Palace. The chimney would cough grey smoke if anyone entered the chamber without deactivating the trigger. He could see the signal all the way from his estate on the northwest edge of Eheene. Unless it was raining.

It was far from a perfect system, something he'd conceded when he designed it, but it had only been temporary. He was close now. A few weeks more, maybe less, and he would have all he needed from Anna. Now it was a few weeks he didn't have.

Syrina had triggered the alarm. He knew it deep in his bones. Kalis Sal and Kalis Orda were down there now, between her and his life's work, but he didn't think they would be enough.

Ten minutes. In ten minutes, he would be at the palace. There he could gas the chamber, as long as Orda and Sal could keep Syrina occupied long enough for it to matter. Their loss would be regrettable, but he could get over them. Anna's loss would be worse, but if his theory was correct, her mind would still be high above, trapped in the daystar she had joined with. Eventually, with all he'd discovered, he'd be able to access her again.

Setbacks, setbacks, setbacks.

Ormo's steam car tore through Eheene. Out of the mist, the Syndicate Palace loomed into view.

In life, there are those moments that hang, heaped with regret. Actions done or left undone, words said or left unsaid. Ideas that come too late or too early. Moments that exist in all mortal lives. Even Kalis.

Syrina thought she already had enough such moments in her past to bog her down with a lifetime of remorse. But there's always room for one more.

Getting through the Foreigner's District and over the wall into the city was as easy as she remembered, and moving through the darkened streets of Eheene filled her with a nostalgia she wasn't expecting but forced herself to ignore.

The best way into the Syndicate Palace was still through the side entrance used by Kalis and other agents of the High Merchants who needed to keep their names off the books. There were Seneschal, but as far as Syrina knew, they couldn't tell one Kalis from another. At worst, Ormo would find out about her presence the same time she got to Anna. That wouldn't give him enough time to prepare.

She hoped.

The Seneschal gave a subservient nod as Syrina made eye contact with her, and stepped aside.

Now came the hard part. Ormo would know the moment she opened the door beneath his dais, if she even got that far. If she could even open it. He would show up with a swarm of Kalis if he wasn't there already. If he was, she was screwed. Her abilities honed by the voice or not, that would be a fight she knew she couldn't win. Not if he was ready for her, and this time he would be. He'd know it was her breaking into the chamber, now. Even if he didn't know why, he'd assume the worst. The ship of trust had left the harbor between them a long time ago.

When Syrina got to the entrance to Ormo's audience hall, she hesitated. Two Seneschal stood at the door, bored but attentive.

Ormo didn't keep guards at his hall unless he was expecting trouble.

They're not on edge, the voice pointed out. *Meaning they're probably always here. I wonder what the other High Merchants think of Ormo's newfound paranoia.*

There was that. If it were only Ormo acting paranoid, it meant he was the only one who thought he had something to worry about. And if he was worried about it here of all places, he was protecting himself from the rest of the Syndicate. The other High Merchants wouldn't like that.

Syrina would bet her tattoos and the voice in her head it had to do with Anna.

That's a sucker's bet.

"Probably," Syrina conceded. "They'd be a sucker to want a smart-ass voice muttering behind them all the time."

You had one of those before I was around. I'm just more obvious than it used to be.

Syrina didn't have a response to that.

She considered her options. Removing the two Seneschal wouldn't be difficult, but she didn't know if she could do it before they sounded the alarm, nor what sort of protection Ormo had inside.

Still, she was running out of time, and she didn't know any of the other ways in or out of Ormo's hall and the chamber beneath it, nor did she did have time to look for them.

Her solution came a minute later, while she still hunkered in the shadows of the courtyard, undecided. A low, booming rumble echoed across the plaza from somewhere to the south, followed a few seconds later by another one.

Ves.

A jumble of shouts echoed from the gate. Something about the harbor being under attack.

The Seneschal were too well trained to leave their post, but a group of palace guards came running by and stopped to talk to the two standing at the door, who took a few steps forward as they conversed.

Use the Door, the voice advised. *No, not that door. The Papsukkal Door.*

Syrina scoffed. "And be unconscious before I get out of the palace?"

No, I don't think so. I mean, I think I can help you with that. Something else I learned when we were connected to the library. I've been meaning to try it.

"You're telling me this now?" Syrina was so incredulous she almost shouted the words aloud and bit her tongue. "You had how many months to tell me about this, and you're telling me now? To try now? It's maybe something we could have practiced once or twice, don't you think?"

It didn't come up until now, the voice said, but it sounded sheepish.

Choices, Syrina thought. Always stripped away until only the worst one remained. "Fine," she whispered, annoyed.

She stepped through the Papsukkal Door.

The guards, locked in their conversation, froze in place as her heart stopped, and her skin began to tingle. Not even moving in slow motion. Frozen, or at least so slow they didn't seem to be moving at all. It had been ages since she'd needed to use the Door. True to its word, the voice had made her even better at it than she had been, and it had always been one of her strengths.

The important part, though, would be what happened when she came out of it, but there was no point in worrying about that yet.

She slipped between them, nothing more than a brief, fierce wind, and pressed the combination of switches that unlocked the entry to the audience hall. She didn't know if it was even possible to change it, but she was glad Ormo hadn't as it swung open, then slammed behind her.

Inside, six more Seneschal, standing around Ormo's empty dais, began to turn at the sound, but Syrina was already across the floor and on top of them. The room whistled and tweeted as the music of the floor reacted to her passing.

She approached them at a leisurely jog. She didn't have any desire to kill them, but they would make her life difficult if she was leaving with Anna. Depending on how long it took her in Ormo's chamber, she wasn't sure if she could keep up the Door that long, with the voice or no.

Don't take the time, the voice advised. *We can get through the Door again.*

Syrina was surprised the voice was electing to spare lives for once, but she took its advice.

Don't get sentimental. These guys are trained to deal with Kalis, remember? You—we—don't have time to deal with getting hurt, unlikely as that might be.

As the voice justified itself, Syrina pressed the marble tile at the base of the dais. The panel concealing the lever swung open, fast as a snail crawling upstream from the other side of the Door. She yanked the lever down. The door popped open.

She slammed the aperture behind her, hoping none of the Seneschal would open it until Ormo got there, and took the steps five and six at a time. Far away, she heard some kind of booming chime. She wondered if he had set an alarm for her eventuality. Probably, she thought. Ormo considered everything.

Then again, he had told her the first time she'd found her way here a lifetime ago that this place would be off limits to her, and yet here she was.

She pulled open the now-familiar white, non-metal door, half-wondering if it would be sealed, the other half wondering whether Ormo could even lock it beyond the crossbar on the other side.

It pulled open. She streaked in, jamming the crossbar down behind her the same time she saw a hint of motion coming at her from across the room. Beyond, she saw Anna, strapped to the chair, stripped naked, covered in her own waste.

A visceral burst of rage churned in Syrina's chest. Why would Ormo would leave her in such a state?

As her mind raced, she turned toward the movement, lost track of it, then found it again. Brown eyes. All else faded into the background.

As fast as the other Kalis was in her own Papsukkal Door, she couldn't compete with Syrina, who ducked the incoming blow to bring her shoulder up into the woman's armpit.

At the same moment she launched the other Kalis into the barred door, a blow landed in the center of Syrina's back that shoved her twenty hands across the room, into a bank of copper and brass valves. The air in her lungs gushed out, and she spent an eternal moment stunned, still on the other side of the Door, with just enough wherewithal to swear at nobody in particular.

Two Kalis. Of course Ormo would guard his most valuable asset with two Kalis. He would need fewer spies, now that he could watch the world through Anna.

She extracted herself from the tangle of pipes, ripping them from their sockets with the speed of her movement. An explosion of steam scalded her back. Pain screamed through her, but she ignored it, scanning the room for motion. She felt a dull ache in her chest, growing stronger, and she wondered how much longer she could stay on the other side of the Door.

Don't worry about it. Long enough.

Movement flowed next to where Anna was reclining in the chair. Syrina kept her eyes fixed towards the center of the room, keeping track of the Kalis on her left in her peripheral while seeking the other one. Steam churned out of broken pipes like an oncoming storm.

There she was, moving in tandem with the first. On the other side of their own Doors, they were cautious, working together. She wondered if they were a different breed of Kalis, bodyguards trained to work in pairs to protect their Ma'is, and she wondered again how often a Kalis went rogue, when protection beyond the usual Seneschal would be needed.

Just as the Kalis on her left reached her, a fraction of a second before the one on her right, Syrina dropped under the paralyzing blow and spun with her foot extended, sweeping the first attacker off her feet, and used her body to throw the falling Kalis into the other one. Syrina was moving faster than them, and neither could avoid the maneuver, though the second managed to half-twist out of the way. The first glanced off her back and she stumbled head-first into the pipes.

Syrina heard a metallic thunk as the woman's head stuck. Steam billowed as the brass and copper piping bent, then broke from the impact. The Kalis lay, half-upright, head embedded into the piping with her neck twisted at an unnatural angle. Steam hissed around her body.

The other Kalis was already spinning to face Syrina again, but she was off-balance, and Syrina took the opening to streak over, aiming to smash the other's face with her elbow.

Her blow landed low, into the woman's throat, crumpling her trachea. She made a whistling sound and collapsed.

Syrina didn't pause. She stepped out of her own Door, trying to fight off the waves of exhaustion and nausea sweeping over her. Her arm ached, and her scalded back itched and burned. The clouds blasting from broken pipes roiled, and the Kalis' tattoos smoked and burst into flame almost as one. Smoke and the stench of charred meat blended with the churning steam.

The voice did a commendable job forcing everything to the back of her mind as she went over to the second chair and jabbed the needle into her neck.

Again, the room twisted into the infinite mercury of the ceiling and floor blooming above and beneath her, then curved away. Below, the details of Eris glimmered out of the sheen, much closer than it had before, while above, the ceiling formed the orb of the Eye, off to her left, cresting the horizon of the world below. Syrina could make out the jagged cost of Skalkaad, and under her, the irregular, glowing circle of Eheene, near enough that she could make out specks of flame in the harbor. She thought of Ves, and, with a twist in her heart, Pasha.

Immeasurable cold and that pounding internal pressure. She felt panic growing in her.

"Focus," the image of the voice commanded. "Think of Pasha. Talk to Anna and get out. Don't forget, your body is having a nice sauna right now. Hurry up in here so you can get back to it."

She fought down the waves of fear and looked around.

In front of her hovered Anna, the vague form of her voice lingering a little behind. Her image reflected that of her body strapped in the chair—emaciated. Syrina wasn't sure the woman could even walk, much less run without being carried across the city.

"Syrina," Anna said, her eyes dull, her voice expressionless. "You left me."

"I'm so sorry. I made a mistake. What has he done to you?"

Anna looked down at her hovering image, poised as if even her mental projection had become petrified in the chair Ormo had bound her to.

"It didn't start like this," she said. "After you left..." she trailed off and then seemed to remember she'd been talking. "After you left, he let me out for a while. Gave me a room and food and new clothes. He was so nice. But I guess you must know how that is.

"Only, when I came back to the chair, I didn't know how to get back here—" Her bony arms waved. "Without your help, I couldn't find it. I didn't know how to talk to my voice the way you talk to yours. Days and days I tried. He tried to use other Kalis to help me, but they didn't know what to do.

"He got so angry. At first, he just kept encouraging me to try, but

I didn't know where to start. It was my fault. He got angrier and angrier.

"Two weeks, maybe more. And then I found it. I was back! I thought he'd be happy, but he just acted like he'd lost time. He did lose time. That was my fault, too.

"He said he couldn't let me out of the chair anymore. In case I couldn't find my way back again. I tried to tell him I'd figured it out, but he didn't want to risk it. Now he sends Kalis to watch me and make sure I can't leave. They take turns feeding me with a tube going into my stomach so my body won't die. I could hear them talking—I learned to hear things outside this place, where my body is. I learned Skald. Enough, anyway. They hated me. They hated coming, going up and down the stairs. Just me with nothing to do. I heard you fighting them. I guess you won."

Syrina, horrified, only said again, "Anna, I'm sorry. I wouldn't have left you if I'd known." But as she spoke, she wondered if it was a lie.

"He's been making me watch the others. The other High Merchants. He can control this place a little bit, but I need to do the rest. I can see them, and I figured out how to show him what I see on the screen, but I think you broke it when you were fighting. He's not going to like that. He'll need to go back to asking me questions."

"The other High Merchants?" Syrina began to ask, even as she knew the answer. He was learning who they were. Their true identities. With that knowledge, he could manipulate them, even assassinate them, but that wouldn't be his style unless they became a problem. He would seize control of the Merchant's Syndicate, and from there, send his legion of Kalis out to take over everything else.

Ironic, Syrina thought. A few years ago, she'd spent so much time and effort learning the identity of Ma'is Kavik. If he'd waited a few years, Ormo could have figured it out himself. Lucky he didn't, or Ka'id wouldn't have gotten away. Wherever that woman was now, the world was better off with her in it.

"Ormo is coming," Anna blurted, again speaking as if she'd just remembered Syrina was there. "He was on the other side of the city, but he's coming back. The alarm and the fires. I'm sure he knows."

Syrina was sure too. She looked down at the luminous streets of Eheene, now even closer beneath them. So close she could see people moving about like mites, and a steam car, like a black and white ant, wending its way toward the crescent shape of the Syndicate Palace.

"We need to go, Anna."

But Anna shook her head. "It's so cold, and I don't remember how to move. I don't want to go. I don't want anything."

"Come on," Syrina said, beginning to will herself away from the scene and back into the warmth of her body. "I don't know what will happen if I just unplug you from this. Maybe nothing, but I'd rather not find out if I'm wrong. Come on," she said again. "Pasha is waiting. It's warm in the room with the chairs. It's warm on the ship."

"I can't see Pasha. Is he here? I was watching the fires in the harbor. I wasn't looking for Pasha."

"He's still on the boat, Anna. Not one of the burning ones," she added, hoping it was true. "He's safe. He came for you."

But Anna shook her head. "He came for *you.* Tell him I'm sorry when you see him again. I'm sorry I left him."

"Tell him yourself," Syrina insisted, but even as the words left her mouth, something else occurred to her.

"Anna, we're closer to Eris now than when I was here before. I mean, whatever you're looking through is closer. Did you move it?"

Anna, perplexed, nodded. "It's a daystar. That's what they are. Machines floating above Eris. They used to do lots of different things. This one just watches. Ormo wants me to go into some of the others to see what they do, but I don't know how." She paused and gave a sad little smile that made Syrina's heart twist. "Funny, everyone all over Eris is so different, but that's what we called them too, in the valley. Little daystars, winking in and out, shining in the sunlight.

"I think about seeing things closer," Anna explained. "And it can look without moving. Ormo can control that, too. But I can move it to be even closer, or go over different places. He can't do that, so he needs me. To get this close, I have to move it."

"Can you move it even closer?"

"Closer would be dangerous. I think if it gets too close, it would fall." A sudden understanding bloomed in her dull, tired eyes.

"Can you bring it down? All the way to the Palace? What Ormo is doing is dangerous for everyone. You know that. He wants to take control. He's insane. Now I know why he used Triglav to make me, why he tried to turn me against Kavik. This was always what he's wanted—to control the Artifacts. To control Eris with the daystars. If you can make it fall, he won't be a problem for anyone. Not ever again."

Anna hesitated. "What about Pasha?"

Syrina turned to look at her voice, who had been hovering behind her.

"I think so," it said. "It's powered by the same thing that powers the tidal machines, but smaller. A lot smaller. I think it will be okay. Maybe."

Those were the kinds of odds Syrina had played with her whole life, but this time it was Pasha they were talking about, and she hesitated.

"He'll probably be fine," the voice said, exasperated. "But if we do this, we need to do it now."

She glanced at Anna's voice, hovering behind the girl, chrome face blank.

"It won't stop you," Anna said, following her gaze. "It doesn't do anything. Just follows me. Like I said, I don't know how to talk to it the way you talk to yours. I don't think it wants to talk to me."

Syrina studied Anna, chest pounding with guilt, but the girl nodded. "I'm tired of being cold all the time," she whispered. "Tell Pasha it was my choice. I don't want him to blame you."

The pang twisted deeper in Syrina's stomach, but all she said was, "I'll tell him." Then she willed herself back to the room, now full of steam and stale, acrid smoke.

I think we'd better use the Door again, the voice said.

She passed Ormo's steam car as it ground through the palace gates. An odd, out of place urge pulled her eyes to the deep shadows that shrouded the narrow street between the palace wall and the four-level townhouses flanking it, but she saw nothing before forcing her eyes away to navigate the boulevard. She streaked along, sprinting within the Papsukkal Door, the few people in the streets as motionless as statues, the marble edifices on either side reduced to blurs; objects she couldn't see as much as she could sense, as if the tattoos themselves could perceive the world on the other side of the Door. Her body screamed a pounding, high-pitched roar in her ears. She could feel the Door as a presence, chasing her, demanding she step back into normal time, and her tattoos burned and itched as they kept her blood flowing and her body alive. She gripped the pair of long, prism-like rods of Mann's treasure in her right hand. A nudging from the voice had forced her from the stairs back into Ormo's chamber long enough to grab them from their triangular keyholes. *More to be learned*, it had told her, and she hadn't had the time or will to argue.

As she ran, her mind circled, second guessing herself again and again. Would Pasha forgive her? How could he? What else could she have done? Over and over, questions without answers.

And she was dying.

Almost. The voice said, its tone soothing, despite her body disintegrating from the inside. *The other side of the wall. In the District. It should be enough. Hopefully.*

Hopefully.

The addendum wasn't encouraging, but it was that or certain death, so she kept running.

Atop the wall, she collapsed and fell down into the shadows of a burned out warehouse leaning next to one of the main gates. She tried to catch herself, but her mangled hand slipped, and she plummeted the rest of the way onto the packed mud of the alley. A bone in her arm popped. She grunted in pain and crawled into the maw of a blackened door frame to slump against the inside edge, at last leaving the other Door behind her. She couldn't lift her arms, so she left Mann's treasures lying in the muck next to her. The rain had stopped, but there was a steady, *plonk, plonk* of water from somewhere deeper within the old bones of the building.

I don't know if this is the best place to stop, warned the voice. Syrina could feel it trying to get her to her feet, or even crawl, but her resources were dry. *This whole place might—*

The sky brightened, casting harsh shadows around the huge, rubble filled room like a flash of lightning. Then all turned white.

The noise a few seconds later started with a series of cracks like shattering stone, followed by a boom that didn't stop, didn't even fade, but increased into a screaming roar. A living, rabid thing filled with rage. Burning chunks of the upper wall that framed the Foreigner's District careened into the warehouse, which shuddered, sagged, and began to collapse. Syrina, with a strength she didn't know possible, dragged herself like a worm back outside. The building fell to ruin behind her, making no sound over the cacophony of fire and light wailing from the other side of the shattered District wall.

"Oh, shit." Though whether or not her voice made any sound, she couldn't tell. "What have I done?"

And then consciousness fled.

Pasha listened to the conversation through the door. Footsteps clomped up the steps and across the deck. Silence followed.

He knew he was acting like a child, but he couldn't bring himself to care. Since Syrina had come back, that was how everyone treated him. Even before then, Mann and Ves had treated him like a toddler. He just hadn't noticed because he'd been too busy getting drunk and feeling sorry for himself.

He thought about the other cripples he'd known in his life. There weren't many. People healed fast in the valley, and well. There had been some, though, who'd fallen, or been burned in a blackvine forge, or maimed by bora, missing an eye or burdened with a useless hand. Or a limp. They had, he realized, all been treated the same way his friends treated him now. Relieved of responsibilities everyone thought they couldn't handle, talked about on the other side of closed doors as if they'd lost their ears instead of their fingers or legs. Treated like children. He'd always thought their bitterness came from their injuries, but now he knew better. They weren't angry at their condition. They were angry at those around them for turning them into their condition as if nothing else they were mattered anymore.

And Syrina—Syrina with her missing fingers, half of her left hand reduced to a knot of wilted flesh—she should understand, but she didn't. Her hand was a mild inconvenience, something she needed to include with every back-story she created for herself.

With or without Syrina, he didn't want to spend his life as the ears behind closed doors.

He lurched up, scowling at the sharp ache that shot from his knee through his thigh and up his back. Syrina needed him. Anna needed him. If he knew his sister, she wouldn't forgive Syrina. She'd fight and ask questions and refuse to budge until she got answers. She'd slow their escape down enough they might not make it back to the boat if someone was coming after them, and he had no reason to think Syrina was wrong when she said there would be.

Syrina would take the most direct route. He could meet them on the way back, where could convince Anna that Syrina was on her side.

Pasha doddered down the gangplank, onto the creaking dock, and half-limped, half-jogged into the teaming crowds of the District. There was a low overcast, thick enough to hide even a glint of Eyelight, spitting a cold drizzle that reminded him of Fom.

The throng of people ignored him as he moved his way through the press of bodies, loading and unloading the ships as the tide edged toward its peak. He listened for rumors or brooding panic from sailors and dock workers about the Grace's impending attack, but three quarters of the mob were speaking in Skaald, and the ones he could understand talked about the task at hand, or engaged in the mindless small talk the same the world over. Well, Pasha thought, it had only been twenty minutes since Mann and Ves had left. They still had time. Pasha guessed it would be high tide in another two or three hours, which gave everyone another four or five to finish the job or be stranded in Skalkaad for a half a day.

The crowd thinned as he neared the wall between the Foreigner's District and Eheene. He slowed. After all he'd heard about the fantastic wealth of Skalkaad and the Merchant's Syndicate, the drab edifice in front of him was disappointing. Rough cut blocks of granite rose twenty hands, topped with another twenty of unfinished pine—tall, straight trunks, stripped of bark and branches, set into the stone below, pale mortar filling the vertical gaps between them. Solid but unglamorous. Guards stood at gates well-lit with bluish lamps two hundred hands in either direction, but Pasha found himself alone in an alley that branched in a "T" and ran along the wall between the shabby buildings.

He found an even narrower space between two warehouses a half-block back the way he'd come. They were so close together he could shimmy up the space between, using the windowsills as leverage, keeping his weight on his good leg and arms. From the roof, he scaled up the building next to it, in ruin from some long-ago fire, but half of the second story was still intact. He used a collapsed support beam to clamber up to the top of its one good wall, wincing at the dubious creaking under his weight.

At the top, he paused. He was close to one of the guard posts now, just two buildings over and below, but none of them seemed interested in looking up, and even if they did, Pasha didn't think they could see him against the black sky. It had begun to rain in earnest as he'd climbed, and he was thankful for the added cover.

He edged over to the gap between the burned building and the

District Wall. It was a gap of only about twelve hands, but the top of the wall ran yet another twelve above his level. He might have been able to make a jump like that with two good legs, enough to get a hold on the top. Maybe. He couldn't do it now.

Vertical gaps he hadn't noticed below ran between the lodgepole trunks, where the trees narrowed towards their tops, unfilled with mortar this high up. It was hard to tell in the dark, but he thought he'd be able to wedge his hands into the space, though the thought of leaping over a gap wider than he was tall, to jam his hands into a narrow space between unfinished tree trunks, wasn't an appealing one. Not when he didn't know what was on the other side.

Still, there didn't seem to be another way, except through the gate, and there was no way he could talk or fight his way through.

Filtering out any more thought, he took two steps back, made sure he'd be pushing off with his good leg, made an awkward, hobbled run, and jumped.

Burning pain shot first through his leg as he jumped, then through his fingers and hands as he jammed them into the crack. Another, even fiercer pain avalanched down his arms and shoulders as they caught his weight. He forced himself not to scrabble with his good leg, but pressed his body against the damp wood, turning his foot enough that he could shimmy it into the gap and let it bare a tenth of his weight. His bad leg hung, a dead, aching weight, dragging at his hip.

He looked down. The guards had heard nothing over the steady patter of rain, and all but one had retreated into the guard house. The last stood in the center of the road, hunched and miserable.

Pasha pulled one hand free. Warm blood streamed down his fingers and forearms to drip off his elbow. He reached as high as he could, finding a little more space in the gap. He pulled himself up, wrist twisted, biting his tongue against a scream of agony while he pushed with his foot against the wet wood until he could do the same thing with his other hand. And again, ignoring the pain, focused on the rivulets of rain running down rough pine, until he was dragging himself to the top and looking over it into the city of Eheene.

Bland, stone warehouses lined the wall on the city side. Pasha jumped down to a flat roof and rolled to avoid any weight on his bad leg before sliding down the narrow gap between the wall of the building and the barrier to the District. Just as Syrina had said, there were no guards on this side, and it was easy to limp into the city.

The night was quiet. No drunken revelers or beggars roamed the streets. Just the occasional steam car, rickshaw, or palanquin carrying important people to this or that social function, or home again after. Bored looking city watch, wandering in groups of three or five, paced the streets, but they made no secret of their presence. Pasha slipped into doorways or alleys when he heard any coming his way. Shadows pooled the streets that the glow from the naphtha lamps and flames from the upturned marble hands failed to fill, and he skirted around the pockets of light.

He didn't know the way to the Syndicate Palace, but it was so immense he could see it's hazy silhouette down north-running streets and along the canals. It stood on a slight rise, and the fifteen spires speared into the dark sky, glinting in the rain.

A sudden boom startled him into hobbling down a narrow stairway along a canal, where he found shelter under one of the intricate bridges along a ledge that ran its length. Another explosion followed, and soon after, shouts and footsteps thumping across the bridge above him.

Mann and Ves had started their work, and Pasha needed to hurry.

It took him an hour to hobble his way to the palace walls. His leg ached, but there was no time to rest. Syrina might leave with Anna any minute if she hadn't already.

He crept toward the huge, iron gate, still shut. Six guards stood at attention, starring down the main street at the periodic explosions coming from the Foreigner's District. More moved in the shadows across the wall above.

Not that Syrina would use the front gate, but he doubted the guards there would just be standing around staring down the main boulevard if she'd freed Anna yet.

Just then, a deep gong peeled out from the other side of the palace walls and echoed across the city, and he froze, expecting there to be an explosion of activity, Syrina bursting down the street, Anna in tow.

After a few minutes, though, nothing happened except for the guards exchanging glances and whispers, and Pasha wondered whether the sound had something to do with Ves and Mann's attack on the harbor.

He decided to wait and watch the guards. If there was a disturbance inside the Palace they needed to deal with, he could follow them. He knew she was still in there. He could feel her. They'd find each other because they always did.

A long, elaborate steam car, painted all black and white, growled up the wide boulevard to the gate. Angry shouts burst from within, and the guards ran to let it through. Two followed while the others worked the gate shut before Pasha could devise a way to follow. He swore and wondered if he should look for another way in.

A minute later he was still thinking about it when a sudden brightening of the haze made him pull back into deeper shadows.

He looked up. The clouds above the Palace shone with a growing, white light. The guards at the gate turned toward the sky.

That's not the Eye, Pasha thought.

Then the light filled the world around him, an instant before there was nothing at all.

"How would you know a thing like that?"

Mann frowned. For all that Ves had touted his fame, he'd been trying to tell anyone who would listen about the invasion for over an hour, and only three people had recognized him enough to put any weight into what he said. None of them had taken him seriously enough to react with more than a few arched eyebrows. People in the Foreigner's District, just like people everywhere, were too stuck in their ways to panic over rumors, until those rumors got up and punched them in the face. He wished Ves would hurry with whatever he was up to in the harbor.

Before he could announce who he was, someone standing next to him at the crowded bar of the Cranky Maiden did it for him. "Shit!" a man's voice called from behind him. "That's goddamned General Albertus Mann! What's he sayin' about an invasion?"

The woman he'd been speaking to, middle aged and swarthy like she was from the Yellow Desert, dressed in the uniform of a Skald merchant marine, glanced passed his shoulder at who'd spoken, then blinked at Mann's wrinkled face, now hidden behind a month's growth of gnarled, grey beard. "Well, goddamn," she declared in Skald. "I think you're right."

"That's what I've been trying to tell you," Mann sighed, exhausted with telling the same story again and again to people who didn't care. "I know how the Grace thinks. I saw her fleet with my own eyes, heading north from Maresg. Right behind me. Just got into Eheene the last low tide myself. Hoping to be out on the next, if anyone around here would bother to be in a hurry about it."

The woman continued to blink at him. A few other people at the bar had overheard, and had stopped their own conversations to listen. "Well," she said. "Captain's supposed to be docked here for another day while the grunts load the—"

A brilliant flash of yellow and orange light flashed through the grimy windows lining the front of the Cranky Maiden, followed a second later by a tremendous explosion that sent drinks spilling from tables and some of the more unstable patrons to their knees. A second later another followed, then a third.

In the brief, stunned silence that came after, someone standing near Mann shouted, "The Grace! The Grace is attacking the harbor!"

Panic crashed through the Cranky Maiden like a wave as people fought and shoved their way to the doors. Someone smashed out a window with a chair and people tumbled through into the chaos teeming in the street. Mann was glad he was near the back, or he was sure his hip would have given out in the press and gotten him trampled. As the room cleared, he made his way out and back toward the Tar's Gamble at a hurried limp. More explosions ripped through the harbor.

He got back before Ves, after fighting his way through the panicked mobs fleeing the burning ships or dashing towards them to put out the fires. The pirate had done a commendable job burning or blowing up every ship docked at the far ends of the piers, blocking the view beyond with rolling smoke so no one on shore could see that there were no attacking ships.

Ves dragged himself from the cold, greasy water on the far side of the dock a few minutes later, and they greeted each other with nods before turning to watch the commotion in the Foreigner's District. They had tied the Gamble at the western most pier, now the only one that hadn't suffered any sort of calamity. Their immediate area was calm, though Mann suspected that would soon change.

"You stirred them up good enough," Ves observed with a slight grin, though it wasn't as broad as Mann expected it to be.

Mann didn't answer.

Ves looked at him for a moment, then nodded. "By the time they realize there's no attack, we'll be gone."

Mann shrugged. "That realization will be longer than you think. I heard talk on the way back that the Grace's fleet wasn't here, but her agents were aground, sabotaging the harbor. Funny how fast rumors take on a life of their own."

Ves studied the old man's dour expression again. "What's your problem? Plan worked. Better than expected. As long as our goddamned Kalis can get back here with Anna before the whole Foreigner's District burns to the ground, us included." He nodded toward the city. "Should be easy enough for her to lose anyone in that mess."

Mann continued to frown, looking at the expanding chaos along the waterfront. Screams of pain and fear rolled at them from across the docks. A burst of blue-white naphtha flame bloomed close to the District wall, and he wondered what had caused it. A warehouse set alight, maybe. Or too many people trying to flee into the city proper, so the watch had taken drastic measures.

He sighed. "I spent too many years worried about the life of every man under me. After that I fretted over every life in Pasha's valley that I helped snuff out, or at least did nothing to save. Then I go and cause this." He gestured to the District. "I'm seventy-one years old, and I don't know what I am anymore."

He expected some witticism from Ves, but the big pirate only said, "Come on. We'd better go check on Pasha. I'm surprised he hasn't come up here to see all the commotion, however pissed off he is."

I've gone to help Syrina. I know Anna. They'll need me.

They found the cabin door ajar, the letter sitting at the end of Pasha's bunk. Mann read it aloud.

They looked at each other. "Syrina's not going to like this," Ves observed.

"That idiot. How does he even expect to find a Kalis?" Mann said. His hand holding the note was shaking. All this, all this because he had some driving need to save two lives from a valley he'd helped destroy. Now they were both lost behind a wall of chaos and fear he'd helped create.

"Come on," Ves said. "We'd better get back on deck. If a crazed mob is about to kill us while we wait for these shits, I want to see them coming."

They'd just emerged together from the cabins below deck, Pasha's letter in hand, when a flash opened a hole in the clouds. It streaked down and blossomed into a new sun over the spires of the

Syndicate Palace, which stood out, etched black for an instant, before breaking apart and vanishing in white light.

The light spread, faster than they could comprehend, to crash against the District wall, which shattered. A wall of heat smashed over them, knocking them to the deck, and with it, a booming, rushing sound, escalating to a scream. The single mast splintered and the Tar's Gamble lurched on its moorings, then broke free and capsized, spilling Ves and Mann into the churning water. Fires erupted across the shanties of the Foreigner's District, twisting and spiraling upwards in the mad frenzy of wind blasting from Eheene over the remains of the wall.

Ves swam over to Mann, who was spluttering and coughing, and began dragging him towards the half-dozen steamships anchored in the deep water south of the harbor. But the sea was too turbulent even for Ves, and after a few minutes, he heaved Mann onto the ruins of a drifting rowboat, one side of it burned to charcoal to just above the waterline. He dragged himself up after the old man.

Neither said anything, and they turned to watch the City of Eheene fall into hell.

Fires burned across the Foreigner's District, from the fishermen's shanties on one end to Exporter Row on the other. Through roiling clouds of black smoke, they could see fragments of the dividing wall. Beyond, only shadows here and there within the flames—the skeletons of a few marble buildings that hadn't been reduced to rubble. Between and around those rose a wall of blue-white fire streaked with yellow and black, roaring two thousand hands into the sky, illuminating the clouds in a mockery of daylight. The clouds, which were clearing in an ever-widening, perfect circle centered over where the Syndicate Palace used to be.

"The naphtha reserves are burning," Ves muttered to himself, his voice filled with awe. "All of them."

Mann stared up at the unnatural hole growing in the clouds. "Something came from the sky." He fell silent again before asking, "Syrina?"

Ves shook his head. "I don't know. I don't know how even a Kalis could do something like that. Or why." He looked at Mann, his face streaked with tears. "Pasha," he said.

Mann looked again at the inferno that had once been one of the great cities of the world. "It was my fault. I was supposed to watch him." He gestured at the burning remains of the Foreigner's District. "And nothing we did mattered anyway."

Ves shook his head again, more vigorously. "Hindsight, old man. You should've learned to live with it by now. And I told you. He was going to do what he wanted. You really think you would have stopped him? If I hadn't talked you out of trying to keep him here, he would have." He paused. "Do you think Syrina and Anna made it?"

Mann stared at the chaos of burning warehouses and shanties, and the wall of fire beyond. "If anyone finds a way out of that, it will be Syrina."

Ves nodded. "And if she didn't have anything to do with it, I'd bet my balls she at least knows something." He looked at Mann. "She'll kill you, you know, if she blames you for Pasha."

"Probably," Mann agreed.

Ves nodded, the issue settled, and wiped his eyes. One oar still lay on the floor of the dingy, and he picked it up and started rowing back toward the capsized remains of the Tar's Gamble.

Pain and light overwhelmed Syrina. Her eyes were closed. There was some jagged, pressing weight grinding her into hot mud, but when she pushed, it shifted. She shoved harder, and she heard a crunching, popping sound. The weight fell away, so she risked opening her eyes. The searing light was burning through her eyelids anyway.

Fires burned here and there around her in the charred ruins of warehouses, but the heat that rolled over her was flooding from a wall of white fire growling nine hundred hands in front of her, beyond the shattered ruins of the district wall.

No, I didn't help you crawl, the voice answered her unasked question. *The explosion threw you. I did manage to help you land without breaking your neck and both your legs, though, so you can thank me if you want.*

Syrina clawed her way to her feet, coughing. Her whole body itched and burned beneath the tattoos, and her arm hung limp and aching at her side, but all she could think about was a growing, directionless emptiness spreading from the pit of her stomach, horrible and familiar. Mann's rods were gone, too, but that wasn't what haunted her, and the voice didn't seem inclined to look for them any more than she was. *Triglav,* she thought, then: "Pasha." She said his name aloud, but it came out as a choked sob.

He's back at the boat. The voice sounded unconvinced.

Syrina began running.

She was oblivious to the blur of fire that lay behind her. Oblivious to the frantic, desperate cries and agony of the people around her. Oblivious to everything but the shattered ruins of the Tar's Gamble capsized, half-sunk at the end of the pier, and, beyond that, drifting in a broken dingy, the hunched, grief-stricken figures of Ves and Mann.

Ves and Mann. Ves and Mann. The names ricocheted in her mind, the third one, the only important one, absent, absorbed in the vacuum in her chest that was turning her inside out. "Not again," she said to herself. "Not again, not again, not again."

But she knew. She had known since she'd opened her eyes in the burning ruins of the Foreigner's District.

Ormo was gone. Disintegrated along with the entire corrupt, sculpted marble cesspool of Eheene.

But with him—with them all—she had somehow sacrificed Pasha.

A new, black hole in her soul merged with Triglav's absence and the hollow void of her revenge.

She watched the pair in the little boat for a long time as they scanned the docks, until Ves picked up one singed oar and began rowing towards the anchored steamships, trailing behind a trickle of other survivors seeking to leave the ruins of Eheene. Mann still starred back toward the docks, his desperation palatable even from where Syrina stood.

She watched until they reached the nearest steamship, her sharp eyes picking them out among the others as they climbed up the waiting ladders. Cargo freighters and naphtha tankers turned to rescue ships for the few survivors of a city that had once been home to two million people.

She turned and walked back into the remains of the Forcigner's District, without a goal, willing herself to cry, but finding only an abyss where her grief should be.

The voice was silent.

EPILOGUE

Ehrina Ka'id stood at the edge of her terrace that overlooked Heaven's Plaza at the center of Tyrsh, sipping wine and frowning. "There must be some mistake," she said at last.

"No mistake, Ma'is." Kalis Kirin hovered behind Ka'id in the doorway to their apartments. She'd dressed as the maid today, which usually amused Ka'id to no end, but Ka'id wasn't amused now.

"Four separate confirmations," Kirin went on. "Including two eye witnesses who escaped from the Foreigner's District. Eheene is gone."

Ka'id put down her cup on the broad railing and turned to face her last Kalis and the woman she loved. "I told you before, I don't know how many times: I am not your Ma'is, nor anyone else's. The High Merchants paint their faces in Eheene. I drink wine in Tyrsh."

"Yes, Ma'is. I'm sorry."

Ka'id sighed. "Eheene is gone. Annihilated by fire from the sky. So say your witnesses."

Kirin nodded. "According to the gossip in the Port of Pom, it's still burning. Or at least it was two weeks ago. They can smell the smoke in Maresg when the wind is right." She paused. "So they say."

Ka'id turned again to look off the terrace. The sun was sinking low to her left, turning the white marble of the pavilions and array of churches and cathedrals gold. People still scurried through the markets and in and out of the temples dedicated to their various Heavens, but there had been a tension in the air since the war had started. If this mad report was true, it would only get worse.

"Yes," she said. "That would further confirm this news. The naphtha reserves and unrefined tarfuel under Eheene might burn for years. What on Eris happened?"

She took another sip of her wine and turned back to Kirin, still holding the glass. "I suppose there's no news of the High Merchants —how many were in the city?"

The Kalis only shook her head.

"No, there wouldn't be. Some would have been away, but I dare say this means the Merchant's Syndicate as we know it has been disbanded." She took a few steps to sit down at the round, glass table at the center of the balcony. After filling a second glass, she gestured for Kirin to join her.

Ka'id went on. "This could be a disaster for Tyrsh. Without the support of the Syndicate, the Arch Bishop won't have the resources to keep pressing the Grace. If people need to stop using naphtha in Tyrsh to support the war effort, well, I suspect the promise of Heaven will only get so far. But without the Syndicate to produce the stuff, they will have to ration, eventually, even if peace were declared this afternoon. It could get ugly. People expect a certain level of comfort living in the capital. To most of them, the Grace's rebellion is something others need to sacrifice for.

"Fom, of course, has no such concerns. Even most of their warships are tarfuel. It makes me wonder how long the Grace has been planning this little war."

Kirin blinked. "So the rumors were true? The Syndicate was supporting the Arch Bishop?"

Ka'id smiled and sighed again. "I forget sometimes how much we enjoyed keeping our servants in the dark. Yes, forgive me. These are things I should have told you the moment we left Eheene. My dear, the Merchant's Syndicate wasn't just supporting the Arch Bishop in the war effort. We *made* the Church."

Kirin sipped her glass and leaned forward. "What do you mean? Why?"

"Because quite a long time ago, the Syndicate realized that wealth was only wealth when not everyone had it. The poor need to be poor for the rich to be rich. To keep power, they need everyone else to be weak. The problem with that is, the poor get tired of being poor, the weak, weak. And then, well, the rich and powerful are in trouble, aren't they?"

The Kalis nodded.

"So, the Church. Something for the poor to give themselves over to—a higher aspiration than hating those who stand above them, proverbial whip in hand. Who cares about being poor when you get to go somewhere better when you die?"

"But there's so much tension between the Church and the Syndicate," Kirin protested.

"Of course. There must be. The Church of N'narad is everything the Merchant's Syndicate is—was—not. It wouldn't make any sense if they got along. But think of it, all that tension for thousands of years, and never one major war?"

Kirin gave a reluctant nod. "Until now."

"Until now," Ka'id agreed. "The Grace was once a pawn of the Syndicate, too, of course, but Fom never needed the wealth of Skalkaad the way Tyrsh has always been dependent on it. For centuries, faith had been the only thing keeping them in check, but over those centuries, the Grace's power grew to rival that of the Arch Bishop of Tyrsh. Until... well, one's faith might make one resent how their 'infallible' leader is dependent on a group that is their ideological antithesis. So. Here we are."

"Here we are."

They fell into silence, but Ka'id's mind was whirling. She was thinking of that other Kalis. The one that had killed Carlaas Storik and warned her that it had been Ormo who'd been after Ma'is Kavik. Ma'is Kavik, who used to be Ehrina Ka'id.

Ka'id had thought of that mysterious Kalis a lot since she'd fled Eheene with her last loyal servant; wondered how Ormo's Kalis could have put together everything, and she could only ever come up with one answer. That Kalis had been to Ristro, and for some reason, the Astrologers had helped her. There was no other place on Eris that she could have gotten the information she needed to convince Ormo that Storik had been the High Merchant Kavik. No matter how much Ormo trusted her, he'd need something more indisputable than her word to act on something likc that.

That Kalis had hated Ormo so much that Ehrina had tasted it as she'd stood there in Ka'id's office. Was she behind the destruction of Eheene? Unlikely. Not much chance even a Kalis could pull something like that off.

It was, however, likely that Kalis hadn't been in Eheene when the city went up in flames. There would be hundreds of Kalis without masters, now, and odds were, her mysterious savior was among them. And it was also likely that, if that Kalis had been in contact with the Astrologers, she still would be. Ehrina Ka'id could use someone like her in the days to come.

"Kirin, my love," Ka'id broke the comfortable silence between them. "How would you like to take another trip to Ristro? There's someone I'm hoping they can help me find."

ACKNOWLEDGMENTS

Thank you Joe and Cary for your invaluable feedback.

Thank you, mom, for being you.

Thanks most of all to Tomomi and Taiki, for supporting my dreams, no matter how insane they might be.

Dear reader,

We hope you enjoyed reading *The Black Wall.* Please take a moment to leave a review, even if it's a short one. Your opinion is important to us.

Discover more books by R.A. Fisher at https://www.nextchapter.pub/authors/ra-fisher

Want to know when one of our books is free or discounted? Join the newsletter at http://eepurl.com/bqqB3H

Best regards,

R.A. Fisher and the Next Chapter Team

You could also like:
Cradle of the Gods by Thomas Quinn Miller

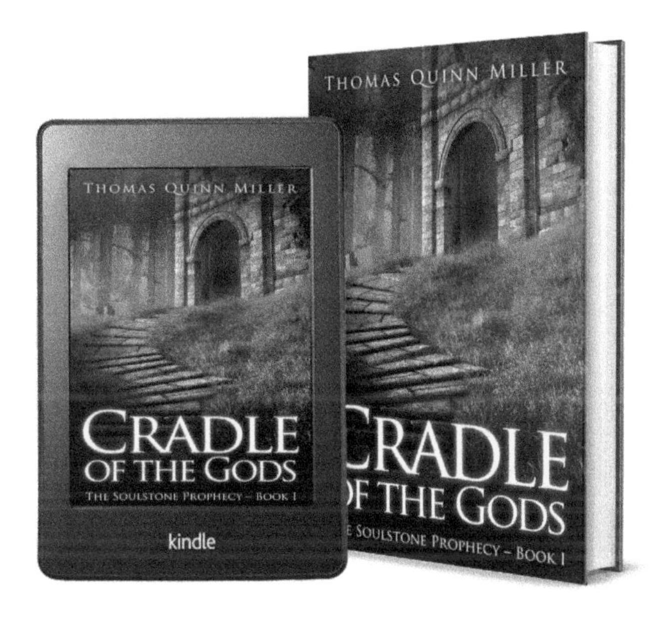

To read the first chapter for free, please head to:
https://www.nextchapter.pub/books/cradle-of-the-gods-epic-fantasy-adventure

ABOUT THE AUTHOR

Robert Fisher has lived in Hiroshima, Japan with his wife and son since 2015, where he occasionally teaches English, writes, and pretends to learn Japanese. Before that he lived in Vancouver, Canada where he worked in the beer industry and cavorted about, getting into trouble and eating Thai food. He placed fourth in The Vancouver Courier's literary contest with his short story *The Gift,* which appeared in that paper on February 20, 2009. His science fiction novella *The God Machine* was published by Blue Cubicle Press in 2011.

Lightning Source UK Ltd.
Milton Keynes UK
UKHW011854290121
377940UK00008B/314/J